Secrets

FIONA LOWE
MELANIE MILBURNE
EMILY FORBES

First Published in Great Britain 2016
By Mills & Boon, an imprint of HarperCollins*Publishers*
1 London Bridge Street, London, SE1 9GF

SECRETS IN SYDNEY © 2015 Harlequin Books S. A.

Sydney Harbour Hospital: Tom's Redemption, Sydney Harbour Hospital: Lexi's Secret and *Sydney Harbour Hospital: Bella's Wishlist* were first published in Great Britain by Harlequin (UK) Limited.

Sydney Harbour Hospital: Tom's Redemption © 2012 Harlequin Books S. A.
Sydney Harbour Hospital: Lexi's Secret © 2012 Harlequin Books S. A.
Sydney Harbour Hospital: Bella's Wishlist © 2012 Harlequin Books S. A.

Special thanks and acknowledgement are given to Fiona Lowe, Melanie Milburne and Emily Forbes for their contributions to the *Sydney Harbour Hospital* series

ISBN: 978-0-263-92049-9

05-0116

Our policy is to use papers that are natural, renewable and recyclable products and made from wood grown in sustainable forests.The logging and manufacturing processes conform to the legal environmental regulations of the country of origin.

Printed and bound in Spain
by CPI, Barcelona

SYDNEY HARBOUR HOSPITAL: TOM'S REDEMPTION

BY
FIONA LOWE

Always an avid reader, **Fiona Lowe** decided to combine her love of romance with her interest in all things medical, so writing Mills & Boon Medical Romance was an obvious choice! She lives in a seaside town in southern Australia, where she juggles writing, reading, working and raising two gorgeous sons with the support of her own real-life hero!

With special thanks to Leonie and Steve:
two terrific doctors who generously shared
their medical knowledge.

CHAPTER ONE

TOM JORDAN—Mr Jordan to almost everyone—stood on the balcony of his top-floor penthouse apartment with the winter sunshine warming his face. The harsh cry of seagulls wheeling above him clashed with the low and rumbling blast of a ferry's horn as the tang of salt hit his nostrils. All of it was quintessentially Sydney. The emerald city. *Home.*

He gazed straight ahead towards the Opera House with its striking sails and architectural splendour, before turning his head toward the iconic bridge on his right. He knew the scene intimately, having grown up in Sydney, although a *very* long way from this multimillion-dollar vantage point. As a kid he'd once taken the ferry to Taronga Park Zoo on a school excursion and been awed by the size of the mansions that clung to the shoreline for the breathtaking views. The teacher in charge had noticed him staring and had said, 'Dream on, Jordan. People like you only ever clean their floors.'

Tom had never forgotten that hard-nosed teacher or his words, which had eventually driven him to prove that teacher wrong. Prove everyone in Derrybrook wrong— well, almost everyone. Two people hadn't needed convincing because they'd always believed in him.

The penthouse and the Ferrari were his way of giving

those bastards from Derrybrook 'the finger'. The long, hard journey to being head of the world-renowned neurosurgery department at Sydney Harbour Hospital was another beast entirely—a personal tribute to one of life's special men.

His nostrils twitched as a slight musty aroma mixed in with the sharp citrus of cleaning products, drifted out from inside and lingered on the afternoon air. His cleaning lady had been both liberal and vigorous with their use in meeting the challenge of ridding the apartment of stale air—the legacy of having been closed up for well over a year. A year that had started out like any other, on a day that had been so routine it would have gone unnoticed in the annals of history yet for one tiny moment of mistiming, which had changed everything. Irrevocably. Irreversibly and indelibly.

For twenty-two months he'd stayed away from Sydney, not ever imagining he could return to the *one* place that represented everything he'd lost, but, just like that one moment in time, things had once again changed. Two months ago on Cottlesloe beach in Perth, the wind had whipped up in him an urge so strong it had had him contemplating heading east, but to what? A week later he'd received a joint invitation from Eric Frobisher, Medical Director of SHH, and Richard Hewitson, Dean of Parkes University's School of Medicine, inviting him to give a series of guest lectures over six weeks for staff and medical students. His initial reaction had been to refuse. He wasn't a teacher and lecturing wasn't what he wanted—it didn't even come close, but on a scale of necessity it was better than doing nothing at all. Doing nothing had sent him spiralling into a black hole that had threatened to keep him captive.

He gripped the balcony rails so tightly that the skin on

his knuckles burned. This past year had been all about 're-education' and was the first step onto the ladder of his new life. Once before he'd dragged himself up by the bootstraps and, by hell, he could do it again. He *had* to do it again. Only this time, unlike in his childhood, at least he wouldn't see their pity or disdain.

A nip in the air bit into him, making him shiver, and he turned slowly, reaching out his hands to feel the outdoor table. Having made contact, he counted five steps and commenced walking straight until his extended left hand pressed against the slightly open glass door. Running the fingers of his right hand down the pane, he kept them moving until they touched and then gripped the rectangular handle. He pulled the door fully open and stepped inside, barely noticing the change in light.

'And we're done. Good work, everyone. Thank you.' Hayley Grey, final-year surgical registrar, stepped back from the operating table and stripped off her gloves, leaving her patient in the capable hands of the anaesthetist and nursing staff. The surgery would later be described in the report as a routine appendectomy and only she and her night-duty team would know how close it had come to being a full-on disaster of septic shock with a peritoneum full of pus. Kylie Jefferson was an extremely lucky young woman. Another hour and things could have been very different.

Hayley pushed open the theatre swing doors, crossed the now quiet scrub-in area and exited through another set of doors until she was out in the long theatre suite corridor. She rolled back her shoulders as three a.m. fatigue hit her, taunting her with the luxury of sleep. Glorious and tempting sleep, which, she knew, if she gave in to and snuggled down in her bed, would only slap her hard and instantly depart with a bitter laugh. No, after years of experience she knew better than to try. She'd stick to her routine—type up her report on the computer, have something to eat, do an early round—and only then, as dawn was breaking, would she head home.

'Hayley, we've got cake.'

'What sort of cake?'

Jenny, the night-duty theatre nurse manager, rolled her eyes as Hayley walked into an unexpectedly busy staff lounge. Earlier in the night a road trauma case had put everyone on edge and Hayley had seen the tension on their faces when she'd arrived for her case. Two hours later, with the RT patient in ICU, the adrenaline had drained away, and the nursing staff was debriefing in the low-lit room, curled up on the couches and tucked up in warm theatre towels.

She automatically switched on the main bank of lights to make the room reassuringly brighter.

Hands flew to eyes as a chorus of 'It's too bright. Turn them off', deafened her.

Jenny compromised by turning off the set over the couches. 'After a month here, do you really have to ask what type of cake?'

Hayley gave a quiet smile. 'In that case I'll have the mud cake. Lucky I like chocolate.'

Although she'd only been at 'The Harbour' for four weeks, she'd already learned that the night-duty theatre team had an addiction to chocolate and caffeine, which, given their unsociable hours and the types of cases they often dealt with, was completely understandable. They were also an outgoing crew and although Hayley appreciated their friendliness, she often found it a bit daunting. Once she'd had a sister who had been as close a friend as a girl could ever have and, try as she might, she'd never been able to find the same sort of bond with anyone else. Sure, she had friends, but she always felt slightly disconnected. However, she could feel The Harbour staff slowly drawing her in.

'Everyone loves chocolate.' Jenny plated a generous triangle of the rich cake and passed it over.

'Tom Jordan didn't.' Becca, one of the scrub nurses, cradled her mug of coffee in both hands.

An audible sigh rolled around the room—one that combined the bliss of an en masse crush along with regret. This happened every single time someone mentioned the previous head of neurosurgery. Hayley had never met the man, but apparently he'd left the hospital without warning almost two years ago.

Hayley forked off some cake as she sat down. 'Is a man who doesn't like chocolate worth missing?'

'Hayley! You know not of what you speak.' Becca pressed her mug to her heart. 'Our Tom was divine. Sure, he took no prisoners, was known to reduce the occasional obtuse medical and nursing student to tears, but he never demanded more of you than he demanded of himself.'

'Which was huge, by the way,' added Theo, the only male nurse on the team. 'The man lived and worked here, and patients came ahead of everything and everyone. Still, I learned more from him than any other surgeon I've worked with.'

'Watching Tom operate,' Jenny gave a wistful smile, 'watching the magic he wove with those long fingers of his, you forgave him any gruff words he might have uttered during tense moments. One look from those sea-green eyes and we'd lay down our lives for him.'

'Suzy lay down with him,' Theo teased the nurse sitting next to him. 'But he got away. Who's your man of the moment? Rumour is it's Finn Kennedy.'

Suzy punched Theo hard on the arm. 'At least I experienced him once. You're just jealous.'

'Of Finn Kennedy? Not likely.' But the muscles around Theo's mouth had tightened.

Suzy shot Hayley a cool look. 'Theo quite fancied Tom, and the fact he's an amazing lover just makes Theo even sadder that he doesn't bat for his team.'

Hayley was used to the nurses teasing, but this time it all seemed way over the top. Laughing, she said, 'Gorgeous, talented, dedicated and a lover beyond Valentino? Now I *know* you're making this up.'

The aura of the room changed instantly and Jenny shot her a reproving look. 'No one could make Tom up. He's one of a kind.'

Hayley let the chocolate float on her tongue before swallowing another bite of the delicious cake. 'If he's so amazing and at the top of his game, why did he leave the prestigious Harbour?'

Becca grimaced. 'That's what we don't know. Tom took leave and then, without warning, management announced that Rupert Davidson would be acting head of Neuro while they searched the world for a new head. Then they clammed up when we asked questions.'

Jenny nodded. 'We've phoned Tom, but his number's no longer in use, we've done online searches, wondering if he took a job in the States or the UK, but the last entry about him was his final operation here. The man's gone to ground and doesn't want to be found.'

'I just hope that, wherever he is, he's working. Talent like that shouldn't be wasted.' Theo rose as the PA called the team into action. 'Oh, and, Hayley, we're competing against ICU to win the "Planet Savers" competition.

You're our weak link. Can you *please* turn off the lights when you leave?'

She bit her lip. 'I'll try.'

Having checked on her appendectomy patient, who was stable and sleeping, Hayley was now in the lift and on her way home. She leaned against the support rail and gave a blissful sigh. She loved this time of the night when dawn was close, but the hustle and bustle of the day was yet to start. It was a quiet and peaceful time—not always, but today all was calm and experience had taught her to savour the moment. The ping of the lift sounded and she pushed herself off the rail as the silver-coloured doors opened into the long, long corridor that connected the hospital with the basement staff car park. Sensor lights had been installed as part of the hospital's environmental policy, especially down here where, after the morning and evening's arrival and departure rush, the corridor was rarely used.

As she stepped out of the lift, she commenced counting in her head, expecting the lights to come on halfway between numbers one and two. She got to three and was now standing in the corridor, but there was still no greeting light. Not a single flicker. The lift doors closed behind her with a soft thud, stealing the only light, and inky, black darkness enveloped her. A shiver raced from head to toe, raising a trail of anxious goose bumps and her heart raced.

Just breathe.

Fumbling in her pocket, her fingers clamped around her phone. The lights had failed two nights ago and in a panic she'd rung Maintenance. Gerry had arrived in his overalls, taken one look at her terror-stricken face and had said, 'We've been having a bit of trouble with the sensor, but we've got a new one on order. If it ever happens again, love, you just do this,' and he'd quietly shown her where the override switch was located.

Why didn't I just walk to work?

Because it was dark. Come on, you know what to do.

She pressed a button on her phone and a tiny pool of light lit up her feet as she edged her way along the wall. Sweat dripped down her neck as the darkness pressed down on her, making it hard to move air in and out of her lungs. She thought she heard a sound and she stopped dead. Straining her ears to hear it again, she didn't move a muscle, but the moment passed and all she could hear was the pounding of her heart. She started moving again and stopped. This time she was sure she'd heard a *click-click* sound.

It's the bowels of the hospital. There are all sorts of noises down here. Just keep walking.

She wished she'd counted steps with Gerry last week, but she'd stuck to him like glue, listening only to his re-assuring voice. She continued edging along the wall until she felt the turn of the corridor pressing into her back. *You're halfway.* Knowing she was closer was enough to speed up her feet.

Click. Click. Tap. Tap. Tap. The sounds echoed around her like the boom of a cannon.

Her feet froze. Her breath stalled. *It's probably the furnace. Or pipes.*

God, she hated this. She was one exam away from being a fully qualified surgeon. She duelled with death on behalf of her patients every single day, winning more often than not. Facing down blood, guts and gore didn't faze her at all so she absolutely loathed it that the dark could render her mute and terrified.

You're close to the lights. Keep going.

Ten, nine, eight, seven... She silently counted backwards in her head as she scuttled sideways like a crab. Finally, she felt the bank of switches digging sharply into her spine. *Yes!* She swung around, pushed her eight fingers against the plastic and started pressing switches.

Bright, white light flickered and then filled the space with wondrously welcome light and Hayley rested her forehead against the cool wall in relief. She gulped in a couple of steadying breaths and just as her pulse stared to slow, she heard a click. She swung around and her scream echoed back to her.

'Are you hurt?' A tall man in black jeans, a black merino sweater and a black moleskin jacket turned from three metres away, holding something in his hand that she couldn't quite make out.

Her heart jumped in her chest and then pounded even harder, making her head spin, but somewhere buried in her fear a shot of indignation surged. 'No, I'm not bloody hurt, but you scared the living daylights out of me.'

'Why?' The question sounded surprised and he stared at her, but he didn't move to close the gap between them.

She threw her arms out as if the answer was self-evident. 'I didn't know you were here!'

His mouth twitched, but she didn't know if it was the start of a smile or the extension of a grimace. 'I've known you were here for the past few minutes.'

She blinked. 'How? It was pitch-black until a moment ago.'

His broad shoulders rose slightly and his empty hand flexed by his side. 'I heard the ping of the lift.'

'But that's in the other corridor and I might have gone in the opposite direction.'

'True, but you didn't. I could also smell you.'

Her mouth fell open at the matter-of-fact words and she

couldn't stop herself from raising one shoulder as she took a quick sniff of her armpit before looking back at him. His gaze hadn't shifted and offence poured through her. 'It's been a long night saving lives so sue me if I don't smell squeaky clean and fresh.'

'I didn't say it was offensive.'

Something about the way the deep timbre of his voice caressed the words should have reassured her and made her smile, but the fact he was still staring at her was utterly disconcerting. He hadn't made any move towards her, for which she was grateful, even though she could see a hospital ID lanyard hanging out of his pocket. With his black clothes, black hair, bladed cheekbones, a slightly crooked nose and a delicious cleft in his stubble-covered chin, he cut a striking image against the white of the walls. Striking and slightly unnerving. He wasn't a fatherly figure like Gerry the maintenance man in his overalls, neither did he have the easygoing manner of Theo. Neither of those men ever put her on edge.

Even so, despite her thread of anxiety, she would have had to be blind not to recognise he was handsome in a rugged, rough-edged kind of a way, and that was part of her unease. She had the feeling that his clothes were just a veneer of gentrification. Remove them and a raw energy would be unleashed that would sweep up everything in its path.

An unbidden image of him naked exploded in her mind, stirring a prickle of sensation deep down inside her. It wasn't fear and that scared her even more.

'Scent aside...' he tilted his head '...which, by the way, I believe is Jenson's Floral Fantasy.'

How did he know that? She frantically glanced around, looking for a camera or any sign that this was some sort of a set-up, a joke being played on her because she was a new staff member, but she couldn't see anything. She turned back to him and his tight expression suddenly faded, replaced by a smile that crawled across his face, streaking up through jet stubble and crinkling the edges of his eyes. It lit up his aura of darkness and she wondered why she'd ever been scared of him.

His rich laugh had a bitter edge. 'I would need to be deaf not to hear the argument you were having with your feet.'

He knows you were scared.

Stung into speech, she tried for her most cutting tone— the one she knew put over-confident medical students in their place. 'I was *not* arguing with my feet.'

'Is that so? What else would you call that stop-start shuffle you were doing?'

'It was dark and I couldn't see.'

'Tell me about it.'

The harshness of his words crashed over her and still he kept staring. It was as if he could see not only her fear of the dark but so many other things that she kept hidden. His uncanny detective skills left her feeling vulnerable and exposed. She hated that and it harnessed her anger. 'Will you *stop* staring at me?'

He flinched and turned forty-five degrees. 'I apologise.'

The tension in his body was so taut she could have bounced a ball off it and his broad shoulders seemed to slice into the surrounding air. As ridiculous as it seemed, she got the impression she'd just insulted him. 'I'm sorry, that was rude. It's just I'm not used to meeting anyone down here at this time of the day and, as I said before, I got a fright.'

He didn't look at her. 'Please be assured I have no plans to rape, assault or hurt you in any way.'

The harsh edge of his voice did little to reassure her. She'd never met anyone who spoke so directly and without using the cover of social norms. 'I guess I'll take that in the spirit it's intended, then.'

'You do that.' A silence expanded between them and was only broken by his long sigh. 'The only reason I'm in this corridor is because it's the mirror image of every other corridor in this wing of The Harbour. If you were on level one, what would be on your left?'

She shook her head as if that might change his question. 'Is this some sort of test?'

'Something like that.'

His muttered reply didn't ease her confusion. 'Um, we're underneath the theatre suite.'

'We're standing directly under theatre *one*.' He almost spat the words at her.

She'd had enough. 'Look, Mr um…?'

'Jordan.'

'Okay, Jordan, I've been at The Harbour for a month, but you know this, right? You're in on some crazy initiation joke at my expense.'

He turned back to face her, his cheeks suddenly sharper. 'Believe me, none of this is a joke, Ms…?'

This was ridiculous. Everything about this encounter held an edge of craziness, including her reaction to him, which lurched from annoyance at his take-no-prisoners attitude to mini-zips of unwanted attraction. She closed the gap between them and extended her hand in her best professional manner. 'Grey. Hayley Grey. Surgical registrar.'

Sea-green eyes—the electric colour of the clear waters that surrounded a coral cay—bored into her, making her heart hiccough, but his hand didn't rise to meet hers. She dropped her gaze to his right hand and now she was closer she could see it gripped what looked like black sticks. With a jolt and a tiny but audible gasp, she realised it was an articulated cane.

Her cheeks burned hot. Oh, God, she'd just accused a blind man of staring at her.

Before she could speak, the doors to the car park opened and a young man wearing elastic-sided boots, faded jeans and a hoodie crossed the threshold and stood just inside the doors.

Jordan immediately turned toward the sound of cowboy heels on lino. 'Jared?'

'Yeah.' The young man grinned and shot Hayley an appreciative look that started at her head and lingered on her breasts.

Jordan turned back and this time his blind stare hit her shoulder. 'Now you have light, can I assume you're able to find your way to the car park alone?'

His tone managed to combine a minute hint of concern with a dollop of superciliousness and it undid any good intentions she had of apologising for her massive faux pas. Her chin shot up. 'I wouldn't dream of holding you up.'

'Goodbye, then, Hayley Grey.' He flicked out his cane, clicked his tongue and started walking.

She watched his retreating back and slow and deliberate stride as the clicks echoed back to him, telling him where the walls were.

As he approached the door he said, 'You're late, Jared.'

The young man jangled the keys in his hand. 'Sorry, Tom.'

Hayley froze. Tom? She'd thought his first name was Jordan.

Mr Jordan. Tom Jordan.

The conversation about the mysterious disappearance

of The Harbour's favourite neurosurgeon came back to her in a rush.

No way.

It had to be a coincidence. Both names were common. There'd have to be a thousand Thomas Jordans living and working in Sydney. But as much as she tried to dismiss the thought, the Tom Jordan she'd just met knew the hospital intimately. Still, perhaps one of those other thousand Tom Jordans worked at the hospital too. He could easily be an I.T guy.

We're standing directly under theatre one.

She might not know the complete layout of The Harbour, but she knew the theatre suite. Theatre one was the neurosurgery theatre, but the man walking away from her was blind. It was like trying to connect mismatching bits of a puzzle.

The man's gone to ground and doesn't want to be found.

And just like that all her tangled thoughts smoothed out and Hayley swallowed hard. She'd just met the infamous missing neurosurgeon, Tom Jordan, and he had danger written all over him.

CHAPTER TWO

TOM worked hard not to say anything to Jared about his driving as the car dodged and wove through the increasing rush-hour traffic. Tom knew this route from the hospital to his apartment as intimately as he knew the inside of a brain. In the past he'd walked it, cycled it and driven it, but he'd never been chauffeured. Now that happened all the time.

Being a passenger in a car had never been easy for him, even before he'd lost his sight. Whenever he'd got into a car he'd had an overwhelming itch to drive. Perhaps it was connected with the fact he'd grown up using public transport because his mother couldn't afford a car. Whatever the reason, he remembered the moment at sixteen, after a conversation with Mick and Carol, when he'd decided that one day he would own his own car. From his first wreck of a car at twenty, which he'd kept going with spare parts, to the Ferrari that Jared was driving now, he'd always been the one with his hands on the wheel, feeling the car's grip on the road and loving the thrum of the engine as it purred through the gear changes.

Tom stared out the side window even though he couldn't make out much more than shadows. 'Give cyclists a good metre.'

'Doing it. So, did you crash into anything this morning?'

Tom could imagine the cheeky grin on Jared's face—the one he always heard in the young man's voice whenever he'd given him unnecessary instructions. 'No, I didn't crash into any walls.'

'What about that woman you were talking to?'

Hayley Grey. A woman whose smoky voice could change in a moment from the trembling vibrato of fear to the steel of 'don't mess with me'. 'I didn't crash into her.'

'She looked pretty ticked off with you just as you left.'

'Did she?' He already knew she had been ticked off by his ill-mannered offer—an offer generated by the anger that had blazed through him the moment he'd heard her realisation that he was blind. He refused to allow anyone to pity him. Not even a woman whose voice reminded him of soul music.

Jared had just given him a perfect opportunity to find out more about her. Making the question sound casual, he asked, 'How exactly did she look?'

'Stacked. She's got awesome breasts.'

Tom laughed, remembering the gauche version of himself at the same age. 'You need to look at women's faces, Jared, or they're going to punch you.'

'I did start with her face, Tom, just like you taught me, but come on, we're guys, and I thought you'd want to know the important stuff first.'

And even though Jared was only twenty, he was right. When Tom had had his sight, he'd always appreciated the beautiful vision of full and heavy breasts. He suddenly pictured that deep, sensual voice with cleavage and swallowed hard. 'Fair enough.'

If Jared heard the slight crack in Tom's voice he didn't mention it. 'She's tall for a chick, got long hair but it was tied back so I dunno if it's curly or straight, and she's kinda pretty if you like 'em with brown hair and brown eyes.'

Knowing Jared's predilection for brassy blondes, Tom instantly disregarded the 'kinda'.

'Her nose wasn't big but it wasn't small neither but her mouth…' Jared slowed to turn.

A ripple of something akin to frustration washed through Tom as he waited for Jared to negotiate the complicated intersection he knew they'd arrived at. The feeling surprised him as much as the previous rush of heat. He hadn't experienced anything like that since before the accident. Even then work had given him more of a rush than any woman ever had—not that he'd been a recluse. He'd had his fair share of brief liaisons, but he'd always ended them before a woman could mention the words, 'the future'.

The car turned right, changed lanes and then took a sharp left turn. Tom's seat belt held him hard against the seat as they took a steep descent toward the water and his apartment. He broke his code and said, 'What about her mouth?'

'Her mouth was wide. Like it was used to smiling, even though it wasn't smiling at you.'

'I gave her a fright.' He wasn't admitting to more than that.

He heard the crank of the massive basement garage door opening, and as Jared waited for it to rise, Tom assembled all the details he'd just been given, rolling them around in his mind, but all he got was a mess of body parts. It was a pointless exercise trying to 'identikit' a picture because all of it was from Jared's perspective.

His gut clenched. He'd lost his job, his career and, damn it, now all he ever got was other people's perspectives.

Stick with what you know.

His ears, nose and skin had become his eyes so he concentrated on what he'd 'seen'. Hayley Grey was a contradiction in terms. Her fresh scent of sunshine and summer gardens said innocence and joy, but it was teamed with a voice that held such depth he felt sure it had the range to sing gut-wrenching blues driven by pain.

'Tom, Carol rang from Fiji. She said, "Good luck with today, not that you'd need it." I told her you'd call her back. She's sort of like a mum, isn't she?'

'Sort of.' He smiled as he thought of Carol working with kids in the villages, glad she'd actually respected his wishes and had not come rushing back to Sydney when he'd finally told her about the accident and his blindness. She'd be back in a few weeks, though.

Thinking about Carol's message grounded him—centring him solidly where he needed to be: in the present. Reminding him he had far more important things to be thinking about than a surgical registrar. Just like before he'd lost his sight, work came ahead of women and now he had even more of a reason to stick to that modus operandi. Sure, he'd given the occasional lecture before he'd gone blind, but he wasn't known for his lecturing style. No, he'd been known for a hell of a lot more.

What was the saying? 'Those who can, do, and those who can't, teach.' Bitterness surged. Lecturing was hardly going to set the world on fire. The accident had stolen so much from him and was now forcing him to do something that didn't come naturally, but until he worked out if he was staying in medicine or not, it was all that was open to him. He couldn't fail. He wouldn't allow that to happen, especially not in front of his previous colleagues.

He wasn't afraid of hard work—hell, he'd been working hard since he was fourteen and Mike had challenged him to improve at school so he could stay on the football team. His goals had changed, but his way of achieving them had not—one hundred per cent focus on the job at hand with no distractions from any other quarter. This morning's trip to SHH had been all about navigating his way around the hospital in preparation for his first lecture. He was determined to show everyone at The Harbour that although his domain had changed and had been radically curtailed, he was still in charge and in control, exactly as he'd been two years ago.

Jared was his sole concession in acknowledging that with driving he required assistance. The fact that Jared had turned up in Perth and refused to leave had contributed to the decision.

'I've got two lectures. One at one p.m. and the other at six.' Tom hoped he'd hidden his anxiety about the lectures, which had been rising slowly over the last two days. 'I'll need you to set up the computer for me both times.'

He heard Jared's hesitation and his concerns rose another notch. 'Is there a problem with that?'

'You know I'd do anything for you, Tom.'

And he did. He'd saved Jared's life and now Jared was making his life more tolerable.

'I've got a chemistry test at six and I asked the teacher if I could sit it with the full-time students, but that's the same time as your lecture.'

It had taken Tom weeks to convince Jared to return to school and he wasn't going to let him miss the test, even though it meant he was going to have to ask for assistance from The Harbour. He swallowed against the acrid taste in his mouth that burned him every time he had to ask for anything. 'You can't miss a chem test if you want to get into medicine.'

'Yeah, but what if someone sets up your computer all wrong?'

Tom gave a grim smile. 'They wouldn't dare.'

'Push fluids!' Evie Lockheart tried not to let the eviscerating scream of the monitors undo her nerve. She had a patient with a flail chest and she knew without the shadow of a doubt that he was bleeding, but from where exactly she was yet to determine.

'See this bruise?' She hovered the ultrasound doppler over her patient's rigid abdomen.

James, a final-year medical student, peered at it. 'From a seat belt?'

'Yes. So we're starting here and examining the spleen and the liver first.'

'Even though he's got a haemothorax?'

'With his pressure barely holding, we're looking for a big bleed.'

Everyone stared at the grainy black-and-white images on the small screen. 'There it is.' Evie froze the frame. She pointed to a massive blood clot. 'Ruptured liver, and they bleed like a stuck pig. He needs to go to—'

'Why the hell isn't this patient upstairs yet?'

Evie's team jumped as Finn Kennedy, SHH's head of surgery, strode into the resus room, blue eyes blazing and his face characteristically taut under the stubble of a two-day growth. His glare scorched everyone.

'Catheterise our patient,' Evie instructed the now trembling James, before flicking her gaze to Finn. He looked more drawn than usual but his gaze held a look of combat.

In the past she might have thought to try and placate him, but not now. Not after the night he'd obviously spent with Suzy Carpenter, the nurse from the OR who had the reputation of sleeping with any male who had MD after his name. That Finn had slept with that woman only a few hours after what they'd both shared in the locker room left her in no doubt that she, Evie, meant nothing to Finn.

She lifted her chin. 'If you want him to bleed out in the lift on the way to Theatre, by all means take him now.'

'It looks like he's doing that here.'

'He's more stable than he was ten minutes ago when his pressure was sixty over nothing.'

'Better to have him on the table stopping the bleeding than down here pouring fluids into a leaky bucket.'

'Five minutes, Finn.' She ground out the words against a jaw so tight it felt like it would snap.

His eyes flashed brilliant blue with shards of silver steel. 'Two, Evie.'

'Catheter inserted, Ms Lockheart.'

'Excellent.'

'Packed cells.' A panting junior nurse rushed in, holding the lifesaving red bags aloft.

'Check O positive.'

'Check O positive.' The nurse stabbed the trocar through the seal and adjusted the flow.

'Ninety on sixty. Good job, people. James, get the lift,' Evie instructed, before turning to Finn. 'He's all yours.'

'About damn time.' Finn kicked off the brakes of the trolley and started pushing it despite the fact that the nurse was putting up a bag of saline. 'Move it, people!'

A minute later Evie stood in the middle of the resus room with only the detritus of the emergency as company. She could hear Finn barking instructions and knew the nurses and the hapless med student would be shaking in their shoes. The staff feared Finn Kennedy. She had been the one SHH staff member to see a different side of him—the one where she'd glimpsed empathy and tenderness—yet it had been shadowed by overwhelming and gut-wrenching pain.

She swallowed hard as she remembered back to their moment of tenderness in the locker room two weeks ago after one of the worst days of her career. How he'd leaned back into her, how she'd rested her head against his shoulder blade and they'd just stood, cradled together as one with understanding flowing between them. Understanding that life can be cruel. Understanding that some days fear threatened to tear you down. Understanding each other.

Hope had flared inside her, along with flickering need.

And then he'd slept with Suzy.

Don't go there. She bent down and picked up the discarded sterile bag that had held the intravenous tubing and absently dropped it into the bin. It wasn't her job to clean up but she needed to keep moving and keep busy because thinking about Finn made her heart ache and she hated that. She wouldn't allow it. Couldn't allow it. Letting herself care for Finn Kennedy would be an act of supreme stupidity and if growing up as a Lockheart had taught her anything, it was that being self-contained was a vital part of her life.

'Move the damn retractor,' Finn yelled. 'It's supposed to be helping me see what I'm doing, not blocking me.'

'Sorry.' James hastily moved the retractor.

Finn wasn't in the mood for dealing with students today. Two minutes ago he'd made an emergency midline incision and blood had poured out of the patient's abdomen, making a lake on the floor. As he concentrated on finding the source of the bleeding, pain burned through his shoulder and down his arm, just as it had done last night and most every other night. It kept him awake and daylight hadn't soothed it any. Even his favourite high-land malt whisky hadn't touched it.

'Pressure's barely holding, Finn.' The voice of David, the anaesthetist, sounded from behind the sterile screen. 'Evie did a great job getting him stable for you.'

'Humph.' Finn packed more gauze around the liver. He sure as hell hadn't been in the mood to see Evie. The sharp tilt of her chin, the condemning swing of her honey-brown hair, which matched the reproving glance from those warm hazel eyes, had rammed home how much he'd hurt her the night he'd slept with that nurse from OR.

He'd had no choice.

You always have a choice. You chose to hurt her to protect yourself.

The truth bit into him with a guilt chaser. Giving in and letting his body sink into Evie's and feeling her body cradling his had been one of those things that just happened between two people in the right place at the right time, but the rush of feeling it had released had been wrong on so many levels. Letting people get close had no value. It just paved the way to heartache and despair, so he'd done what he'd needed to do. But a kernel of guilt burrowed in like a prickly burr, and it remained, making him feel uncomfortable, not just for Evie but for the nurse, whose name he couldn't remember.

Finn grunted his thanks as the surgical registrar kept the suction up while he zapped another bleeder. The blood loss appeared to be easing, and with the patient's pressure holding he was confident he was winning the battle. 'You're new. Who are you?'

Tired eyes—ones that could match his for fatigue and lack of sleep—blinked at him for a moment from above the surgical mask. 'Hayley Grey. I've been at The Harbour a few weeks, but mostly on nights.'

More blood pooled. His chest tightened. God, this liver was a mess. 'I don't need your life story.'

She spoke quietly but firmly. 'I'm not giving it. This is my final rotation. By the end of the year I should be qualified.'

'You hope. The exam's a bastard.' The packs around the liver were soaked again. 'More packs.' He removed the old ones and blood spurted up like a geyser. Monitors screamed with deafening intent.

'Hell, Finn, what did you do?' David's strained voice bounced off the theatre walls. 'More blood. Now.'

'It's under control.' But it wasn't. Blood loss like this only meant one thing—a torn hepatic vein. Damn it, the packs had masked it and he'd been dealing with minor bleeders as a result. He pushed the liver aside and gripped the vein between his thumb and forefinger. 'David, I'm holding the right hepatic vein shut until you've got some more blood into him.' He raised his gaze to his pale registrar. 'Ever seen a rapid trauma partial liver resection?'

She shook her head. 'Will you use a laser?'

'No time.' With his left hand he pointed to a tear in the liver. 'I learned this in the army. We start here and do a finger resection. I can have that liver into two pieces in thirty seconds.' He was gripping the vein so hard that his thumb and index finger started to go numb. 'Ready, David?'

'One more unit.'

'Make it quick.' He pressed his fingers even harder, although he couldn't feel much. 'I'll need a clamp and 4-0 prolene.'

'Ready.' The scrub nurse opened the thread.

'Be fast, Finn.' There was no masking of the worry in the anaesthetist's voice.

'I intend to be. Keep that sucker ready, Ms Grey.'

He released his grip and slid his fingers through the liver. The expected tingling of his own blood rushing into his numb fingers didn't come. They continued to feel thick and heavy. 'Clamp!'

He grabbed it with his left hand and saw surprise raise the scrub nurse's brows.

'Hurry up, Finn,' David urged. 'Much longer and there'll be more blood in the suction bottle than in the patient.'

Blood spewed, the scream of monitors deafened and sweat poured into his eyes. *You're losing him.* 'Just do your job, David, and I'll do mine.' He snarled out the words as he managed to apply the clamp.

He flexed his fingers on his right hand, willing the sensation to return to his thumb and index finger. He could do some things with his left hand but he couldn't sew. He accepted the threaded needle from the scrub nurse and could see the thread resting against the pad of his thumb. He couldn't feel it. With leaden fingers he started to oversew the vein but the thread fell from his numb fingers. He cursed and tried to pick it up but the lack of sensation had him misjudging it. He dropped it again.

Another set of fingers entered the field, firmly pushing the sucker against his left palm and deftly picking up the thread. With a few quick and dexterous flicks, the registrar completed the oversewing before taking back the suction.

Finn's throat tightened and he swallowed down the roar of frustrated fury that she'd taken over. That she'd needed to take over. He barked out, 'Remove the clamp.'

Hayley removed the clamp. All eyes stared down.

The field mercifully stayed clear of blood.

'Lucky save, Finn,' said David from behind the screen.

Except David hadn't seen who'd stopped the bleeding.

Brown eyes slowly met Finn's but there was no sign of triumph in the registrar's gaze, or even a need for recognition that she'd been the one to save the patient. Instead, there was only a question. One very similar to the query he'd seen on Luke's face. And on Evie's.

Don't go there. He stared at Hayley. 'And next, Ms Grey?'

'We complete the resection of the right side of the liver?'

'And you've done that before?'

'I have, yes, during elective surgery.'

The pain in his arm grew spikes and the numbness in his finger and thumb remained. Any hope that it would fade in the next few minutes had long passed. 'Good. You're going to do it again.' He stepped back from the table and stripped off his gloves then spoke to remind her of hospital protocol.

'Oh, and, Ms Grey, as surgical registrar you must attend the series of lectures that start today. They count toward your professional hours. Your log book needs to be verified and notify my secretary of the conferences you wish to attend so they can be balanced off with the other registrars' requirements.'

He didn't wait for a reply. As chief of surgery it was his prerogative to leave closing up to the minions. The fact that today he'd needed to scared him witless.

Hayley accepted the tallest and strongest coffee the smiling barista said she could make and hoped the caffeine would kick in fast. The plan for the day had been to sleep and arrive just in time for the six o'clock lecture, but the moment her head had hit the pillow she'd been called in to work again due to a colleague's illness. This time she'd found herself scrubbed in with the chief of surgery. Finn

Kennedy was everything everyone said—tall, brusque and brilliant. The way he'd finger-dissected their patient's liver to save his life had been breathtaking. But his gruff manner and barked commands made it impossible to relax around him. Cognisant of the fact that he was her direct boss, she'd been determined to make a good impression. Ironically, she'd effectively killed that idea by acting on pure instinct and taking over in mid-surgery when he hadn't been able to make the closure. She'd fully expected Mr Kennedy to order her out of his theatre, but instead he'd been the one to leave. She wondered if she'd be reprimanded later.

Probably. She sighed, not wanting to think about it, so she set it aside like she did a lot of things—a survival habit she'd adopted at eleven. She'd deal with it if it ever happened. Right now, she needed to deal with no sleep in twenty-four hours and staying awake through an hour-long lecture. Some of the lecturers were so dry and boring that even when she wasn't exhausted she had trouble staying awake. She'd been so busy operating she hadn't even caught up with the topic, but she hoped it was riveting because otherwise she'd be snoring within five minutes.

Gripping her traveller coffee mug, she walked toward the lecture theatre and stifled a slightly hysterical laugh.

She'd always known that training to become a surgeon would be a tough gig and she wasn't afraid of hard work, but it had become apparent that operating was the easy part of the training. It was all the lectures, tutorials, seminars and conferences that came on top of her regular workload that made it unbelievably challenging. Even with all the extra work and the fact she had no desire for a social life, she could have just managed to cope, but lately her chronic insomnia, which she'd previously be able to manage, was starting to get on top of her. Had she been able to get more than three hours' sleep in twenty-four she could function, but that wasn't possible now she had to work more days than nights. She preferred night work, but as she was in her final year, she needed more elective surgery experience, which meant working more days.

She paused outside the lecture theatre, wondering why the foyer was so quiet, and then she glanced at her watch. She was early. No matter, she'd take the opportunity to hide up at the back of the lecture hall and take a quick ten-minute power-nap. She'd doze while she waited for the coffee to kick in. Her colleagues always used the dark on-call room but for her the brighter the light, the better she slept. She gripped the heavy door's handle and pulled.

Tom heard the click of the door opening and immediately breathed in the heart-starting aroma of strong, black coffee. A buzz of irritation zipped through him. Had the IT guy stopped for coffee, even though he'd already kept him waiting for fifteen minutes? Tom had deliberately booked him half an hour earlier than his lecture start time to avoid any stress on the run-up to the Jared-less evening lecture, but right now he could feel his control of the situation slipping due to his unwanted dependence on others. He tried to clamp down on the surge of frustration that filled him, but it broke through his lips.

'It's about damn time. I've attempted to connect the computer myself, but there's no sound.' The person didn't reply and Tom turned, seeking out the shadowy outline. As he did, he caught the hint of an undertone of a floral scent. A very feminine scent. He let out a low groan. 'You're not the IT guy, are you?'

'Should I be?'

'I would have preferred it.'

'Sorry to disappoint you.'

Her seductively husky voice, edged with a touch of sarcasm, swirled around him, leaving him in no doubt he was speaking to Hayley Grey. An image of soft, creamy breasts exploded in his head and he tried to shake it away. 'That's hellishly strong coffee you're drinking.'

'It's been a hellish kind of a day.' She sighed as if standing in the lecture hall was the last place on earth she wanted to be.

He knew exactly how that felt.

'Do you need a hand, Mr Jordan?'

I need eyes. He forced his clenched fingers to relax and ran them over his braille watch, realising that the IT technician was now twenty minutes late. Need won out over pride. 'Do you know anything about computers?'

A lilting laugh washed over him. 'I can turn one on and off.'

'I suppose I'll have to work with that, then.' God, he hated incompetence and right now he was ready to lynch the absent IT professional. It was bad enough having to ask for help let alone be supported by someone who didn't have the skills he needed. 'Can you follow instructions?'

He heard her sharp intake of breath at his terse question. 'I can follow *civil* instructions, yes.'

He found himself unexpectedly smiling. He couldn't remember the last time someone had spoken back to him and just recently most people—with the exception of Jared—tiptoed around him, making him want to scream. 'Good. We're in business, then. Follow me.'

He used his cane to tap his way to the lectern because when he was stressed he didn't do echolocation at all well, and falling flat on his face in front of Hayley Grey or anyone else from The Harbour wasn't going to happen. 'I can see light on the screen so I assume the picture is showing?'

'Your screensaver is. Nice picture.' Genuine interest infused her voice. 'Is that the Ningaloo Reef in Western Australia?'

He had no clue which one of his pictures Jared was currently using and he really didn't care. 'Probably.' He ran his hands around his computer until his fingers located the cord he knew he'd plugged into the sound jack. 'Is this green?'

'Yes.'

'Look on the lectern. Have I plugged it into a matching green jack?'

He felt strands of her hair brush his cheek as she leaned past him and this time he caught the scent of coconut and lime. It took him instantly to a beach in the tropics and for some crazy reason he thought of a bright red bikini and a deep cleavage. He felt a tightening against his pants.

It had been so long since anything had stirred in that region of his body that part of him was relieved it still all worked. Most of him wasn't.

Stop it. Concentrate on work.

Out of habit, he closed his eyes to rid himself of the image. The irony hit him hard—the only images he saw now were in his imagination and darkness didn't affect them one little bit.

'You only missed by one.'

The admiration in her voice scratched him. Once he'd been admired around the world for groundbreaking brain surgery. Now he needed help with basic technology. 'Just push the damn plug into the damn jack.'

He thought he heard her mumble, 'I'd like to plug it somewhere else.' A moment later music blared through the speakers. 'Good. It works.'

'So it does.' She paused as if she expected him to say

something. Then she sighed again. 'If that's all, I'll leave you to it.'

Her tone reminded him he should thank her, but it was bad enough having to ask for help without then having to be permanently grateful. He almost choked on a clipped 'Thank you'.

'Any time.' Her polite response held a thread of relief that she could now leave and that 'any time' really meant 'not any time soon'.

He could hear the clack of heels and the firm tread of rubber as people entered the auditorium in large numbers. There'd been a reason his first lecture earlier in the day had been to the medical students. He'd warmed up on a less demanding audience—practised even—but now his colleagues were filing in and taking their seats. Some had come to hear him speak, some had come merely to confirm if the rumour that he was now blind was true, and he knew that a small number of people he'd ticked off over the years would have come to gloat that the mighty Tom Jordan had taken one of life's biggest falls.

His right hand fisted. He would not fail in front of them. Even when he'd been sighted he'd known how fickle technology could be and there was no way was he going to have an equipment stuff-up or malfunction that he couldn't see. He would not stand alone at the front of the theatre, hearing twitters of derision or pity.

He checked the time again with his fingers, and his chest tightened. The IT person still hadn't arrived and Jared's worst-case scenario had just come true. He thought of how he'd once commanded a crack team of surgeons, nurses and allied health professionals, and how their groundbreaking surgery had made headlines around the world. He'd demanded perfection but he'd never asked for anything.

But *everything* in his life had changed and he was being dragged kicking and screaming in the slipstream. His throat tightened and he gripped the lectern so hard the edge bit into his palm, but that pain was nothing compared to what was about to happen. Summoning up steely determination, he made himself say the words he never wanted to utter. 'I need you to stay and be my eyes.'

CHAPTER THREE

'I'M NOT saying there weren't moments when I thought that the surgery might result in brain damage. In fact, there were many such moments, but as a surgical team we were committed to trying to offer these little twin boys, conjoined at the head since birth, a better life.'

Hayley listened spellbound as Tom Jordan's deep and confident voice boomed through the speakers while he presented his most groundbreaking neurological case. Something fell on her feet and with a rush of surprise she realised the printed version of his presentation had slipped off her lap. Initially, she'd done as Tom had asked and had turned each page of the document when he'd pressed his remote control to change the slide on the screen. This meant that she would know exactly what slide he was up to should something go awry with the computer, the data projector or the microphone.

Tom had been brusquely specific about the job he'd imposed on her, making her repeat his instructions back to him as if she was a child and not a nearly qualified surgeon. She'd almost told him to stick his lecture notes where 'the sun don't shine', but the edge of anxiety that had dared to hover around his commanding, broad shoulders had made her stay.

It hadn't taken long before she'd become so caught up

in the story and the technicalities of the surgery that she'd forgotten all about page turning. Instead, she was having a series of mini-moments of hero-worship as the implications of what Tom Jordan and his team had achieved sank in. It had been the 'moon landing' of surgeries.

'This surgery was the culmination of two years of work, and innovation was key.' Tom stared at the back of the room as he spoke. 'Not only were we successful, we paved the way for other neurosurgeons, and earlier this year a similar operation took place in the UK.'

She leaned down, picking up the folder, and then glanced up at Tom. The tense, angry and pedantic man who'd greeted her earlier was gone. In his place was a brilliant surgeon, his long, lean and tanned fingers resting purposely on his braille notes. Notes he didn't need because she knew he could 'see' the surgery. At this very moment he was inside those little boys' brains, and his passion for their well-being and giving them the chance at a normal life filled the auditorium, along with a sense of humility that he and his team had been given such an opportunity.

There was nothing dry and dusty about Tom Jordan and he held the silent audience in the palm of his hand. No one was nodding off to sleep or fiddling with their phone or doodling. Everyone was leaning forward, interested and attentive, and fascinated by the report of brilliant surgery told in an educative yet entertaining style.

All too soon the lecture was over and Hayley felt a zip of disappointment. She could have listened to Tom for a lot longer, but after he'd fielded questions for fifteen minutes he wound it all up. People started to leave and although some lingered for a moment as if they wanted to speak with Tom, most left without talking to him, their faces filled with a mixture of sympathy and embarrassment—what did you say to someone who'd lost their career?

Finn Kennedy stopped and gave his usual curt greeting before moving off quickly when Evie stepped up with Theo. Both of them greeted Tom warmly and as they departed, two men passed and started chatting to each other before they were out of earshot. 'Damn shame. He was the best and now—'

Hayley saw Tom's shoulders stiffen.

He heard them.

Of course he'd heard—the man had almost bionic hearing. She rushed to speak in the hope of drowning out the thoughtless remarks. In her post-lecture awe, she spoke more loudly than she intended. 'That was amazing.'

Tom flinched and turned toward her, his face granite. 'I'm blind, Hayley, not deaf.'

'I realise that, it's just that…' She didn't think he'd take kindly to her saying she'd had a crazy urge to protect his feelings when he didn't seem to have any problem with trampling on hers. *Stick to the surgery topic.* 'I was in the UK when I heard about that surgery. I didn't realise it was you who'd led the team.'

'So now you know.' He turned away from her and pushed down the lid of his laptop with a sharp snap.

Her mind was flying on the inspirational lecture and the fact she was in the presence of the man the world media had declared 'a trailblazer'. 'It must have been the most incredible buzz when you realised you'd pulled it off.'

His generous mouth pulled into a grim smile. 'It's something you never forget.'

'I bet. I would have loved to have been there and seen you operating.'

His hands stilled on the laptop case. '*That* chance is long gone.'

A tingle of embarrassment shot through her. 'Sorry. I didn't mean to remind you that…' *Oh, God, oh, God, shut up!* She closed her eyes and stifled a groan. She'd managed to wrong-foot herself twice in two minutes.

'You didn't mean to remind me that I can no longer operate? How very thoughtful and considerate of you, Hayley.'

His sarcasm stung like the tail of a whip and this time she was the one to flinch. 'I think I need to start over. What I was trying to say was that your lecture was the best one I've heard. Ever heard.' She smiled and tried to joke. 'And, believe me, I've heard a lot of boring lectures in the last ten years. You're a gun lecturer and The Harbour's fortunate to have you.'

He slung his laptop bag abruptly across his chest. 'Aw, shucks. Stop now, you're embarrassing me.'

But his icy tone sounded far from embarrassed and with a wicked flick he extended his cane. She jumped sideways, narrowly avoiding being hit.

'I'm so glad that you're honouring me with the title of "gun" lecturer,' he continued. 'I mean, after all, that's what the last twenty years of my life have been about. Forget neurosurgery. Forget saving lives or improving lives and lessening pain. All of that pales into insignificance compared to giving a *gun lecture*, especially to a group of people who'll probably never come close to achieving the level of technical expertise I was known for.' He started walking. 'But you wouldn't understand that, Hayley.'

His words fired into her like a shot, and she crossed her arms to stop herself from trembling from his unexpected verbal assault. To stop herself shaking from an incandescent fury that was fuelled by his deliberate misconstruction of her sentiments, and his belief that he alone had suffered in life. She knew far too intimately about loss and how life went on regardless.

He was blind, not dead, and she wasn't treading carefully around him any more. 'Were you this rude before you went blind?'

He stopped walking and his roared reply echoed around the now empty auditorium. 'I was a neurosurgeon.'

She swayed at the blast. 'I'll take that as a "yes", then.'

For a moment he didn't speak. His sightless emerald eyes continued to stare at her but his previously hard expression had softened a touch. 'Out of curiosity, Hayley, are you new to The Harbour because you were asked to leave your last post?'

As a woman in the very male-dominated world of surgery, she'd learned early to stand her ground. Something told her this was the only approach with the darkly charismatic Tom Jordan. Her chin shot up. 'My recommendations from The Royal in London make the paper they're written on glow in the dark.'

She waited for a sarcastic put-down but a beat went by and then he laughed. A big, bold, deep laugh that made his eyes crinkle up at the edges and sparkle like the sea on a sunny day.

'Which is why I imagine you got a coveted surgical registrar's position at The Harbour.'

She dropped her arms by her sides and relaxed slightly, knowing his statement was as close as a man like Tom Jordan would ever come to a compliment. 'It was the top of my list because of its association with Parkes University.'

'Mine too.' His brows drew down for a moment and then he seemed to throw off the frown. 'You said before you had a hellish day and mine, as you've adroitly deduced, wasn't much better. How about we end it in a more pleasant way and I buy you dinner?'

Shocked surprise sent her blood swooping to her toes and was instantly followed by a flare of heat. *Dinner?* The idea of dinner with Tom Jordan the surgeon delighted her because she'd love to hear more about his pioneering operations. The idea of dinner with Tom Jordan the man didn't generate quite the same feelings. An evening of verbal sparring would be exhausting and she was already beyond tired, but there was also a tiny part of her that was intrigued. He was heart-stoppingly handsome, just as the nurses had told her, but his soul had a shadow on it darker than his cocoa-coloured hair. That was enough to warn her that dinner wasn't a good idea.

That and the fact that she generally didn't date.

Vacillating, she bit her lip. 'That's very kind of you but—'

'But what?' The thin veneer of politeness that covered all that raw energy and 'take no prisoners' attitude cracked yet again.

She almost snapped at him and said, 'Because of that', but as she opened her mouth she saw a different tension in his jaw. *He's expecting you to say no.* The thought made her stomach squirm. Did he really think she'd reject his invitation because he was blind?

Rude, yes, blind, no.

She thought of all the people at the lecture who'd known him when he'd been head of neurosurgery and who'd prevaricated and then chosen not to speak to him because they didn't know what to say to the man who'd once held the pinnacle of all surgery positions. She wouldn't do that to him even if the thought of dinner came more under the banner of duty than pleasure.

Decision made, she pulled her shoulders back. 'I was going to say I'm not really dressed for dinner.'

'Dressed or naked makes no difference to me, but I assume you have clothes on.'

Her breasts tingled at the lazy way his mouth roved over the word 'naked' and she was thankful he couldn't see her pebbled nipples pushing against her T-shirt. As she tried to get her wayward body back under control she managed to splutter out an inane 'Of course I've got clothes on.'

His brows rose and he extended his arm. 'Then you're dressed for dinner. Hurry up before I change my mind.'

She rolled her eyes but slid her arm under his. His fingers immediately curved around her elbow, his warmth seeping through her long-sleeved T-shirt. 'I'm completely bowled over by your charm.'

'Of course you are.'

He smiled at her and her knees sagged. Dimples carved through evening stubble, changing everything about him. The hard planes of his face yielded to the softer lines of humour, light replaced dark and bitter gave way to sweet. Everything inside her melted. *What have I just gone and done?*

The sarcastic, bitter man was easy to resist. This more human version of Tom Jordan—not so much.

What the hell possessed you?

Now that Tom was seated opposite Hayley at Warung Bali, a casual restaurant a short walk from the hospital, the reality of inviting her to dinner hit him hard. He'd shocked himself with the unanticipated invitation, which had come out of nowhere. One minute he'd been livid with the injustice of everything that had happened to him and not being able to operate, and the next he'd found himself smiling and the anger had faded slightly.

Still, dinner?

Yes, that had probably been overkill, but after the lecture, part of him had wanted to hold on to something that resembled normality. Before blindness had stolen more than his sight, he'd often dated and more than once he'd taken a nurse or a resident for an impromptu drink at Pete's. He'd avoided Pete's tonight because revisiting the social hub of The Harbour on 'half-price Wednesdays' would have been more than he could bear.

The reaction of the medical students to his lecture at lunchtime had been in stark contrast to that of his colleagues this evening. It had taken him close to an hour to deal with the number of students who'd wanted to speak to him at the end of the lecture. Only a few of his previous colleagues had made themselves known to him and he understood why. If his career had been chopped off at the knees from one act of fate, then so could theirs be, and it terrified them. So they'd avoided him.

Now he was avoiding them.

He'd brought Hayley to this restaurant because he often ate here and it was a short walk from his apartment. Prior to tonight, he'd only ever eaten here alone so he hadn't anticipated that Wayan, the owner, would give Hayley such a rapturous welcome and offer champagne.

Tom had quickly gone into damage control. This wasn't a date. It was just a meal with a fellow doctor and an attempt at reality—nothing more, nothing less. In the past, he'd rarely taken anyone out more than once so the chances of this ever being repeated were exceedingly slim.

'Hayley is a colleague at the hospital, Wayan.'

'Hello, Wayan.' Her smoky voice had been infused with

warmth. 'As much as the idea of champagne is tempting, I'm on call and iced water would be wonderful.'

They'd discussed the menu, ordered their food, which had arrived promptly, and the pungent bouquet of lemon grass, coriander, peanut satay and chilli hadn't disappointed. The flavours on his tongue matching the promise of the tantalising aroma. Wayan had placed the food on the table and as Tom had instructed him on his very first visit said, 'On your plate, satay's at twelve o'clock, rice at three and vegetables at nine.'

Both he and Hayley had eaten in relative silence with only an occasional comment about the food. When he'd finally balled his serviette and dropped it on his plate he heard the clink of ice against glass, but it wasn't the movement caused by someone taking a sip. It was more continuous and he knew Hayley was stirring with her straw and staring down at her drink, probably wondering why she'd come.

He understood totally.

He swallowed, knowing he needed to break the silence. He'd never seen the point of chitchat with no purpose and he sure as hell wasn't going to talk about the weather or the lecture he'd just survived. He thought about the first time he'd met her. 'How long have you been scared of the dark?'

She coughed as if she was choking and he realised he'd missed the moment she'd taken a sip.

'How long have you been blind?'

Again he found himself smiling. Three times in one day had to be a record. 'I take it that your fear of the dark is off the conversation list.'

'Is your blindness?'

He thought about it. 'Yes and no.'

Her blurry outline leaned forward. 'Okay, I'll cut you a

deal. If either of us asks a question that goes beyond what we're comfortable answering, we just say, "Enough."'

He'd never met anyone quite like her. Women usually wanted to know every little detail and got offended if he didn't tell all. This suggestion of hers, however, was perfect—conversation with a get-out-now option. 'You're on.'

'Good.' The table rocked slightly as if she was pressing her hands down on it. 'I've been scared of the dark since I was a child and *don't* tell me I should have grown out of it by now.'

The heartfelt punch behind her words hit him in the chest and left behind the trace of a question he could easily ignore. 'I've been living in the dark for two years after an urban four-wheel drive, complete with a dirt-free roo bar, ran me off my bike when I was in Perth for a conference. I slammed into the road headfirst.'

Flashes of memory flitted in colour across his mind. Memories he'd learned to control. 'Ironically, I'm told that my skin's healed perfectly and I don't have a single scar but the impact stole my sight.' He forced his hands to stay in his lap and not grip the edge of the table as he braced himself for the platitudes he'd grown used to hearing.

'That sucks.'

He blinked. She'd just done it again—defied convention. 'It more than sucks, and coming back to Sydney is proving to be—' *Never admit weakness.* He cut himself off before he said more than he intended.

'Challenging. Purposeful. A relief?' The words hung in the air, devoid of anything other than their natural sound.

'I'm not sure it's a relief.' He ran his fingers along the edge of the spoon Wayan had put on the table as his marker to find his drink which was on a coaster directly above it.

'Why did you come back?'

He shrugged, not really understanding the decision himself. 'There's something about the pull of home.'

'Family?' Her usually firm voice suddenly sounded faint.

He shook his head and tried not to think about his mother. 'No, but I grew up here.'

Understanding wove through her voice. 'And you worked at The Harbour. That's got to be a strong pull too.'

It was like a knife to his heart. 'Don't tell me that lecturing is as important as surgery because you know it doesn't even come close.'

He'd expected her to object but instead she gave a heartfelt sigh. He knew exactly what that sound meant. Before he'd thought it through he found himself saying, 'There's something about holding the scalpel just before you cut.'

'I know, right?' Animation played through her voice. 'There's an exhilaration that gives you this amazing feeling, but there's also some tiny ripples of concern because no matter how routine the operation, there's always the threat of the unknown.'

Her words painted the perfect picture, describing with pinpoint accuracy that *one* moment every surgeon experienced. The image floated around him but instead of bringing on a cloud of bitterness, it brought back the buzz. A buzz he hadn't known in two long years.

Hell, he missed talking with a colleague—with a fellow surgeon. Sure, he'd talked to doctors in the last two years, but he'd been the patient and those conversations had been very, very different. 'And in neurosurgery even the known can bite you.'

He felt a flutter of air against his face and his nostrils

flared at the softest soupçon of magnolia. He realised she'd leaned forward again.

'Even with an MRI?'

He responded to the interest in her voice. 'They're a brilliant roadmap, certainly, but just like a photograph often it's all about what isn't in the picture.'

'The human body being a variation on a theme.'

The enthusiasm in her voice pulled him in. 'Absolutely. I remember once when I'd—' The strident notes of techno music split the air.

'Sorry, that's my phone.' The noise was immediately silenced. 'Hayley Grey.'

Tom had no choice but to sit and overhear one side of a conversation. A conversation so familiar that he'd said similar words in the past at dinners, from his bed, in the car and on his bike.

Hayley sucked in a sharp breath. 'When…? A and E…? How many…? Five minutes… Okay, two, then. Call David Mendez… Bye.'

His pulse rate had inexplicably picked up. 'Problem?'

'Road trauma.' The scrape of her chair screeched, matching the urgency in her voice. 'I have to get back.'

He carefully moved his chair back a short distance and rose to his feet, hating it that he didn't know exactly where she was standing, although he could smell her— smell the exhilarating combination of her perfume mixed in with her heady aroma of excitement. The thrill of the unknown—a surgeon's addiction.

'Tom.' Her hand slipped into his, her skin soft, warm and fragrant.

A wave of heat hit him so hard he had to fist his other hand to stop it from reaching out and pulling her against him. It was like his body had just woken up from a long, deep sleep and was absolutely starving. He craved to trace every curve and swell of her body, and he hungered to learn if her body was as lush and as sexy as her voice promised it would be, as her summer garden scent taunted that it was.

She squeezed his hand. 'Thank you for the best satay I've tasted outside Asia.'

'No…' Huskiness clung to the word and he cleared his throat. 'No problem. I'll walk you back.'

'Thank you, but I have to run.'

He'd heard the regret in her voice before she'd even said the word. He couldn't run.

She quickly withdrew her hand. 'I won't ask if you're all right to get home because you'd probably bite my head off.'

He forced a smile against the cold grimness that was washing through him and leaving behind a film of bleakness on every part of him that it touched. 'You're right about that.'

'I'm right about a lot of things. Goodbye, Tom.'

'Good night, Hayley.'

He heard her rapid footsteps, the tinkle of the bell as the door opened, the jet of winter night air that raced in around his ankles, and then the thud of the heavy door closing. And she was gone, running down the street with adrenaline pumping through her veins and her mind alert with every diagnostic possibility.

And he couldn't even freaking escort her back to The Harbour, let alone be involved with the emergency.

His hands fumbled with fury as they sought the back of the chair and with a curse he sat down heavily and felt his hand collide with the plate. Cold rice squelched through his fingers. He swore again and pushed the plate away. A crash followed.

The disappointments of the day and the bitter fury that

had been his companion since the accident rolled back in like a king tide. With a gasp he realised their arrival meant they'd been absent. Gone for the hour he'd spent at dinner.

The hour you spent with Hayley.

But now every single feeling was back with a vengeance—stronger and more devastating than before. It swamped him with the reminder that his current life was a very poor relation to the one he'd lived before. It clawed at him, pulling him down and forcing him back toward the pit of despair he'd only half dug himself out of.

Hayley would be operating within the hour. She would be saving lives. And what was he doing? Sticking his hand in cold food and making a damn mess. He fought for his breath against a tight and frozen chest. So what if she smelled like summer sunshine or if the timbre of her voice stroked him like a hot caress, sending his blood direct to his groin? If attempting normality meant being reminded of everything he'd lost, he wasn't ever doing it again.

'Wayan!' He heard himself yell and didn't care that probably every other patron in the small restaurant was staring at him.

'Yes, Tom?'

'Bring me the rest of that bottle of red wine. Now.'

He intended to lose himself in Connawarra's finest merlot and forget everything about Hayley Grey.

CHAPTER FOUR

HAYLEY woke up slowly, blinking against the sunlight that streamed in through her open curtains, and stretched out with a sigh. The brighter the light, the better she slept, and today was an exceptionally sunny day. It was also her day off—a day she usually spent studying.

At high school she'd spent her weekends studying instead of partying, and that had continued through medical school. Now her days off often came during the week but the pattern hadn't changed. She'd sleep really late and then study well into the night until she fell asleep at her desk under the glow of her reading lamp. There she could get a few hours' sleep, unlike in her bed.

She threw back the covers and got up, padding directly to her small kitchen to make a huge pot of Earl Grey tea and a plate of hot, buttered toast. While she waited for the kettle to boil, she opened up her study planner to see what the next topic of revision was, only this time her usual buzz of enthusiasm didn't stir. Instead, she had an overwhelming urge to do something totally different with her day. An urge so unexpected that it swooped in and changed the shape of her loneliness.

She bit her lip. She was intimate with loneliness—it had been part of her from the moment death had stolen not only her twin sister's life but a part of her life too.

Over the years it had become a living thing—a constant companion—despite other friendships. She'd thrown herself into study and then work, and she enjoyed being part of a huge institution, but the empty space inside her had never filled. She'd tried a few times to be a girlfriend, but she'd never found the connection strong enough. Eventually she'd accepted that there was always going to be a space between her and others. Still, she was a healthy woman with needs like anyone else so in the past she'd settled on two 'friends with benefits' arrangements— one at university and another last year in the UK. Both men had eventually wanted more than she could offer so she'd let them go, and happily watched each of them fall in love with a woman they deserved. A woman who was whole and could love them the way she never could. Now she was back in Sydney she didn't have time for anything other than work and her exam preparation. She'd spent years working toward this exam so she could proudly hang up a brass plate with her name on it—Ms Hayley Grey. Surgeon. FRACS.

Finn Kennedy was right. The exam was a bastard and the pass rate first time round was very low. She was determined to pass on her first attempt and for that to happen, study must be her priority. *Nothing* was going to derail her from her goal.

You enjoyed having dinner with Tom Jordan.

The kettle boiled and she poured the water over the fragrant leaves and breathed in deeply. To her total and utter surprise, the quick dinner she'd shared with Tom hadn't been the horror she'd anticipated. Sure, Tom had his own set of demons, but the flipside meant he wasn't interested in hers. Added to that, his conversation style was in such sharp contrast to the usual 'first date' scene that it had been both refreshing and stimulating.

It was hardly a date.

I know that.

She quickly buttered her toast but she couldn't deny that Tom's rough-edged charisma and wickedly deep voice kept coming back to her at all times of the day and night, making her feel flustered and tingly all at the same time. God, maybe she did need to have sex with someone soon.

Tom Jordan is not that one.

And she knew that. Dark and brooding was not for her. She needed light. She needed sunshine and happiness, which was why the two men she'd chosen in the past had been benign in comparison with Tom's rugged cynicism. But the problem was, she'd glimpsed the man who was buried under all that anger and sadness, and she wanted to see him again.

Her cheeks suddenly burned when she thought about how during the emergency surgery three nights ago she'd asked Theo in a roundabout way where Tom lived.

'*You* had dinner with Tom Jordan?'

Theo's eyes had widened so much that Hayley had thought they would explode and she'd realised she'd just given out information to a hard-core gossip.

'Yes, and I had to dash back here. I was just wondering if he'd chosen the restaurant because it was close to his place. If I was blind, I think I'd stick to known places.'

Theo had nodded and said, 'His apartment's on the top floor of the Bridgeview Building. I can't believe that all this time he's been blind and living in Perth, and none of us knew. Did he say what happened?'

Hayley didn't like to gossip but as she'd been the one to bring the topic up she took the middle road. 'I only met the man this morning and he said he was knocked off his bike. I'm sure now that he's back in Sydney he'd appreciate a call from friends and he'll probably tell you a lot more that he did me.'

Theo had almost dropped the Yankauer sucker. 'Tom Jordan was incredibly well respected amongst the staff but he wasn't someone you made friends with or saw much outside the hospital. Believe me, many of the nurses tried but he pretty much held himself apart. Tom could talk surgery for hours, but put him in a staffroom with a group discussing last night's favourite TV show and it was like sticking him in a foreign country where he didn't speak the language. Put it this way, the man doesn't do small talk.'

How long have you been scared of the dark?

Hayley smiled at the recollection as she bit into the toast. Theo was right. Tom still didn't do small talk but, then again, neither did she—or when she tried she didn't do it very well. She totally understood what it was like to feel completely at sea when surrounded by an animated discussion about who would be eliminated next from the phenomenally popular cooking show on television. She hardly watched any TV and if she did have some downtime she tended to re-watch her favourite movies on DVD.

She gave herself a shake. Enough of straying thoughts and Tom Jordan. It was time to knuckle down to her day. But as she rinsed her plate and mug, the need to move, to do something different, intensified. It was as if her entire body was fidgeting. With a sigh she tossed the tea towel over the dish drainer.

Go for a run. She smiled at the thought. Exercise was the perfect solution to working off this unusual lack of focus and after a long run she'd be able to settle down to study.

Five minutes later and with her MP3 player strapped to her arm, she slipped a key into her pocket and headed out the door. She usually ran down towards Luna Park, but today she just started running, letting her feet take her wherever, and it didn't take long before she realised she was almost at the hospital. When she reached it, she ran along the back boundary, past Pete's and the crashing sound of bottles being thrown in the dumpster for recycling, and then across into the strip shopping centre. Dodging through the building lunchtime crowd, she automatically slowed as she passed Wayan's.

What are you doing? Tom won't be there.

She looked anyway.

Told you he wouldn't be there.

Shut up.

She continued the run, silencing the chatter in her head by pushing her body hard and turning her mind over to the demands of keeping one foot in front of the other until she reached a small park close to the sparkling waters of Sydney harbour. As always, the harbour was busy with yachts, motor launches and the ever-present green and yellow ferries that carried commuters all over Sydney. Panting, she stopped at a water fountain and quenched her thirst before leaning over a park bench and doing some necessary stretching. She'd taken a zigzag route from home but now she was at the lowest point. It was going to be a long, uphill climb all the way back.

Giving her body some recovery time, she walked slowly through the small park and came out on the high side, away from the water. It took her a moment to work out exactly where she was and then she saw the gold letters on the building in front of her. Bridgeview.

Tom's building?

She crossed the street and peered at the list of names next to the pad of doorbells. His name was at the top of the list. A zip of heat shot through her and without stopping to think she pressed her finger to the button.

Her brain instantly engaged. *What are you doing?* She pulled her finger off the button as if it was on fire, but it was too late. The peal of the electronic bell sounded back at her from the intercom.

'Did you forget your key, Jared?'

Horrified, she stared at the intercom.

'Jared?'

Say something or walk away. 'I'm not Jared.'

'Who is it?'

Tom's voice sounded deeper than ever through the intercom and her heart skipped a beat.

'It's, um…' *Oh, for heaven's sake, you know your own name.* She gave herself a shake and tried to settle the cotillion of butterflies that had taken over her stomach. 'Hayley.' She quickly added, 'Grey' for clarification, and then gave a silent groan of humiliation.

She stood there in her running gear, dripping in sweat and feeling incredibly foolish. What on earth had possessed her to ring his doorbell? Worse still, what was she going to say if he actually asked her why she was there? "Just passing. Thought I'd drop in…"

With a groan she rested her head against the wall and closed her eyes, lamenting the fact she hadn't thought this through at all and hating that she'd allowed her wayward body to make decisions for her. Meanwhile, the silence extended beyond the time it would take to reply and had moved from a polite pause into seriously uncomfortable nothingness.

Just go home.

She pushed off the wall and then jumped as the buzzing sound of amplified silence blared out of the speaker.

'Are you still there?' Tom demanded.

Say nothing. Pretend you've left. 'I am.'

'I suppose you'd better come up, then.'

Her lips twitched into a half-smile. As invitations went, it summed up Tom perfectly—direct and straight to the point.

The door buzz sounded for a long moment. *You're committed now so open the door.* After a short hesitation she bit her lip, pushed against the heavy glass and stepped into the foyer. A whisper-quiet lift whizzed her to the top floor and then she was standing in front of an ivory-coloured door. Tom's front door. As she knocked, another zip of panic ricocheted through her. Oh, God, what was she doing? She was hot, sweaty and probably bright red. She wiped her hands down her running shorts and for one purely selfish moment she was glad he was blind.

The door opened and Tom stood in front of her, his chocolate-noir hair spiked as if his hands had ploughed through it a thousand times and strands of silver caressed his temples. Deep lines pulled around his bright green eyes and bracketed his generous mouth, and the familiar aura of strain circled him. Today, instead of being dressed head to toe in what she'd assumed was his signature black, he wore dark brown cord, slim-fit pants, a white shirt with a button-down collar and a chocolate-brown moleskin jacket. His clothes were all perfectly colour-coordinated and although there was no sign of any tweed, he looked every inch a university professor. Not that he technically was one, but she wondered if one day in the future he might just choose that path. His ruffled hair added to the look, although Hayley knew that was all to do with him not being able to see, because there was *nothing* about Tom that was absent-minded.

She smiled. 'Hello, Tom.'

He didn't offer his hand but gave her a nod and stood back from the door. 'Come in.'

She stepped into his apartment and stopped abruptly, instantly struck by a sense of space. It took her a moment to realise this was because he had hardly any furniture and what he did have was spaced a good distance apart. She noticed dents in the carpet and realised that once there'd been a lot more furniture, but the side tables and coffee table had now gone. A glossy black grand piano was the only piece of non-essential furniture.

As if reading her mind, he said in a manner-of-fact voice, 'Less to bump into and no sharp corners, which are murder on shins.' He stretched his hands out in front of him. His palms collided with her breasts.

For a split second his fingers brushed across her skimpy Lycra running top. A rush of delicious tingles swooped through her breasts, making them push against her bra and filling the curve of his palm. The rest of her body moaned as a shiver of need rocked and coiled between her legs with a jealous throb.

Tom quickly dropped his hands and stepped backwards, colliding with the now-closed door. Pain and discomfiture streaked across his face before he spoke through tight lips. 'I apologise.'

She wanted to die on the spot. Not because he'd touched her breasts—that had been pure pleasure—but because she'd caused him embarrassment and hurt in his own home. 'Please, there's no need to apologise.'

His eyes deepened to moss green and there wasn't a trace of humour on his face. 'So you're happy with men you barely know touching your breasts, are you?'

Her chin shot up. 'No, of course not. It's just that—'

'What?' He folded his arms over his chest and glared ever so slightly to her left.

'Well, it was an accident. I should have given you more space by moving further into the room.'

He'd stepped forward while she was speaking, all predatory intent, and a sizzle of something very strong arced between them, draining her brain and making her sway towards him.

'I might be blind, Hayley, but, believe me, I'm still very much a man.'

He stood so close that she felt his low words vibrating against her face. She could smell the crisp, fresh scent of his cologne, which mocked her as it was in stark contrast to the dangerous currents of lust and leashed restraint that circled him.

Currents that circled her too, buffeting her and taunting her. She slowly raised her hand and placed it on his chest in the exact place he'd put his hand on hers. When she spoke, her voice came out slightly breathless. 'Not for one moment have I *ever* doubted you were a man.'

His nostrils flared as he breathed in deeply and for a moment his face shed its tension and his sightless eyes flared with the same need she knew burned hotly in hers. His hand touched her bare waist and she rose on her toes, ready to brush his lips with hers.

A heartbeat away from her kiss, he tensed under her palm. Without a word he lifted his hand away from her waist, peeled back her fingers from his body and with a firm grip put her hand back by her side.

A chill like an arctic wind cooled her from the inside out.

He took five careful steps away from her. 'Why are you here, Hayley?'

Because you fascinate me. Because my subconscious led me to you, knowing I would have fought it otherwise.

Neither reply would work so she thought on her feet,

making up a reason for a visit that had none. Ignoring the fact she wasn't dressed for lunch, she said, 'I had to leave abruptly the other night but today's my day off. I thought we could try lunch, only this time we can manage to finish an entire meal.'

His fingers flexed. 'I believe we'd both finished eating our meal before you had to leave.'

She laughed. 'But I didn't get dessert.' *Shut up.* The moment the words left her lips she wanted to bury her face in her hands. The quip was supposed to have come out light-hearted and breezy, but instead her body had betrayed her by dropping her voice to an alto purr, making her sound like she was trying to seduce him.

He instantly raised a brow, but not even a hint of a smile cracked the tension on his face. 'It might be your day off, Hayley, but I have to work. I'm giving an afternoon lecture.'

'Oh. Right.' It was crazy to feel so disappointed when a moment ago the idea for the invitation hadn't even existed. Perhaps it was because she'd enjoyed their dinner the other night or perhaps it was some other reason altogether, but she surprised herself by asking, 'What about tonight, then?'

He shook his head. 'I have a dinner with Eric Frobisher.'

Against growing regret, she made herself sound very casual. 'Perhaps another time, then? Consider it an open invitation between two friends.'

The shadows that dogged him darkened even more, placing his cheekbones in sharp relief. 'I don't think so.' He turned away from her, out toward the multimillion-dollar view. The one he couldn't see.

There was no ambiguity in his words or his stance. This was an unequivocal rejection.

He doesn't like you.

She stood staring at his back, feeling out of place and completely in the way. How had she got this so wrong? The other night they'd got along in a funny sort of way and a few moments ago an attraction had pulsed so strongly between them that every part of her still vibrated with the remnants of desire.

She couldn't possibly have imagined it all, could she? And yet right now every fibre of his being screamed at her to leave.

More than anything she wished the floor would open up and swallow her or that she could just wave a wand and vanish. If this was what happened when she gave in to impulsive thoughts then she was done with them. She stomped down hard on the new and unsettling feelings that had led her straight into this demoralising situation. Gulping in a steadying breath, she accepted she had to leave but, damn it, she was going to exit with grace, style and good manners.

Rolling her shoulders back, she said, 'If you regret your decision, the hospital switchboard can give you my number.'

He didn't turn around or say another word.

A spark of anger flared at his rudeness and total disregard for her feelings. 'I won't impose on you any longer. Goodbye, Tom. I'll let myself out.'

Tom didn't hear her feet moving against the sound-absorbing plush carpet, but he heard the quiet click of the door and he knew she'd gone. His trembling hands found the doorhandle to the balcony and he hauled the door open. Once outside he let out an almighty roar—one that was filled with anger, pain and frustration, and he let the winter breeze take it away and dump it out over the harbour.

Breathing heavily, he tried to find some calm. The

last person he'd ever expected to ring his doorbell was Hayley. Hayley, who'd felt as soft and as warm as a kitten but whose voice had told another story—the story that promised tangled sheets, sweaty bodies and the bliss of ultimate release.

He'd sensed the change between them, hell, he'd smelled it on her, and heard it in her voice after he'd accidentally pressed his hands to her breasts. Her soft, round breasts that had felt so glorious in his hands. It had been a clear invitation from her to explore and to see what might happen—a man's perfect fantasy and he'd kicked her to the kerb.

He slammed his hand hard against the metal railing, trying to silence the itch that had pleaded with him to touch her again, but the impact of the blow didn't affect it. Neither did it cool his body, which burned to feel hers moulding to his. No, all it had achieved was to make him want to kiss her even more and taste the scent of her. That potent scent he'd been inhaling from the moment she'd walked in, the interplay of sweat and desire, culminating in a powerful aphrodisiac that had made him hard and ready to lose himself in her.

But he'd also smelled sweetness and that scared him because it was a sweetness unsullied by the bastard that was fate. The bastard that had stolen his sight and continued to mock him.

He pulled his phone out of his pocket and said, 'Jared,' to activate the call, before pressing it against his ear.

'Hey, Tom.' Jared's voice sounded muffled due to the hands-free device. 'I'm pulling in now. I just saw that doctor you met the other day, only this time she was smokin' in Lycra. She's got one hot body, dude.'

Lycra he'd just had his hands all over. One nipped-in

waist he'd cupped, and soft, soft skin he'd longed to explore. Skin he couldn't explore. Damn, he'd wanted her.

She offered you friendship.

The tempting thought tried to settle but he shrugged it away. There was no point. His life had changed the moment his brain had been jolted violently on its axis and dinner the other night had left him in no doubt that being with Hayley only reminded him of everything he'd lost. That's why he'd hurt her feelings and sent her away. He couldn't risk her coming back.

It was all about survival, pure and simple.

His survival.

He thought about the lecture hall full of medical students waiting for him, and waiting for him to make a mistake. How long would it take before they considered his experience passé?

'Tom, do you want me to come up?'

'No, stay there, Jared. I'm coming straight down.'

He picked up his computer and his cane, patted his pocket for his wallet and keys and opened the door. He paused for a moment, visualising the route: thirteen steps to the lift and avoid the ornamental palm in the unforgiving ceramic pot at step nine.

Yes, it was all about survival.

CHAPTER FIVE

'HAYLEY, come talk to us.' Theo winked and patted the space on the couch next to him. 'Been having any more dinners with dark-haired doctors?'

All the other night-duty nurses' heads turned toward her so fast she could hear cervical vertebrae cracking. Damn it, why had she asked Theo about Tom?

'I know it won't be Finn Kennedy.' Jenny looked up from her cross-stitch, sympathy in her eyes. 'I see you're back on the night-duty roster again. That's his way of saying, "Behave and don't usurp your superiors."'

Thank you, Jenny, for moving the conversation away from Tom and thank you, Mr Kennedy, for a week of nights and seven days of sleep. 'I promise I'll be well-behaved from now on.'

'Good.' Theo pulled a green badge from his pocket and handed it to her.

She stared at the picture of a light bulb with a red line through it. 'What's this?

'It's to remind you to turn out the lights. You're my worst offender. Do you realise everywhere you go you leave a trail of light behind you and that's adding to global warming? Meanwhile, ICU is whipping us and I want to win the sustainability grant. Everyone…' he paused and glared at all the staff '…has to get on board. If you're not in a room, turn out the lights.'

'I didn't realise you had a scary side, Theo.' Hayley forced a smile and stuck the badge on her scrubs, knowing that was the easy part. Turning lights off went against years of ingrained behaviour, years of using light as a refuge from fear.

'And now back to who you're dating.' Suzy Carpenter's mouth was a hard, tight line.

'Don't stress, Suzy,' Theo teased. 'There's no new doctor on the block so she's not stealing anyone from you.'

Thankfully, Hayley's pager started beeping because, short of torture, she refused to tell anyone how she'd made a fool of herself with Tom. As she read the page she quickly rose to her feet. 'This can't be good. Evie wants me downstairs stat for a consult. Gear up, gang, we could be operating soon.'

Hayley took the fire-escape stairs two at a time rather than waiting for a lift, and a couple of minutes later she was in the frantic emergency department. Nurses were speed-walking, doctors looked harried and she glimpsed three ambulances standing in the bay. It all pointed to a line-up of serious cases.

'Hayley!' Evie gave her an urgent wave while she instructed a nurse to get more dexamethasone. 'We've got a problem.' She tugged her over to a light box where a CT scan was firmly clipped. She tapped the centre of the film. 'Gretel Darlington, a nineteen-year-old woman presenting with a two-month history of vague headaches, but tonight she's had a sudden onset of severe, migraine-type headache. She's in a lot of pain, slightly disorientated, and on examination has shocking nystagmus. She's not got control over her eye movements at all.'

Hayley frowned as she stared at the black and white

image of the patient's brain, wondering exactly why Evie was showing it to her. 'She hasn't got a migraine. That tumour's the size of an orange.'

Evie moved her pen around the perimeter of the tumour. 'And she's bleeding. She needs surgery now to relieve the pressure.'

'Absolutely.' Hayley had no argument with the diagnosis or the treatment plan, but she was totally confused as to why Evie had paged her. 'Exactly what's this case got to do with me?'

The usually unflappable Evie had two deep lines carved into her forehead and her hazel eyes radiated deep concern. 'You have to do the surgery.'

Tingling shock whooshed through Hayley so fast she gaped. 'I'm a general surgical registrar, Evie, and this girl needs a neurosurgeon!'

'You think I don't know that?' Evie shoved her hair behind her ears with an air of desperation. 'Rupert Davidson is at a conference with his registrar and Lewis Renwick, the on-call neurosurgeon, is already in surgery over at RPH. By the time he finishes there and drives over the bridge to here, it could be three hours or more. She doesn't have that much time.'

Hayley bit her lip. 'There *has* to be a neurosurgeon in private practice we can call.'

'Tried that. The problem is that most of Sydney's neurosurgeons are at the Neurosurgical Society of Australasia's conference.' She shrugged, the action full of resignation. 'It's in Fiji this year and because it's winter more than the usual number went, leaving all the hospitals stretched.'

'What about Finn Kennedy? He's got all that trauma experience from his time in the army.'

Evie flinched. 'He's not answering his pages. It's you, Hayley.'

Brain surgery. A million thoughts tore around her mind driven by fear and ranging from whether she could actually do the surgery without damaging the patient to possible law suits against her. She was in Sydney, NSW, not Africa. This lack of appropriate surgeons shouldn't have happened here and yet circumstances had contrived to put her in this position. To put her patient in this position.

She stared at the scan again, but it didn't change the picture. The brain fitted snugly inside the bony protection of the skull and the design didn't allow for anything else. No extra fluid, no blood, no extra growths. Nothing.

She was between a rock and a hard place. If she didn't operate, the woman would die. If she did operate, she risked the life of her patient and her career. She could just see and hear the headlines of the tabloid papers and the sensational television current affairs programmes if something went wrong.

'Evie, it's so damn risky, and not just for the patient.'

The ER doctor's hand gripped her shoulder. 'Believe me, if there was another option, I would have taken it. Pretend we're in Darwin, Hayley. All emergency neurosurgery up there is done by general surgeons.'

She shook her head. 'That doesn't reassure me.'

The scream of sirens outside muted as Hayley forced herself to block out everything except the task at hand. Slowly the chaos that Evie's request had generated started to fade and her thoughts lined up in neat rows—problem, options for best outcome, solution.

Tom.

The thought steadied her. There was a neurosurgeon close by. Now wasn't the time to think about what had happened the last time they'd met. About his completely unambiguous rejection of her. This was a medical emergency and the stakes were life and death. All personal feelings got set aside. Must be set aside no matter how hard.

'Evie, go grab a taxi and send it to the Bridgeview Building.' She grabbed the phone on the wall and punched 9 for the switchboard. 'It's Hayley Grey. Connect me to Mr Tom Jordan, now. It's an emergency.'

The shrill ring of the phone on Tom's bedside table woke him with a jerk. Once he'd always slept lightly, used to being woken at all hours by the hospital, but two years on from the last time he'd worked as a surgeon and his body clock had changed. Now the only thing that woke him at three a.m. was his own thoughts.

Completely out of practice, he shot out his hand and immediately knocked into the lamp. He heard the crash and swore before reaching the phone. Hell, this had better not be a wrong number or he'd just sacrificed a lamp for nothing. Not that he technically needed it. Hating not being able to read caller ID, and not recognising the ringtone, he grunted down the phone. 'Tom Jordan.'

'Tom, it's Hayley.'

This time he instantly recognised her sultry voice and his gut rolled on a shot of desire so pure that it couldn't be mistaken for anything else. He immediately chased it away with steely determination. The sort of single-mindedness that had driven him to become the youngest head of neurosurgery, and now drove him to master braille and attempt echolocation so he could be as independent as possible. He wouldn't allow himself to want Hayley. It would only make him weak.

She wanted you. He sighed at the memory and now it was the middle of the night and a week since he'd been beyond rude to her to keep her away from him. Was this a drunken booty call or a drunken 'how dare you reject me?' call? Either way, he didn't need it. He ran his free hand through his hair. 'Hayley, don't say anything you're going to regret in the light of day.'

'I need you, Tom.'

And she'd just gone and said it. 'Look, Hayley, I tried to make it clear the other day that—'

'This is *nothing* to do with the other day.' The cutting tone in her voice could have sliced through rope. 'Just listen to me. There's a young woman in ER with a brain tumour and an associated bleed. There isn't a neurosurgeon available between here and Wollongong and I have to operate. Now. I need you in Theatre with me, Tom. I need you to talk me through it. Be my guide.'

He heard the fear in her voice and it matched his own. There was a huge difference between being able to see the operating field whilst guiding a registrar through the procedure and depending on Hayley telling him what she was seeing so he could tell her what to do next. 'Can dexamethasone reduce the swelling enough to hold her until the guy from Wollongong arrives?'

'No.' Her tone softened slightly. 'Believe me, Tom, if I had any other choice I would have taken it but there isn't one. We are this girl's only chance.'

He swung his legs over the side of the bed. 'Hell, she's having a really bad day, then.'

'She is.' Hayley's strained laugh—the one all medical personnel used when things were at their darkest—vibrated down the line, bringing with it a camaraderie that called out to him.

'I've sent a taxi, which is probably arriving any minute. I'll see you at the scrub sinks, Tom.'

The line went dead.

The scrub sinks.

She'd rung off, leaving him with no option.

He was going back to Operating Room One. Going home. Only home was supposed to be a place of sanctuary and safety and this felt like walking off a cliff.

'You didn't shave off all her hair, did you?'

Tom sat on a stool behind Hayley, noticing the varied array of smells in the operating room that he'd never noticed when he'd been sighted. Disinfectant mixed in with anaesthetic gases and blood, plus a couple of other aromas he couldn't quite identify and wasn't certain he wanted to. But no matter how pungent the odours, Hayley's perfume floated on top of them all in a combination of freshness, sunshine and summer flowers. He wanted to breathe in more deeply.

'No, we only shaved off half her ponytail.'

'Good. Neurosurgery is a huge invasion and I always make it a point to shave the bare minimum out of respect for the patient.'

Made it a point. You're not operating any more.

Being back here felt surreal—he was in his theatre that wasn't his any more, part of a team rather than leading it. He wasn't scrubbed. Hell, he couldn't remember the last time he'd been in the OR and not scrubbed. Probably when he'd been a med student. He interlocked his fingers, keeping his hands tightly clasped together in his lap.

He heard Hayley murmuring to the anaesthetist and then she said, 'Tom, I have Theo scrubbed in, David's the anaesthetist, Jenny is scouting and Suzy—' she seemed to hit the name with an edge '—is assisting David.'

He and Suzy had shared a fun night three years ago after one of the OR dinners, but he'd never called her. He'd never called any woman because work and patients had always come first and he would never allow anyone to derail him from his goal of staying on top and keeping the demons of his childhood at bay.

He could feel the gaze of many on him and then came the chorus of 'Hello, Tom', just as it had when he'd owned this space and had been called in for a night-time emergency. He knew everyone and he also knew, despite all their idiosyncrasies, they worked together as a team. Given the circumstances, Hayley had the best support she could have.

'Tom, the pinion's in place, holding Gretel's head in position, so let's start.'

To someone who'd not met her before, Hayley's voice would have sounded confident, but Tom detected her massive stress levels in the tiny alto quavers. She'd explained the scan to him earlier and he could picture it all very clearly in his mind. 'Due to the position of the mass, you're making a lateral incision and then performing a suboccipital craniotomy.'

'Removing a bone flap to relieve the pressure,' Hayley muttered as if it was a mantra. 'That's the easy part.'

It is. 'One step at a time and we'll get through this.' But he too was talking out loud to reassure himself as much as everyone else. So much could go wrong in so many unpredictable ways and he couldn't see a damn thing.

He'd always operated with music playing, but not soothing classical. His OR would vibrate with hard rock and, during extremely tense moments, heavy metal. Hayley was operating in silence so he sat listening to the whoosh of the respirator and the hiss of the suction, which only ramped up his agitation. He started to hum.

'Tom, I've turned the skin flap and I can see bone.'

'Now you use the high-speed drill and make three small burr holes into the skull.'

The shrill shriek of the drill against bone always made

medical and nursing students jump the first time they heard it. Tom had always teased and laughed at their re-action, but he didn't laugh today. Instead, his fingers clenched against nothing, wishing they were holding the drill, wishing he was able to do the job, not just for him-self but for the patient. *For Hayley.*

The shriek died away. 'Done.' Hayley swallowed. 'What's next?'

He visualised the silver instruments all laid out in neat rows on the green sterile sheet. 'Use the Midas Rex drill to create the bone flap.'

'Oh, my, it's like a can opener.' Hayley gave a tight laugh and a few moments later said, 'The bone flap's re-moved and I can see the dura.'

Like an illustrated textbook, Tom's mind beamed the image Hayley was looking at. 'Excellent. Now you need the grooved director. It's your atraumtic guide. Using the scalpel, cut the dura over the groove and this protects the brain tissue underneath.'

'Too easy.'

But the everyday slang expression was laden with her anxieties. He moved to reassure her. 'You're doing fine, Hayley. David, how's our patient?'

'She's holding her own at the moment, but I'll be hap-pier when Hayley's stopped the bleeding.'

'You're not alone there.' Tom counted to ten because he didn't want to rush Hayley, but he also needed to keep her within a particular time frame. 'Can you see brain tissue, Hayley?'

'I've found the clot.' Her relief filled the theatre.

'Theo, position the microscope.'

The rustle of plastic-covered equipment being wheeled into place was the only sound and Tom hated not being able to see what was going on. 'Hurry up, Theo.'

'It's in position now, Tom,' Theo said.

'Good. Hayley, have you found the bleeding?'

'Give me a minute, I'm still looking.'

Her normally mellow voice rose as her semblance of calm shredded at the edges. Tom wished he could take over, relieve her of this unwanted task that was stretching her and forcing her to go places she'd never been before. But he was powerless to help so he did the next best thing. 'Theo, suction the clot and keep the field clear. She needs to be able to see.'

'On it, Tom,' the nurse replied.

For a moment all he could hear was the gurgle of suction and he couldn't stop his foot from tapping on the floor.

'Okay.' Hayley's breath came out in a rush. 'I see it.'

Thank you. 'Stop the bleeding with the bipolar forceps.'

'What if that doesn't work?'

Don't panic on me now, Hayley. He infused his voice with a calm he didn't feel. This surgery was something he'd perfected over years of training. Hayley was being thrown in feet first. 'We've got the option of clipping, but try the electrical coagulation first because it will probably work.'

Please let it work. The sooner she stopped the bleeding, the better it was for their patient.

He held his breath while Hayley worked, but he could only guess at what was going on because, apart from a few muttered words, she was silent. He'd always grunted, yelled, talked and even sung his way through surgery. Her silence was unnerving.

'Suction, Theo,' Hayley snapped.

'Her intracranial pressure's still rising.' David sounded seriously worried.

'Has it worked?' Tom hoped like hell it had.

'Pray that it has,' Hayley said. 'This is the moment of truth, team.'

No one said a word. Only the buzz and whirr of the machines dared to make a sound as time slowed down, stretching out interminably and reaching into infinity.

'Yes!' Hayley's woot of relief bounced around him. 'Field is clear. Bleeding's stopped. Clot's evacuated. We did it. Thank goodness I'm sitting down or my legs would collapse.'

'Great job. You've done well.' Tom grinned, wanting to high-five her. She'd held her nerve in a tight corner and now step one was complete. He immediately focused. 'Don't get too excited. You've stopped the bleeding, but we've still got the problem of the pressure. With a mass that size you're going to have to excise a part of it so the brain can get some relief and relax. This takes the risk of her brain herniating down to zero. We also need a biopsy for pathology so we can hand over to Lewis Renwick, who'll operate to remove the rest of the tumour in a day or so.'

'You make it all sound so simple.'

'It's just brain surgery.'

Like a pressure valve being released, everyone laughed. Despite the life-threatening emergency, the fraught conditions and the fact he couldn't operate, something inside Tom relaxed. Something that hadn't relaxed in a very, very long time.

Hayley felt utterly shattered as she walked toward ICU. Even though it had only been three and a half hours since she'd operated on Gretel, it felt like years ago. Having used up every ounce of her concentration whilst operating on her neurological patient, she'd expected to be able to fall in a quivering heap the moment the surgery was over.

Instead, just as Tom and David had left the OR to escort Gretel to ICU, she'd been called back down to Emergency for another consultation. Half an hour later she'd been scrubbed again and busy resecting an ischaemic bowel. It hadn't been an easy operation either.

Now pink streaks of dawn clung to the clouds and all she wanted was her bed, but she couldn't go home without calling in to see Gretel. She pushed open the doors, checked the patient board, and walked directly to cubicle four. She stood at the end of the ICU bed and blinked. Twice. Shooting out her hand, she gripped the edge of the bed as her legs threatened to collapse in shock. She didn't know what stunned her more, the fact that Gretel—whose head she'd had her hands inside a few short hours ago—was sitting up, awake and talking to two doctors, or that Tom was one of those doctors.

He was sitting by the bed, holding Gretel's hand. His face had lost its taut expression—the one she'd become convinced was a permanent part of him—and he looked almost happy.

Tom turned slowly and his nostrils flared. 'Hayley?'

A buzz of hope streaked along her veins. *He knows it's you.*

It's not personal. He's got ninja olfactory skills.

She nodded automatically and then realised her mistake. 'Yes, Tom, it's me.'

'Lewis…' Tom threw his arm out toward her '…meet Hayley Grey, the registrar who operated on Gretel.'

A man in a crumpled suit extended his hand in greeting along with a tired smile. 'Lewis Renwick. Last neurosurgeon in Sydney, it seems. Sorry I was tied up at RPH, but Tom's been telling me that you coped admirably. Looking at the most recent scan, I agree. You've done a wonderful job.'

Hayley grinned with relief. 'Thank you, but I'm pretty good at following instructions.'

Lewis laughed. 'Which is fortunate as Tom's pretty good at giving them.'

Tom's dark brows rose but a grin clung to his lips. 'Only because most people need them.'

Gretel smiled and touched her hair. 'Thanks, Dr Grey, not just for saving my life but for saving most of my hair.'

'You're very welcome, but it was very much a team event, with Mr Jordan guiding me through it.'

'I know, he told me all about it.' Gretel glanced between the three of them, but spoke directly to Hayley. 'I can't believe all this has happened to me, but at least the tumour isn't cancerous. I'm so lucky that you and Mr Jordan were here tonight and now to have Mr Renwick looking after me.'

Tom patted Gretel's hand and gave her a big wink. 'He's almost as good a neurosurgeon as me except for his lousy taste in music.'

'So now you're taking on Mozart?' Lewis folded his arms in mock effrontery.

'I always let my patients choose their playlist for the awake part of their surgery.'

The joking faded from Tom's voice and Hayley saw how much he missed hospital life. It wasn't just the surgery but his patients as well. Perhaps the patients even more than the surgery? The thought hovered for a moment before she discarded it.

'I tell you what, Gretel...' Lewis made a note on her chart '...ask your family to bring in your MP3 player and as long as there's no hip-hop on it, you can listen to your music while I'm removing the tumour and the anaesthetist is asking you questions.'

'That's awesome, Mr Renwick. Thank you.' Gretel

touched the bandage on her head. 'It's going to be weird being awake while you're operating on my brain.'

Hayley gave Gretel's foot a pat. 'I'll leave you to talk to Mr Renwick about the surgery as I'm heading home now, but I'll call by later tonight when I'm back on duty.'

'I'll come with you.' Tom rose and flicked out his cane.

Hayley's feet stayed still in surprise. He'd been brilliant in Theatre, but she could still vividly remember what he'd said when he'd first answered the phone. Now he wanted to leave with her? It didn't make sense.

He's in ICU with machines everywhere. He'll need some guidance to get to the safety of the corridor.

Yep, that would be it.

Logic didn't stop the sneaking fizz of disappointment.

'You're in good hands, Gretel.' Tom's voice suddenly took on a parental tone with an underlying warning. 'Take care of her, Lewis.'

Hayley stepped up to Tom and said quietly, 'Would you like to put your hand on my shoulder or tap your way out?'

His entire body stiffened. 'I'll take your elbow.'

She lifted his hand and guided it to her left elbow. 'Are you ready?'

'As I'll ever be.'

The prickly man was back and she didn't try to make polite conversation. She walked normally, but she did slow just before the nurses' station. 'Do you want to speak to any staff before you leave?'

He frowned and his mouth flattened. 'Is there any point? Gretel isn't my patient.'

She didn't even try to stop the snarky tone in her voice. 'Oh, right. How could I have possibly forgotten that you don't do social niceties?'

The corner of his mouth twitched, but he didn't say a word.

She kept walking and was about to say 'The door is just ahead' when Tom got in first.

'Five steps to the door,' he said. 'If you open it, I'll walk through the doorway and meet you on the other side.'

'Okay.' She did as he asked and then rejoined him in the corridor. She wondered if he might insist on walking on his own but he took her arm again.

As the music played around them in the lift, he said, 'You did a great job today.'

'Thank you.' The ping sounded and the doors opened.

He gave a brisk nod. 'I'm going to use the exit into the lane.'

She thought about where she'd run the other day. 'The one where Pete's got the rubbish dumpster?'

'That's it.'

It was on the other side of the hospital from the exit she usually used, and she wondered if it was Tom code for *I'll walk on my own now*? But he hadn't let go of her arm so she kept walking with him toward the door. Just as Hayley pushed open the heavy external door, a ward clerk, hurrying in for the morning shift, stopped to let them through.

'Mr Jordan?' The woman's face lit up with a huge smile. 'It's Penny. It's so great to see you. You've been missed.'

Tom extended his hand, which the clerk pressed warmly. 'Penny, it's great to hear your voice. How's Ben doing?'

'He's thriving, thanks to you. Can you believe that he's even playing football in the under nines?'

Tom moved his head toward her voice. 'I can believe it. He was a determined kid and I'm pleased to know he's doing so well.' He gave her a warm smile. 'You take care, Penny.'

Hayley stared at him, hardly able to recognise the man standing next to her.

Be fair. He was like this with Gretel.

Just not with me. Her silent sigh dragged her shoulders down a touch.

'You take care too, Mr Jordan.' Penny squeezed Tom's hand again. 'Goodbye.' She hurried inside to work and the door slammed shut behind her.

Tom's grip on Hayley's arm increased ever so slightly and he leaned in towards her, his deep voice caressing her ear and sparking such a swirl of longing that she wanted to move her head so her lips would brush his.

'And you thought I didn't do social chitchat.' He tapped his cane and grinned. 'Time to pick your jaw up off the ground, Hayley Grey.'

Just when she thought she'd got Tom Jordan figured out, he went and did something totally unpredictable like this. She tried to close her gaping mouth, but before she could, a giggle escaped, and then another and another, until she couldn't stop. It was like her veins were full of laughter bubbles and they just kept rising to the surface, being carried up on a wave of fatigue and sheer relief that the night was finally over. Everything seemed uproariously funny and she gave in to it, loving the reckless feeling and the joy that came with it.

Tom's bass laugh joined hers, making her laugh even harder until tears streamed down her face, her sides ached and she could hardly hold her head up. She let it fall onto his shoulder as she gasped for breath. 'I don't even know why I'm laughing.'

'The non-technical term is slap happy.' He pressed his

free hand gently against her hair. 'It's a release for the pressure of the last few hours.'

She raised her head, loving the way his hand now curved around the back of her neck. 'It doesn't usually happen to me.'

'You don't usually do brain surgery.' Now his fingers were stroking her neck and then they moved along her jaw, tilting her chin. His eyes that couldn't see her darkened with desire. 'You were amazing. Are amazing.'

Her laughter faded at his voice—husky, filled with admiration and undisguised attraction. Unlike the last time they'd almost kissed, this time there was no ambiguity. This time his words and tone of voice matched his expression. Nothing about him was pushing her away.

Her brain melted into a puddle of need as he traced her mouth with the tips of his fingers. Zips of sensation tore through her, detonating heat, lust and a desperate yearning all over her body. Then his mouth pressed against hers— gentle yet firm and, oh, so scorching hot. She heard a soft moan as she opened her mouth under his and realised it had come from her. His taste flooded her—coffee, peppermint and hunger for her—swirling into her mouth, diving deep and strumming the strings of her need. It knocked her off her feet.

She sagged against him. He stumbled slightly at the unexpected weight and she flung her arm around his waist to steady him. She didn't want to give him any reason to pull away. She closed her eyes and let him kiss her, giving him full rein to explore her mouth, to nip her lips with his teeth, to caress and explore with his tongue and to brand her with his flavour of arousal. Sinking into the kiss, his heat simmered her blood, making every pulse point throb, and she never wanted it to end.

She'd been kissed before but nothing like this. It was

as if he was stealing part of her and she was giving it up freely, but still he demanded more and she could feel the pull. Suddenly her blissed-out body woke up and demanded him. She cupped his cheeks, felt his stubble grazing her palms and she kissed him back.

Hard.

Fast.

Her tongue duelled with his and dominated his mouth, seeking his fire and merging it with hers. She heard him moan, heard his cane fall to the ground and felt his mouth plunder hers with a weight that stole her breath.

Panting, he tore his mouth away from hers and she shivered from the loss of his touch.

His hand ploughed through his hair. 'Hell, I used to have a lot more finesse than this. We're standing next to a rubbish dumpster.'

'I hadn't noticed.' She touched his cheek, wanting to keep the contact. Not wanting him to change his mind.

He laughed and brought his hand up to cover hers. 'Your sense of smell is hopeless.'

'I thought we were dealing with a whole lot of other senses and, believe me, you still have loads of finesse.' She kissed him quickly and decided to act. 'I don't have my car, but my place isn't far. It's over on Northcliff.'

He smiled and his eyes seemed to sparkle like the phosphorescent green waters of the Great Barrier Reef. 'Mine's closer. Walk fast.'

CHAPTER SIX

Tom stretched out in his bed, feeling completely sated. The musky smell of sex, the sweet scent of Hayley and the warmth from her body circled him, and he realised he hadn't felt this relaxed since— Hell, he had no clue how long it had been and at that moment he didn't care. He just was. He grinned at the play of light and dark in the room, shadows cast by the morning light. They'd made it to his apartment—just. Somehow he'd got his trembling hand to insert the key into the lock and had managed to turn it and open the door. In a tumble of clothes, they'd kicked off shoes, popped buttons, got arms tangled up in sleeves and shucked pants until finally they'd fallen into his bed and come together in a rush of blood-pounding desire and screaming lust—hot, fast and breath-stealing. Nothing about it had been slow. Nothing about it had been measured. It had been all about need—his and hers—two people equal in their quest to lose themselves in each other, taking more than giving.

Now, as his lungs refilled with air and his blood came back to his brain, the full impact of what had just happened hit him. He had a woman in *his* bed. A woman in his apartment. Before he'd gone blind, he'd always had sex with a woman at her place. That way he had been the one in control. He could get up and leave when he was ready, sometimes before he was ready if the hospital called him out—but either way his departure took place prior to the woman snuggling up and falling asleep on his shoulder. He'd always mumble something about 'work' and 'calling later', which, of course, he never did. Work had always come first because it protected him from tumbling back to poverty and the griminess of his childhood.

The mattress moved and he reached his hand out to touch Hayley's silky hair, surprised at the need he had to feel her presence.

You never went in for touchy-feely stuff.

The last time I had sex I wasn't blind. This is my way of seeing her.

If you say so.

He blocked out his internal argument. 'You okay, Hayley?'

'I'm fine. Why?'

He heard the smile in her voice. 'It was pretty fast.'

She gave a throaty laugh. 'Fast, but good, I hope.'

'Very good.' And it had been. Intoxicatingly good, and his blood still sang with her taste and touch. The buzz reminded him of the high he'd always got from riding his 1000 cc motorcycle fast along the coast with the throb of the powerful engine vibrating through him, and the wind and salt pounding him. It was amplified exhilaration and totally addictive. But as much as he'd loved the speed of his motorcycle and his sports car, he'd also enjoyed long, leisurely walks. That had given him a totally different buzz and that was the one he wanted now. He knew the urgent feel of Hayley's arms and legs around him, the hot press of her body against his, and her gasps of breath as she begged for him. This time he wanted to feel and hear her shatter from a long, slow build-up. From a seduction so unhurried in its approach that it would sneak up unannounced and render her deliciously helpless with its power. And then he'd join her.

Hayley felt Tom's fingers in her hair and the unhurried way they explored its length until they reached her scalp and traced the width of her forehead. The touch was gentle as opposed to urgent, which was how it had been from the moment they'd stumbled into his apartment. How she'd managed to stand next to him in the hall, watching him miss the door lock three times without lunging for the key and ripping it out of his hand and slamming it into the lock, still amazed her. Both of them had been crazy with lust and had given themselves over to it completely. Now the exhilaration was fading and exhaustion from her huge night at The Harbour was sending out its cloying tendrils. His fingers soothed and her eyes fluttered shut.

'What happened here?'

Her eyes flew open as she felt his fingers on her hairline, caressing the small scar that nestled there, hidden under her hair. No one ever saw it and yet Tom, who couldn't see, had found it. She looked up at him as he stared down at her through beautiful yet sightless eyes, knowing she was only a shadow to him. 'I fell off my bike when I was nine.'

He nodded slowly as if he was compiling a picture of her. 'What colour's your hair?'

'I say it's brown but my hairdresser insists it's chestnut. However, we both agree that it's dead straight.'

His mouth tweaked up in a half-smile. 'That I knew. Not one single curl snagged my fingers.' He breathed deeply as he ran strands of her hair across his face. 'It smells like lime and coconut.'

Her short laugh showed her embarrassment. 'I have a bit of a thing for body lotions, perfumes and shampoo, but I also know that often patients are scared before surgery so I think I should smell nice for them.'

He pressed his lips to her forehead. 'I appreciate it.'

A silly quiver of happiness shoved her embarrassment away.

His palms cupped her cheeks and his thumbs met at the bridge of her nose. He stroked outwards with a delicious amount of pressure—not firm but not soft either—and she let his touch roll over her, stripping her muscles of all their tension as she sank into the mattress. She'd never been touched quite like this. It was an almost reverent exploration that put sighted lovers in the shade. His hands brushed her eyebrows and then outlined her closed eyes.

Again Tom's voice called her back. 'Are they chestnut too?'

She struggled to concentrate as his fingers sent rivers of relaxation washing through her. 'What?'

'Your eyebrows. Are they chestnut?'

It seemed odd to be describing herself—almost vain—but she'd enjoyed watching Tom and studying him over the last ten days and this was his turn. 'No, they're darker and so are my eyelashes. With my brown eyes and long brown lashes my sister used to—' She bit off the words. She didn't want to think about Amy right now. This wasn't the real world with all its pain and heartache. This was pure escapism.

'Call you a Jersey cow?'

She gasped in surprise. 'How did you know?'

He grinned. 'Big brown eyes and long, thick lashes. It doesn't take a rocket scientist to work that one out.'

His thumbs continued to explore her face. 'Your nose is cuter than a Jersey cow's.'

'Gee, thanks.' She laughed half-indignantly and then

reached out her hand, running it along the length of his very distinctive nose and lingering on the slight bump. 'Mine hasn't been broken.'

'You probably grew up on the Northern Beaches.' It was said without rancour, but it inferred that her childhood had been easier than his.

She didn't confirm her middle-class upbringing because she knew more than anyone that money didn't protect a child from death or a family from loss. Instead, she let him capture her hand from his nose, place it by her side and then kiss her.

Deep beyond her tiredness, her body stirred.

The length of his body edged hers lightly, moving against it and then away with each breath he took. His hands brushed her chin and her neck, and then he stroked her collarbone with a feather-soft touch, lingering on the slightly raised area on the right-hand side. 'The bike accident?'

A delicious tingle spread around her body, demolishing the fatigue and waking her up in the most wonderful way. 'Who knew my body was a road map of my life? There's an appendix scar further down.'

'Poor Hayley.'

He kissed the spot where the bone had knitted, his tongue caressing her skin, and her legs twitched as the shimmers joined together into one wide river of glorious sensation. Then his hands reached her breasts and his touch became almost reverent. Cupping them, he took their weight and a deep line of concentration carved into his brow.

She was instantly self-conscious, wondering what was wrong with her breasts. 'What?'

'They're just as I imagined.'

She didn't understand. 'But you've touched them before.'

He smiled a knowing smile. 'That was a mere brush of the hand, which to a blind man is nothing more than a passing glance. Now, this…' his thumb stroked her nipple '…is really seeing them.'

A hot arrow of longing darted straight down between her legs and her body jerked against his.

This time he grinned widely. 'If you like that, you might just enjoy this.'

His mouth closed around the areola of her other breast while his thumb continued to brush the nipple. Her breasts tightened and her nipples puckered, desperately seeking more. Her breath hitched in her throat as showers of colour and ribbons of heat followed, making her head thrash against the pillow. She never wanted it to stop and her hands plunged into his hair in a combination of wanting to touch him and not wanting him to stop what he was doing.

His wicked laugh rained down on her as he dawdled his tongue and his hands down her belly, stroking her, tasting her and branding her with his stubble until her body was quivering and slick with throbbing need for him.

Her arms flailed out toward the bedside table and she managed to gasp, 'Condoms.'

He shook his head as his fingers reached the only thatch of hair on her body that was curly. 'We're not ready for that just yet.'

She stared at his face as she tried hard to bring her eyes into focus. 'We're…not?'

'No.' His fingers sneaked slowly lower and lower with blissful intent, and then he slid one inside her. Then another.

She gasped with delight and instantly tightened around

his fingers before closing her eyes and joining the ride to oblivion. Nothing existed except the ever-increasing ball of sensation that he was building inside her with his talented hands.

Suddenly, his fingers stopped and then withdrew.

Shocked surprise and begging need snapped her eyes open, fast. 'Don't stop.' She heard the desperation in her voice and didn't care. 'Please, don't stop.'

His face was wreathed in one enormous smile that crinkled the edges of his eyes, which now glowed with a light she'd never seen before. With his other hand he drew a lazy circle on her lower belly. 'Just tell me, what's the colour of the hair down here?'

She heard words, but her completely melted brain frantically scrambled, trying to find some neurons that would still connect. It tried, but the colour eluded her. 'You're a shocking tease, Tom Jordan. Does it even matter?'

'Yes. It completes my picture of you.'

The tenderness in his words touched her and the permanent emptiness around her heart shrank a little. She pressed her hand against his chest and the almost black hair that rested there. 'This colour.'

'Beautiful.'

He moved and she felt his hair lightly brush her belly and then his lips pressing kisses on her inner thigh before finding the perfect place.

Deep within, her scream of need ignited and she cried out for him, wanting him to fill her, aching for his width, but then her body took over, riding the pounding waves of wonder, sweeping her higher and higher until the ball of bliss exploded, flinging her far beyond herself to a place she'd never been.

When she floated back to earth, she pulled his face to

hers and kissed him. 'Thank you. Now I want to give you the same gift.'

'And you can.'

He rolled her over so he was under her and then he pressed a foil square into her hand. She rolled the condom over his erection, marvelling at his long, silky length, and she kept stroking him, loving the feel of him against her palm.

He groaned and his face flushed. 'Listening to you come almost undid me so if you want the full experience you need to stop doing that right now.'

'Really?' She leaned forward, letting her hair sweep across his chest, surprised but loving the fact that her orgasm had turned him on when she'd seen it as a selfless gift from him.

He grabbed her buttocks and lifted her. 'Believe me. Really.'

A surge of power filled her—her femininity rising to dominate for the very first time in her life. This sightless man desired her and wanted her, and just as he'd held the key to demolishing all her restraint, she now held the key to his. She also knew that by giving him release she too would receive it. Lowering her body slowly, she felt herself opening up layer upon layer to take him, to absorb him, and then she closed tightly around him.

His guttural groan filled the room and then his hands gripped her hips. In a rhythm as old as time they moved together, driving each other upward, taking and giving, needing and demanding, until they both cried out with the glory of touching the stars.

Warmth cocooned Hayley. Warmth, cosiness and blissful rest. Everything around her was fuzzy—a sort of soft focus—and she had an overwhelming feeling of being safe. She didn't know how she'd come to be on a beach, lying on a large and lovely soft towel, or how long she'd even been here, but it didn't matter. She had sunshine on her back, the soporific lapping sounds of a gentle tide against the sand, and the sleep she always craved beckoned her with an addictive serenade. The Sandman with his dancing eyes said, 'Sunshine so you can sleep in a lovely pale red glow. I did this just for you. You know you want to sleep so close your eyes and leave the rest to me.'

And she was so very tired. Chronically tired from years of not getting enough sleep and this was all so perfect. She let her book fall from her hands as she laid her head down and then she let her eyelids fall shut.

The promised pink glow surrounded her and all her stress and fatigue rolled away, absorbed by the heat of the sand. The beguiling Sandman was right. This was the perfect place to sleep. Why had it taken so long to find this beach? She might never leave. As she stretched out with a sigh, the pink glow deepened to a claret-red. She fell deeper into sleep. A shiver ran along her spine as a cool breeze sneaked in around her back. She rolled over, chasing the sun, but it vanished, leaving darkness in its place. Her hand shot out, grasping for the heat of the sand, but instead of warm silica and quartz crystals she touched cold, lifeless marble. She pulled her hand back in fright as the inky darkness intensified, roaring in, settling over her like the membrane of suffocating plastic and denying her breath.

Her heart slammed against her chest as panic screamed in her ears. She gasped for breath, desperately trying to flee the dark and find the light. The more she fought the dark, the stronger its grip on her became until it pinned her down, trapping her in its clutches. She tried to stand but her legs were tied and everything she touched burned her with desolate cold.

Get out. Get out now before you die.

Panting hard, she gave an almighty push and kicked hard. Her eyes flew open and she realised she was now awake—abruptly jolted out of a nightmare. Her tight chest formed a band around her and she could hardly move any air and her head spun while her fingertips tingled.

Breathe in, breathe out. Count it in, count it out. Gradually, her eyes adjusted to the dark. Her skin was drenched in sweat, her legs felt constricted and slowly she realised she was in a bed and tangled up in a sheet and duvet. A tiny chink of light squeezed through a small gap at the closing point of the curtains.

Curtains? She never closed the curtains during the day.

And then she remembered. She was in Tom's bed.

Her arm reached out and patted cold sheets. Alone in Tom's bed.

Kicking her legs free of the rope-like sheet and pushing the duvet back, she jumped up and whipped open the curtains. Sunshine flooded the room and she fell back onto the bed and pushed herself up onto a pile of pillows. She was safe. A half laugh and half groan rumbled up from deep inside her and she automatically turned toward the bedside table, seeking a clock. But no green or red digital display greeted her. Instead, there was a large black cube with a big button on top. She pressed it and then jumped in surprise when an automated male voice said, "It's three-seventeen p.m., Wednesday, August nineteen."

She'd been asleep for seven hours? That totally stunned her. Despite the nightmare wake-up, she'd slept soundly, and in a foreign bed. She never slept very well and what sleep she was able to get always occurred in her own bed with the blinds wide open. It had been light when she'd fallen asleep and Tom must have closed the curtains for her when he'd got up, thinking it would help her sleep.

Mind-blowing sex was why you slept so well.

She grinned like a child who'd just been given a lollipop. Tom had been the most amazing lover and going by his moans and groans and panting breath she hadn't been too shoddy either. She could feel the ache of muscles that hadn't been used for a long time and just the thought of what had made them ache made her tingle.

Three o'clock. She had four hours before she had to be at work. It was time to get up and bring Tom back to bed for an hour or so before she had to head home and get ready for work. Maybe they could even grab an early dinner. Ignoring the crumpled scrubs on the floor, she whipped the sheet off the bed. Wrapping it around herself like a strapless gown, she was aiming for a seductive look—or, for Tom, a seductive feel—and she walked out into the open-plan room saying, 'Thanks for letting me sleep. I… Oh.'

The same young man she'd seen the first morning she'd met Tom was sitting at the large table in front of a laptop with a couple of textbooks open next to him. His face wore a wide grin as he stared at her, appreciating the look.

'Hello.' His blue eyes rested on her cleavage.

She gripped the top of the sheet more tightly and pulled the trailing section forward, making sure her back and legs were fully covered. Her chin shot up in an attempt to make her look a lot more in control than she felt. 'Hi. I'm Hayley.'

'Yeah, I know. Tom said.' He kept on grinning as if he'd witnessed exactly what had gone down in the bedroom seven hours earlier.

Oh, God, shoot me now. 'And you're…?'

He jumped to his feet as if her question had suddenly

woken him up and kick-started his manners. 'Jared. Jared Perkins.'

'Jared.' She took a breath to slow down her delivery and keep a handle on her embarrassment. 'Is Tom home?'

He shook his sandy-coloured head. 'No.'

'Are you expecting him back soon?'

'He's at work.' He picked up a printed piece of paper and consulted it. 'He's got an evening lecture and I'm picking him up at seven.'

'Right.' Her brain started churning over times and dates. Tom finished work at seven and she started work at seven. 'Did he leave a message?'

'No.'

Disappointment slugged her and she tried to brush it away. It wasn't like they'd made an arrangement to meet. Rational thought zoomed in, making her practical. She was standing dressed in nothing but a sheet for a man who wasn't even here. It was time to go home. She ducked back into the bedroom, dumped the sheet, pulled on her clothes and ran her fingers through her hair before snagging it back into a ponytail with a hair-tie she found in her pocket. She didn't look in the mirror because it would be far too depressing and gave up a quick wish that she didn't meet anyone she knew on the walk home, which was a sure-fire guarantee that she would.

When she returned to the living area, Jared was sitting back at the table, reading one of the textbooks. In his bright-coloured board shorts and surfing T-shirt, he looked as if he belonged more on Bondi Beach than inside, studying. Who was he? Tom's brother? Nephew? She realised she didn't know anything about Tom except he'd been a neurosurgeon and now he wasn't.

'Do you live here, Jared?'

'Nah. Wouldn't mind it, though.' He swung his arm out toward the balcony. 'It's an awesome view.'

'It is.' What exactly was his connection to Tom? 'Do you work for Tom?'

He shook his head emphatically. 'No, but I do stuff for him. Driving, shopping, anything he wants.'

She guessed Jared was in his late teens or early twenties and his broad accent and lack of social etiquette hinted at the possibility that he came from a less affluent suburb. Being on call for a taciturn blind man without any financial incentive struck her as unusual. 'That's very good of you.'

Jared's shoulders rolled back and he sat up straighter, as if she'd just offended him. 'No, it isn't. Tom's an awesome bloke and he saved my life.' The sincerity in his words put her rightfully back in her place.

She aimed for a conciliatory tone. 'Everyone at The Harbour says he was a brilliant surgeon.'

'Yeah.' He fiddled with the edge of the textbook, folding up the corner of the page.

Hayley waited for him to say more, to say exactly what operation Tom had performed on him, but he didn't elaborate and instead stuck his finger back on a line of text in the book and stared at it with a deep frown.

Okay. 'I'll leave you to it.' She walked to the door and had her hand on the handle when Jared said, 'You any good at chemistry?'

She stopped and turned to face him. 'Excuse me?'

'Chemistry.' His voice rose slightly with aggression, and his previously friendly and open face tightened. He picked up a sheaf of papers covered in red pen and waved them at her. 'The teacher says if I want to get into medicine I need an A and Tom says it's easy but it bloody isn't. You're a doctor, right? So you get chemistry.'

His blue eyes held the duelling expressions of 'I'm a macho guy' with 'I need help, Mum'. She realised it had cost him something to ask her. Just like she knew it cost Tom something every time he had to ask for help. She was struck by the similarity and she knew she couldn't ignore his request.

She walked back to the table and dropped her bag on a chair. 'Can you make coffee, Jared?'

'Yeah. Tom's got a machine.'

She smiled. 'Good. You make me a latte and I'll read what's causing you problems and see if I can help. Deal?'

Relief washed over his face. 'Deal.'

'If we grab some take-away, Jared, I can help you with that chemistry homework when we get home,' Tom offered as he fiddled with the seat-belt buckle, finally sliding it into the holder with a snap.

'Thanks, but I got it sorted. But if you're buying, I'll stay for take-away as long as it's pizza.'

'You finished the chemistry?' Tom wished his voice hadn't risen in surprise. He knew how hard Jared was working and chemistry wasn't something that came easily to him, but he had dogged determination and that often served a person better than natural ability without the drive to succeed.

'Don't sound so surprised, old man. You're not the only person good at this stuff.'

Jared's cocky tone was in stark contrast to the down-in-the-mouth voice he'd used earlier in the day when Tom had told him he could help him, but not until after work. He instinctively knew something else was now at play. 'Enough of the old man, kiddo.' He hit the word, teasing the youth back. 'So, just like that, you totally understand electrochemical series order, which five hours ago had you ready to quit school?'

'Yep.'

'Good for you.'

A moment of silence passed between them and then Jared said, 'Hayley helped.'

Hayley.

Hayley, who'd been fast asleep in his bed when he'd left his apartment. He'd left it way earlier than necessary because he hadn't wanted to be there when she woke up. Hell, he'd even invited Jared over under the guise of a fast internet connection and a quiet place to study well away from the noise of younger siblings, but the invitation had been all about Jared being in the apartment with him if Hayley woke up before he left for work. Insurance so they wouldn't be alone together again, because if they had been he didn't trust himself not to take her back to bed.

Blood pooled in his lap. Hell, just the thought of her had him wanting to retract his decision, but when he'd been sighted he'd never slept with a woman more than once. Well, not since he'd been a second-year registrar. He'd had one short-lived relationship with Karen, a radiographer, but he'd found within three months of dating that she'd had expectations of being considered first in his life, well ahead of study and his job. It had been a distraction he hadn't wanted or needed. At first putting study first had been all about fear of failure and fear of poverty, but then it had become so much more and nothing and no one had been allowed to come ahead of medicine and his plan to become a neurosurgeon. He'd owed Mick that. He'd owed Mick and Carol everything. Once he'd qualified he'd set his sights on heading his own department. Work had always come first and from the moment he and Karen parted, he'd only ever spent one night with any woman.

The fact he'd achieved the pinnacles of surgical success and had now lost it all didn't seem enough of a reason to change his habits. Financially he was secure and the threat of poverty was long gone but, hell, he was still learning how to be blind. He didn't need any distractions from conquering the dark and living an independent and meaningful life.

'Hey, Tom, as well as being totally hot, she's an awesome teacher.'

Jared's enthusiasm for Hayley rang out loud and clear and Tom's jaw instinctively tightened. 'I'd appreciate it if you referred to her in terms of a surgeon and a teacher.'

'Sorry. I'm not gonna steal her from you, dude. I'd never do that.'

The apology in the young man's voice was unmistakeable and Tom regretted being short with him. He still wasn't totally certain why he had been. Yes, this morning had been amazing, but now it was over.

'Besides,' Jared continued, 'she's a bit old for me, but she's perfect for a bloke like you who's nearly forty.' He made the number sound ancient.

Tom gave a strangled laugh. 'I'm thirty-nine, thank you, and if you keep on about it I'll buy Chinese instead of pizza.'

'You're the same age as my dad.' The teasing had vanished from Jared's voice, leaving only regret.

Tom flinched. He hadn't meant to remind the boy of his absent father or of his tough home life. He turned toward the sound of his voice and smiled. 'I'm thinking two large La Dolce Vita specials with the lot.'

'And a garlic pizza. Order them now and make sure they throw in the gelato because last time you let them rip you off and you don't want me saying you're getting old and soft.'

Tom's mouth tweaked up into a smile. 'Just drive the damn car, Jared.'

CHAPTER SEVEN

As the tinny beat-bop music filled the operating theatre, Hayley looked up from the screen, which showed the magnified image of Mrs Papadopoulos's stone-filled gallbladder and she asked, 'Is that my phone?'

The moment the four little words were airborne, she wanted to pull the words back. She'd forgotten that Jenny wasn't scouting for this operation.

'I'll check,' said Suzy.

Dread crawled along her skin. Why did it have to be Suzy? For the first time in days Hayley willed that the phone call *not* be from Tom.

It was close to the end of a long shift—twelve midnight to twelve noon—the result of a crazy idea from someone in Administration who thought it might help diminish the surgical waiting list. It meant the team had a foot in both the night shift with its emergencies and the elective routine of the day shift morning.

'Answer it quickly, Suzy.' Theo rolled his eyes as if the sound was burning his ears. 'Hayley, of all the ringtones that state-of-the-art phone of yours has, why did you choose that one? You have to change it.'

'I can't.' She dropped her gaze back to the screen as she manoeuvred everything into position in preparation to sever the gallbladder from its anchoring stump. 'I accidentally washed my lovely phone and now it's tucked up in rice in a vague hope it might work again. Meanwhile, I've bought a temporary cheap phone and it only comes with one ringtone and one volume.'

'My ears are aching already.' With a gloved hand Theo held out a kidney dish.

Hayley dropped the badly scarred gallbladder onto the silver monometal and tried not to glance around at Suzy and ask who was calling. It had been five days since she'd seen Tom. Five days since she'd experienced the best sex of her life and then slept the most deeply she could ever remember, but since she'd left his apartment there'd been no messages, no texts, no emails, nothing. Just one long and empty silence that dragged through each day, seemingly extending it way beyond its twenty-fours.

Get over it. He never said he'd call. You never expected him to call.

Logically, she knew that they'd only acted on their simmering attraction and had come together to defuse the stress after a huge operation—that meant it had been a one-off fling. This sort of thing happened between staff occasionally, especially after a life-and-death situation. It was a type of coping mechanism—a way to share the crisis with the only other person who really understood exactly what had happened and the ramifications of how close it had come to going horribly wrong.

At least I had him.

She bit her lip as she realised with a hollow feeling that she now had something in common with Suzy. She'd used Tom and she'd let him use her. Not that she wanted to keep Tom as hers, or at least she didn't think she did, but she hated that she'd allowed herself to become a phone vulture. Twenty-four hours after leaving Tom's penthouse, she'd started circling her phone, constantly waiting for it to either ring or beep with a message, and when either of those two things happened, diving for it and hoping it was Tom. Now she'd even allowed her guard to fall and had asked out loud in front of her gossipy staff.

It's time to get a grip.

Her reaction to the whole Tom situation was totally new to her and, if she was honest, scared her just a little bit. She'd certainly never been this jumpy or spent this much time thinking about Richard or Sam. Or any other man.

'Dr Grey's phone.' Suzy's voice held the same thread of dislike that was always present when she spoke to Hayley, but never seemed to be in attendance when she spoke to the other staff. 'Oh, hello.' Warmth suddenly infused her voice. 'It's Suzy Carpenter.'

Hayley heard the change in her tone and panic made her swing around.

Suzy mouthed, 'Lachlan McQuillan.'

Relief rolled through Hayley that it wasn't Tom and she wasn't about to become the target for gossip.

Suzy continued talking to Hayley's counterpart on the other side of the surgical registrar's roster. Lach usually called Hayley for a handover just prior to starting his shift.

She let Suzy flirt with the Scot while she stitched up the four small incisions she'd made. 'David, I'm done. Thanks, everyone.' She stepped back and stripped off her gloves, leaving the nurses to clean up and the anaesthetist to extubate the patient before handing her over to the care of the recovery nurses.

Suzy was still talking to Lachlan when Hayley put out her hand out for her phone. Suzy glared at her before purring down the line, 'See you at Pete's soon.'

The nurse slapped the phone into Hayley's hand before stalking off, and Hayley rubbed her temples as she put the phone to her ear. Lachlan was just coming back after two days off so the chances of Suzy catching him at Pete's anytime soon were slim.

'Hey, Lach, it's been a quiet night, but if you can keep an eye on Mrs Papadopoulos's blood pressure for me, that would be good.'

'Not a problem, Hayley, lass. Enjoy your sleep.'

'Study more like it. I've got two days off and the exams get closer every day.'

'Aye, they do. It's a shame you missed Finn Kennedy's talk on the surgical considerations of gunshot wounds this morning. The man might be a devil to work for but he knows his stuff.'

'Have you operated with him?' Hayley hadn't told anyone what had happened in the OR with Finn because everyone was allowed a bad day, but it still niggled at her and she wanted another person's opinion.

'Aye, last week. He makes it all look so easy while the rest of us struggle just to finish the job.'

So that was it, then. She'd caught Finn Kennedy on a bad day.

Lachlan continued. 'I stayed on afterwards and caught Tom Jordan's lecture for the final-year medical students about extratemporal epilepsy.'

Tom. Her heart jumped, filling the empty space around it and she had to force herself to sound casual. 'Anything interesting?'

'Aye. Fascinating.' His Scottish accent always sounded stronger when he was excited about something. 'His patient kept spinning and experiencing memory gaps and Tom had a hunch. So, using electrodes for a month, he charted the electrical impulses and from there he removed a three-centimetre-diameter piece of brain from the seventeen-year-old. Turns out it was at the bottom of a malformation called a sulcus dysplasia and the boy's stopped spinning. Amazing stuff.'

'He gives a good lecture, that's for sure.' Worried that her voice would give her away, she switched topics. 'But listen, can you email me any notes from Kennedy's lecture, which is more our area?'

He laughed. 'Sure, although I hear you've taken to brain surgery. I'd better be careful or you'll be making me look second-class.'

'I was lucky, Lach. Believe me, you don't need the stress.'

'Aye, you're right. Enjoy your break.'

Thanks, Lach—' But he'd hung up before she could finish. She slipped her phone into her pocket and rubbed her chest, unused to it feeling this way. The fuller sensation hadn't vanished when her heart had finally resumed its normal rhythm. It was an odd feeling and left her unsettled.

Seeing Tom will help. He might still be in the lecture theatre.

That's stalking.

No, it's not! I have to walk past it to go home.

Opening the door and looking in isn't part of your way home. What happened to getting a grip?

She conceded that point to her conscience. Her time with Tom had been wonderful, but it probably wasn't going to happen again and this jumpy-heart stuff was just fatigue.

As she gathered her jacket, bag and MP3 player out of her locker, acid burned her gut and she realised she hadn't eaten anything more than almonds and chocolate in hours. The thought of a breakfast of bacon, eggs, tomato, sausages and golden buttered toast had her salivating. She checked her watch. Twelve twenty p.m. There was only one place she knew that served breakfast until midafternoon and that was Café Luna, which was a long drive from The Harbour but only a short ferry ride away.

You need to sleep and then study.

Her stomach groaned so loudly that the nurse at a locker further down the room turned around and laughed.

'You better get something to eat fast or you'll need peppermint water for wind pain.'

Hayley joined in the laughter. 'I think you might be right.' She couldn't sleep or study on an empty stomach and if she listened to some lectures on her MP3 player during the journey there and back, that would justify the travel time. Decision made, she slammed her locker shut, shoved white earbuds into her ears and started walking.

Tom had asked Jared to drop him off at a café he'd once visited frequently but hadn't visited since the accident. He'd told Jared that he'd catch a taxi home because he didn't want him to miss out on any classes. Jared, to his credit, hadn't questioned him about why he wanted to come to this out-of-the-way place, given it was a bit of a drive, which was fortunate because Tom wasn't certain he had an answer that made much sense. All he knew was that he'd woken up that morning and had instantly thought about the little beach café. Lately, when he'd been teaching the medical students, he'd experienced odd moments of total focus—the sort of intensity he'd known when he'd been operating. It surprised him because he wasn't at all certain he wanted to teach long-term, but then again he had few other options within medicine and when he thought about working outside medicine, nothing sprang to mind.

Focus in today's lecture, however, had been seriously lacking because the idea of the café had kept interrupting him. By the time he'd answered the final question, it was like the memory of the café had taken hold of him and was demanding to be visited.

Before the accident, he'd often ridden his bike here on a Sunday morning and then he'd sit and read the papers and watch the world go by while gorging himself on the best breakfast in Sydney. Those happy memories had filled him with a zip of anticipation so by the time he'd taken his seat at his favourite outdoor table, he was almost excited. It wasn't an emotion he experienced much any more because the *one* thing that had excited him beyond anything in his life had been surgery and now that was denied him.

Thirty minutes after taking his seat, it wasn't going well. The coffee was still as aromatic and full of the caffeine kick he remembered, and the eggs on the crisply toasted English muffins were deliciously runny and the hollandaise sauce decadently creamy, but he couldn't read the paper and the sounds and smells of the busy café dominated, preventing him from getting any sense of the beach despite it only being three steps away.

The cacophony disoriented him and he hated that. He cursed himself for getting into this position. He should have asked Jared to stay. *No.* What he should have done was not given in to a stupid memory and come to the café. He knew better than giving in to memories because he couldn't relive anything any more. Nothing was ever the same now he'd lost his sight and right now was a perfect example of why he never acted on impulse. When he did, it left him stranded in unfamiliar environments and dependent on others.

'Ah, sir?' The waitress sounded uncertain.

Tom looked towards her, not because he could see her but because he knew sighted people needed him to look at them or else they thought he wasn't listening. In fact, he'd heard her footsteps well before she'd spoken, although he hadn't been certain they belonged to the waitress due to so much passing foot traffic. 'Yes?'

'Can I get you anything else? We've got some lovely cakes today.'

'I'll have another coffee. Are you busy today?'

'You arrived at the peak of the rush, but it'll be quiet again soon. I'll be right back with your espresso.'

He leaned back in the chair and breathed in, trying again to smell the sea, and this time, instead of the dominating smell of onions, bacon, coriander and chocolate, he caught a whiff of salt. He heard the excited shout of a child, but any responding voices were drowned out by an almighty crash of crockery. He sighed. Ironically, he'd never noticed any noise in the café when his entire perspective of the world had been absorbed through the visual.

His coffee arrived at the same time he heard the rumble of a ferry's engine and the cheery toot of the horn. Soon after, just as the waitress had predicted, the café quietened, which allowed the sounds of the beach to finally drift in and the salt on the air make his nostrils tingle. A second later he caught the sudden scent of summer flowers and his gut tightened.

A woman in the café or walking past on the beach was wearing the same perfume as Hayley.

Damn it. He'd managed not to think about her very often today, but it didn't take much to bring her front and centre in his mind. He'd been battling errant thoughts of Hayley for five long days, which made no sense to him at all. In the past, although he'd enjoyed his encounters with women, he'd never thought about them afterwards and he'd never had his thoughts interrupted by memories of them.

He heard a woman's voice from somewhere off to his left. 'Oh! You've dropped your teddy. Here you are.'

Tom's head swung toward the voice, which sounded identical to Hayley's.

You're totally losing it. Let's look at the facts. 1. Other women have been known to wear that perfume. 2. You're nowhere near the hospital or where she lives so that rules out Hayley. He reached out his fingers, feeling for the edge of the saucer in preparation for picking up the small coffee cup.

Noise buzzed behind him—murmured thanks, the squeak of wheels, possibly from a stroller, and then soft footsteps. Jerky almost. The exact same stop-start gait he'd heard the night he'd met Hayley on the way to the car park.

Stop it.

He ran his hand through his hair, pulling at the short strands as if that slight pain would shake the ridiculous thoughts from his head.

A cloud of coconut and floral scent floated over him and he gripped the edge of the table. He had no clue who was standing near him, and yet everything in him screamed it was Hayley. A bitter surge of vitriol at his useless eyes duelled with the surge of heat that rolled through him, taunting him with the memory of what he'd been doing the last time he'd breathed in that combination of fragrances.

'Tom? What on earth are you doing here?'

Hayley. She sounded stunned, indignant and happy all at the same time. He understood the emotions exactly. He somehow got this throat to work. 'Having breakfast for lunch.'

She laughed. 'That's why I'm here. I finished work and all I could think about was the big breakfast. May I join you?'

Say no now to avoid problems later. 'Sure.'

'Great.'

He started to move so he could stand up for her, but she said, 'There's a stroller wedged in behind you. Have you eaten?'

He welcomed her matter-of-fact tone of voice and how she'd just slipped in the information quietly without making a fuss and then continued with her conversation. 'I had the eggs Benedict.'

'Ohh, fancy. I'm going for straight grease today with an extra side of hash browns. It's crazy but sometimes I dream about these breakfasts and when I do I think it's my body telling me that I need some salt and fat.'

He remembered her delectable curves and how he'd appreciated them, unlike the feel of a woman who fought with food. He grinned. 'Sounds reasonable to me.'

She quickly gave her order to the waitress and sighed.

'Problem?'

'No, not at all.' She sounded relaxed and happy. 'It was a catching-my-breath sigh.'

He knew what she meant. 'I used to do that here.'

'Used to? Simple deduction tells me you're still doing it.'

He shook his head. 'Today's the first time I've been here in over two years.' He expected his words to be greeted with an embarrassed silence due to the indirect reference to his accident. Instead, he heard the creak of her chair as she moved in it.

'I love coming to this café and here's a perfect example why. There's an elderly couple walking hand in hand along the pier. They're deep in conversation and wearing hiking boots so I guess they're going to walk to the next cove along the cliff-top path. To your left, on the beach, there's a little boy about three and he's trying to wrestle a bright red ball from his toddler sister.'

He heard a high-pitched squeal. 'I gather the sister doesn't want to give up the ball.'

Hayley laughed and the rich, smoky sound carried both the warmth and softness of velvet. 'No, she's holding on tight and he's just sat on her. Their mother, who's on her mobile phone, hasn't paused her conversation for a second. She's just picked him up by the back of his T-shirt and he's flailing his arms and legs about.' She dropped her voice. 'Just behind you is a boy who looks about eighteen. He's got heavily tattooed arms, piercings on his face, but he's cuddling a puppy as if it's the most precious thing in the world.'

Tom instantly remembered the dog he'd adopted as a child and how devastated he'd been when it had died. His father had taken off when he'd been a baby and had never made contact again. Although his mother had loved him, she'd loved the contents of a bottle more. The dog, however, had loved him unconditionally and he could understand why the tough-looking young man was showing the puppy affection. The animal was probably the only thing in his life that gave him positive vibes. 'What sort of dog is it?'

The screeching scrape of the chair legs against concrete sounded and then he heard Hayley saying, 'Excuse me. Could we have a look at your puppy, please?'

He tensed. 'Hell, Hayley I didn't mean you to—'

But Hayley ignored him and starting talking to someone he assumed was the tattooed young man.

'Oh, he's just gorgeous,' she cooed. 'He's going to be a huge dog if he grows into those feet. This is my friend,

Tom. He's blind but he wanted to know what sort of dog it is.'

'Do you wanna hold him, mate?'

Tom suddenly felt the wriggling, warm softness of a puppy being shoved into his lap and he quickly brought his hands up to support and contain the dog. Its heart pounded hard and fast against his hand, and a wet tongue licked his thumb. He smiled as he traced the outline of its big, silky ears.

The waitress's brisk steps hurried to their table and with a clanking slam a plate hit the tabletop. 'Here's your big breakfast and no dogs are allowed in the café.'

'Technically, we're outside and this young man is on the beach so he's not in the café,' Hayley replied mildly. 'And Tom's blind so by law you have to allow his dog.'

Tom stifled a laugh at the ludicrous argument and heard the waitress's sharp intake of breath.

'That's not a seeing-eye dog.'

'Not yet.' Hayley had that tone in her voice that dared the waitress to prove her wrong. 'A great deal of training happens before a dog is old enough to wear the harness and it all starts when they're this young. It's important that they're out and about amongst people.'

Somehow Tom managed to keep a straight face and nod as well, adding gravitas to what was an outright lie. 'We have to see if we get along.'

The puppy laid its head against his forearm as he stroked the length of its back.

'Just keep it contained, okay?' The waitress walked away, her shoes slapping the ground crossly.

'Can I have me dog back now?' the young man asked.

'Sure.' Tom held the puppy out toward the voice. 'Thanks. I enjoyed the cuddle.'

'No worries. See ya.'

'Bye,' Hayley said with a smile in her voice.

Tom leaned forward, propelled toward her by a lightness of being he hadn't experienced in years—if ever. 'So tell me. What sort of a mutt were you trying to pass off as a potential seeing-eye dog?'

Her laugh matched his. 'What sort of dog did you feel?'

He thought about the picture he'd painted in his mind. 'Drop ears, wide head, long snout, strong legs, big paws, short coat and a healthy wet nose.'

'Exactly.' He heard the scratch of cutlery on china and a soft sigh of delight as she tasted her food. 'You wanted to know what sort of dog it was and now you've seen it.'

A spark of frustration flared. 'I have no clue of its colour.'

'A gorgeous golden blond.'

Her perfume eddied around him and he realised she'd leaned forward. He fought against the distraction and thought about the dog and its short coat and immediately ruled out a golden retriever. 'You've got to be kidding me. That dog was actually a golden Labrador?'

'I know you want to cast me as a con artist and, granted, I was pushing the envelope, but technically that dog could have been a trainee guide dog. Besides, you looked happy and we weren't upsetting any customers. I would have said the same thing if it had been a Jack Russell.'

He fought the traitorous cosy feeling of being cared for by using the stark reality of abandonment as the weapon. Experience had taught him not to let himself be tricked by caring because it always let him down. A long sigh shuddered out of him. 'Hayley.'

She responded with an exaggerated sigh. 'Tom.'

It made him want to smile, but it was time to be frank. Time to lay his cards on the table and kill any illusions she might have about the two of them. 'About the other day. You do know it wasn't the start of anything between us. I've never done relationships and I don't intend to start now. It was what it was. Great sex.' He heard her put her cutlery down and he braced himself for her reply. He'd had this conversation before.

'I'm glad we agree. It *was* great sex. Nothing more and nothing less so now you can stop worrying that I've booked the church and put a deposit on a dress.'

He wished he could see her face—see if her expression matched her voice, which sounded very normal and without the strain of a lie. But he wasn't totally convinced. Before he'd lost his sight he'd never met a woman who hadn't held a hint of hope in her eyes that a relationship would grow from a casual fling.

Her hand settled over his, her fingers stroking the back of his hand. 'I can see you don't believe me, but you should. I like you, Tom, but I've got exams looming and my whole life at the moment is work and study. I hardly have any time to sleep, my parents have taken to visiting me in the cafeteria at The Harbour because I can never manage to get home to see them, so if I can't even manage that, I know I don't have the time or the energy to give to a relationship. But…'

The 'but' worried him. However, her touch had his pulse racing and it took every bit of willpower he had not to link his fingers with hers. 'But what?'

She doodled lazy circles around each knuckle. 'You remember what it was like just before you qualified?'

Through the growing fog of desire that was building inside him, he located a memory. 'Sheer hell.'

'Exactly. Stress city, and it's well documented that sex releases tension and I have a very stressful time coming up.'

Was he hearing right? He didn't dare to believe it so

he asked, 'Are you saying you want to have sex without the relationship part?'

Her other hand linked fingers with his. 'Ever heard of friends with benefits?'

He had. 'I didn't think it really existed.'

She laughed. 'Oh, it does. It works well for busy people. Unlike a relationship, we're not at each other's beck and call, but when it suits us both we get together. A sort of win-win situation.'

She's right about the final year of surgery. There's no time for anything other than work.

There'll be a catch. Women don't suggest this sort of thing. Guys do.

But the memory of being buried deep in Hayley was so strong and the thought of being there again was so tempting that it stampeded over the faint echoes of his concerns.

'When do we start?'

CHAPTER EIGHT

'I SHOULD go.' Hayley sat forward, having spent the last twenty minutes leaning back on Tom's chest as he sat propped up against a tree.

Two weeks had passed since she'd run into Tom at Café Luna. Seeing him sitting alone in the café had brought up a mix of contrary emotions, starting with shocked surprise, moving into relief and then finishing up with something that made her feel unexpectedly bereft at the thought of not seeing him again. That had propelled her to suggest being 'friends with benefits'. It was the perfect solution. Obvious even.

She knew what she was getting into and it wasn't like she'd never done it before. It suited her and if the past fortnight was anything to go by, it was the best decision she'd made in a long time. Not that they'd seen a lot of each other, but when they could coordinate their schedules, the sex had been as wondrous as their first time. Still, as amazing as the sex always was, it was times like the hour they'd just spent having a picnic in the park close to her cottage that she was really starting to treasure. They could talk for hours about all sorts of things and equally she could sit in companionable silence with him and not feel the need to talk. She hadn't experienced anything close to that sort of ease with someone since Amy.

Tom's arm, which had been resting casually across her chest, tightened against her and he nuzzled her neck. 'Come back to my place.'

She turned and pressed her lips to his, loving that she could do that whenever they were alone. 'Later. First I have to do another three hours of study and then you're my treat for working hard. Will you be home about seven?'

'Tonight, yes.' He stroked her hair. 'It seems I'm surrounded by people who are studying.'

'How's Jared going?' She'd enjoyed helping the young man with the chemistry and had appreciated his rough but honest manner.

'He's working hard.'

It was the perfect segue to ask the question she'd long pondered. 'How did Jared go from being your patient to your friend?'

The edges of Tom's mouth tightened a fraction. 'I don't really know, but it was probably because he wouldn't go away and now I'm stuck with him.'

But although he might think he sounded resigned and put upon, she saw his affection for the young man shining clearly on his face. 'What's the real story?'

The doctor moved to front and centre. 'I clipped an aneurysm in his brain two months before I left for Perth. He came through Outpatients as a public patient and he was a bright kid, but, like a lot of kids from the western suburbs, life wasn't easy and he had a massive chip on his shoulder. I don't think I got more than grunts out of him before the operation.'

She smiled. 'And let me guess, you chatted to him just like you talked to Gretel.'

Two deep lines carved into a V at the bridge of his nose. 'I talked to him like I talk to all my patients.'

She shrugged. 'Maybe you think you did, but I find

some patients are easier to deal with than others. You might not realise it but you have a knack with young people.'

'No, I don't.'

'Yeah, you do. Look at the medical students. It's standing room only at your guest lecture spots.'

'Only because they'll be failed if they don't turn up.'

She dug him in the ribs with her elbow—half joking and half serious. 'That's not the only reason and you know it. You're a good lecturer because you speak to them, not at them.'

A muscle twitched in his jaw. 'I'd rather be operating.'

She flinched, absorbing the hit of his pain, but then she took the reality road—a path she'd always taken with him because she knew the 'if only' road was a dead end filled with unrelenting despair. 'I know you'd rather be operating, but you can't so why not embrace this avenue of medicine? You enjoy young people's company, you must or you wouldn't have Jared over at your place so often.'

His shoulders rose and fell. 'I think I must have seen something in Jared that reminded me of myself at a similar age. That and the fact he lives five streets away from where I grew up.'

She recalled the comment he'd made about her Northern Beaches upbringing. 'And that wasn't the Northern Beaches?'

His laugh was harsh and abrupt. 'As far from there as you can possibly get.'

She wanted to know. 'Where?'

'Derrybrook Estate.'

She'd heard of it, but had never been there. 'What's it like?'

'It's got the highest unemployment rate in the city, is a

hub for crime and drugs, and most kids drop out of school by sixteen.'

She thought about his polished veneer and how whenever he was angry or stressed it cracked, exposing the rough edges he'd obviously worked hard at smoothing over. Now it all made sense. She found herself imagining a struggling family with a bright son. 'Studies have shown that no matter the economic circumstances, if a family values education that's the one thing that makes the difference.'

He flinched and his high cheekbones sharpened. 'I wouldn't know about that. The fact I stayed at school had absolutely *nothing* to do with my family.'

His words stung like a slap. 'Oh. I just assumed that—'

'Yeah, well, don't.' He flattened his spine against the tree as if he wanted to move away from her.

'I'm sorry. Obviously, though, you not only finished school, you went on to have a brilliant career.'

'Had.'

'Do.' She didn't realise she could sound so much like a school teacher. 'The fact it's different doesn't make it any less.'

'If you say so.'

She knew he didn't believe her and she ached for him because for some reason he didn't seem to recognise that he was a great teacher. 'Can you just answer my original question, please?'

The stubble on his now drawn-in cheeks made him look thunderous and she wondered if he was going to say anything more. She'd just about given up when he spoke.

'You're not going to stop asking, are you?'

'No.'

He sighed. 'At fourteen, I hated school. I was bored by everything and I was heading straight toward the juvenile justice system. Ironically, the fact I was acting out saved me.'

She wanted to know everything but all parts of her screamed at her to go slowly. If she rushed him for information, he'd clam up. As hard as it was to stay silent, she managed it, but only just.

His haggard expression softened. 'One night the football coach caught me on the roof of the school with cans of spray paint in my hand. I was seconds away from graffitiing the windows. It wasn't the first time I'd been in trouble, but instead of calling the police, he held it over me and made me go to training. I hated him for it, but at the same time part of me wanted to go. I hated being there but I missed it when I wasn't, and it confused the hell out of me. The fact Mick put up with my smart mouth and gave me more than one chance was a miracle and once I started to achieve in footy, I started to settle at school and attended regularly.'

'But I don't understand. With your brain, why were you bored by school?' The question slipped out before she could stop it.

He snorted. 'You went to an all-girls private school, didn't you?'

His accusatory tone bit into her. 'I did but—'

He held up his hand. 'Don't give me "buts". You had teachers who cared, parents who valued education and facilities that weren't broken or falling down around your ears.'

She sat up straight, propelled by a mixture of guilt and anger. He made her childhood sound idyllic and what it had been was so far from that it didn't bear thinking about. 'By the sounds of things, *you* had a teacher who cared.'

'Yeah. I had a couple.' He sighed. 'Mick's wife, Carol, was a maths and science teacher. Looking back, I now see what they really did for me. What I thought was a casual invitation of "come home for dinner" after footy training was really "we'll give you a healthy meal, a quiet place to study and any help you need". *They're* the reason I passed year twelve and got into medicine. That, and a burning desire to prove the bastards wrong.'

His pain swamped her and she instinctively pressed her hand to his heart. He'd not once mentioned his parents. 'Which bastards?'

The set of his shoulders and the grimness around his mouth reminded her of the first time she'd met him when he'd been practising navigating around the hospital. 'Everyone who ever told me I wouldn't amount to anything because my mother was drunk more than she was sober. Her drinking started when my father took off, leaving her a single mother at seventeen and gradually got worse after every other man she'd tried to love did the same thing. Everyone who's still telling kids from the estate the same thing.'

'I bet Mick and Carol were really proud of you.'

He swallowed and seemed to force the words up and out from a very deep place. 'Mick never saw me graduate. He died when I was in fifth year, taken out hard and fast by a glioblastoma, the most aggressive type of brain tumour a person can have.'

'Oh, I'm so sorry.' But she suddenly understood. 'And that's why you drove yourself to be a neurosurgeon.'

He nodded as if he was lost in the clutch of memories and then his lips formed a quiet smile. 'For Mick first and then for the Ferrari.'

She smiled and slid her hand into his. 'Proving the bastards wrong?'

He gripped it hard. 'Hell, yeah.'

Her own heart swelled as she glimpsed the man's giving heart that he seemed to want to hide more often than not. 'So now you're paying it forward and giving Jared the same sort of support that Mick and Carol gave you?'

He shook his head. 'Carol was born to help, but I'm no saint, Hayley. I didn't seek Jared out or offer to mentor him, like Mick did for me. Jared tracked me down in Perth and then refused to go away.'

'But now you're helping him. He probably tracked you down because of how you related to him when he was sick.'

The admiration in Hayley's voice couldn't be mistaken for anything else, but Tom didn't want to hear it. Their conversation had taken him far too close to the memories of his mother. Hell, he hated thinking about her because it took him back to a place he'd fought so hard to escape. Hayley had no clue about the eroding nature of abject poverty. How it slowly ate away at self-esteem and corroded hope, making the seduction of alcohol and drugs so tantalising as a temporary escape.

Only it wasn't an escape at all. It was an extension of the poverty trap, which then gripped people like his mother permanently until death claimed them. Her death had been her release and he ached that she'd wanted death more than she'd ever wanted him.

He shivered as he pushed the memories away and then realised the wind had changed. He reached out his hand for his cane. 'Feel the cold in that wind? What does the sky look like?'

'Gunmetal.' She shivered. 'Oh, it's really spooky.'

He heard her tossing things into the picnic hamper as the sun vanished. The temperature plummeted and the south-buster wind picked up speed. Dust made his eyes water and he could imagine the leaves and any debris being tossed every which way by the ferocious wind that howled around them.

He stood up and wished he knew the area better. 'We need to find shelter.'

'My place is less than two blocks away.'

He shook his head. 'I know storms like this and we don't have that much time.'

As if on cue, huge drops of rain started falling, but the violence of the wind blew them horizontally, stinging his face.

'Ouch.' Hayley caught his hand. 'Since when does rain hurt?'

'When it's sleet. I was here in 1999 for Sydney's most expensive hailstorm ever and this feels like the start of that.' He yelled to be heard over the wind. 'Get us to the nearest shelter. Now.'

Thunder cracked around them and Hayley squealed. 'Sorry.' She jammed his hand on her shoulder. 'There's a bandstand a hundred metres away.'

As they started walking, the sleet became hail—stones of ice that dive-bombed them with sharp edges, and stung, bruised and grazed any uncovered skin. It was the most painful hundred metres he'd ever walked and he hated that his blindness meant Hayley had to endure it too instead of being able to run to safety.

'Three steps,' Hayley yelled over the noise of the hail on the bandstand's tin roof.

He navigated the steps and he knew he must be inside the bandstand, but they were still being pummelled by hail. Bandstands generally had only hip-height walls, which gave scant protection when the wind was driving the hail in at a thirty-degree angle. 'We need to get down and huddle.'

'We can sit on the ground wedged in against the seat.

That puts us lower than the height of the wall.' She moved his hand and he felt wooden slats before he lowered himself down and sat cross-legged on the wet and icy concrete.

Another crack of thunder seemed almost overhead and Hayley's arms wrapped around his head so tightly he risked neck damage. He reached out and wet strands of her hair plastered themselves against his palm. 'I gather you don't like thunder.'

She shivered against him. 'I think I must have been a dog in a previous life.'

'Get the picnic rug out and we'll use it as extra protection.'

'Okay.' She sounded uncertain but she pulled away from him.

He heard her cold fingers fumbling to untie the toggles, followed by the emphatic use of a swear word he'd never heard her say. In fact, he'd never heard her swear, not even in the OR when she'd been operating on Gretel. She really was scared. The next minute she scrambled into his lap and her whole body trembled against his as she wrapped the rug around their shoulders. 'I hate this.'

'I'm getting that impression, but usually storms like this are over quickly.' He stroked her wet back as an unfamiliar surge of protectiveness filled him and then he pulled the rug over their heads to protect their faces.

Her fingernails instantly dug into his scalp as sharp and as tenacious as a cat's claws. 'Hell, Hayley, what are you doing?'

But she didn't speak. Instead, her chest heaved hard and fast against his and the next moment she'd torn back the rug and was panting hard.

He reached out his hand, trying to feel the rug. 'We need the protection.'

'You have it.' She threw the rug over his head and he immediately blew it away from his mouth. The instinctive action made him think. 'Are you claustrophobic as well as scared of the dark?'

There was a moment's silence before she said, 'It's easing. The hail's turned into rain.' She grabbed his hand. 'Let's go to my place. Please.'

The pleading in her voice both surprised him and propelled him to his feet. 'Lead the way.'

As they reached the bottom of the bandstand's steps, Hayley said, 'I can't believe some hailstones are the size of cricket balls.'

'I'll trudge, then.'

After navigating flooded gutters and hail-covered footpaths for five minutes, Hayley said, 'We turn left and then we're home. It's a tiny cottage and nothing like your penthouse.'

The rain was now trickling down Tom's collar and the cold seeped into his bones. So much for mild Sydney winters. Still, perhaps the storm wasn't all bad. He now had the perfect excuse to entice Hayley into bed—he needed to keep warm while his clothes dried in front of her heater. Then he'd go home and leave her to her study.

With a loud gasp Hayley suddenly stopped and he crashed into her as water flowed over his feet. 'Is your house flooded?'

'I don't think so. The water hasn't quite reached the front door.'

'You might want to make a bit of a levee between the front door and the road, then.' He kept his hand on her shoulder, following her, all the while trying to tamp down his rising frustration that he had no idea what she was seeing and that the only help he could give was advice.

He heard her slide a key into a lock and then the grating squeak of a door swinging open.

'Oh, God.' She pulled away from him and the sound of her running feet against bare boards echoed around him, leaving him with the impression he was standing in a long corridor. Her wail of despair carried back to him.

'Hayley?' Using his cane, he tapped his way along the corridor. 'What's happened?'

'My roof's collapsed, my windows are almost all broken and I have a house full of hail.' She sounded utterly defeated.

Tom instantly recalled the billion-dollar damage that the huge storm of 1999 had inflicted on the city. He pulled out his phone. 'Show me where I can sit down and I'll call the State Emergency Services to come and tarpaulin your roof, and then I'll wait in the phone queue of your insurance company. They're going to be inundated so it might take a while and you can sweep up the hail.'

'I don't even know where to start.' Her voice rose with every word. 'There's more plaster on the floor than on the ceiling and I can see sky!'

Seeing sky wasn't good. He ran his hand through his hair. 'You can't stay here, then, even with a tarpaulin.'

He heard a chair being pulled out and a thud. 'What a mess. I really don't need this with my exams looming. My parents live too far out for me to get to the hospital when I'm on call so I guess I'm going to have to find a motel.'

Tom didn't like her chances. 'You'll be lucky to find a place if every house is as badly affected as yours.'

'Are you trying to cheer me up?'

He could imagine the mess she was sitting amidst and his heart went out to her. Before he'd thought it through he heard himself saying, 'Go pack up your textbooks and computer, throw some clothes in a bag and come back to my place.'

What the hell have you just done? You live alone. You've always lived alone. More than ever you need to live alone.

I can't just leave her here and it will only be a few days. I can handle a few days.

Her hand touched his cheek and then her lips pressed hard against his mouth. 'Thank you. I'm so glad you're here bossing me around because I'm not sure I would have known where to start.'

'Bossing people around is what I do best.' He dug deep and managed to muster up a smile to cover how useless he felt and how he hated it that he couldn't do more. Once he would have been on the roof, lashing down the tarpaulins, or wielding a broom and sweeping out the mud and muck left by flood waters or removing sodden plaster. Now all he could offer in the way of help was phone calls and letting her stay for a bit. It was a poor man's offer and it didn't feel like he was contributing at all.

Finn Kennedy gripped the silver arm of the pool ladder with his left hand as every muscle in his body frantically tried to absorb the lactic acid his obsessively long swim had just generated. He'd started swimming soon after the hail storm, ploughing up and down the Olympic pool, willing his neck pain away. Or at least giving the muscles in his neck some rest by supporting them in warm water. He'd rather swim for an hour than wear the damn cervical collar Rupert Davidson forced on him. It was bad enough that the staff at The Harbour were whispering about him and giving him furtive glances. He sure as hell wasn't giving them an obvious target like a soft collar so they felt they could ask him questions.

Pressing his foot into the foothold, he swung up and stepped onto the pool deck, the air feeling chilly after the heat of the water. He scooped up his towel and hurried to the locker room. He reached the door just ahead of Sam Bailey, The Harbour's cardiac surgeon, who raised his hand with a smile. Avoiding eye contact, Finn gave a brisk nod of acknowledgment before heading straight to the showers. He cranked up the hot tap until the temperature was just shy of burning and let the heat sink into his skin and the constantly stressed muscles below. After doing his neck exercises under the heat of the shower, the skill lay in getting dry and dressed fast so his clothes could trap the heat for as long as possible. It was almost as good as the anti-inflammatories and he used it once a day to stretch out *one* time period between the pills.

With his towel looped low on his hips, he quickly grabbed hold of the combination lock, spun the black dial three times and then pulled down hard to open the lock so he could retrieve his clothes. The silver U stayed locked. 'Blast.' His fingers felt thick and uncoordinated. He tried again, but still the lock stayed firm. He slammed his hand hard against the unyielding door and the crash resonated in the cavernous room.

'These locks can be bastards,' Sam said quietly, having appeared at the locker next to his. He spun his own lock slowly and methodically. 'If you don't hit the exact spot, they won't open.'

'You don't say,' Finn ground out as he tried again, feeling the sideways glance of his colleague along with the fast-fading power of the heat from the shower. Beads of sweat formed on his forehead and one trickled down into his eye. Hell, he was a surgeon. He could sew the finest and smallest stitches so that his patient was left virtually scar-free. He sure as hell could open a bloody lock.

A registrar rescued you when you couldn't tie off that bleeder.

That was once. It hasn't happened again.

It's happening now.

His fingers on his right hand were doing exactly what they'd done during that operation and he couldn't control their gross movements let alone make them execute a fine task. He brought his left hand up to the lock, and in what seemed like slow motion he finally got it to open.

Sam slammed his locker shut. 'Will I see you in the gym?'

Finn shook his head. 'I'm done.'

'Catch you later, then.'

Finn didn't reply. With a pounding heart he pulled his clothes on, wrapped a scarf around his neck and with legs that felt weak he sank onto the wooden bench between the lockers, dropping his head in his hands.

You can't even open a blasted lock.

He rubbed his arm and swore at the offending fingers. He couldn't deny it was happening more often—this loss of sensation that had him dropping things. Hell, he'd already had some time off and rested exactly as Rupert had suggested. He hated following instructions, but he'd done everything the neurosurgeon had suggested. On his return to work he'd cut back his surgery hours so he wasn't standing for long periods. He'd taken up swimming, he'd even tried Pilates, which galled him, and none of it was working. He was still swallowing analgesia tablets like they were lollies and he refused to think about his Scotch intake.

He ran his left hand over the back of his neck, locating the offending area between cervical vertebrae five and six. Wasn't it enough that the bomb had killed Isaac, stealing his only brother from him? Apparently not. Its remnants now lingered with him way beyond the pain of grief. The blast that had knocked him sideways, rendering him unconscious, had jarred his neck so badly that the soft nucleus of the cushioning disc now bulged outwards, putting pressure on the spinal cord. That something so small could cause so much chaos was beyond ironic. It was sadistic and it threatened to steal from him the one thing that kept him getting up in the mornings. His reason for living. The one true thing that defined him.

Surgery.

So far he'd been lucky. So far he'd been able to survive without mishap the few times his weak arm and numb fingers had caused him to stumble in surgery. So far his patients hadn't suffered at his unreliable hand and they wouldn't because he now made sure he only operated with a registrar present.

His gut sent up a fire river of acid and his chest constricted as the horrifying thought he'd long tried to keep at bay voiced itself in his head.

How long can you really keep operating?

CHAPTER NINE

HAYLEY was exhausted, but at least she was now warm. It always amazed her how therapeutic a hot shower could be. She'd finally got back to Tom's place at eight p.m., after the SES guys had boarded up her windows and lashed a tarpaulin over her roof. She still couldn't believe that ten minutes of freaky weather could wreak so much havoc. She smiled and hugged herself whenever she thought of how Tom had quietly and methodically organised things, including helping her neighbour, a single mother with a young baby. Thea had rushed in crying and he'd calmed her down, asked Hayley to make tea for everyone and had then made phone calls for her as well.

Hayley knew that if she'd been on her own she would have made herself cope with everything, but having Tom deal with the SES and the insurance company while she busied herself with the practical clean-up had made it all much more bearable. They'd made a great team, but whenever she'd tried to tell him that and thank him, his mouth had flattened into a grimace and he'd brushed her appreciation aside. Oddly, he'd accepted Thea's thanks with grace, which Hayley didn't understand at all, and it had left her feeling disgruntled.

Hunger had her quickly brushing her hair and padding out to the main living area, which was cloaked in darkness except for the glow of Tom's computer screen. She automatically reached for the light switches and flicked them all on.

Tom immediately turned toward her and smiled. 'My light bill has plummeted since I went blind.'

She jumped. 'I'll pay the electricity bill while I'm here.'

He frowned. 'I was making a joke, Hayley.'

She forced out a laugh because as far as she was concerned the dark was *nothing* to joke about. She crossed the room and, with her heart racing, quickly closed the curtains. Despite the pretty twinkling lights, there was too much dark around them and it made her feel anxious. Shutting out the night was an evening ritual for her no matter where she was so she could bathe in the glow of artificial light and pretend it wasn't dark at all.

Her stomach rumbled and she said brightly, 'Do you actually cook with that flash stainless-steel gas stove or is it just for decoration?'

'Even with the lights on, can't you enjoy the night view of the city lights?'

The quietly asked question was tinged with surprise and it made her shiver. 'Of course I can, but it's cold tonight so I'm keeping the heat in.' She sucked in a breath and rushed on. 'Theo, at work, he's been hammering us with sustainable living information and closing curtains at night cuts greenhouse gas emissions and saves you money. So, what are we doing about dinner? I'm starving.'

He closed his laptop. 'I have three recipes I can manage in emergencies, but Gladys keeps my freezer filled with her home-cooked specialities, which has made me a brilliant defroster and re-heater. I'm also excellent at ordering take-out and dining at Wayan's.' He rose to his feet and walked into the kitchen, his gait the most relaxed bulbs is another thing entirely. I live in semi-darkness, Hayley, it's not that scary.'

She instinctively shuddered at the thought and then regretted it.

His lips grazed her shoulder. 'Who's Amy?'

No way. No. She threw back the covers as panic consumed her. 'Go back to sleep, Tom.'

She grabbed her pyjamas and rushed towards the kitchen, flinging on lights wherever she saw a switch until the entire apartment was lit up like a Christmas tree. With trembling hands she filled the kettle and set it to boil and then she frantically opened cupboards, searching for some sort of soothing tea.

'What are you looking for?' Tom stood in a pair of boxers and a T-shirt that fitted his toned chest like a glove and made him look like an underwear model.

But it did nothing to dent her panic. 'Chamomile tea, peppermint tea, any bloody tea!'

One corner of his mouth tweaked up. 'I don't have any.'

Ridiculous tears pricked the back of her eyes. 'That's not helpful at all.'

He put out his arm and caught hers, pulling her into him. 'How about hot milk and brandy? The nurses swear by it for calming down crazy old ladies who try to climb over the cot sides.'

Her worst fear made her sharp. 'I'm not crazy.'

His hand stroked her hair. 'Not usually, but you are tonight and I'd hazard a guess you've been like this many times before. Isn't it wearing you out?'

Yes. The sympathy in his voice unlocked something inside her and tears started to fall. 'I'm so tired, Tom. I'm so very, very tired.'

He held her, his arms circled tightly around her and he pressed kisses in her hair. She could have stayed there for ever with his strength flowing through her. She felt protected, cared for and safe in a way she hadn't felt in years. Eventually he dropped his arms and said, 'You go sit on the couch and I'll make you that milk.'

She almost said, 'I'll do it', but the determination on his face stopped her. Instead, she did as she was told and cuddled up on the couch with a light polar fleece blanket draped around her shoulders, and she came to a decision.

Tom picked up the mug of hot milk. Heating it was the easy part. Getting the damn thing to Hayley without spilling it was another thing entirely, but if he could do it anywhere it was here. Once he was out of the kitchen it was twelve steps to the couch. He started walking, concentrating on making each step smooth. 'Where are you?'

'On the right-hand side of the couch.'

He turned and counted five more steps. At least her voice sounded stronger than it had a few minutes ago and no milk had scalded his hand. Miracles could happen. He held out the mug. 'Here.'

'Thanks.' She accepted it, her fingers brushing his, and a moment later she started coughing. 'How much brandy's in this?'

Obviously too much. He hated that he had no clue how much he'd put in, and that what was supposed to be a helpful act had her coughing like an asthmatic. He sat down next to her. 'Tell me about Amy.'

She gave a long sigh. 'Amy's my…' She gulped and then her words rushed out. 'Amy was my twin sister. She died suddenly when we were eleven.'

A shock of guilt flared through him, making him regret his previous accusations that, unlike him, she'd had a perfect childhood. The guilt tumbled over empathy. Although he didn't have siblings, he'd experienced enough loss to have a form of understanding. 'I'm sorry.'

'Yeah.' She sounded sad and resigned. 'It was a long time ago. Too long ago.'

But time didn't mean squat with grief. 'Doesn't make it any easier.'

'No. I still miss her. I know that can't be right but I do.'

She paused and he wished he could see her face, but he couldn't make out anything but shadows. He heard her shudder out a breath.

'For eleven years my life was happy and relatively care-free. Amy was my best friend, my conscience and my other half. Sometimes we didn't even have to talk to find out what the other was thinking, we just knew. Once when Dad took Amy to buy me a birthday present she came home having chosen the exact same gift I had bought for her.'

He wondered what it was like to be that connected to another human being. He'd never got close. Never allowed himself to get that close.

Until now.

He shook his head against the words. 'Were you identical?'

'Yes.'

He let her silence ride, knowing she had to tell her story in her own time.

'I'm the eldest by twenty minutes and I took my job as the "big sister" very seriously.'

He smiled. 'I can picture you doing that.'

'Is that code for saying I'm bossy?'

He reached out, patting the couch until he felt her leg, which he gave a gentle squeeze. 'You know what you want and there's no crime in that.'

'I guess I've been trying to live my life for Amy too.' Her voice sounded small and she lifted his hand, folding it in hers and gripping it hard. 'One night, Amy crawled into bed with me, saying she felt weird. We'd been to a party and had eaten way too much junk food and we didn't want to confess that to Mum because she was huge on eating healthy, so I cuddled her and we both fell asleep. I woke up and my clock said 3:03. Amy was still in bed with me, only…'

Her fingers crushed his but he didn't move. He now understood exactly why she feared the dark so much and he wished he could turn back time and change what had happened to her. Change the fact she'd woken up with her sister dead in her arms. But, hell, he couldn't change a thing. He kissed her hand.

'She'd died of bacterial meningitis and I didn't even get sick.' Her voice rose on a wail and he waited, giving her a chance to compose herself.

'I was a kid and I didn't understand any of it.' Her voice sounded stronger. 'I thought it should have been me who died and for a long time I refused to accept she was dead. My parents were inconsolable and I spent a lot of years being the perfect child so as not to give them any more stress and maybe to honour Amy. I felt so guilty that she'd died and I lived. I went to school, I worked hard and achieved, but I was living in a fog. I didn't do the normal teenage stuff like parties and boyfriends, and I couldn't sleep at night. I took to napping in the day, which worked at university between lectures, and once I'd qualified, I always offered to do night shift. Over the years I've become the power-nap queen.' Her laugh was hollow. 'I worked out that if I sleep in the light the nightmares are less. As you've just found out, sleeping in the dark is an invitation for fear to invade.'

'You're chronically exhausted.' He ran his fingers over the back of her hand. She was an intelligent woman and a brilliant doctor, but she couldn't see that she also had post-traumatic stress disorder. 'You sleeping with the lights on isn't going to bother me, but you know it isn't helping you.'

The couch vibrated as she dropped his hand and shifted. 'I think I know what works best for me.'

Her defensive tone told him to back off, but he wasn't having a bar of it. 'Hayley, not very long ago you told me that you're exhausted. If you don't deal with this you're going to fall apart in a monumental breakdown and climbing back from that will be beyond hard.'

'Suddenly you're a psychiatrist?'

Her sarcasm whipped him but he let it wash over him. 'Hell, no. I treated brains with surgery, but even if I could still operate, I wouldn't be able to fix this.' He closed his eyes for a moment, seeking the strength to share something he'd never told anyone.

You never share anything with anyone.

But he knew he had to expose his own weakness to help her. 'After the accident I thought death was preferable to being blind. I couldn't see a damn thing, but when I shut my eyes I relived the accident in all its Technicolor glory. The shock of the car hitting me, the cool zip of the air as I flew through it still on my bike, and the terrifying crunching sound as my head slammed into the pavement. All of it was pushing me deep into a very black pit. Reluctantly, I agreed to hypnotherapy.'

'I can't imagine you doing that.'

He understood her surprise. 'Neither could I, but it was better than talking about my damn feelings to someone who had no bloody clue and could only look at me and think, thank God, that's not me.'

It was suddenly really important to him that she seek professional help. He wanted her to be well and get the most out of her life. He moved closer to her, smelling the citrus of her hair and using it to find her face. He traced her cheek and with his finger. 'Promise me you'll try it.'

He felt her hesitation, smelt her scepticism, apprehension and doubt, and just when he thought she'd refuse, she leaned her forehead against his and whispered, 'Thank you.'

He immediately shrugged off her heartfelt words. 'There's nothing to thank me for. I'm just doing what any friend would do.'

She sighed as if she didn't quite believe him. 'Well, thanks for caring.'

He opened his mouth to say 'You're welcome' but the words stalled in his throat as his heart suddenly ached without reason. Something in her voice had skated too close to it for comfort. *Caring?* He tried to shrug it off, tried to rationalise his wanting to help her as a normal reaction to a patient or friend. It wouldn't stick. Hayley wasn't a patient and he'd never had a friend like her.

She's special.

A flutter of panic skittered through his veins.

Hayley's fingers caressed the keys of Tom's piano, revelling in the rich sounds, and she lost herself in one of Chopin's nocturnes. As soon as her house was habitable again, she was going to buy a piano. She'd moved so much in the last ten years that she didn't own one, but this last ten days she'd found the music was helping her.

She felt Tom's hand settle on her shoulder and she leaned back into him, loving his strength and his iron-clad determination that flowed into her. It inspired her every time. He'd arrived home a few minutes ago, but she'd learned he had a routine and it was best not to disturb it so she'd kept on playing. He looked as divine as ever in a blue-and-white checked shirt, navy collared light jumper and the palest of grey chinos.

Before she'd started living at the penthouse, she'd wondered how he managed to coordinate his clothes so well, when his hair always looked slightly unkempt and rumpled. Now she knew. He bought an entire season of clothes from a particular men's store and his cleaning lady hung them in colour groups.

She smiled up at him. 'Before I forget, Carol rang to say she's home and she suggested dinner soon.'

'Let me know your roster and I'll call her later.'

Delicious surprise flowed through her that he wanted her to meet the woman who'd been more of a mother to him than his own and she hugged it close. 'Will do. You're back early.'

He dropped a kiss onto her head. 'And you're not studying.'

'Your powers of deduction amaze me, Watson.'

He smiled gently. 'You're rolling your eyes at me.'

How did he know that? 'No, I'm not.'

His fingers played with her hair. 'You're also a hopeless liar, Hayley. I can hear it in your voice. Bad day?'

It had been an awful day, starting with a young motorcyclist who'd wrapped himself around a tree and almost bled to death on the table, and it had ended with what should have been a straightforward division of adhesions, but when she'd opened up the patient's peritoneum it had been riddled with cancer. She'd immediately closed up, stitching each layer with great care, and two hours later had broken the bad news that the woman had only weeks to live. After all of that she'd had her second appointment with the hypnotherapist. She hadn't wanted to go to the first appointment, but Tom had pushed and chivvied and walked her there to make sure she'd followed through on her promise. It hadn't been the ordeal she'd expected and today's return visit had left her feeling oddly light inside. She kept rubbing her chest, expecting the familiar heavy weight to return.

While she'd been living with Tom, she'd got used to talking about her day with him, as well as chatting about all sorts of things from medicine to politics and books. Their taste in books was poles apart, but she didn't care because the discussions that stemmed from their differences was invigorating. She hadn't felt this alive or shared her thoughts like this with a friend in…

Never as an adult.

Or as a teenager. When Amy died, she'd stopped sharing her thoughts with others and she'd never experienced a strong connection with anyone since, but now with Tom, it felt…right.

Her arm crossed her chest as she placed her hand on top of his. 'It was a seriously lousy day, but how did you know?'

'You're playing the piano.'

She laughed. 'I've been known to play the piano after a good day.'

He raised his brows and put his hands on the piano stool, feeling for the edges. She moved along, creating some space, and he sat down next to her. His hand pressed on her thigh and a tingle shot through her.

'Just as I thought.' He smiled at her. 'You're wearing what I assume are old and faded tracksuit pants. They're your comfort clothes.'

She stared at him, aghast that he'd worked that out about her. She only wore them because he couldn't see how tatty they were. 'How do you even know I own tracksuit pants?'

He laughed. 'You're chronically untidy, Hayley, and I tripped over them once in the bedroom.'

'Oh, hell, I'm sorry.' Learning to share a house with someone after years of living alone was one thing. Sharing with a blind man was something else entirely. 'I can move out if it's not working.'

Please say no.

He squeezed her thigh. 'My offer stands, but I think I've worked out the reason you're still single.'

His teasing made her smile. 'Your logic is flawed. If I'm single due to being messy, how come you're single when you're a neat-freak?'

'I tried living with a woman once, but the relationship got in the way of what I wanted to achieve and I can't see that ever changing. What's your excuse?'

She blinked at his unexpected reply. He wasn't known for volunteering that sort of information about himself and his question to her caught her unprepared. 'I don't think I'm the sort of person who falls in love.'

Her heart suddenly rolled over and she rubbed her chest at the ache.

'I knew you were a sensible woman.'

His words circled her, adding to the ache and bringing with them an unaccountable sadness that swamped her. She tried to shrug it away but it wouldn't leave. She sighed as confusion added to the mix. 'That's me. Pragmatic and sensible.'

He leaned in, his hand seeking her cheek, and then he kissed her gently. 'Talking of sensible, while you're here, can you please try and pick up and put things where they belong so I don't break a leg?'

She bit her lip. It was incredibly generous of him but she was compelled to tell him about the phone call she'd received earlier in the day. 'I spoke to the insurance assessor today and although the job's been approved, the problem is finding tradesmen because they're swamped with work.' She took in a deep breath. 'It could be a month or longer.'

He didn't say anything and for a moment she thought she read regret on his face. Regret that he'd offered so quickly that she should stay for as long as it took to fix her house. Then he nudged her arm with his. 'At the rate you're going I'll have just got you house-trained and it will be time for you to leave.'

'Hey.' Indignation flowed through her on the back of relief. 'I'm not that bad.'

This time he rolled his eyes. 'Even Gladys commented on the spare room mess.'

'Gladys complains about everything.'

'True, but I knew her before I went blind and I know she cleans everything to within an inch of its life so I'm keeping her.'

She pondered that. Did Tom think people would take advantage of his lack of sight? He fought the limitations of his blindness every single second of every single day and his quest for independence was almost a religion. Apart from her lapses in tidiness, she'd quickly learned to unobtrusively assist him only when it was absolutely necessary and that usually only happened when they were out. When they were home, she forgot he was blind—to her he was just Tom.

Smart, gorgeous, wickedly ironic and with a caring streak a mile wide—not that he'd admit it. He made her feel special, cared for and safe. Very safe. These last ten days, sharing his apartment and living with him, had been the best ten days of her life. She loved being here with him.

You love him.

No. That's not possible. I don't fall in love. We're good friends. Mates.

You're way more than that and you know it. The empty space around your heart's vanished. It's why you just felt so sad when he called you sensible. It's why the thought of moving out of here hurts.

Oh, hell, she loved him.

Her breath caught in her throat as the reality hit her so hard she almost swayed. How had it happened? How had she fallen in love? What she and Tom shared was supposed to be sex and friendship, and falling in love was never part of the deal. He was adamant he didn't want a relationship and it had never even crossed her radar as something to be cautious of because she'd never given her heart to anyone. When Amy had died, she'd closed down to avoid any more hurt. She specialised in keeping things light with everyone and maintaining distance. She'd never anticipated falling in love.

But it had sneaked up on her so slowly she hadn't even realised it was happening.

Are you sure it's not just lust?

But she knew it was way beyond that. The feeling was so different from the hot, burning need she experienced every time they had sex. No, this was like the steady warmth from an Aga stove—it eddied around her in a blanket of comfort and filled her with an all-encompassing happiness that made her smile all the time.

His right hand started playing the top notes of 'Heart and Soul' and she automatically started playing the bass to the well-known piece. It triggered a memory, but it didn't douse her with pain like it might have done once. 'I used to play this with Amy.'

'It's all I can play.' He gave her a gentle smile, reached for her right hand and squeezed it.

Her heart swelled in a rush and she glanced at his handsome profile. Did he love her? Had love slowly arrived with him as well?

The relationship got in the way of what I wanted to achieve.

That was when he was living a different life. He comes home early from work when he knows you're home.

That he cared for her she was in no doubt.

Caring was part of love.

Was the gap between caring and love so very big? She hoped not.

She kept playing the continuous loop with one hand while her other snuggled in his, adoring their close connection and wanting to build on it. Build a future. 'Why do you have such a beautiful grand piano if you don't play?'

His hand slowed on the keys. 'When you grow up with nothing, once you have money you tend to spend it on things the inner child was deprived of.'

'An expensive home, a fast car and a piano?'

'Got it in one.'

'Anything else?' She had an overwhelming need to know much more about the man she loved.

His head tilted in thought. 'I'd always planned on getting a dog, but I was never home enough.'

'And that's why you didn't get around to piano lessons?'

'Running The Harbour's neurosurgery department didn't leave me with any time. I was never home.'

She suddenly had a brilliant idea. 'So learn now.'

He stopped playing altogether and let go of her hand, his body bristling with intransigent tension. 'Why? Because once the lecture series is over I'm unemployed and will have all the time in the world?'

'No.' She held her voice steady, refusing to fall into his

argument trap. 'Look, I know you're not certain what's coming next or what you want to do and that's unsettling, but if learning the piano is something you've always wanted to do, it won't happen if you don't make it a priority.'

Shoving himself to his feet, he caught the edge of the piano with his hip as he moved away. He swore and rubbed the bruised skin with his hand. 'Learning to live blind is my priority. That's my focus for the coming year.'

She bit off her automatic 'Are you okay?', saying instead, 'It's been your priority and it's paid off in spades. You're already doing amazingly well. Do you really need to take off another year?'

He made a strangled sound. 'When I can use echolocation exclusively and walk without a cane, *that* will be doing amazingly well.'

His derisive expression ripped through her and she chewed her lip, feeling anxious for him. 'Tom, that's an admirable goal, but is it realistic?'

Anger scored his face. 'Of course it bloody is.'

She rose to her feet and ran her hand along his arm, wanting to soothe. 'If you hate the cane so much, why not think about a guide dog?'

'No.'

He shook her arm away, his expression full of hurt. It was like she'd just mortally offended him.

'Tom, I was only trying to—'

He held up his hand. 'Look, we've both got work to do before dinner. You need to study and I have to convert my notes into braille for my final few lectures. I'll leave you to it.'

He turned and walked away from her, the action as

sharp and loud as a door being slammed in her face. Her heart took the hit, and the deep purple stain of a bruise spread out across it.

CHAPTER TEN

'BLOODY bow tie. I could never tie the damn things when I could see. Why does the vice chancellor's dinner have to be formal?'

Tom almost flung the offending piece of silk onto the floor, but restrained himself because Hayley was sitting on the bed. There was something about her that made him want to control his frustration, which was odd because all his life he'd never experienced the urge to do that. Tonight it was hard to control because he needed to go to this dinner, but a large crowd in a noisy room meant a tough night for him.

Although he'd never admit it out loud, the fact Hayley had accepted his invitation to be his guest had mitigated some of his concerns about attending. She, unlike most people, had the knack of knowing when he needed the hated assistance and when he didn't. Well, most of the time. She'd both crossed the line and shocked him when she'd suggested a guide dog. He'd thought she understood how important it was to him that he be totally independent.

Now, under the thread of his controlled anxiety about the evening was a simmer of anticipation. Hayley was fun to be with and her presence would temper any boring speeches that might be part of the event, given that Guy

Laurent was retiring. Tom could remember attending lectures given by 'The Prof' when he'd been a med student and Parkes wouldn't be quite the same without him.

'It's a formal affair because a hundred and fifty years ago, when the first dinner was held, the tuxedo was de rigueur and you would have had a valet to dress you,' Hayley said. 'Besides, some traditions are worth holding on to. Plus, it fits in with Parkes's amazing sandstone cloisters and the dining room with its high vaulted ceiling.'

She sounded almost wistful and the rustle of material as she stood up evoked a bygone era. 'But most importantly...' she gave a wicked laugh '...it makes all the men look as sexy as hell.'

'So you plan on scoping out the talent this evening, do you?' He'd intended the words to come out as joke, but they sounded unexpectedly tight and if they were to be awarded a colour, it would have been green.

'Absolutely.'

Her smoky voice rode on top of a cloud of musky sandalwood scent, which wrapped around him as she stepped in close. The deeper and sexier evening fragrance was a delicious assault on his nostrils and in stark contrast to her more innocent summer-fresh scent of flowers with a citrus tang. His pulse quickened.

Hayley's fingers brushed his neck as she pulled the material of the tie toward her and he moved with it, his lips meeting hers in a kiss she immediately deepened.

His arms instantly wrapped around her waist and he matched the kiss, wanting nothing more than to tear whatever she was wearing off her and follow the trail of that intoxicating scent. He broke off the kiss, the thought of staying in with Hayley burning strong. 'We could just stay home.'

'And waste my *one* opportunity of the year to get out of scrubs and wear a dress? I don't think so.'

Her knuckles brushed his skin as her fingers tied and tugged at the bow tie. 'There you go. Now you're complete. You look all dark and decadent, like a man of mystery.'

'And what do you look like?' His hands settled on her hips, and then dropped lower, fisting into an ocean of soft, filmy material he couldn't name. He then trailed upwards, across a tight fitted bodice that outlined the nip of her waist and the swell of her breasts and then his fingers touched skin. Warm, smooth skin that dipped and rose until his fingers nestled between her breasts. He swallowed hard and his voice came out hoarse. 'Strapless?'

She laughed. 'Totally strapless. It's black with a band of white satin at the top of the bodice so I match you in black and white.'

An ache unlike anything he'd ever experienced took hold of him. 'I wish I could see you.'

She caught his hands and placed one on her back and one on her chest and her voice came out soft and low. 'You've already seen more of me than I've ever shown anyone.'

Her words vibrated deep down inside him before echoing back and he realised that over the last few weeks he'd shared more about himself with her than he'd ever shared with any other person. He hadn't intended that to happen—it just had. She'd slipped into his life and into his home with an ease that stunned him. Since arriving back in Sydney, his home had been his sanctuary from the world—the one place he could really relax. He'd thought Hayley would damage that and he'd be spending more time at work, but instead she'd made his home even more of a refuge. Just lately he'd even had moments of wondering what it might be like if she stayed.

Great sex every night.

Huh! In your dreams. If you ask her to stay it will turn into your worst nightmare with her thinking white dresses, redecorating and babies.

Children?

The thought rolled around in his head with burgeoning roots, eagerly trying to find a place to settle. A slight tremor of panic ruffled his equilibrium.

His watch beeped seven o'clock, interrupting his anomalous daydream and bringing him firmly back to the present. 'I told Jared we'd get a taxi because he had a party to go to so we'd better head downstairs. Are you ready to go?'

She slid her arm along his. 'I'm all yours.'

Hayley watched Tom walking across the empty dance floor on his way back to their table, his shoulders square and his face stern, but she knew it was from concentration, not ill-humour. He'd been tense when they'd arrived earlier in the evening, but she'd quietly given him the layout of the room and once they'd taken their seats for dinner, he'd relaxed. It had been Tom, with his humour and entertaining stories, who had been the glue at their table, setting everyone at ease and making her laugh along with the rest of the guests. She could hardly believe she'd thought him taciturn and rude when she'd first met him.

Tonight had been pretty much perfect. Tom had kept his arm draped casually over the back of her chair for most of the evening and more than once his fingers had caressed her bare shoulders in a public display of affection she hadn't ever expected in her wildest dreams. She hugged it to herself as a sign that perhaps she wasn't the only one falling in love.

Tom stopped just short of the table. 'Hayley?'

She rose and crossed to him. 'Right here. You've said your farewells to Guy?'

He nodded. 'He's pretty excited about his retirement and takes off for France next week.'

'Lucky Guy.'

He groaned at the play on words. 'I think he's heard that a lot this evening. Are you ready to leave?'

'Sure, I'll just grab my things.' She took five short steps to the chair, picked up her evening bag and wrap, and when she turned back Tom was in conversation with Richard Hewitson, the dean of the school of medicine. She'd chatted to him earlier in the evening.

He nodded at her in recognition. 'I was just asking Tom if he'd made up his mind.'

'Oh?' Hayley had no idea what Richard meant and she glanced at Tom for a clue, but his face was expressionless except for a line of tension along his jaw.

Richard smiled. 'Guy's retirement has opened up a spot in the faculty and Tom would bring new vigour to the position, but he's holding out on us. It would be great if you could convince him to join us on staff.'

Joy for Tom rocked through her and she opened her mouth to speak but Tom got in first.

'Richard…' His voice had the 'don't push me' tone, which anyone who knew him well would recognise. 'I'll be in touch.'

Richard shook Tom's hand, completely missing the warning. 'Looking forward to it, but don't wait too long.' He then extended his hand to Hayley. 'Lovely to meet you and I hope we'll all be seeing a lot more of each other.'

She quickly murmured her goodbyes and caught up

with Tom, who'd already started walking in the direction of the exit with a white-knuckled grip on his cane.

Tom needed to move. He needed to walk off his anger at Richard. The cool outside air hit him the moment he stepped out the door and although he couldn't see the bare jacaranda trees he remembered how they cast long shadows against the sandstone buildings. As a student he'd often sat in the quad, staring at the clock tower, not quite believing that he'd come so far from Derrybrook and was studying in such hallowed halls. He'd also felt inspired by the sight just before exams and he'd missed his time at university when he'd qualified. But that had been years ago and he wasn't ready to come back. He couldn't believe the dean had mentioned the job to Hayley with the sole intent of forcing him to make a decision quickly.

Hayley's feet slowed. 'Did you call a taxi?'

'No.' His raw and restless energy surged. 'It's not far. Can you walk home in your shoes?'

'They're high but comfortable but I won't be striding out.' Her hand touched his elbow. 'Which way do we go?'

He turned forty-five degrees and started walking. 'Straight down The Avenue, through Graffiti Pass—'

'Is it lit at night?'

'Yes. And then out onto the main road. It's only five minutes from there.'

'That will be handy if you decide to take the job.'

He swung his cane in wide arcs, knowing this route home well. 'I won't be taking it.'

'Why not?'

He heard her surprise and it bit him. 'Because it's beneath me.'

'You're going to have to explain that to me.'

'You think I should take a job teaching anatomy and physiology to first-year medical students?'

'You'd be really good at it.'

'I'd hate it.' He stabbed the ground with his cane. 'I was a neurosurgeon, for God's sake. I should be lecturing in neurology at the very least.'

'Guy lectured in other areas. Perhaps this is just a starting position.' Her mild tone meant she was working hard not to sound cross. 'Look at the positives. It's a professorship at a prestigious university connected to one of the world's best teaching hospitals. It would open up all sorts of opportunities for you. Given that you can no longer operate, this is about as perfect as it gets.'

He railed against her common-sense words. 'It isn't bloody perfect. It's settling.' He stopped suddenly, his anger having taken over so much that he'd forgotten to count steps and he had no clue where he was.

As if she could read his thoughts Hayley said, 'Graffiti Pass. Four steps down.'

'I know.' He ground out the words, cross with himself and furious at the world.

'Of course you do.' Her voice softened. 'Tom, let's just walk and we can talk about this when we get home.'

'Let's not.' He moved away from her, tapping down the four steps, and continued into the tunnel, hearing the echo of Hayley's steps behind him. Then he heard the sound of running feet. He stopped because the sound was bouncing off the concrete walls and he wasn't certain if the running was coming from behind him or in front of him. He moved to the side.

The noise got louder and the next moment pain exploded in his gut and then in his shoulder. He tumbled backwards and as he hit the wet and gritty floor of the tunnel, he realised he'd just been punched and pushed.

'Hey!' Hayley's yell reverberated around him.

The running feet stalled for a moment and then

Hayley's scream tore through him like a jagged knife. Fear poured through him, burning like acid. Was she hurt? Had she been knifed? Had she been dragged off?

He pushed himself to his knees, primal fear driving him. He had to help her. Protect her. 'Hayley!'

No one replied. All he could hear were the echoes of the running feet being joined by other, sharper echoes. Shock rendered his fledgling echolocation inadequate and he stretched out his hand, trying to find his cane. He needed the damn thing more than ever. Needed it to help Hayley. Something sharp sliced into his hand, but he didn't care, he kept on feeling, spreading his hands over what was probably broken glass in an ever-increasing circle, but all he could feel was the floor of the tunnel.

You can't protect her. You can't even find a bloody cane.

The thought barrelled into him hard and fast, sucking his breath from his lungs and drenching him in cold sweat.

You're totally useless to her.

Hayley dabbed the cuts on Tom's hand with antiseptic and tried to infuse some lightness into her voice after the shock of seeing him being pushed to the ground. He'd been eerily quiet from the moment she'd handed him his cane in the underpass and, despite having had a shower and a finger of whisky, he still seemed detached and a million miles away from her. Shock could do that.

'The police say it's unlikely they'll catch whoever snatched my bag, but at least the bastard only got a cheap phone with a crappy ringtone and ten dollars.'

Tom didn't reply. She put a plaster over the deepest cut and then kissed his hand. 'I've removed all the gravel so they should heal up fast.'

'Thank you.' A muscle twitched under his left eye as he put his hands in his lap. 'I should never have suggested we walk home.'

'We walk most places. It's one of the things I love about inner-city living.' She rose and walked around the table, putting her hands on his shoulders and dropping her head onto his. 'What happened tonight was not your fault. It was just one of those things. The underpass was well lit and there's security all over the campus. I think this guy just made a split-second decision.'

He gave a snort of derision. 'Because I was blind.'

The bitterness in his voice dried her mouth. 'Because we were in evening dress and we looked rich.' She wanted him to put his hand up and touch her cheek, like he often did, but he sat perfectly still like he was carved out of stone and she could feel her reassurances just sliding off him.

She walked around and picked up his hands and then leaned in, pressing her lips to his forehead. 'I'm just glad you weren't seriously hurt. It's really late so let's go to bed. Tomorrow's a new day.'

He shook his head. 'You go.'

A skitter of unease shot through her. Not once in all their time together had he ever said no to her when she'd suggested they go to bed, no matter the time of day or night. 'I sleep better with you when it's dark.' She snuggled onto his lap and ran her finger along his lips. 'Not that I intend to go to sleep right away.'

He started to rise, effectively tipping her off his lap. 'You can't depend on me to sleep, Hayley. You can't depend on me for anything.'

His words carried the sting of a slap and her heart cramped. 'Tom, what's going on?'

He'd walked over to the couch and gripped the back

with his hand. 'You could have been seriously hurt tonight and I couldn't do a damn thing to stop it.'

His feelings mirrored hers. 'I saw you get pushed to the ground and I couldn't do a damn thing to stop it either. I agree it was horrible.'

He swung back toward her, the movement stiff. 'You're deliberately being obtuse. If I'd been able to see, I would have made sure you were protected.'

She crossed the room and put her arms around him, wanting to disabuse him of the thought. 'You don't know that for a fact. It all happened so fast and every day the paper's full of assaults on sighted people who can't defend themselves or the people they're with during an attack.' She stroked his face. 'But I love that you wanted to protect me.'

'Of course I want to protect you.'

His granite expression had softened and his quietly spoken words lined up perfectly with all the care and concern he'd showered her with over recent weeks.

He's made the leap too. He loves you.

Sheer joy expanded her heart so much she almost cried and she kissed him deeply. Then the words she'd been saying silently to herself for days slipped out. 'I love you, Tom.'

For a tiny moment panic closed her throat. Had she misconstrued his words? But Tom didn't stiffen or pull away. Instead, he brought his hand up to her hair and caressed it gently before breathing in deeply as if he was inhaling part of her to keep.

He kissed her hair. 'My Hayley.'

My Hayley. She was his. She rested her head on his shoulder and gave a blissful sigh, knowing that he loved her and they belonged together. The future rolled out in front of her like a magic carpet—the two of them together and sharing life's journey. She'd never known such happiness and it swam through her, warming her until she was bathed in a rosy glow.

He slowly brought his hands to rest on her arms and then he set her apart from him. 'I think it's best if you move out tomorrow.'

Her knees sagged in shock and her chest refused to move. She scanned his face but couldn't read it. Of all the words she'd expected him to say, those weren't among them. 'You…you want me to leave?'

He gave a curt nod, his expression blank. 'It's been fun, Hayley, but it's over.'

A million thoughts zoomed around in her head but none of them fully formed because all the foundations had been stripped away. 'I don't understand. You just said "my Hayley". I thought you loved me.'

'Love's got nothing to do with it.' He sounded ragged and worn out. 'You and I are never going to work.'

A surge of hope pushed her shock aside momentarily and she sought to clarify his words. 'But you do love me?'

'I don't know.' He ran his hand through his chocolate-noir hair and his face sagged, making his five o'clock shadow darker than ever. 'Love wasn't in my house when I was growing up, and the lack of it ruined my mother's life. Being with someone isn't something I've ever wanted, and being with you is the closest I've ever come to that.'

I don't know. She tried not to let his words wound and instead concentrated on trying to hear what he was really saying. 'So you've thought about us being together in the future?'

'Occasionally.'

Hope shot up. *That's better than never. Build on that.* 'When you thought about us, what were we doing?'

A mellow smile softened his expression but then his

mouth hardened. 'There's no point talking about this, Hayley. I've never wanted to be in a relationship and added to that I'm now blind. Tonight just made everything more clear to me and ably demonstrated that I can't protect you, let alone children.'

She gasped, totally stunned as her heart did somersaults. 'You've thought about us having children?'

His bladed cheeks sharpened. 'Only how they'd be in danger with me and I wouldn't be able to be a proper father and take care of them.' His fist slammed into his palm with a slap. 'Hell, they could walk out the door and I wouldn't know they'd gone. We wouldn't work, Hayley.'

She grabbed his hands—desperate to connect with him and show him that they did have a future. A future he'd glimpsed but was now rejecting. 'We can make it work. Together we're a team and we complement each other, you know that. It's what we've been doing these last few weeks.'

She tried to think of an example but her brain was still recovering from the shock of him asking her to leave. She grabbed on to the first thought that floated past. 'You know I'm hopeless at computer stuff and you're sensational at it, so you can teach them all the technology and I'll—'

'Do everything else?' His brow shot up in a sardonic tilt as he pulled his hands away and strode across the room.

Desperation made words flood out of her. 'We'd get help. That's what housekeepers and nannies are for.' She thought of her mother and smiled. 'And grandmothers.'

He gave a harsh laugh that sliced through the air, leaving a chill in its wake. 'I can't contribute one of those.'

She refused to let him wallow in self-pity. 'You're *not* without family, Tom. Carol would love to help and Jared can be the bachelor uncle who lets the kids stay up all night watching inappropriate films and eating too much chocolate.'

He shook his head. 'Stop dreaming, Hayley. It would all fall apart.'

'No, it won't.'

'Yes, it will.'

She wanted to shake him free of this crazy notion. 'It would only happen because you believe it will.'

'This is nothing to do with believing and everything to do with knowing.' His yelled words settled over them like a shroud. 'I'm a realist, Hayley.'

Her heart hammered hard and fast as she fought for their future. 'No, this isn't realism. This is you being a fool, and that's exactly what you'll be if you walk away from what *will* be a wonderful and amazing life together.'

He didn't respond and her shoulders slumped. 'Tom, this makes no sense.'

'It makes all the sense in the world.' His shoulders rolled back in a familiar action of determination. 'I'm doing you a favour. Ending it now will save us long-term pain. You'd only end up resenting me and resenting the blindness. Hell, I resent it. It will tear us apart and then you'll leave, like everyone else.'

Her heart spasmed for him. How could she argue against a childhood of abandonment?

With the truth. 'I don't care that you're blind. To me you're just Tom, the most giving and caring man I've ever had the fortune to meet. You're the man I love and I won't ever leave you.'

'You say that now, but everyone does.' He flinched, the tremor moving across his shoulders and ricocheting down his legs. 'This is the reason I've stayed single and now that I'm blind it's even more important. You have no idea what it was like for me tonight in that underpass and

I'm never allowing myself to feel that vulnerable again. I've never depended on anyone and I'm not about to start.'

She wanted to scream and rage at him, but she knew he'd just tune her out completely. 'Tom, I have twenty-twenty vision and I depend on you in so many ways, big and small. Without you, I'd still be chronically exhausted, but you forced me to deal with my PTSD and I'm making progress. There's nothing wrong with needing people. No one is completely independent of others and if they are, well, it's a sad life and they're not happy.'

He turned slowly and she saw that the warm glow that had been living in his eyes for a few weeks had now vanished. A knife-sharp pain tore through her heart and she knew right there and then that she'd lost the argument.

Lost him.

'You don't want to fight for us, do you?'

'I'm sorry.' He walked toward the spare room, 'I'll sleep here tonight and Jared can help you move tomorrow. Have a good life, Hayley.' He closed the door softly behind him.

'I never took you for a coward, Tom Jordan,' she yelled as she hurled a couch cushion at the door and then watched it fall with a quiet thud to the floor. Her shaking legs gave way completely and she collapsed onto the couch, her breath coming in ragged runs. For years she'd held herself apart from people, but Tom had slipped under her guard and into her heart, digging in for the long haul and making her dream.

Now he'd killed the dream, but the love stayed on, lamenting what might have been.

She buried her face in her hands and silently wept.

CHAPTER ELEVEN

EVIE arrived at Pete's, glanced around and sighed. She couldn't see Lexi anywhere. Her sister had texted her twice in the last hour, reminding her to meet her here, and now Evie had not only arrived but arrived on time and Lexi was nowhere to be seen.

She headed toward the bar, but stalled at a table tucked away in a corner. 'Hayley?'

'That's me.'

Even in the mood lighting of the bar, Evie could see the registrar's drawn expression and sorrow-filled eyes. Hayley wasn't a regular at Pete's—in fact, she was a bit of a loner, although The Harbour gossip mill had her linked with Tom Jordan but no one seemed to know too much about it. The fact she was sitting here meant something was up. 'May I join you?'

Hayley sighed and pushed out an adjacent chair. 'Sure.'

Evie noticed Hayley was drinking mineral water and she called over to the bar. 'Hey, Pete, I'm off the clock so can you please bring me one of your Harbour Specials?'

Pete gave her a wave. 'Anything for you, Dr Lockheart.'

Evie returned the wave and sat down. 'Are you okay? You look absolutely wiped.'

Hayley fiddled with a coaster. 'It's been a long day on all fronts.'

'Of course. Sorry, I should have realised.' Earlier in the day, a twenty-three-year-old had wrapped his car around a pole, injuring himself and his three passengers. All available staff had been called in and she knew that Finn and Hayley had been in Theatre most of the day, dealing with the emergency as well as trying to clear their delayed surgical list. 'Has Finn Kennedy been giving you hell?'

'I wish.' Hayley leaned back and laughed, but the sound was neither happy nor ironic. 'Actually, I got a rare compliment from Mr Kennedy today.'

'A compliment?' Evie couldn't hide her astonishment and yet at the same time she was unaccountably happy that Finn had been able to voice praise. She knew he found expressing any sort of positive emotion incredibly difficult.

'There you go, Evie, a Harbour Special, as requested.' Pete put the glass of beer down with a grin and returned to the bar.

Hayley stirred her mineral water with her straw and gave a half-smile. 'You know our chief of surgery, Evie. He's taciturn and a man of few words, but after we'd patched a frayed femoral artery courtesy of an impacted steering column, he said, "When you qualify we'd consider an application from you."'

That's so Finn. 'You know it means he wants you working here as a consultant and part of his team.' She raised her glass. 'Congratulations, Hayley.'

'Thanks.' She picked up her glass and clinked it against Evie's, but the action lacked enthusiasm.

'You don't sound very thrilled.' Evie realised she didn't know much at all about Hayley except that she was always obliging when the ER requested a surgical consult and she hadn't shied away from the tough decisions or the hard asks. 'You're not long back from the UK, are you? Were you planning on going back or working somewhere else in Oz?'

Hayley shook her head and compressed her lips. 'No. My heart was set on settling down in Sydney, here, in fact, but—' Hayley's phone honked like a ferry horn and she glanced down at the liquid display and sighed. 'Sorry, Evie, I'm on call and that's Mia McKenzie from ER. Sounds like it's a good night for you to be off duty and out of there. Enjoy yourself.' She rose and hurried out the door.

Evie realised that once again Hayley had been friendly and yet had managed not to give out much information about herself at all. While they'd been talking, Pete's had filled up but there was still no sign of Lexi and with the first few sips of the beer warming her veins, Evie had no desire to sit on her own. She stood up, looking for someone from The Harbour, but none of the chattering groups in the deep and comfy booths were people she knew. Picking up her drink, she headed to the bar to chat with Pete, who was always entertaining, but stopped short a few steps away, instantly recognising the taut set of broad shoulders and long legs that were wound around a barstool.

Finn.

She swallowed hard.

Sure, they saw each other at work but there was always a patient and a team of staff between them. The last occasion they'd been alone together had been when time had stood still. He'd leaned into her and she'd pressed herself against his warm, broad back, wanting nothing more than to stay there for ever. Her surge of feelings for him then had been so unexpected that they'd both terrified her and filled her with a hope she'd never dared to dream of. Then he'd lurched away from her, to this very bar, and straight into the arms of another woman.

She didn't want to relive *that* particular memory of him flirting with the OR nurse when he'd known that she was still in the bar with a full view of what he was doing. Deliberately hurting her.

She swayed slightly. Seeing him at work was one thing—she didn't have a choice there, but she did have a choice now. She didn't have to see him socially.

'Something wrong with your drink, Evie?' Pete enquired as he flung a bar towel over his shoulder.

Finn immediately turned around, his vivid blue gaze torching her. She hated that she stood stock-still like a rabbit caught in headlights. Hated that she hadn't moved half a second earlier before Pete had seen her. Before Finn had seen her.

Put on your mask.

She tilted her chin and strode toward the bar, standing next to the seated Finn. 'All alone tonight?'

'Not any longer.' He raised his glass of malt whisky to her and his eyes simmered with a swirl of caged emotions, none of which held form long enough to be named.

She gulped her drink as she felt herself being pulled in by them. 'Oh, I'm not staying.'

'No?'

She slammed the empty glass down on the long counter. 'No. I make it a rule not to spend any time with people who are immersed in self-destruction.'

His right brow lifted. 'That rules out all the interesting people. Does it feel good, living a vanilla life, Evie?'

Anger drove caution to the wind and lifted the mask on her heart. 'Does it feel good rejecting everyone around you who cares, Finn?'

His fingers tightened around his glass and he tossed back his drink. 'Do-gooders don't interest me.'

His words slashed her, breaking open her barely sealed emotions, and a rush of hurt spouted like a geyser. 'In that case you can hope that Suzy Carpenter will be along soon to keep you company.'

His blue eyes narrowed. 'I suppose I can.' He tapped the edge of his glass. 'Pete, give us another one.'

Nausea gripped Evie at his brutal dismissal. She grabbed her bag off the bar and strode toward the door, no longer caring if Lexi was going to arrive or not. She had to leave. Had to get out before she threw up and added to her utter humiliation. Pulling open the heavy wooden door, she stepped out into the night and gulped in a lungful of cool evening air.

Why had she been so foolish? Why? What was it about Finn that made her act so out of character? She was always in control and yet, with a few poorly chosen words, she'd just exposed her jumbled feelings for him. Feelings that she'd wanted to keep hidden because telling a man who was so emotionally shut down that she cared was like putting a match to an incendiary bomb. The ensuing explosion only hurt her.

Not Finn.

No, Finn hadn't been affected at all. He'd read her face, he'd heard her words, and he'd instantly rejected them and her. There had been no ambiguity. He had no feelings for her and he'd made that abundantly clear.

Tom was running late and the day had been quickly going downhill from the moment he'd overslept. The irony that he'd been wide awake at four a.m. wasn't lost on him.

'Jared? Where the hell are my keys?'

'You always leave your keys in the dish by the door.'

'And if they were there, would I be asking you?'

Jared's heavy footfalls headed toward the door. 'I dunno. You've been grumpy and losing things ever since Hayley's house got finished. It's kinda funny because when she was living here you complained that her mess made it hard for you but now everything's all neat again you're losing more stuff than ever.'

Jared's words cut too close to the bone to be comfortable. It was true, his concentration had been all over the place since he'd asked Hayley to leave, but no way in hell was he admitting to it. 'I'll have you know that she lost more things than I ever did.'

Jared snorted. 'Yeah, right. Hey, Tom, did you drink a lot last night?'

Was a bottle of merlot and a whisky chaser a lot? 'Why?'

'Because…' Jared laughed '…I've found your keys in the fruit basket.'

Damn it, how had he done that?

The same way you put your wallet in the fridge. You were thinking about Hayley.

Tom banished the unwanted thought and snapped his hand out for the needed items. 'Thanks. Let's go. Now. The last thing I need is smart-arse late jokes from one hundred and twenty med students.' He slung his computer satchel over his chest, flicked out his cane and headed toward the lifts.

'Excuse me.'

An accented and unknown voice hailed Tom as he prepared to leave the lecture hall. He sighed. The day had been a long one. The whole damn week had been excruciatingly long without Hayley in it, but finally it was Friday and he'd survived the first week without her. He'd survive the next and the one after that and the one after that, stretching well into the future.

He hated that he'd hurt her but, no matter what she believed, he knew he'd made the right decision. With each passing week she'd come to realise that he'd actually freed her.

So, if it was the right decision, why does it feel like hell?

'Mr Jordan?'

The foreign accent reminded him he was supposed to reply. 'Yes?'

'I'm Akim Deng, medical student, and I follow your lectures with most great interest.'

Tom put out his hand on hearing the formal sentence structure so often used by people where English was a second or subsequent language. 'Where are you from, Akim?'

'Blacktown.'

Tom smiled. The western suburbs continued to be a melting pot of nationalities, just like it had been when he'd been a kid. 'I used to live near there, but I meant where did you live before Blacktown?'

'Oh, I am from the Sudan, but before Australia I lived in Kenya for some years.'

Tom mentally filled in blanks that the 'some years' had most likely been spent in a refugee camp. He knew how hard the struggle out of poverty was and he'd not had to cope with the language barrier. 'How are you finding medical school?'

'I am honoured to be here.'

'I'm sure you'll make the most of your opportunity, then. Good to meet you, Akim.' Feeling that the conversation was over, Tom unfurled his cane.

'Not every teacher is like you.'

Blind? An ex-surgeon? The zip of fury that had lessened in recent weeks roared through him and he worked on keeping the edge out of his voice. 'No. They're not.'

Akim sighed. 'Sadly, no.'

Tom's feet, which had been ready to move, suddenly stilled. 'What do you mean?'

The student hesitated for a moment before saying, 'I do not need to seek help from other students to understand your lectures.'

Shock at the frankness of the student lit a fire under his collegiate support. 'I'm sure my colleagues would be happy to explain things if you're not following their lectures.'

'Often they use the same words over and over, which does not help in understanding.'

Sadly, Tom knew what he meant. Some of the older lecturers had been in the job for years and hadn't realised that the world had changed, students had changed, and lecturing styles needed to keep pace.

'I like how you use examples. It makes the theory real.' Akim's voice filled with appreciation. 'I can picture it all and this helps when I am meeting patients. I can hear your voice and see the pictures in my head. I am now thinking of neurology for my future.'

'Not neurosurgery?' Tom joked. 'I can't have been doing my job very well, then.'

Akim's hand touched his arm. 'Believe me, Mr Jordan, you do your job very well. I am sad your lectures are finishing.'

You're a fantastic teacher, Tom.

Hayley's voice suddenly broke through the barrier he'd imposed on everything to do with her, but as he patched up the breach he found himself fishing in his pocket for a business card, which he held out to Akim. 'Give me a call if you ever need a hand with your studies.'

Akim gasped. 'You are very generous. Are you certain it would not bother you?'

You know, mate, you can call by any time.

How many times had Mick said that to him? Every single time he'd seen him, whether it had been at Mick's house or at school or on the footy field. Mick, who'd freely given so much of himself and by default had provided Tom with everything he needed to achieve and create a positive life. Every patient he'd ever operated on to remove a brain tumour he'd done with Mick in mind.

You can't do that any more.

I bloody know that.

Yeah, but can you see what you can do?

It was like hearing Mick's voice again and right then he knew how he could keep Mick's legacy going. Helping Jared had been done unconsciously. *This* would be different.

He reached out his hand and Akim gripped it. 'The only bother would be if you didn't ask me.'

'In that case, I will not bother you often.'

Tom laughed. 'Sounds like a plan, Akim. I'll talk to you soon.'

On the walk home he thought about Akim and wondered how many other medical students there were whose English was their second language and who might need extra tutorial time. This led to thinking about Jared who'd headed back to finish school after realising that education was the key to improving his life, but still needed a lot of support to achieve his dream. By the time Tom slipped his key into the front door, his head was filled with ideas and excitement churned his gut. He hadn't experienced such a work-related buzz since the accident and for the very first time he could actually see a work future. One that he was driving rather than having it imposed on him. He couldn't wait to share his thoughts and ideas with Hayley.

He stepped into the apartment and, like a punch to the chest, he remembered she'd gone. The piano was silent, her lingering perfume was now only a faint scent, and the clicks of his tongue as he navigated around the apartment reinforced to him that her clutter was long gone.

You asked her to go.

It's for the best.

The first time he'd come home after she'd left he'd expected a rush of relief, but it hadn't come. Neither had it come the next day and with each passing day it continued to be elusive. He didn't understand because he knew he'd made the right decision. Made the right decision for both of them. Love didn't survive what life threw at it. His parents were a perfect example of that.

Mick and Carol had made it work.

Mick wasn't blind.

He dumped his stuff on the table. He'd ring Carol and tell her his ideas. Why hadn't he thought of telling her first anyway, especially as the whole idea had been generated by his connection to Mick? Flicking open his phone, he said, 'Carol.'

It started ringing and then a warm and familiar voice answered. 'Tom! How lovely. I was just about to call you so how's that for timing? I so enjoyed meeting Hayley at dinner the other night.'

A flicker of guilt washed through him that she telephoned him a lot more than he called her. He immediately told her about his idea, rather than talking about Hayley. 'Of course, I have to sell it to Richard Hewitson, but I think I've some bargaining power.'

Carol laughed. 'You've always had that. You were a

star negotiator at fourteen. I was surprised you didn't go into law.' Her voice sobered. 'Mick was so proud of you the day you got your results and we both knew that you could go to uni and do whatever you put your mind to. If he was still with us he'd be thrilled at what you achieved before the accident and even more so about what you're doing now. So what does Hayley think?'

He closed his eyes out of habit and blew out a slow breath. 'I haven't told her.'

'Oh?' The small sound was loaded with a thousand questions.

He rubbed the back of his neck. 'It was never going to be a long-term thing.'

'Why on earth not?'

He sighed, wishing he'd not answered Carol's first question about Hayley. 'You've always known I don't do relationships, Carol, and I especially don't do them now.'

'You're not seriously telling me that you've broken up with her because you're blind?'

Carol's incredulity spun around him, pulling and pushing at him until he felt unsteady on his feet. 'I appreciate your concern, but it's my life.'

'You don't appreciate my concern in the least, Tom,' she snapped, 'so don't give me that nonsense. I know that anything to do with feelings always makes you uncomfortable and sends you into retreat. I've sat back for years watching you bury yourself in work so you can hold everyone who has ever wanted to care for you at bay. I might have only met Hayley once, but I could see the love she has for you clear on her face and how happy she makes you. If you've let her get away then you're not only blind, you're bloody stupid.'

Carol had never spoken to him like that in his life and

he didn't know if he was shocked, angry or both. 'Are you done?'

'No. Do you love her?'

Carol's question, so familiar to Hayley's, hammered him. He hadn't been able to answer it a week ago and he still couldn't. He knew he cared for her, but love? 'How the hell do I know if I do?'

She let out a long and exasperated sigh. 'Do you enjoy being with her?'

'Yes, but—'

'No "buts", Tom. Only "yes" or "no" answers. Is she the last person you think about when you go to sleep at night and the first person you want to see when you wake up?'

He thought of the last week when he'd hardly slept at all because he'd been constantly thinking of Hayley. He answered with a reluctant, 'Yes.'

'Since you broke it off with her, have you felt like you've been wading through mud and going through the motions of living?'

He tugged at his tie, which suddenly seemed to be choking him. 'Yes.'

'Did you think about telling her about your university plans before you rang me?'

Damn it.

'Tom?'

'Yes.'

Carol's excruciating questions continued. 'Does the idea of spending the rest of your life with her scare you?'

He swallowed in relief. Finally, she'd asked a question where the answer didn't feel like it was being hauled up with a piece of his soul. 'Yes, which is why—'

'Tom.' Carol invoked her best schoolteacher tone.

'When you think about *not* spending the rest of your life with her, does it scare you?'

The words sounded innocent enough and his immediate answer to himself was no, but as his mouth went to form the word he heard the clicking sound of a land mine being engaged. Abject fear tore through him, sweat beaded on his brow and he threw off his jacket. The answer ripped through him with the velocity of an exploding bomb.

Yes.

Oh, hell, he loved her. He truly loved her. 'Carol, I love her, but I can't ask her to spend her life with me when I can't offer her what she needs.'

'And what does she need?'

'A man who doesn't need her.'

Carol gave a confused huff. 'Coming from the most logical male I know, that answer makes no sense at all.'

His heart hammered hard and fast and despite feeling like he was being torn in two he admitted his worst fear. 'I found myself depending on her and I've never depended on anyone. Not before I was blind and especially not now. She doesn't need that in her life.'

'No, she needs a man who loves her.' Carol's voice was quiet but the impact of her words was ear-shattering. 'Tom, you've never been in love before and the logical people are the ones who are thrown most by love. It scares you, but know this. With love comes an amazing interdependence that strengthens individual independence. You're stronger with her than you are without her.'

No one is completely independent of others and if they are, well, it's a sad life and they're not happy.

Hayley's words that he'd so quickly discarded were almost identical to Carol's. Carol, who'd shared her life with Mick for twenty-five years and truly knew what love was through good times and through bad.

So does Hayley. Catch up!

He tried to moisten his dry lips with his tongue, but his mouth was parched. 'Carol, I have to go.'

He didn't wait for her reply.

CHAPTER TWELVE

HAYLEY stared up from her computer at the freshly painted plaster and the beautifully renovated decorative cornices, and wished her heart could be restored so easily. Her little cottage glowed from its hailstorm-imposed redecoration, looking like a woman after a complete make-over. She, on the other hand, knew her hair was lank, that her comfort clothes needed a wash and that she looked a total mess. Sadder still, she was having trouble caring.

The irony of it all was that because of her therapy she was actually getting more hours of uninterrupted sleep than she'd had in years, but not even that was enough to remove the black rings from under her eyes or to fill in the hollows in her cheeks. The theatre staff had noticed and Theo had fussed, Evie had tried to draw her out the night she'd tried to forget everything at Pete's, but it was when Finn Kennedy had glanced at her in ER and said, 'You look like hell. Don't let it affect your work,' that she'd known she must have hit rock bottom.

She turned back to her lecture notes. Her personal life may have fallen apart, but the examiners didn't care about that. They expected her to be an expert on all things surgical and anything less meant failing. Her fingers gripped the computer's stylus overly hard. She would not fail. Being rejected by the man she loved was one thing. She wouldn't allow failing to qualify as a surgeon the first time round to add to her humiliation.

You're doing what Tom does.

What?

Burying yourself in work so you don't have to deal with your feelings.

But what was there to deal with? She'd told Tom she loved him. He'd said, 'Goodbye.'

The loud rap of her door knocker made her jump. She wrapped her fleecy hoodie around her, slipped her feet into her sheepskin boots and walked up the hall, still surprised that the floor no longer dipped. The knocker sounded a second time, and impatience vibrated through the house. 'Okay, just a minute.'

She picked up her keys from a bowl by the door—a habit she'd picked up at Tom's. She shook the thought from her brain as she slid the key into the deadlock before pulling the door open. Her mouth gaped, her throat closed and her heart cramped.

'Hello, Hayley.'

Tom's deep voice spun around her as he stood on her front mat, his height and breadth filling the tiny porch. His hair was dishevelled and for the first time ever he wasn't perfectly colour-coordinated. He wore his royal blue scarf with his brown jacket and black pants. More than the usual amount of black stubble covered his cheeks, giving him a rugged and raw look at odds with the urban-chic clothes. A tingle shot through her and she jumped on it, hating that her desire for him still burned despite how much he'd hurt her. It faded away, leaving her feeling raw and wounded.

She crossed her arms to protect herself. 'That's an interesting combination of clothes. I see as part of your insane drive to be totally independent of anyone you've asked Gladys to leave as well?' Hayley's unexpected response to his greeting thundered into Tom, completely discombobulating him. On the drive over, as Jared had excitedly told him about his A in chemistry, Tom had silently been rehearsing everything he planned to say to her. All of it had been predicated on her saying, 'Hello, Tom.'

He breathed in deeply, savouring the scent of the woman he loved, and tried a smile. 'I've been a bit distracted this last week.'

'How interesting for you.'

Her frigid words almost froze the Sydney winter sun. He steadied himself. 'May I come in?'

'Why?'

Her hurt and anger encased him like the metal bars on a cell. *Did you expect this to be easy?* 'I want to talk to you.'

'I'm not sure—' her voice wavered slightly '—that I want to talk to you.'

He heard the squeak of hinges and he shot out his hand, hoping to stop the door from closing. His knuckles hit something soft.

'Ouch.' Her fingers closed around his hand, pushing it away. 'Hell, Tom. First you break my heart and now you want to give me a black eye?'

His gut rolled on guilt and frustration. 'I'm sorry, but I can't bloody see and I thought you were closing the door on me.' He went for contrition. 'You know I'd never intentionally hurt you.'

'I don't know any such thing.'

His heart shuddered at the hardness in her voice and he sighed. 'Fair call. I deserved that. All I'm asking is for ten minutes and after that you can throw me out.'

Please don't.

'Okay.' Her voice sounded utterly resigned as if she didn't have the energy to say no but that talking to him was something she was being forced to endure. 'It's ten steps down the hall.' She didn't offer her arm. 'Stick to the right to avoid the hall table and there are two steps down into the kitchen. The table with chairs is on your left.'

He wanted to sit next to her without a table between them. 'Do you have a couch we could sit on?'

'I don't think so, Tom.'

Undiluted fear scuttled along his veins at her intractable manner and it took all his concentration to walk to the table without stumbling into something.

Soon after that he heard the legs of her chair scraping on the floor and he realised she was sitting adjacent to him. He folded his hands loosely on the table in front of him. Once he'd thought staying at high school was hard. Once he'd thought the battle to rise out of poverty and carve out a name for himself in neurosurgery was hard, and more recently he'd thought learning how to function as a blind person in a sighted world was the hardest thing he'd ever done. But right now, sitting next to the woman he loved, and feeling the waves of her animosity dumping all over him, he knew that all of it—every other struggle he'd ever endured—paled into insignificance. This was the fight of his life.

He felt her stillness next to him and turned to face her, remembering the soft and curvy feel of her. He stuck to his rehearsed script. 'Hayley, this last week's been the longest of my life. I've missed you so much. I've missed your mess, your music, the way you spread-eagle yourself across the bed and how you talk to me so passionately about your work. You filled my apartment with life and when you left, an emptiness moved in. For the first time in my life I've experienced real loneliness.'

'You did ask me to leave and loneliness is easily fixed. Get a dog or ask Jared to move into the spare room. He's good company.'

Her words shredded him like razor wire and he licked his lips. 'Did you miss hearing the bit where I said it was *you* I missed?'

'No.' The word sounded positively breezy. 'I heard you quite clearly.'

This wasn't going anything like he'd planned and in desperation he abandoned his script. 'Hayley, I love you.'

Her gasp of surprise gave him an injection of hope.

'I don't think you do, Tom.'

Her words crashed around him, shattering his dreams. *You're losing her.* He opened his hands palms up in supplication. 'I'm so sorry that I was slow to realise it, but you must believe me when I tell you that I do love you.'

'I think you've confused love with loneliness.' Her chair scraped back. 'I can't be your friend or your back-up girl with benefits any more, Tom. Goodbye.'

Hope spluttered out like a candle starved of oxygen and he almost doubled over from the visceral pain. His arrogance and pride, which had stood him in such good stead in all other aspects of his life, was worth nothing here. It was as if he'd been cut adrift from everything he'd ever known and he was drowning by inches. He felt for his cane, which he'd hung over the back of his chair, and rose. Her scent twirled around him and he knew she was very close. Like a dying man, he grasped at one last straw. If he could just touch her then perhaps that would connect him to her in a way his words had so miserably fallen short. 'Hayley?' He reached out his hand and prayed she'd take it.

Hayley stared at Tom's face, knowing all the contours and planes so well, having gazed at it for hours and traced it with her fingers and her lips. A face that at times could be as expressionless as granite and at other times open and responsive. Right now, it combined desperation with pleading—two emotions she'd not seen on him before. She wanted to believe what he said, believe that he truly loved her, and she wanted to take his hand, but he'd hurt her too much for her to trust him.

I love you, Hayley.

'Tom, I don't understand. A week ago you locked me out of your life because you believed you couldn't protect me and that as a couple we'd fall at the first hurdle. Over the last seven days you haven't regained your sight so how does the fact you think you love me change anything?'

His hand rested in midair, hovering between them with fingers splayed and a slight tremor at the tips. Her hand tingled and her fingers flexed, but she fisted them to keep them under control.

He cleared his throat. 'The thought of spending the rest of my life without you scared me rigid.'

She pushed her hair out of her eyes as her heart sent new rafts of pain through her with every beat. 'So now you love me out of fear? Great, Tom, I think that's worse than telling me to go.'

The tremor in his hand increased and his jaw tensed as if it didn't want to move and allow the words to come out. 'Apart from Mick and Carol, I've essentially been alone my whole life and I've never allowed myself to need anyone because I was so focused on getting out of Derrybrook and staying out. It drove everything I did. Then you wandered into my life and turned it upside down and you opened my heart to knowing what I'd been missing all these years. Suddenly I wanted all things I'd believed I'd never have. A woman who loved me. A family.' His voice cracked. 'The night in the tunnel when I thought you'd been hurt and I couldn't do a thing to help you terrified me. I never wanted to feel like that again and I asked you to go. I'm beyond sorry.'

She bit her lip against his sorrow, trying to stand firm until she knew exactly what he was really saying. 'Sorry for what?'

His other hand ploughed through his hair as pain scored his face. 'For retreating into a lifelong habit of locking people out and focusing on work. You're right. I try to be insanely independent and losing my sight has only made me worse. It took meeting you to show me how wrong that choice is.'

Her hurting heart hiccoughed. *Be careful.* But her arm lifted and she passively slid her fingers between his.

He instantly encased her hand with both of his, gripping them like a drowning man. 'I love you, Hayley. You make me a better person and I'm begging you for a second chance.'

A picture of a future with Tom beamed in her mind, but she stalled it. 'Tom, I never want to relive this last week. Sighted or unsighted, no one can totally protect me, just like I can't totally protect you. How do I know that you're not going to retreat on me again?'

'Because I *never* want to relive this last week again either and should I ever fall back on old habits, you'll remind me of how miserable I was without you and how much I need you.' He brought one hand up to cup her cheek. 'You've taught me more than you'll ever know, but most importantly you've opened my eyes and shown me that my life with you is stronger, richer and happier. I can only hope that you believe your life with me is stronger, richer and happier too.'

His heartfelt words all but demolished her doubts and she put her finger under his chin, tilting his head slightly so she could look directly into his eyes. She saw a deep and abiding love, and a pledge of commitment to her. He spoke the absolute truth. He really did love her. Warmth spread through her, clearing away the remnants of her misgivings, and the axis of her world righted itself, spinning on joy.

She touched his cheek. 'I found a peace with you I've never known. I love you, Tom Jordan.'

Relief flooded his handsome face and he pulled her close, his lips seeking hers. She met them with her own, welcoming the heat of his desire, and at the same time recognising the change in it. This time love underpinned his need and it flowed through her as a living thing, touching every organ, bone, muscle, tendon, tissue and cell until she almost cried out from the intensity of it.

When he finally broke the kiss he said, 'You love me and I'm the luckiest man alive.'

She leaned into him, still not quite believing that he'd come back and found her. 'Don't ever forget it,' she half teased.

'I won't. I promise.' He stroked her hair. 'Hayley?'

Her senses reeled with the musky smell of him, the solid feel of him in her arms, and she never wanted to move. 'Mmm.'

'I spoke to Richard Hewitson today.'

She raised her head to look at him, holding her breath before she finally spoke. 'And?'

He grinned. 'I'm the new associate professor at Parkes School of Medicine, and as well as lecturing I'm setting up a support structure for disadvantaged students. Not only for those enrolled in the programme but for students who aren't here yet, like Jared. I'm going to help create pathways into medicine and then support the students when they're here, like Mick and Carol did for me.'

He's found his way. Happiness flooded her and she kissed his cheek. 'That's fantastic, Tom. I've always said you had great rapport with young people.'

His mouth kicked up at one corner. 'And I finally heard you.' He pressed a kiss into her hair. 'You know, not being able to operate will always feel like I've lost a limb, but there's nothing I can do to get my sight back. I have to move on, and being blind has led me to this new job and the possibility of helping kids just like me. I know it's going to challenge me in new and different ways, and that feels exciting. Most importantly, my blindness led me to you.'

His love and sincerity cocooned her and she rested her forehead against his. 'If I've opened your eyes then you've given me back the dark. Thank you.'

His hand curved around the back of her neck. 'Like you told me, we make a good team. Will you make us a permanent team by marrying me?'

She didn't even try to stifle her squeal of delight as she enthusiastically threw her arms around his neck. 'Yes. Oh, yes.'

He swayed from her body slam and grinned at her. 'I love your answer, but do you have a couch we could sit on before you knock me off my feet?'

'No.' She dropped her voice to the smoky timbre she knew he adored. 'But I do have a bed.'

His eyes flared with love and desire. 'Even better.'

'I'm full of good ideas.' She took his hand. 'Follow me.'

His fingers closed around hers. 'I'll follow you anywhere, Hayley.'

Her heart melted with happiness. 'And I'll walk beside you for the rest of my life.'

Smiling, he brought her hand to his mouth and kissed it, and she knew she was home.

EPILOGUE

Tom Jordan—Prof to almost everyone—felt his academic robes slide over his knees as he rose to his feet and joined in the applause for the graduating class. Sixty new doctors would be commencing their internships in hospitals across Australia and Jared was one of them. Tom could only remember a couple of other times in his life that he'd felt this proud.

Hayley's hand slipped into his and he thought he heard her sniff. 'I can't believe he's going to be working at The Harbour.'

'Daddy, why is Jared throwing his funny hat in the air?'

He looked down at the daughter he'd never seen, but his picture of her was crystal clear in his mind. He'd held her within seconds of her birth, counted her fingers and toes, felt her snub nose, tangled his fingers in her masses of hair and had recognised the differences in her cries ahead of Hayley. 'He's celebrating, Sasha. This is his special day.'

'Like my party?' Sasha had recently turned five and her voice sounded hopeful. 'Is there cake?'

His hand ruffled her silky hair. 'Yes, Nanna Carol made Jared a great big cake.'

'When Mummy was at the hospital?'

'That's right.' Hayley was now a consultant at The Harbour and had two registrars working under her.

People started moving around him and Hayley said, 'We should probably go now so we're home before our guests arrive. Sasha, hold my hand, please.'

Tom reached down, his left hand clasping leather. 'Forward, Baxter.'

His guide dog rose and safely guided him through the crowd, the way he'd been doing for seven years, and it constantly amazed Tom how expert he was at it. He smiled when he thought back to when he and Hayley had got married and how hard she'd worked to convince him that a guide dog would suit him perfectly. Years on, he knew that Hayley understood him almost better than he understood himself, and as a result he was much more open to her suggestions. He loved having a dog and couldn't imagine himself without one.

Two hours later, the party was in full swing. Tom had made a speech and was taking a breather from all the noise out on the balcony.

'Hey, Prof.'

Tom turned toward the voice. 'Hey, Dr Jared Perkins.'

Jared came and stood next to him. 'I've imagined being called "Doctor" for so long, but now it's here it sounds so weird. Six long years and I'm a doctor.'

Tom smiled. 'If you want to do neurosurgery, you're preparing to scale another mountain. Seven to ten more years.'

'Yeah, but it will be worth it. Without neurosurgery and without you I wouldn't be here. Thanks, Tom.'

The emotion in his friend's voice stirred the well in Tom he no longer hid, and he found Jared's shoulder and gave it a squeeze. 'It goes both ways, mate.'

'What does?'

Hayley's perfume and quick steps had preceded her, and Tom dropped his arm from Jared's shoulder and extended it toward his wife. 'Thanks go both ways.'

'They do.' Her smile sounded clear in her voice. 'Now you're dealing with rosters, Jared, Sasha's going to miss your Friday night visits. No other babysitter lets her get away with pizza in front of her favourite DVD.'

'Forget Sasha, we're going to miss our date night,' Tom teased. 'I wonder if there's another student in the Pathways Programme who might be interested in paid babysitting.'

'Jared!' Sasha's running feet hit the tiles of the balcony. 'Can you cut your cake, please?' She managed to elongate the 'please' with endearing charm.

Jared laughed. 'For you, Sash, anything.'

'Daddy, I can cut some cake for you.'

'Thank you, darling, but let Jared help you. Mummy and I will be there in a minute.'

When he heard the sound of their retreating feet ebb into the carpet, he pulled Hayley in close and a rush of tenderness made him smile. 'I just felt the baby bump.'

Hayley's hands slipped around his neck and she kissed him. 'In four months our life is going to change.'

He stroked her cheek. 'Life's always changing. We're going to have a new baby and a new puppy.'

'Poor Baxter. His retirement's going to be noisy and busy with a baby human and a puppy in the house. Sasha can't wait to play with him and I think she plans to dress him up for her tea parties.'

Tom still pinched himself every day that he'd been so blessed in his life. Hayley had changed his world and then Sasha had arrived and added to it in more ways than he could count. Now he could hardly wait to welcome their second child.

Tom laughed. 'Poor Baxter indeed. I had to be the tea-party guest last Wednesday.'

Hayley giggled. 'The work of a father is never done.'

'And I wouldn't have it any other way.'

'I might have known you two would be out here ca-noodling,' Carol interrupted with a chuckle. 'Akim and his wife have just arrived and they've brought basboosa cake.'

'We'll be right there, Carol.' But he didn't move his feet.

Hayley sighed. 'We should go.'

'We should and we will.' With the fingers of both hands he traced Hayley's face and then he brought her lips to meet his. He savoured her taste and felt her love pouring through him, and then he gave her all his love in return.

* * * * *

SYDNEY HARBOUR HOSPITAL: LEXI'S SECRET

BY
MELANIE MILBURNE

To Ricki Peres for her friendship and support,
and also for her help in the research for this
novel in the field of transplant surgery.
Thank you!

CHAPTER ONE

It was the worst possible way to run into an ex, Lexi thought. There was only one parking space left in the Sydney Harbour Hospital basement car park and although, strictly speaking, she shouldn't have been parking there since she wasn't a doctor or even a nurse, she was running late with some things for her sister, and it was just too tempting not to grab the last 'Doctors Only' space between a luxury sedan and a shiny red sports car that looked as if it had just been driven out of the showroom.

She opened her door and winced when she heard the bang-scrape of metal against metal.

And then she saw him.

He was sitting in the driver's seat, his broad-spanned hands gripping the steering-wheel with white-knuckled force, glaring at her furiously when recognition suddenly hit him. Lexi saw the quick spasm of his features, as if the sight of her had been like a punch to the face.

She felt the same punch deep and low in her belly as she encountered that dark brown espresso coffee gaze. Her throat closed over as if a large hand had gripped her and was squeezing the breath right out of her. Her heart pounded with a sickening thud, skip, thud, skip, thud that made her feel as if she had just run up the fire escape of a towering skyscraper on a single breath.

It was so unexpected.

No warning.

No preparation.

Why hadn't she been told he was back in the country? Why hadn't she been told he was working *here*? He clearly was, otherwise why would he be parking in the doctors' car park unless—like her—he had flouted the rules for his own convenience?

OK, so this was the time to play it cool. She could do that. It was her specialty. She was known all over the Sydney social circuit for her PhD in charm.

She shimmied out of the tight space between their cars and sent him a megawatt smile. 'Hi, Sam,' she said breezily. 'How are things?'

Sam Bailey unfolded his tall length from the sports car, closing the driver's door with a resounding click that more or less summed up his personality, Lexi thought—decisive, to the point, focussed on the task at hand.

'Alexis,' he said. No "How are you?" or "Nice to see you" or even "Hello", just her full name, which nobody ever called her, not even her father in one of his raging rants or her mother in one of her gin-soaked ramblings.

Lexi's winning smile faded slightly and her hands fidgeted with the strap of her designer bag hanging over her shoulder as she stood before him. 'So, what brings you here?' she said. 'A patient perhaps?'

'You could say that,' he said coolly. 'How about you?'

'Oh, I hang out here a lot,' she said, shifting her weight from one high heel to the other. 'My sister Bella's in and out for treatment all the time. She's been in for the last couple of weeks. Another chest infection.

She's on the transplant list but we have to wait until it clears. The chest infection, I mean.' Lexi knew she was rambling but what else could she do? Five years ago she had thought they'd had a future together. Their connection had been sudden but intense. She had dreamed of sharing her life with him and yet without notice Sam had cut her out of his life coldly and ruthlessly, not even pausing long enough to say goodbye. Seeing him again with no notice, no time to prepare herself, had stirred up deeply buried emotions so far beneath the surface she had almost forgotten they were there.

Almost...

'Sorry to hear that,' Sam said making a point of glancing at his silver watch.

Lexi felt a sinkhole of sadness open up inside her. He couldn't have made it clearer he wanted nothing to do with her. How could he be so...so distant after the intense intimacy they had shared? Had their affair meant nothing to him? Nothing at all? Surely she was worth a few minutes of his precious time in spite of the different paths their lives had taken? 'I didn't know you were back from wherever you went,' she said. 'I heard you got a scholarship to study overseas. Where did you go?'

'America,' he said flatly.

She raised her eyebrows, determined to counter his taciturn manner with garrulous charm. 'Wow, that's impressive,' she said. 'The States is so cool. So much to see. So much to do. You must've been the envy of all the other trainees, getting that chance to train abroad.'

'Yes.' Another frowning glance at his watch.

Lexi's gaze went to the strongly boned, deeply tanned wrist he had briefly exposed from the crisp, light blue business shirt he was wearing. Her stomach shifted like a pair of crutches slipping on a sheet of cracked ice. Those wrists had once held her much smaller ones in a passionate exchange that had left her body tingling for hours afterwards. Every moment of their blistering two-week affair was imprinted on her flesh. Seeing him again awakened every sleeping cell of her body to zinging, pulsing life. It felt like her blood had been thawed from a five-year deep freeze. It was racing through the network of her veins like a flash flood, making her heart hammer with the effort.

Her gaze slipped to his mouth, that beautiful sculpted mouth that had moved against hers with such heart-stopping skill. She still remembered the taste of him: minty and fresh and something essentially, potently male. She still remembered the feel of his tongue stroking against hers, the sexy rasp of it as it cajoled hers into a sizzling hot tango. He had explored every inch of her mouth with masterful expertise, leaving no corner without the branding heat of his possession.

And yet he had still walked away without so much as a word.

Lexi lifted her gaze back to his. Encountering those unfathomable brown depths made her chest feel like a frightened bird was trapped inside the cage of her lungs. Did he have any idea of the hurt he had caused? Did he have any idea of what she had gone through because of him?

She swallowed in anguish as she thought of the heart-wrenching decision she had made. Would she ever be able to summon up the courage to tell him? But, then, what would be the point? How could he possibly understand how hard it had been for her back then, young and pregnant with no one to turn to? She hadn't felt ready to become a mother. A termination had seemed the right thing to do and yet…

'I have to get going,' Sam said, nodding towards the hospital building. 'The CEO is expecting me.'

Lexi stared at him as realisation slowly dawned. 'You're going to be working here?' she asked.

'Yes.'

'Here at SHH?'

'Yes.'

'Not in the private sector?' she asked.

'No.'

'Do you ever answer a question with more than one word?'

'Occasionally.'

Lexi gave him a droll look but inside she was screaming: *This can't be happening!* 'Why wasn't I told?' she asked.

'No idea.'

'Wow, that's two.'

'Two what?' he said, frowning.

'Words,' she said. 'Maybe we can work on that a little. Boost your repertoire a bit. What are you doing here?'

'Working.'

She mentally rolled her eyes. 'I mean why here? Why not in the private system where you can earn loads and loads of money?' *Why not some other place where I won't see you just about every day and be reminded of what a silly little fool I was?*

'I was asked.'

'Wow, three words,' Lexi said, purposely animating her expression. 'We're really doing great here. I bet I can get you to say a full sentence in a month or two.'

'I have to go now,' he said. 'And, yes, that's five words if you're still counting.'

She lifted her chin. 'I am.'

Sam looked into those bluer than blue eyes and felt as if he had just dived into the deepest, most refreshing ocean after walking through the driest, hottest desert for years. Her softly pouting mouth was one of those mouths that just begged to be kissed. He could recall the dewy soft contours under his own just by looking at her. He could even remember the feel of the sexy dart of her tongue as it played catch-me-if-you-can with his. Her platinum-blonde hair was in its usual disarray that somehow managed to look perfectly coiffed and just-out-of-bed-after-marathon-sex at the same time. He felt the rocket blast to his groin as he remembered having her in his bed, up against the wall, over his desk, on a picnic blanket under the stars...

Stop it, buddy, he remonstrated with himself.

She had been too young for him before, and in spite of the years a world of experience separated them now. She was still a spoilt, rich kid who thought partying was a full-time occupation. He was on a mission to save lives that were dependent on transplant surgery.

Other people had to die in order for him to give life to others. He was *always* aware of that. Someone lost their life and by doing so he was given the opportunity to save another. He didn't take his responsibility lightly. He had worked long and hard for his career. It had defined his life. He had given up everything to get where he was now. He could not afford, at this crucial time in his journey, to be distracted by a party girl whose biggest decision in life was whether to have floating candles or helium balloons at a function.

He had to walk away, just as he had before, but at least this would be his choice, made of his own free will.

'You dented my car.' It was not the best line he could have come up with but he had just taken delivery of the damned vehicle. To him it just showed how irresponsible she was. She hadn't even looked as she'd flung open her door. It was just so typical of her and her privileged background. She had no idea how hard people had to work to get things she took for granted. She had been driven around in luxury cars all of her life. She didn't know what it felt like to be dirt poor with no funds available for extras, let alone the essentials.

Just take his mother, for instance. Stuck on a long transplant list and living way out in the bush to boot, his mother had died waiting for a kidney. His working-class parents hadn't had the money to pay for private health cover. They hadn't even had the money to afford another child after him. He knew what it felt like to want things that were so out of your reach it was like grasping at bubbles, hoping they wouldn't burst when your fingers touched them. In his experience they always burst.

Lexi was another bubble that had burst.

'You call that a dent?' Lexi bent over to examine the mark on the door.

Sam couldn't stop his gaze drinking in the gorgeous curve of her tiny bottom. She was all legs and arms, coltish, even though she was now twenty-four. It didn't seem to matter what she wore, she always looked like she had just stepped off a catwalk. Her legs were encased in skin-tight black pants that followed the long lines of her legs down to her racehorse-delicate ankles. She was wearing ridiculously high heels but he still had a few inches on her. The hot-pink top she had on skimmed her small but perfectly shaped breasts and the ruby-and-diamond pendant she was wearing around her neck looked like it could have paid off his entire university tuition loan.

She smelled fabulous. He felt his nostrils flaring to breathe more of her fragrance in. Flowers, spring flowers with a grace note of sexy sandalwood, or was it patchouli?

She suddenly straightened and met his eyes. 'It's barely made a mark,' she said. 'But if you want to be so pedantic I'll pay for it to be fixed.'

Sam elevated one of his brows mockingly. 'Don't you mean Daddy will pay for it?' he asked.

She pursed her mouth at him and he had to stop himself from bending down and covering it with his own. 'I'll have you know I earn my own money,' she said with a haughty look.

'Doing what?' he shot back. 'Painting your nails?'

She narrowed her blue eyes and her full mouth flattened. 'I'm Head of Events at SHH,' she said. 'I'm in charge of fundraising, including the gala masked ball to be held next month.'

Sam rocked back on his heels. 'Impressive.'

She gave him a hot little glare. 'My father gave me the job because I'm good at what I do.'

'I'm sure you are,' he said. *After all, partying was her favourite hobby.* 'Now, if you'll excuse me, I have a meeting to get to.'

'Is this your first day at SHH?' Lexi asked.

'Yes.'

'Where are you living?'

'I'm renting an apartment in Kirribilli,' he said. 'I want to have a look around before I buy.'

A small frown puckered her smooth brow. 'So you're back for good?' she asked.

'Yes,' Sam said. 'My father's getting on and I want to spend some time with him.'

'Is he still living in Broken Hill?' she asked.

'No,' he said. 'He's retired to the Central Coast.'

Sam was surprised she remembered anything about his father. It didn't sit well with his image of her as a shallow, spoilt little upstart who had only jumped into bed with him as an act of rebellion against her overbearing father.

That had really rankled.

Damn it, it *still* rankled.

Their red-hot affair had only lasted a couple of weeks before her father Richard Lockheart had stepped in and told him what would happen to his career if he didn't stop messing with his baby girl. To top it all off, it turned out she was six years younger than she had told him. It had been a jolting shock to find the young woman he had been sleeping with had only left high school the year before. Nineteen years old and yet she had looked and acted as streetwise and poised as any twenty-five-year old.

Sam had told her things during that short affair he had told no one else. Things about his mother's death, like how hard it had been to watch her die, feeling so helpless, his father's endless grieving, his own dreams of making a difference so no one had to go through what his family had suffered. For once in his life his emotional guard had come down and it had backfired on him. Lexi had used him like she used her social standing to get what she wanted. He had almost lost everything because of her puerile, attention-seeking little game.

When it came down to it, it had been a choice between relocating or sitting back and watching his career implode. To a working-class trainee who had lived on Struggle Street for most of his life, Sam knew that the well-connected and powerful Richard Lockheart could have done some serious damage to his career. He hadn't taken those threats lightly. He had been lucky enough to be able to switch to the US training programme, and while it had cost him a packet, it had been the best thing he'd ever done. He had worked with some of the world's leading transplant surgeons and now he was considered one of the best heart-lung surgeons on the planet. Everyone back home had believed he had transferred on a scholarship and he hadn't said anything to contradict the rumour. Interestingly, neither, it seemed, had Richard Lockheart.

The appointment to SHH had been timely because he had been keen to come home for a couple of years. He missed his homeland and his father. The man was the only family he had. It was time to come home and put the past behind him.

Lexi was a part of his past but she had no place in his future. He had been captivated by her beauty and her alluring sensuality. But her party-girl mentality had been at odds with his career-focussed determination back then—just as much as it was at odds with it now. He couldn't afford to be distracted by her. Even though the eleven-year age gap was no longer such an issue he didn't want anything or anyone—particularly not red-hot little Lexi Lockheart—derailing his career plans.

Lexi flicked a strand of hair away that had drifted across her face. 'How will I contact you?' she asked.

Sam's brows snapped together. 'About what?'

'About your car,' she said, with another little mocking quiver of her eyelids. 'About the dent you need a magnifying glass to see.'

'Forget about it,' he said.

'No, I insist,' she said, taking out her mobile. 'I'll put you in my contacts.' Her slim, beautifully manicured fingers poised over the data entry key.

And that's when he saw it.

The diamond engagement ring on her finger seemed to be glinting at him like an evil eye, mocking him, taunting him.

Engaged.

He felt his throat seize up.

Lexi was engaged.

His mouth was suddenly so dry he couldn't speak. His chest felt as if someone had backed over it with a steamroller. He couldn't inflate his lungs enough to draw in a breath. His reaction surprised him. No, damn it, it shocked the hell out of him. She was nothing to him. What did it matter if she was engaged? It wasn't as if he had any claim on her, certainly not an emotional one. He didn't do emotion. He didn't even like her, for goodness' sake. She was an attention-seeking little tramp who thought bedding a boy from the bush was something to giggle about with her vacuous, equally shallow socialite girlfriends. Good luck to the man who was fool enough to tie himself to her.

Lexi looked up at him with an expectant expression. 'Your number?' she prompted.

Sam reluctantly rattled it off in a monotone he hardly recognised as his own voice. He had changed his number five years ago as a way of completely cutting all ties. He hadn't wanted her calling him or texting him or emailing him. He didn't want that soft sexy voice purring in his ear. It had taken years to get the sound of her voice out of his head.

Engaged.

Sam wondered what her fiancé was like. No, on second thought he didn't want to know. He'd bet he was a preppy sort, probably hadn't done a decent day's work in his life.

Lexi was engaged. Engaged!

It was a two-sentence chant he couldn't get out of his head. Cruel words he didn't want to hear.

'Do you want mine?' she asked, tucking another wayward strand of platinum-blonde hair away from her face with her free hand. It had snagged on her shiny lip gloss. He guessed it was strawberry flavoured. He hadn't eaten a strawberry in five years without thinking of the taste of her mouth.

He blinked. 'Your…er what?'

'My number,' she said. 'In case you want to contact me about the repairs?'

Sam swallowed the walnut-sized restriction in his throat. 'Your car isn't damaged.'

She looked at him for a moment before she closed her phone and popped it back in her bag. 'No,' she said. 'It's made of much tougher stuff, apparently.'

Sam's gaze kept tracking to her ring. It was like a magnet he had no power to resist. He didn't want to look at it. He didn't want to think about her planning a future with some other nameless, faceless man.

He didn't want to think about her in that nameless, faceless man's bed, her arms around his neck and her lips on his.

'You're engaged.'

He hadn't realised he had spoken the words out loud until she answered, 'Yes.'

'Congratulations,' he said.

'Thank you.'

Sam's gaze tracked back to the ring. It was expensive. It suited her hand. It was a perfect fit. It looked like it had been there a while.

His chest cramped again, harder this time.

He brought his eyes back to hers, forcing his voice to sound just mildly interested. 'So, when's the wedding?'

'November,' she said, a flicker of something moving over her face like a shadow. 'We've booked the cathedral for the tenth.'

The silence crawled from the dark corners of the basement, slowly but surely surrounding them.

Sam heard the scrape of one of her heels as she took a step backwards. 'Well, I'd better let you get to work,' she said. 'Wouldn't be good to be late for your first day on the job.'

'No,' he said. 'That might not go down so well.'

The silence crept up to his knees again before he added, 'It was nice to see you again, Alexis.'

She gave a tight smile by way of answer and walked off towards the lift, the sound of her heels click-clacking on the concrete floor striking totally unexpected and equally inexplicable hammer blows of regret in Sam's heart.

CHAPTER TWO

LEXI got out on the medical ward floor with her heart still racing. She had to control her spiralling emotions, but how? How was she supposed to act as if nothing was wrong?

Sam was back.

The shock was still reverberating through her like a dinner gong struck too hard. Her head was aching from the tattoo beating inside her brain.

Sam was back.

She drew in a calming breath. She would have to act as if nothing was wrong. It wouldn't do to reveal to everyone how shocked she was by his appointment. Had no one told her because they were worried how she would react or because they thought she wouldn't even remember him? And how could she ask without drawing attention to feelings she didn't want—*shouldn't want*—to examine?

'Hi, Lexi,' one of the nurses called out to her. 'I just bought my tickets for the ball. I can't wait. You should see the mask I bought online. It's fabulous.'

Lexi's face felt like she was cracking half-dry paint when she smiled. 'Great!'

The ball was the thing she was supposed to be focussed on, not Sam Bailey. It was the event of the year and she was solely responsible for it. It was no secret that some people at SHH were sceptical over whether she would be up to the task. Rumours of nepotism abounded, which made her all the more determined to prove everyone wrong. The proceeds she raised would go to the transplant unit for the purchase of a new state-of-the-art heart-lung bypass machine. Government funding was never enough. It took the hard work of her and her fundraising team to bring to the unit those extras that made all the difference for a patient's outcome.

And her older sister Bella was one of those patients.

Lexi pushed open the door of Bella's room, a bright smile already fixed in place. 'Hi, Bells.'

'Oh, hi, Lexi…' Bella said, her voice sagging over the weight of the words.

Lexi could always tell when Bella had just finished a session with the hospital physiotherapist. She looked even more gaunt and pale than usual. Her sister's thin, frail body lying so listlessly on the bed reminded her of a skeleton shrink-wrapped in skin. She had always found it hard to look at her older sister without feeling horribly guilty. Guilty that she was so robustly healthy, so outgoing and confident…well, on the surface anyway.

She knew it was hard for Bella to relate to her. It put a strain on their relationship that Lexi dearly wished wasn't there but she didn't know how to fix it. Everything Bella did was a struggle, but for Lexi no matter what activity she tried she seemed to have a natural flair for it. She had spent much of her childhood downplaying her talents in case Bella had felt left out. She'd ended the ballet lessons she'd adored because she'd sensed Bella's frustration that she could barely walk, let alone dance. Her piano lessons had gone the same way. As soon as it had become obvious Bella hadn't been able to keep up, Lexi had ended them. It had been easier to quit and pretend disinterest than to keep going and feel guilty all the time.

But it wasn't just guilt Lexi felt when she was around Bella. It was dread. Gut-wrenching, sickening dread that one day Bella was not going to be around any more.

The Lockheart family had lived with that fear for twenty-six years. It was as if the looming shadow of the Grim Reaper had stepped uninvited into their family, and for years had been waiting on the fringes, popping his head in now and again when Bella had a bad attack to remind them all not to take too much for granted, patiently waiting for his chance to step up to centre stage for the final act.

Everyone knew Bella would not reach thirty without a lung transplant. The trouble was getting her healthy and stable enough to be ready for one if a donor became available.

And then there was the waiting list with all those desperately sick people hoping for the same thing: a suitable donor. It was like a weird sort of live-or-die lottery. Even being a recipient of a healthy lung meant that some poor family somewhere else would be mourning the loss of the person they loved.

Life was incredibly cruel, Lexi thought as she put on her happy face for Bella. 'I've brought you a surprise.'

Bella's sad grey eyes brightened momentarily. 'Is it that new romantic comedy everyone is talking about?' she asked.

Lexi glanced at the portable DVD player her sister had on her tray table. Bella was addicted to movies, soppy ones mostly. The shelves the other side of the resuscitation gear held dozens of DVDs she had watched numerous times. 'No, it's not out until next month,' Lexi said. She put the designer shopping bag she'd brought on the bed beside her sister's frail form. 'Go on,' she urged. 'Open it.'

Bella opened the bag and carefully took out the tissue-wrapped package inside. Her thin fingers meticulously peeled back the designer-shop logo sticker keeping the edges together. Lexi was almost jumping up and down with impatience. If it had been her receiving a package the tissue paper would have been on the floor by now in her haste to see what was inside. But Bella took her time, which was sadly ironic really, Lexi thought, when time was one thing she had so little of.

'What do you think?' she asked as Bella had finally unwrapped the sexy red lacy negligee and wrap set.

Bella's cheeks were about as red as the lacy garments. 'Thanks, Lexi, it was very kind of you but...'

'You need to break out a little, Bells,' Lexi said. 'You're always wearing those granny flannel pyjamas. Passion-killers, that's what they're called. Why not live a little? Who's going to notice in here if you wear something a little more feminine?'

Bella's cheeks were still furnace hot. 'I'm not comfortable in your type of clothes, Lexi. You look stunning in them. You look stunning in anything. You'd turn heads wearing a garbage bag. I'll just look stupid.'

'You don't give yourself a chance to look stunning,' Lexi said. 'You hide behind layers of old-fashioned drab clothing like you don't want to be noticed.'

'Don't you think I get enough attention as it is?' Bella asked with a flash of her grey eyes. 'I have people poking and prodding me all the time. It's all right for you. You don't have to lie in here and watch the clock go round while another day of your life passes you by. You're out having a life.'

There was a little tense silence, all except for the squeak of a nurse's rubber-soled shoes in the corridor outside as she walked briskly past.

Lexi felt her shoulders drop. 'I'm sorry,' she said. 'I just thought something bright would cheer you up.' She began to collect the lacy items from Bella's lap.

Bella put her hand out to stop her taking away the negligee set. 'No, leave it,' she said on a heavy sigh. 'It was sweet of you. I'll keep it for when I'm better.'

The unspoken words *if I get better* hung in the air for a moment.

Lexi summoned up a smile. 'Actually, I only bought it because there was a two-for-one sale. You should see the little number I bought myself.'

'What colour is it?'

'Black with hot pink ribbons.'

'Are you saving it for your wedding night?' Bella asked.

Lexi averted her gaze. 'I'm not sure…maybe…'

'Have you heard from Matthew?'

'I got an email a couple of days ago,' Lexi said. 'It's hard for messages to get through. His team are building a school in a remote village in Nigeria.'

'I think he's amazing to be volunteering over there,' Bella said. 'He could have just as easily stayed at home in the family business.'

'He'll come back to the Brentwood business once he's done his bit for humanity,' Lexi said.

'It's nice that you're both are so passionate about helping others,' Bella said.

'Yes… ' Lexi dropped her gaze again. 'Oh, and before I forget…' She rummaged in another bag and took out the latest editions of the fashion magazines Bella loved and spread them like a fan on the tray table. 'You should check out page sixty-three in that one. There's a dress design just like the one you drew last week, only yours is better, in my opinion.'

'Thanks, Lexi,' Bella said with a shy smile.

There was the sound of a firm authoritative tread coming down the corridor.

'I bet that's your doctor,' Lexi said, rising from the end of the bed where she had perched. 'I'd better vamoose.'

'No, don't go,' Bella said, grabbing at Lexi's hand. 'That will be the transplant surgeon. You know how much I hate meeting people for the first time. Stay with me? Please?'

There was a cursory knock at the door and then a nurse came in, followed by a tall figure with shoulders so broad they almost filled the doorway.

Lexi felt her stomach hollow out and her heart did that hit-and-miss thing all over again. Could this really be happening to her? What twist of fate had led Sam to be her sister's surgeon? She'd thought he'd planned to be a renal transplant surgeon. She hadn't for a moment suspected he would be Bella's doctor. It would be even harder to avoid him now. There would be ward rounds and consultations in his rooms, follow-ups if the surgery went ahead. Lexi was the one who mostly ferried Bella around. How was she going to deal with being confronted with the pain of her past on such a regular basis?

'Bella,' the nurse said cheerily. 'This is Mr Sam Bailey, the heart-lung transplant surgeon newly arrived from the US. We're very lucky to have someone of his calibre working for us. And lucky you, for you are his very first patient at SHH. Mr Bailey, this is Bella Lockheart.'

Sam held out his hand to Bella. 'Hello, Bella,' he said. 'How are you feeling?'

Bella blushed like a schoolgirl and her voice was nothing more than a soft mumble. 'I'm fine, thank you.'

'And this is Lexi Lockheart,' the nurse continued with a beaming smile as she turned to where Lexi was standing. 'You'll see a lot of her around the place. She's a tireless fundraiser for SHH. If you have spare cash lying around, watch out. She'll be on to you in a flash.'

Lexi cautiously met Sam's gaze. How was he going to play this? As strangers meeting for the first time? Surely he wouldn't acknowledge their previous relationship, not in a place like SHH where gossip ran as fast as the wireless broadband network, sometimes faster. His professional reputation could be compromised if people started to speculate about what had happened between them in the past.

He put out his large, capable hand, the same hand that had once cupped her cheek as he'd leant in to kiss her for the first time, the same hand that had skimmed over and held each of her breasts, the same hand that had stroked down to that secret place between her thighs and coaxed her into her first earth-shattering orgasm. Lexi slowly brought her hand to his, trying to ignore the way his warm palm sent electric zaps all the way to her armpit and back.

'How do you do?' he said in his deep baritone voice.

So it was strangers, then. 'Pleased to meet you, Mr Bailey,' she said, keeping her expression coolly polite. 'I hope you settle in well at SHH.'

'I'm settling in very well, thank you,' he said, his

eyes communicating with hers in a private lock that made her flesh tingle from head to foot.

She slipped her hand out of his and stepped back so he could speak to Bella. Her hand fizzed and tingled and she shoved it behind her back as she watched as he interacted with her sister with a reassuring mix of compassion and professionalism.

'I've been going over your history in a lot of detail, Bella,' he said, 'especially your lung function over the last couple of years. I guess I don't have to tell you that there's been significant deterioration.'

Bella's grey gaze looked shadowed with worry. 'Yes, I've been admitted to hospital more often with chest infections and it takes longer and longer to clear things up. I've only just started to improve and I've been in here almost three weeks.'

Sam gave an understanding nod. 'I've looked at your latest CT scans and lung function studies. The lungs are very scarred. That's making them stiff, so it's no wonder you're struggling to breathe when you exert yourself or when you get even a minor infection.'

Bella bit her lip and dropped her gaze to the magazines on her tray table. It was a moment before she looked up at Sam. 'Am I getting to…to the end? How much time do I have left?'

Sam gave her thin shoulder a gentle squeeze. 'We're getting to the stage of needing to do a lung transplant within the next couple of months. I've started the active search for a matching transplant donor. If we find one we need to move straight away before you get another bout of pneumonia. We could find a donor in a day, a week or a couple of months. I'm afraid that longer than that and the chances get worse of keeping you well enough to survive the surgery.'

Lexi listened with dread, feeling like a ship's anchor had landed on the floor of her stomach. It was such a massive operation. What if it didn't work? What if poor Bella died on the operating table or soon after? So much of it seemed up to chance: the right donor; whether Bella was well enough at the time to be the recipient; whether she would survive the long operation. So many factors were at play and no one, it seemed, had any control over any of it, least of all Bella.

Bella must have been thinking the very same thing as she said, 'What are my chances of coming through the operation?'

Sam was nothing if not professional and knowledge-able and encouraging in his manner. 'With modern anti-rejection therapy there's better than an eighty-five per cent chance that you'll survive the surgery and live a good-quality life for the next ten years. After that there's not much data, but expectations are that anti-rejection management will continue to improve and that you could end up living a fairly normal life.'

'You're in good hands, Bella,' the nurse said. 'Mr Bailey is considered one of the world's leading heart-lung transplant surgeons.'

Sam acknowledged the nurse's comment with a quick on-off smile as if he was uncomfortable with praise. Perhaps he was worried about operating on someone to whom he had a connection, Lexi thought. Not that he had ever met Bella before, but he had been intimately involved with Lexi. Clinical distance was paramount in life-and-death surgery. A surgeon could not afford to let the pressure of a relationship, no matter how distant or close, interfere with his clinical judgement. She hoped her involvement with him in the past wasn't going to complicate things for Bella.

'I'll keep you informed on things as we go along, Bella,' Sam said. 'You'll stay in the medical ward until your health improves. If a donor becomes available and you're healthy enough, we'll move you across to the transplant unit. Otherwise we'll send you home until something comes up.'

'Thanks for everything, Mr Bailey,' Bella said blushing again. 'I really appreciate you taking me on.'

Sam smiled and gave Bella's shoulder another gentle touch. 'Hang in there, Bella. We'll do all we can to get you through this. Just try and keep positive.'

He gave Lexi a brief impersonal nod as he left with the nurse to continue his rounds.

Lexi didn't even realise she was holding her breath until Bella looked at her quizzically. 'It's not like you to be so quiet when there's a handsome man in the room,' she said.

Lexi felt her face heating and tried to counter it with an uppity toss of her head. 'He's not that handsome.'

Bella raised her brows. 'You don't think? I thought you had a thing for tall muscular men with dark brown eyes.'

Lexi gave a dismissive shrug. 'His hair is too short.'

'Maybe he keeps it short for convenience,' Bella said. 'He's in Theatre a lot. Any longer and it would get sweaty under the scrub hat during long transplant operations.'

Lexi made a business of folding each sheet of the tissue paper into a neat square, lining them up side by side on the bed.

'He's got nice eyes, don't you think?' Bella said.

'I didn't notice.'

'Liar, sure you did,' Bella said. 'I saw you blush. I've

never seen you blush before. That's my specialty, not yours.'

'It's hot in here,' Lexi said, fanning her face for emphasis. 'How do you stand it?'

'Did you notice his hands?' Bella asked.

'Not really…' Lexi remembered how those hands had felt on her body. How they had lit fires under her flesh until she had been burning with a need so strong it had totally consumed her. Those hands had wreaked havoc on her senses from the first moment he had touched her. She opened and closed the hand he had taken in his just minutes ago. The tingling pins and needles feeling was still there…

'He wasn't wearing a wedding ring,' Bella said.

'Doesn't mean he's not involved with someone,' Lexi said, feeling a tight ache in her chest as she pictured his partner. Would she be blonde, like her, or brunette? Or maybe a redhead like Bella. Would she be a doctor or nurse? Or a teacher perhaps? A lawyer? 'Dad's got a new girlfriend,' she said, to change the subject.

'Yes, Evie told me.'

'I haven't met her yet.'

'I don't know why he bothers introducing them,' Bella said with an air of resentment. 'None of them stay around long enough for us to get to know them.'

'Dad's entitled to have a life,' Lexi said. 'It's not like Mum's ever going to come back and play happy families.'

'You always defend him,' Bella said irritably. 'You never let anyone say a bad word about him.'

'Look,' Lexi said, hoping to avoid the well-worn bone of contention between them. 'I know he's not perfect but he's the only father we have. The only parent when it comes down to it. Mum's not much use.'

'Maybe Mum couldn't handle Dad's philandering,' Bella said. 'Maybe it wasn't just because I was sick. Maybe she was left on her own too much and couldn't cope. Maybe she wouldn't have left if he had offered her more emotional support.'

Lexi knew Bella felt terribly guilty about the break-down of their parents' marriage. Her illness had taken its toll on everyone, but their mother had been the first to abandon ship, taking the contents of the drinks cab-inet with her. Miranda Lockheart flitted in and out of their lives, not staying long enough to offer any stabil-ity or support but just long enough to remind them of what they had missed out on.

But blaming their father was not something Lexi had ever felt comfortable doing. He had always been there for her. He was her stronghold, the person she looked up to, the person she craved approval from more than any other.

'Dad has always tried to do his best,' she said. 'He was meant to be a father, not a mother. He couldn't do both.'

Bella gave a weary sigh. 'One day you're going to find out that Dad has clay feet. I just hope I'm around to see it.'

Lexi shrugged and then tried another subject change. 'Have you had any other visitors?'

'Phone calls or texts mostly,' Bella said with a de-spondent look on her face. 'People get sick of visiting after the first week. It happens every time. Maybe it'll be different once I've had the transplant…'

Guilt struck at Lexi like a closed fist. 'I'm sorry I didn't get in yesterday,' she said. 'Matthew's mother wanted me to look at wedding-cake designs. Her sister has already made the cake. Now we just have to decide on the decoration. Matthew wants something traditional but I was thinking we could so something more along the lines of...'

Bella was frowning as she looked into space. It was as if she hadn't heard a word of what Lexi had been saying. 'Sam...' she said. 'Sam. It's really been bugging me. Why does that name sound so familiar?'

Lexi felt her stomach drop again. 'Sam's a popular name.'

'I know but it's more than that,' Bella said, frowning in concentration. 'Bailey. Sam Bailey. Bailey. Sam Bailey.'

Lexi closed her eyes. *Please, no*.

'Oh. My. God.'

Lexi winced as she opened her eyes to see Bella's saucer-like ones staring at her. 'Wh-what?' she choked.

'It's him, isn't it?' Bella asked. 'It's the same Sam Bailey. The Sam Bailey you had that naughty little teenage fling with that made Dad almost blow a fuse. Oh. My. God.'

'Will you please keep your voice down?' Lexi hissed.

'It's not like you'll be able to keep it a secret,' Bella said. 'Not for long and certainly not around here. People have long memories and they just love a bit of juicy gossip. You'd better let Matthew know. You don't want him getting into a flap about an ex-lover turning up out of the blue.'

Lexi turned away to look out of the window, crossing her arms over her body as if that would contain the pain that was spreading like an ink spill through her. Was she deluded to hope no one would remember their past connection? Who else would link their names and start the gossip all over again? How would she cope with it a second time?

No one knew about the baby.

No one.

At least that secret was safe.

But everything else was out there for everyone to pick over like crows on a rotting carcass. All the intimate details of her brief relationship with Sam would be fodder, grist for the mill of gossip that SHH was renowned for. She would be painted as the Scarlet Woman, the scandalous Lolita who had lured Sam away from his studies at the most pivotal moment in his career.

'Lexi?'

Lexi pulled in a breath and faced her sister. 'It was five years ago,' she said. 'Hopefully no one will even remember what happened back then.'

Bella looked doubtful. 'I still think you should tell Matthew.'

'I will tell him,' Lexi said, breaking out into a sweat. 'I'll tell him it was a stupid little fling that meant nothing.'

Bella chewed at her lip for a moment. 'Is this the first time you've seen Sam since you broke up?' she asked.

'No, I ran into him in the doctors' car park on my way to see you,' Lexi said, raking a distracted hand through her hair. 'That'll teach me for breaking the rules. I won't park there ever again. Cross my heart and—' She stopped and gave Bella an apologetic grimace as her hand dropped back by her side. 'Sorry, bad choice of words.'

Bella continued to look at her with a concerned frown on her face. 'You're not happy about seeing him again, are you?' she said.

Lexi lifted her shoulders in a couldn't-care-less manner. 'It's always a little difficult running into ex-partners. It's part of the dating life. Once a relationship ends you don't always end up the best of friends.'

'Not that I would know anything about the dating life…' Bella said as she fiddled with the edge of the sheet covering her thin little body.

Lexi sighed and reached for Bella's small, cold hand. 'You're being so wonderfully brave about all this,' she said. 'If it was me I'd be terrified.'

'I *am* terrified,' Bella said. 'I want what you have. I want a life. I want to one day get married and have babies.'

Lexi felt her insides clench like the snap of a rabbit trap. That aching sadness gripped her every time she thought of the baby she could have had if things had been different. It was ironic that Matthew was keen to start a family as soon as they were married. His parents were excited at the prospect of becoming grandparents. But she had come to dread the topic every time he raised it. It wasn't the only thing she argued with him about. Her lack of interest in sex had become a huge issue over the last few months of their engagement. Matthew's trip abroad, she suspected, were his attempts to make her heart grow fonder in his absence. She didn't have the heart to tell him it wasn't working. She missed him certainly, but not in the way he most wanted her to.

'I'll be the only Lockheart sister left childless and lonely on the shelf,' Bella continued to bemoan.

'Is Evie seeing someone?' Lexi asked feeling a little piqued that she hadn't been told by Evie herself. 'I was under the impression there's been no one since she broke things off with Stuart…what was it? Two years ago?'

'I heard one of the nurses talking about Evie and Finn Kennedy,' Bella said.

Lexi laughed. 'Finn Kennedy? Are you out of your mind? He's the last person I would have picked for Evie. He's so grumpy and brooding. I don't think I've ever seen him smile.'

'He's very kind to patients,' Bella said in his defence. 'And he's smiled at me lots of times.'

'In my opinion Finn Kennedy has a chip on his shoulder that it'd take an industrial crane to shift,' Lexi said. 'I hope to goodness Evie knows what she's doing. The last thing we need in the Lockheart family is another difficult person to deal with.'

There was a small silence.

'Has Mum been in to see you?' Lexi asked.

Bella's shoulders slumped a little further as she shook her head. 'You know what she's like…'

Lexi gave Bella's hand another little squeeze. 'I wish I could change places with you, Bells,' she said sincerely. 'I hate seeing you suffer… I hate the thought of losing you.'

Bella gave her a wobbly smile. 'I guess that's in Sam Bailey's hands now, isn't it?'

CHAPTER THREE

IT WAS a week later when Lexi ran into Sam again—
literally. She was coming out of the hospital cafeteria
with a latte in one hand while she texted a message on
her phone in the other when she rammed into his broad
chest. It was like stepping into a six-foot-two brick wall.
The coffee cup lid didn't survive the impact and the
milky liquid splashed all over the front of Sam's crisp
white shirt.

He let out a short, sharp expletive.

Lexi looked up in horror. 'Oops, sorry,' she said. 'I
didn't see you. I was…um, multitasking.'

He plucked at his shirt to keep it away from his chest.
'This is a busy hospital, not a social networking site,'
he said.

Lexi put up her chin. 'If you had looked where you
were going, you could've avoided me,' she shot back.

'You could've burned me,' he said.

'Did I burn you?'

'No, but that's not the point.'

'It is the point,' she said. 'There's no damage other
than a stained shirt, which I will take full responsibility for.'

He gave her a mocking look. 'You mean you'll hand
it to one of the Lockheart lackeys to launder for you?'

Lexi ground her teeth as she looked up at him. Why today of all days had she worn ballet flats? He seemed to tower over her and it put her at a distinct disadvantage. She was faced with his stubbly chin and had to crane her neck to reach his chocolate-brown eyes. 'I'll see to it that your shirt is returned to you spotless,' she said.

'I can hardly take it off and give it to you in the middle of the busiest corridor of the hospital,' he pointed out dryly.

'Then we'll have to arrange a handover time,' she said. 'What time do you finish today?'

He scraped a hand through his hair. 'Look, forget about it,' he said. 'I have my own laundry service.'

'No, I insist,' Lexi said. 'I wasn't looking where I was going.'

'I'm sure you have much better things to do than wash and iron my shirt,' Sam said.

'Like paint my nails?' she said with an arch look.

He shifted his mouth from side to side. 'OK, round one to you,' he said. 'I had no idea you were so actively involved in raising funds for the unit.'

'I did tell you I was Head of Events.'

'Yes, but I didn't know you had been responsible for raising over five hundred thousand dollars last year.'

'I'm going to double that by the end of this year,' Lexi said. 'You can make a donation if you like. I'll give you the website address. You can pay online. All donations over two dollars are tax deductible.'

Sam was starting to see why she had been chosen for the job. Who could resist her when she laid on the Lockheart charm? She looked especially gorgeous today. She was several inches shorter than usual. But she still smelled as delicious as ever. That intriguing mix of flowers and essential oils teased his nostrils. She was dressed in grey trousers and a loose-fitting white cotton shirt with a camisole underneath that hugged her pert breasts. She had dangling earrings in her ears; they caught the light every now and again, making him think of the sun sparkling on the ocean. It had been her brightness that had attracted him like a moth to a flame all those years ago. He had been drawn to her bubbly nature; her positive outlook on life was such a contrast to his more guarded, introverted approach. She had flirted with him outrageously at a charity dinner held by her father in honour of the hospital. Sam hadn't realised who she was at the time, and he often wondered if he would have taken things as far as he had if he had known she was Richard Lockheart's youngest daughter. He couldn't answer that with any certainty, even now.

Put simply, she had been utterly irresistible.

With her stunning looks, charm and at-ease-in-any-company personality, he had temporarily lost sight of his goal. He had compromised everything to be with her because that was the effect she'd had on him.

But finding out the truth about how she had used him had made him cynical and less willing to open his heart in subsequent relationships. He dated regularly but commitment was something he avoided. Friends of his were marrying and having families now but he had no plans to join them any time soon. He didn't want to end up like his father, loving someone so much that he couldn't function properly without them.

His gaze drifted to Lexi's sparkling engagement ring. He felt a ridge come up in his throat as he pictured her walking down the aisle towards that nameless, faceless man. She would be smiling radiantly, looking amazingly beautiful, blissfully happy to be marrying the man she loved.

Engaged.

The word was a jarring reminder.

Lexi was engaged.

The three words were a life sentence.

Sam gave himself a mental shake. 'I'll get my secretary to make a donation on my behalf,' he said. 'Now, if you'll excuse me…' He pushed against the fire-escape door with his shoulder.

'There is a lift, you know,' Lexi said.

'Yes, I know, but I prefer the exercise.'

She glanced at the lift again before returning her gaze to where Sam was holding the fire-escape door open. She gave him a tight little smile that had a hint of stubbornness to it and brushed past him to make her way up the stairs. He felt his body kick start like a racing-car engine when her slim hip brushed against his thigh. It was probably not deliberate as there wasn't a lot of space to spare. She went ahead of him up the stairs, another bad idea in spite of it being chivalrous on his part. He got a perfect view of her neat bottom and long legs as she made her way up. He tried not to think of those long legs wrapped around him in passion and that beautiful hair of hers flung out over his pillow.

He had lain awake for the last week, sifting through every moment he had spent with her five years ago. From the very first second when her blue gaze had met his across that crowded room he had felt the lightning strike of physical attraction. It had rooted him to the spot. He had felt like a starstruck fan meeting their idol for the first time. He had barely been able to string a few words together when she approached him. Whatever he had said must have amused her for he remembered the tinkling bell of her laugh and how it had made his skin lift in a shiver.

They had left the gathering together and they had barely surfaced from his tiny flat for the next two weeks. For the first time during his career he had neglected his studies. The thick surgical textbooks had sat on his desk opposite his bed, staring at him in a surly silence. And he had pointedly ignored them while he had indulged in an affair that had been so hot and erotic he could hardly believe it had been happening to him. The physical intensity of it had surpassed anything before or since. He had relished every moment with Lexi in his arms. She had been an adventurous and enthusiastic, even at times playful lover. He suspected she'd had a fair bit of experience, perhaps much more than him, but they hadn't talked about it. Looking back, he realised she hadn't said much about herself at all, even though he had tried to draw her out several times. In hindsight he could see why she had been so reluctant to reveal herself to him emotionally. There had been no emotional commitment on her part. She had simply wanted to create a storm with her father and had used him to summon up the thunderclouds.

'Why did you pretend we didn't know each other last week when you were visiting Bella?' Lexi asked, stopping in mid-climb to look back at him over her shoulder.

Sam almost ran into the back of her. He felt the warmth of her body and got another delicious waft of her perfume. 'I didn't think it was wise to advertise the fact that we'd once been involved,' he said.

'Not good for your career?' she asked with one of her pert looks.

He frowned up at her. 'It has nothing to do with my

career. I wasn't sure if your sister knew about us. I'd not met her before. I was playing it safe for your sake.'

'She wasn't at the dinner where we met,' Lexi said. 'But she remembered the dreadful fallout after my father found out we were seeing each other.'

Sam's frown deepened. It had niggled at him a bit that he had never actually seen or spoken to her after her father had approached him with that ultimatum. For the last five years he had just assumed she had run back to the family fortress at her father's bidding. Her little show of rebellion had achieved its aim. She had got her father's attention back solely on her. Back then, Lexi had struck Sam as the type of girl who would never do anything to permanently jeopardise her prized position as Daddy's Little Girl. She would go so far and no further. It was her way of working things to her advantage, or so he had thought.

But what if things hadn't been quite the way her father had said? Lexi had implied on his first day at SHH that she'd had no idea he had gone to the States. Why hadn't she been told where he had gone? Why hadn't she asked? Or had her father deliberately kept her in the dark, perhaps forbidding her to mention Sam's name in his presence, like some sort of overbearing aristocrat father from the past? Was it deluded of him to hope she had invested more in their relationship than her father had suggested? Was it his male pride that wanted it that way instead of feeling like some sort of cheap gigolo who had served his purpose and now meant nothing to her? Had never meant anything to her?

'Your father is well-known for his temper,' he said. 'I hope it wasn't too rough a time for you back then.'

A flicker of something moved over her face but within a blink it was gone, making him wonder if he had imagined it. She gave her head a little toss and turned and continued walking up the fire escape. 'I know how to handle my father,' she said.

Sam followed her up another few steps. 'Why didn't you ask him where I'd gone?' he asked.

He saw her back tighten like a rod of steel before she slowly turned to face him at the fire-escape door. 'Here's the fourth floor,' she announced like a lift operator.

'Why didn't you ask your father, Lexi?' he asked again.

Her blue eyes clashed with his, a spark of cynicism making them appear hard and worldly. 'Why would I do that?' she asked. 'I had a new boyfriend within a few days. Did you really think I was pining after you? Give me a break, country boy. You were fun but not that much fun.'

Sam ground his teeth as he joined her on the landing, conscious of the tight space and the warmth coming off both of their bodies from the exercise. Lexi's breathing rate had increased slightly, making her beautiful breasts rise and fall behind her camisole. He allowed himself a brief little eye-lock but then wished he hadn't. She was temptation personified. He had never wanted to kiss someone more in his life. Did she know she was having this effect on him? How could she not? He was doing his best to disguise it but there was only so much he could do. He was a red-blooded male after all, and she was all sexy, nubile woman.

He thrust the door open out of the fire escape and nodded for her to go through. She walked past him, this time not touching him. He felt the loss keenly. His body ached to feel her, to touch her, to bring her close against him, to feel every part of her respond to him as she had in the past. It frustrated him that she still had that power over him. It wasn't supposed to be like this now.

Engaged.

Lexi was engaged.

For heaven's sake, why wasn't his body getting the message?

'Is this your office?' she asked as she came to a frosted glass door halfway along the corridor.

'Yes.' He stood at the door, pointedly waiting for her to leave.

She peered past his shoulder. 'Aren't you going to show me around?' she asked.

'Alexis,' he began. 'I don't think—'

'I want your shirt,' she said with a determined look in her blue gaze.

I want your body, Sam thought. He let out a ragged breath. 'I guess I can hardly see patients wearing this,' he said. 'I'll put on some scrubs.'

Lexi followed him into the suite of rooms he had been assigned. He wondered for a moment if she was going to follow him all the way into his office but she perched her neat bottom on one of the seats in the currently unattended reception area and idly leafed through a magazine.

Sam came out wearing theatre scrubs and handed her his shirt. Lexi took it from him and tried to ignore the fact that it was still warm from his body. She wanted to hold it up to her nose to smell his particular male smell but she could hardly do that in front of him. It was perhaps a little foolish of her, sentimental perhaps, but she had never forgotten his wonderful male smell. He hadn't been one for using expensive aftershaves. He had smelt of good clean soap and a supermarket-brand shampoo that had reminded her of cold, crisp apples.

Lexi put the magazine down. 'Look, all other things aside, I just wanted to say thank you for all that you're doing for my sister.'

'It's fine,' he said, his granite face back on. 'It's what I do.'

The silence stretched and stretched like an elastic band pulled to its capacity.

Lexi couldn't stop looking at him. It was as if her gaze was drawn by a force she had no control over. She longed to know what was going on behind the unreadable screen of his dark eyes. Was he thinking of the time they had spent together? Did he *ever* think of it? Did he regret walking away from her without saying goodbye? Why had he gone so abruptly? She had thought he was different from other men. He had seemed deeper and more sensitive, more emotionally available. Or had that all been a ploy on his part to get her into his bed as quickly and as often as he could? It had certainly worked. She had held nothing back from him physically. Emotionally she had been a little more guarded because she'd been worried about revealing how insecure she'd felt as a person. She'd known how unattractive that was for most men. He, like all the other men she had met, had been attracted to her as Lexi the confident and outgoing party-loving social butterfly. She hadn't felt comfortable revealing how much of an act it had been to compensate for the deep insecurities that had plagued her. How being surrounded by people had stopped her thinking about how lonely she'd felt deep inside. She had wanted to wait until she was a little more confident that their relationship had a future before she revealed that side of herself. But he clearly hadn't been thinking about *their* future. His sights had been solely focussed on his own.

'Alexis.' There was a note of warning in his voice.

'Please don't call me that,' she said. 'I know why you're doing it but please don't.'

He turned and walked behind the reception desk, the action reminding Lexi of a soldier going back into the trenches. He fiddled with the computer for a moment before he spoke in a casual tone that belied the tension she could see in the square set of his broad shoulders. 'I didn't realise you hated your name so much.'

'I don't hate my name,' she said. 'It's just I can't get used to you calling me anything but Lexi.'

He stopped fiddling and turned, his gaze colliding with hers. 'Will you stop it, for pity's sake?'

'Stop what?' she asked.

'You know damn well what.'

'I don't know what.'

His hands went into fists by his sides. 'Yes, you do.'

'You mean acknowledging you?' she asked, coming to stand in front of him. 'Stopping to talk to you in the corridor or on the fire escape? Treating you like a person, that sort of thing?'

'You probably staged the coffee thing to get me alone,' he bit out.

Lexi glared at him in affront. 'You think I would waste a perfectly good double-strength soy latte on you?' she asked.

His frown closed the gap between his chocolate-brown eyes. 'That shirt cost me seventy US dollars,' he said through clenched teeth.

She put her hands on her hips. 'If that's so then you need some serious help when you go shopping, country boy,' she tossed back.

'What's that supposed to mean?'

She gave her head a toss. 'Call me if you want a style advisor,' she said. 'I have connections.'

He glared at her broodingly. 'You think I need help dressing?'

No, but I would love to undress you right now, Lexi thought. She reared back from her traitorous thoughts like a bolting horse suddenly facing a precipitous drop. What on earth was the matter with her? Her fiancé was working hard in a remote and dangerous part of a foreign country and here she was betraying him with her wayward thoughts about a man she should have put out of her mind years ago. 'Yes,' she said. 'You need to buy quality, not quantity. That shirt is not stain-resistant. For just fifty dollars more you could have bought a stain- and crease-resistant one.'

'Oh, for heaven's sake,' he said as he rubbed at the back of his neck. 'I can't believe I'm even having this conversation.'

Lexi headed for the door. 'I'll get this non-stain-resistant, non-crease-resistant shirt back to you as soon as I can but if the stain doesn't come out don't blame me.'

'Careful not to break a fingernail doing it,' he muttered.

Lexi stomped back behind the reception desk, right into his body space, eyes glaring, cheeks hot with anger. 'What did you say?' she asked.

He looked down at her from his height advantage, dark eyes glittering, jaw clenched, mouth flat. 'You heard.'

She stepped forward half a step and stabbed a finger at his rock-hard chest. 'I might be just an empty-headed party girl with nothing better to do than paint my nails in between organising the next shindig, but this unit, your unit, would not be able to do even half of what it does without my help,' she said. 'Maybe you should think about that next time you want to fling an insult my way.'

Suddenly the distance Lexi had been so determined to keep between them had closed significantly. She felt a current of energy pass from his body to hers. It was like receiving a pulse of high-voltage electricity through her fingertip. She felt it run all the way up her arm until her whole body was tingling. She felt the shockingly traitorous drumbeat of desire between her thighs. It was a primitive pulse she could not control. The proximity of his hard male body had jolted hers into a state of acute feminine awareness. She could feel every pore of her skin dilating in anticipation. The hairs on the back of her neck rose and danced. A shiver ran down her spine and then pooled at the base, melting her bones and ligaments until she wasn't sure what was keeping her upright. She looked into his eyes, those gorgeous sleep-with-me-right-now-and-be-damned-with-the-consequences eyes and her heart gave an almighty stammer.

He felt it too.

The air was vibrating with the heat of their past sexual history. Every moment she had spent in his arms seemed to have assembled and joined them in his office. Every steaming kiss, every smouldering slide of a hand over her breasts or thighs, every blistering caress that had left her senses spinning like a top.

Every heart-stopping orgasm.

She quickly pulled her hand away from his chest, stepping back blindly. 'I—I have to go...'

She was almost out of the door when he spoke. 'Aren't you forgetting something?'

Lexi turned back, her heart beating like a humming-bird's wings as she met his dark satirical gaze. In his hand was his stained shirt. She hadn't even registered she had dropped it. She stalked back over to him, her mouth set in a grimly determined line. She tried to pluck it from his hand but his other hand came from nowhere and came down on hers, trapping her.

Her breath stopped.

Her heart raced.

Her stomach folded when she looked at his darkly tanned hand covering her lighter-toned one.

Her flesh remembered his. It reacted to his. It flared with heat under his. She could feel the nerves beneath the surface of her skin twitching to fervent life. She could feel the blood galloping through her veins like rocket fuel.

She could feel her self-control slipping.

She moved her fingers within the prison of his, her fingernails scraping him in her panic to be free. 'L-let me go,' she said, but to her shame her voice sounded weak and breathless, nothing like the strident, determined tone she had aimed for.

His eyes held hers in a sensual tussle that made her spine tingle. It seemed like endless seconds passed with them locked together, hand to hand, eye to eye. But then his fingers momentarily tightened before he finally released her.

She stepped back, almost falling over her own feet, flustered and flushing to the roots of her hair. 'How dare you touch me?' she said, rubbing at her hand as if he had tainted her. 'You have no right.'

His eyes glinted smoulderingly. 'I hate to quibble over inconsequential details but you touched me first.'

'I did not!'

He pointed to his chest. 'Right here,' he said. 'I can still feel the imprint of your fingernail.'

Lexi swallowed as his eyes challenged hers. Her heartbeat sounded in her ears, loud and erratic, her breathing even more so. 'You're exaggerating,' she said. 'I barely touched you.'

'One way to find out.'

Her eyes widened as his hand went to the hem of his scrub top. 'What are you doing?' she said hoarsely.

The door behind Lexi opened and a middle-aged woman came sailing in. 'Oh, sorry,' she said. 'Am I interrupting something?'

'No!' Lexi said.

'Not at all, Susanne,' Sam said with an urbane smile. 'Miss Lockheart was just leaving.'

'I don't think I've met you properly before,' Susanne said, offering a hand to Lexi. 'I'm Sam's practice manager, Susanne Healey.'

Lexi put on a polite smile but her voice sounded wooden when she spoke. 'Nice to meet you, Susanne.'

'How are the plans going for the masked ball?' Susanne asked.

Lexi crumpled Sam's shirt into a ball against her chest. 'Fine… Thank you…'

Susanne swung her gaze to Sam. 'I suppose you've offered your yacht to Lexi for the silent auction, have you?'

'Er…no, I—' Sam began.

Susanne swung her gaze back to Lexi. 'You should get him to donate a cruise around the harbour in it,' she said. 'It'd be so popular. Everyone loves a harbour cruise and his yacht is gorgeous. I saw it down at Neutral Bay marina with my husband on the weekend. You could have a champagne lunch. You'll get heaps of bids. Think of the money it'd raise. I'll put my name down right now. What do you think should be the opening bid?'

Lexi faltered over her reply. 'I—I don't know…two hundred dollars per couple?'

'How does that sound, Sam?' Susanne asked.

Sam spoke through lips that barely moved. 'Fine.'

'You'll have to buy tickets for the ball now, Sam,' Susanne prattled on. 'You can't miss the hospital's most important event of the year. But you must bring a partner. We can't have you dancing all by yourself, can we, Lexi?'

Lexi met Sam's gaze with a flinty look. 'I'm sure Mr Bailey will have no shortage of dance partners,' she said, 'even if he has to borrow someone else's.'

'I wouldn't steal anyone who wasn't already on the make,' he said with an indolent smile.

Lexi felt her cheeks go red-hot but she refused to be the first to look away. She put all the hatred she could into her glare. Her whole body seemed to be trembling with it as it poured out of her like flames leaping from the top of a volcano.

Luckily Susanne had been distracted by the ringing of the phone. She was now sitting behind the reception desk, scrolling through the diary on the computer screen as she spoke to the person on the other end of line. 'No, that should be fine,' she said. 'Mr Bailey is consulting in his rooms that day… Do you have a current referral from your GP? Good. Yes, I'll squeeze you in at five-fifteen.'

Sam raised a dark brow at Lexi. 'You want to continue this out here or take it somewhere a little more private?'

Lexi's eyes flared and her chest heaved with impotent fury. 'Do you really think I would come running back to you at the crook of your little finger?' she snarled at him in an undertone. 'I'm engaged. I'm getting married in less than three months' time.'

His eyes pulsed mockingly as they held hers. 'Is that little reminder for you or for me?' he asked.

'For you, of course,' Lexi said, and swung away, her head high, her cheeks hot, her heart thumping and her stomach an ant's nest of unease, for somehow, even though he hadn't answered, she suspected he'd had the last word.

CHAPTER FOUR

SAM was still sitting at his desk, absently rolling his pen between his fingers, when Susanne announced on the intercom the arrival of Finn Kennedy, the head of department. 'Send him in,' he said.

The door of his office opened and a tall, imposing figure strode in. Even if he hadn't already been aware of Finn's history Sam was sure he would still have been able to tell he had served in the military from the imperious bearing the man exhibited. There was something about the harsh landscape of his face, the commanding air, the take-no-prisoners demeanour and the piercing but soulless blue eyes that spoke of a long career spent issuing orders and expecting them to be obeyed without question.

Brusque at the best of times and reputedly intimidating to many of the junior staff, Finn was a no-nonsense, show-no-emotion type. But Sam had often wondered if Finn's aloofness had less to do with his personality and more to do with the fact that he had lost his brother while they had both been serving overseas. Finn never spoke of it. If he felt pain or grief or even guilt, he never showed any sign of it.

With a solid background in trauma surgery Finn had retrained to become a highly skilled cardiac surgeon.

His formidable manner didn't win him many friends amongst the staff at SHH but his reputation as a dedicated cardiac surgeon was legendary. Unlike most of his colleagues, Finn usually managed to distance his private life from the gossip network. But in the week Sam had been at SHH he had heard rumours of something going on between Finn and Evie Lockheart, Lexi's oldest sister, who was an A and E doctor. But if the rumours were true and Finn was having an affair with Evie, judging from his crusty demeanour, it wasn't going particularly well.

Sam rose from the behind the desk to offer him a hand but Finn waved him back down. 'How are you settling in?' he asked as he sat down in the chair opposite.

'Fine, thanks,' Sam said. 'Everyone's been very welcoming.'

'Accommodation all right?'

'Yes. Thanks for that contact,' Sam said. 'I'm using the same real estate firm to track down a property for me to buy.'

'The press will want an interview,' Finn said. 'You OK with that?'

'Sure,' Sam said. 'I've already spoken to a couple of journalists who've called. They want a photo opportunity but I'm not sure the patient I have lined up is suitable. Bella Lockheart doesn't strike me as the outgoing type.'

Finn grunted. 'Might be her last chance for the spotlight.'

'I hope it's not,' Sam said. 'I'd like to bring her forward on the waiting list but she's got a chest infection. It's a wait and see, I'm afraid.'

Nothing had showed on Finn's face at the mention of the Lockheart name. 'What are her chances?' he asked.

'She needs a transplant within in the next couple of months,' Sam said. He left the rest of the ominous words hanging in the silence.

Still no flicker of emotion on Finn's face.

'We do what we can, when we can, if we can,' Finn said. He rubbed at his arm and then, noticing Sam's gaze, dropped his hand back down to rest along his bent thigh. 'That rumour true about you and the other sister?' he asked.

Sam stiffened. 'What rumour is that?'

Finn's penetrating gaze met his. 'Word has it you and Lexi Lockheart had a thing going five years ago.'

Sam unlocked his shoulder to give a careless shrug. 'We spent a bit of time together, nothing serious.'

Finn gave him a measured look. 'Did her old man have anything to do with you switching to the US training programme?'

Sam frowned. 'What makes you ask that?'

'Just joining the dots,' Finn said. 'You and young Lexi got it on and then a couple of weeks later you were gone. Makes sense that someone had a gun to your head.'

'The truth is I had thought of studying overseas,' Sam said. 'I just wasn't planning to do it right there and then.'

Finn gave a chuckle. 'I'd like to have seen Richard Lockheart's face when he found out you were sleeping with his youngest daughter.'

'It wasn't a great moment in my life, that's for sure,' Sam said wryly.

'I'm surprised he approved of her fiancé,' Finn said. 'I thought no one was ever going to be good enough for his baby girl.'

Sam swung his ergonomic chair back and forth in a casual manner. 'You know much about her fiancé?'

'Met him at a couple of hospital functions,' Finn said. 'Nice enough chap. Comes from bucketloads of money but he's currently doing a stint with Volunteers Abroad. You see the rock on her finger? He made a big donation to the hospital the day the engagement was announced.' He gave a grunt of amusement. 'Hopefully he'll double it once they're married.'

Sam felt his chest tighten but he forced a smile to his lips. 'Let's hope so.'

'There's a drinks thing organised for Wednesday night at Pete's Bar across the road for you to get to know some of the other departmental staff,' Finn said. 'Just another excuse for the staff to get hammered if you ask me, but you might as well put in an appearance. Half-price Wednesdays are a bit of an institution with the registrars.'

'I got the email about it the other day,' Sam said. 'I'll definitely pop my head in the door.'

Finn stood. 'Right, then,' he said. 'I'm off home. It's been a long day and tomorrow's probably going to be no better.'

Sam stood looking out of the window once Finn had gone. The sun was sinking in the west, casting the city in a golden glow. He had missed that iconic view in the years he had been away. Just knowing it would be there waiting for him to come back had helped quell any momentary feelings of homesickness. But the view had changed, or perhaps his memory of it had.

It just wasn't the same.

On Wednesday evening Sam had been caught up with a particularly tragic case and had spent the extra time explaining the sad prognosis to the patient and his young family.

When he came out to the reception area after dictating the letter to the patient's GP, Susanne drew his attention to a wrapped parcel sitting on the counter. 'That came for you a little while ago.'

'What is it?'

'A shirt,' Susanne said, eyes twinkling. 'From Lexi Lockheart.'

Sam took the package, keeping his expression blank. 'Thank you.'

'She said the stain didn't come out so she bought you a new one,' Susanne said.

Sam frowned at his receptionist's intrigued expression. 'She spilt coffee on it when she bumped into me,' he explained. 'She offered to launder it for me.'

'A little bird told me you and Lexi dated a few years back,' Susanne said, leaning her chin on her steepled fingers.

'Your little bird is wrong because we never actually went out on an official date,' he said, leafing through a pile of correspondence. 'Our entire affair was conducted in private.'

Susanne's pencilled eyebrows lifted. 'I sense some angst between you,' she said. 'That little scene I came in on the other day...'

'Susanne,' Sam said sternly as he put the letters down on the desk, 'I need you to type my letters and schedule my theatre lists and organise my diary for me. I do not need you to speculate on my private life. That is totally off-limits, understood?'

Susanne nodded obediently. 'Understood.'

He was almost out of the door when he stopped

and turned to look at her. 'Who was the little bird?' he asked.

Susanne made a buttoning up motion with her fingers against her mouth. 'I promised not to tell. Guide's honour.'

'Oh, for heaven's sake,' Sam muttered and left.

The bar was full and loud with the buzz of conversation and thumping music when Sam finally arrived. He wove his way through the knot of people, saying hello to those he recognised from previous introductions and stopping to greet those who introduced themselves.

Evie Lockheart was one person he remembered from his training years. But as she had been a couple of years behind him in med school they hadn't really socialised. She moved through the crowd and offered a slim hand to him with a polite but contained smile. 'Welcome back to SHH,' she said. 'I'm not sure if you remember me. I'm Evie Lockheart from A and E. You came to a trainee doctor dinner thing my father held a few years ago.'

Sam took her hand as he returned her smile. Did she also remember he'd only had eyes for her knock-'em-out-gorgeous youngest sister that night as well? And had she been a witness to the fallout Lexi had alluded to? 'Of course I remember you,' he said. 'Nice to see you again.'

'I believe you're doing a great job of looking after my sister,' Evie said.

'Um…pardon?'

Evie smiled to put him at ease. 'I understand patient confidentiality, Sam, but under the circumstances, given we're colleagues, I think it's OK for you to discuss Bella's treatment with me.'

Oh, that sister, Sam thought. 'We're working on getting her well enough to receive a donor lung,' he said. 'She's getting better but finding a match is the next hurdle.'

'We've heard very good things about you,' Evie said. 'Mind you, my father wouldn't have approved your appointment unless he thought you were the best.' She gave him a hard little look. 'Not after what happened between you and Lexi. Talk about World War Three. I thought Dad was going to disown her. I've never seen him so furious with her. I was very worried about her. She took it very hard.'

Sam kept his expression impassive but inside he was reeling. 'Lexi seems very settled now,' he said.

'Yes,' Evie said. 'It's a good match. Matthew is lovely. He's just what Lexi needs. He comes from a very stable family.'

'A very rich family, or so I've been told,' Sam said.

'Mega-rich,' Evie said taking a sip of her drink. 'But unlike some of the silver-spoon set, they're good with it. They support a lot of charities. I think that's why Matthew and Lexi hit it off so well. They have a lot in common.'

Sam wondered what Lexi's fiancé would say if he found out about the tense little scene in his office the other day. Perhaps Lexi was feeling a little frisky with her man away for weeks, if not months, on end. She wasn't the celibate type. She was far too sensual for that. Sam had all the blisteringly hot memories of her to vouch for that.

Finn sauntered over with a glass of single malt whisky in his hand. 'So you finally managed to extricate yourself from the mother ship?' he drawled.

'Yes,' Sam said. 'It's been one of those days. Why is the last patient of the day always the hardest?'

'It's always like that,' Evie said, deliberately turning her body away from Finn as if his presence annoyed her.

Finn's lip curled at the all too obvious snub. 'So how is Princess Evie this evening?' he asked.

Evie gave him an arctic glance over her shoulder. 'There's a new barmaid on tonight, Finn,' she said. 'You might want to see if she's free later on.'

'Maybe I'll do that,' Finn said with a smirk.

The air was crackling with waves of antagonism. It was pretty clear Finn and Evie had something brewing between them but Sam wasn't sure exactly what it was. He had noticed Finn's hand trembling slightly as he brought his drink up to his mouth. He didn't want to think about what had caused that slight tremble. Was that what that arm rub had been about the other day? he wondered. Was that why Evie was so prickly and guarded around him? Did she suspect something but wasn't game enough to put her name and reputation on the line in outing Finn? It was a tough gig reporting a senior colleague and most junior doctors would think twice about doing it.

Being new at SHH would make it equally difficult for Sam. He hadn't been around long enough to be certain but even so, calling out a colleague for suspected alcohol abuse would be nothing short of career suicide. He would only do it if he had enough evidence to prove it was actually the case. There could be any number of contributing factors: extreme tiredness, for instance. He had experienced it himself after long operations and too many nights on call. His whole body had started to quake and tremble with exhaustion. Those symptoms could so easily be misconstrued, and if he was wrong it would have devastating consequences professionally.

Finn Kennedy looked like the overworked type. His piercing blue eyes were bloodshot, but the damson-coloured shadows beneath them could just as easily suggest a man who was not getting enough sleep rather than a man who was consuming too much of the demon drink. But, then, who could really know for sure?

'You haven't got a drink,' Finn said. 'What would you like?'

'It's OK,' Sam said. 'I'll make my way over now and grab something soft.' He smiled to encompass them both. 'Nice to chat to you.'

Sam was soon handed a drink by one of the registrars and drawn into their circle. He did his best to answer some of the questions fired at him but the whole time he felt strangely disconnected. It was as if his body was standing there talking to the small group surrounding him but his mind was elsewhere. Lexi was just a few feet away. There was a faint trace of her perfume in the air and every now and again he could feel her gaze on him.

'What about harvesting organs?' one of the junior interns asked. 'Do you have to travel to different hospitals to do that?'

'Sometimes, but not to harvest the actual organs I will end up using,' Sam said bringing his attention back to the group in front of him. 'As you know, it's impossible to transfer someone on a ventilator. It's easier for us to go to them once the family has come to the decision of turning off life support. We notify the recipient once the match has been made and then swing into action. There's a lot of co-ordination and co-operation between campuses.'

After a while the conversation drifted into other areas so Sam moved away from the bar to circulate some more. He had only taken a couple of strides when a cluster of people separated and he came face to face with Lexi.

There was an awkward silence.

'Thanks for the shirt,' Sam said gruffly. 'But you shouldn't have bothered.'

'I underestimated the efficacy of my laundering abilities,' she said. 'No matter what I did, the coffee wouldn't come out.'

'You should've just sent it back to me,' he said. 'You didn't need to buy such an expensive replacement.'

'It wasn't expensive. I got it in a half-price sale.'

Another tense little silence passed.

'You know, if you don't want to donate a cruise on your yacht, you don't have to,' Lexi said with a frosty look. 'I have plenty of other people more than happy to donate items much better than yours.'

Sam felt his back come up. 'I didn't say I didn't want to donate it.'

She rolled her eyes in disdain. 'You weren't exactly super-enthusiastic about it.'

Sam frowned at her. 'What did you want me to do? Cartwheels of excitement down the corridor?'

'I didn't even know you had a yacht.'

He threw her a cutting glance. 'Pardon me for the oversight,' he said. 'Would you like a list of the things I currently own?'

She glowered at him. 'I'll need to inspect it at some point,' she said. 'I can't allow it to be used if it's not suitable. I have to consider the public liability issue.'

'Fine,' Sam said. 'Inspect it. I'm sure you'll find it comes up to your impeccable standards.'

'How many people can you fit on board?' she asked.

'I could push it to ten but eight's probably the max for comfort.'

'And what sort of lunch do you plan on offering?' she asked, looking at him in that haughty manner of hers that seemed to suggest she thought he would think a sausage wrapped in a slice of bread and a can of beer would do the job.

Sam stared at her plump, shiny mouth. He couldn't seem to drag his gaze away. She was wearing lip gloss again. He wondered if it was the same one she used to wear. 'Strawberries…'

A tiny frown appeared between her ocean-blue eyes. 'Just…strawberries?' she asked.

Sam had to give himself another quick mental slap. 'Champagne and caviar,' he said. 'You know the sort of deal. Good food, fine wines, gourmet food.'

'I'll look into it and get back to you,' she said. 'What's your boat called?'

'*Whispering Waves,*' he said. 'It was already named when I bought it.'

'So it's big enough to sleep on?' she asked.

'It sleeps six,' he said, suddenly imagining her in the double bed beside him, rocking along with the waves. His body stirred as the blood began to thunder through his veins.

He had to stop this—right now.

'I didn't know you were into sailing,' Lexi said. 'You never mentioned it when we…you know…'

'I'd never even been on a yacht before I went to the States,' Sam said. 'I got invited to crew for a friend over there. We did some races now and again. I really enjoyed being out on the water so I decided to buy my own vessel. I had it shipped over before I came back.'

'Do you intend to race over here?' she asked.

'I'm not really into the competitive side of things,' he said. 'I just enjoy the freedom of sailing. I like being out on the water. It's a very different environment from a busy hospital.'

Lexi readjusted the strap of her bag over her shoulder, her gaze drifting away from his. She was aware that people would wonder what they were talking about for so long. 'I'd better let you get back to socialising.'

'You can probably tell I hate these sorts of gatherings,' Sam said. 'I'm not one for inane chitchat.'

'You just have to get people to talk about themselves,' Lexi said. 'Everybody will say what a great conversationalist you are, but really they're the ones doing all the talking. Believe me, it never fails to impress.'

He tilted his mouth in a mocking smile. 'Does that come from Lexi Lockheart's *A Socialite's Guide to Charming a Crowd*?'

Lexi gave him another wintry look. 'It comes from years of experience talking to people with over-inflated egos,' she said, shifting slightly to one side so one of the residents could make their way past juggling glasses of beer.

'What's going on between your sister and Finn Kennedy?' Sam asked, before she could step any further away.

Lexi looked at him in surprise. 'What? You've heard something too?'

'Not as such,' he said. 'But you've only got to look at them together to see something's going on. They're like two snarling dogs circling each other.'

'So you think that's attraction?'

'I didn't say that,' he said.

'But you think it's a sign.'

'They either hate each other's guts or they can't wait to fall into bed with each other,' he said.

'So that's your expert opinion?' Lexi asked with a cynical look.

He took another sip of his drink before he answered. 'You know what they say about hate and love and the two-sided-coin thing.'

'I think he's totally wrong for her,' she said, frowning.

'Why's that?'

'He's emotionally locked down,' she said emphatically. 'He can't give her what she wants.'

'And you know exactly what she wants, do you?'

Lexi pushed her lips forward as she glanced at her oldest sister. Evie was glaring at Finn, her mouth tight, her eyes flashing as he leaned indolently against the bar with a mocking smile on his handsome face. Lexi frowned as she turned back to Sam. 'I think she wants what every woman wants,' she said. 'She wants a man who loves her for who she is, someone who will protect her and support her but not crush her.'

His brows moved closer together over his eyes. 'You think Finn would crush her?'

'He's got a strong personality,' she said.

'But so does Evie.'

'You sound as if you know her personally.'

'I don't,' he said. 'I've only exchanged a few words with her, but I've heard she's one of the best A and E doctors this hospital has ever seen. I've heard she's ambitious but compassionate. Not unlike Finn.'

'So you think they'd be a perfect match for each other?' Lexi asked with an incredulous look.

He gave a noncommittal shrug. 'I think they should be left to sort out their differences without the scrutiny or judgement of others,' he said.

'That won't be easy in a place like SHH,' Lexi said, chewing at her lip as she thought of what people would make of her and Sam talking at length. If it hadn't been for his wretched shirt and his wretched yacht, she wouldn't have had to speak to him at all.

'Yes, like most hospitals, it's a bit of a hotbed of gossip,' he said. 'I'm surprised people can find the time to work at their jobs when they're so busy spreading rumours.'

'I didn't realise people would talk so much. I didn't realise anyone would even remember that we…' She grimaced. 'I hope it's not too embarrassing for you.'

'It will blow over,' Sam said. 'But to tell you the truth, I'm not sure we could've been any more discreet back then. We kept pretty much to ourselves. I don't think we left my flat for the first ten days. Perhaps if we hadn't ventured out for that take-away meal at the end of our second week, our affair might have gone unnoticed.'

Lexi wondered if he had ever thought about that full-on time over the last five years, the burning-hot lust that had burned like a wildfire between them. The days and nights of passion that had only been interrupted by the necessities of existence—water, sustenance and the minimum of sleep. They had been in such perfect tune with each other physically. It hadn't seemed to matter that they hadn't really known each other. Their bodies had done the talking for them. Each kiss and caress, each stroke of his tongue and each stabbing thrust of his body had revealed to her the truly passionate man Sam was underneath that cool, clinical facade he presented to the world. There was a streak of wildness in him that she suspected few people ever glimpsed. She wondered with a pang of jealousy if he had been like that with anyone else.

She looked into the contents of her glass again as the silence stretched and stretched. 'I shouldn't have lied to you about my age.'

'I shouldn't have believed you,' he said. 'You were too young for me, not just in years but in experience.'

Lexi brought her eyes back to his in surprise. 'So you knew all along?' she asked.

He frowned at her look. 'Knew what?'

She moistened her lips with the tip of her tongue, her gaze slipping away from his. 'Never mind,' she said, wondering if it was her imagination or was every eye in the room on them right at that point? She glanced nervously over her shoulder but everyone was chatting amongst themselves, apart from her sister Evie who was giving her the eye: the older, wiser, big sister look that said, *Be careful.*

Sam glanced at her empty glass. 'What are you drinking?'

'It's all right,' she said. 'I can buy my own drinks.'

'I'm sure you can, but I'm going to get myself a mineral water so in order to be polite I thought I'd ask if you would like a fresh drink.'

She let out a little breath. 'I'm drinking lemon, lime and bitters.'

He hiked up one brow. 'Nothing stronger?'

'I like to keep my head together at things like this,' she said. 'No one likes to see a drunken woman making a fool of herself, be she young or old.'

Sam had heard on the hospital grapevine about Lexi's mother's issue with alcohol. It seemed the burden of taking care of the chronically ill Bella for all those years had led Miranda Lockheart straight to the drinks cabinet. Gin had been her choice of anaesthesia. Sam had met many parents who had done exactly the same thing. He didn't judge them for it. He felt sorry for them. Sorry that there weren't enough supportive people in their life at that point of crisis to help them through without the crutch of other substances.

He brought their drinks back and handed Lexi hers. 'Your sister hinted at the reaction your father had to our affair,' he said. 'She said he almost disowned you. And that it was a very bad time for you. Is that true?'

Lexi looked at her drink rather than meet his penetrating gaze. 'I'd rather not talk about it.'

'Your father was furious with me,' Sam said after a moment of silence. 'He threatened to derail my career. I knew he had the power and the contacts to do it. It wouldn't have been the first time a trainee has been bumped off the training scheme. I decided to transfer my studies. The way I saw it, it was a case of leave or fail. I figured it was the only way to keep myself on track for qualifying. But I didn't realise he had directed his anger at you too. That hardly seems fair when I had already taken responsibility for everything that had happened.'

Lexi felt her heart give an almighty stumble. Could it be true? Had her father threatened him? Was that why he had disappeared without a trace, without even saying goodbye to her? She thought of how furious her father had been with her when he had discovered she had been involved with Sam. It had been the first time she had been on the receiving end of his wrath and it had totally crushed her. She had always been the one who pleased him. It was her role in the family: Daddy's little girl.

Evie was the academically gifted one, the mother substitute who had taken on all the responsibility of looking after the family after their mother had left. The nannies and au pairs their father had organised had had nothing on Evie. She was the go-to sister, the one who had always made sure they got everything they needed.

Bella was the middle one, the chronically sick and incredibly shy child who had not been expected to live past her early twenties, if that. Their father had made it more than clear that he felt repulsed by Bella's sickness and her shyness was another strike against her. He thought it brought shame to the family name to have a daughter who blushed and could barely string two words together in the company of anyone outside the family.

Growing up without a mother on hand, Lexi had idolised her father. She had come to realise that deep down she was terrified he too might leave if she didn't please him. Being a social butterfly was her way of feeling needed. She loved being surrounded by people, and parties were a perfect place to showcase her talent at working a room. Even as young as five she had been able to pass around plates of canapés like an accomplished hostess four times her age. And it had only got better as she'd grown into young womanhood. She had lapped up her father's approval with every event or party she had helped him organise. His praise had been like an elixir she'd needed to survive. It had been the only way to feel close to him.

Maybe Sam was making it up, maybe it wasn't true. Her father would never have gone that far, would he? The memories, long buried deep inside her, bubbled to the surface—her father's fury, how long it had taken her to get back into his good books, what she'd had to do to prevent him finding out about the baby... Suddenly, it felt like she had been betrayed by him in the most devastating way.

Her teeth sank into her bottom lip as she looked up at Sam's face. She had to know. 'Did my father really threaten to end your career?' she asked.

Sam's expression was impossible to read. 'It's not important now, Alexis,' he said. 'It wouldn't have worked out between us anyway. I was too career-oriented to give you the time and attention you needed. It was just a crazy lust-driven fling. I should've had better control.'

Lexi felt a choked-up feeling at the back of her throat as she looked up at him. If only she had known what had been at stake for him. If only she had known he hadn't really had a choice but to leave. It was so heartbreaking to think about what could have been if only she had known what had gone on between him and her father.

Her chest rippled with a spasm of pain. Would their baby have had his dark brown eyes and light brown hair, or would it have had her blue eyes and blonde tresses? Would it have been a girl or a boy? If things had been different, their baby would be in preschool now. He or she would be learning to recognise letters, making friends, finger painting, making things with Play-Doh: all the innocent things of childhood.

Lexi had made her decision based on what she had known at the time and it had been the hardest thing she had ever done. She had been so frightened of her father's reaction to the news of her pregnancy. She had felt so unprepared for the responsibilities of motherhood. She hadn't been able to talk to anyone about it. She had hidden it from everybody. She hadn't even told her sisters. Not even Evie, who would have surely helped her and guided her. Instead, she had booked herself into a clinic, miles away in the outer suburbs where her name wouldn't be connected with the powerful and influential Lockheart name. She had stoically faced the impersonal removal of Sam's baby, but on the inside she was devastated that she'd had to make such a harrowing decision. The bottomless well of sadness over that time never seemed to ease, no matter how hard she tried to put it behind her.

Lexi was aware that they were still in the bar surrounded by people but she had never felt so utterly alone. It was like a glass wall was around her, a thick impenetrable wall that had locked her inside with her sorrow.

'Why do you keep calling me Alexis?' she asked. 'I don't understand why you can't call me Lexi like you used to do.'

An irritated frown carved deep into his forehead. 'You know why,' he said. 'We need some distance.'

'How much distance do you want?' she asked. 'I'm based at the hospital and I'm not leaving just because you've flown back into town. You can't pretend it never happened, Sam. It did and nothing you do or say will ever change that.'

The strong column of his throat moved up and down as if he was trying to swallow a boulder. 'Don't do this, Alexis,' he said. 'Don't try and pretend our fling was something it wasn't. You only got involved with me to get back at your father. An act of rebellion, he called it.'

Lexi looked at him with tears burning like acid at the back of her eyes but only sheer willpower prevented them from appearing, let alone falling. Could this possibly get any worse? As if her father's threats against Sam hadn't been enough. Had her father really said that, lied like that? How could the parent she had adored for as long as she could remember deliberately sabotage her relationship with the man she had thought might be the only one for her? It was a devastating blow to see her father in such a light. He had put his own interests ahead of her happiness. What sort of parent did that to their child? 'Is *that* what he told you?' she asked.

He closed his eyes briefly as if this was all a horrible dream and she would disappear when he opened them again. 'I don't want to cause trouble between you and your father,' he said. 'Our relationship wouldn't have lasted either way. We had nothing in common. We were on completely different pathways.'

'You being Mr Ambitious and me being an empty-headed social butterfly with no aspirations beyond shopping and partying?' she asked, emotion bubbling up inside her like scalding lava.

He raked a hand through his hair in a distracted manner. 'Alexis...' He caught her glacial look and amended on an out breath, 'Lexi... '

'You think I didn't have aspirations?' Lexi said bitterly. 'You have no idea. Do you think I didn't want to do well at school and go to university? I could have achieved way more than I did but how could I do that to Bella? Tell me that, country boy. I had a sister two years older than me who ended up in the same class as me at school. She had to stay back because of her illness. How could I outshine her? How do you think that would have made her feel? I had to play down my talents so she could feel good about herself for just a few moments each day. I wanted to do well but she was more important. So don't talk to me about my lack of ambition. Sometimes there are situations that require sacrifice, not ambition at the cost of those you love. I chose the former, so shoot me.'

It was a great exit line and Lexi used it. She pushed past the knot of people blocking the exit and stumbled out into the street. But home was the last place she wanted to be. She wasn't ready to face her father after this evening's revelations.

Right now she desperately needed to be alone.

CHAPTER FIVE

SAM was walking along the corridor after finishing a ward round on the following Monday afternoon when he saw Lexi coming towards him. As soon as she saw him she swiftly turned on her heel and started walking quickly back the way she had come.

'Lexi, wait,' he said, increasing his strides to catch up. 'Can I have a quick word?'

She stopped and turned, sending him a hard little glare. 'I'm on my way to visit Bella.'

'Bella's resting,' he said. 'I've just been in to see her. She's having some oxygen to boost her levels. Just give me a couple of minutes, OK?'

She let out a long hissing breath. 'All right, if you insist.'

'I insist,' Sam said. 'But not here in the corridor.' He pushed open the door of the on-call room and waited for her to go in.

Lexi brushed past him with her head at a haughty angle. 'This had better not take long,' she said.

'It won't, I promise.'

Sam closed the door and allowed himself the luxury of sweeping his gaze over her. She was breathtakingly beautiful, dressed in corporate wear that on another woman could have looked conservative and boring but on her looked absolutely stunning. The prim white blouse hugged her breasts and the narrow skirt teamed with high heels gave her a sexy secretary look that was distinctly distracting. Her perfume drifted towards him as she folded her arms across her body and a tendril of hair escaped from the neat chignon she had fashioned at the back of her swan-like neck. Everything about her fired his blood to fever pitch. It was impossible to be in the same room as her and not want to take her in his arms and kiss her senseless.

His body remembered every contour and curve of hers: her sensual mouth and the way it had fed so hungrily off his; her soft hands with their dancing fingertips that had set his skin on fire; the way her long, slim legs had wrapped around his waist as he'd plunged into her hot moistness; the way her body had gripped him tightly as if she'd never wanted to let go; the way her hips had moved in time with his, her breathing just as frantic as his own gasps; the way her platinum-blonde hair had spread like a halo around her head in the throes of passion; and the way she had gasped his name, her body convulsing in ultimate pleasure, triggering his own cataclysmic release. No matter how hard he tried he couldn't remove the memory of her touch from his mind, much less his body. She wore another man's ring but, heaven help him, he still wanted her.

She tapped her foot on the floor impatiently. 'Well?'

Sam let out a long breath. 'Lexi, I owe you an apology. I should've come to see you before I left for the States. It was wrong of me to just up and leave like that. I didn't think about your end of things at all. I just believed what your father said about you and left it at that. I realise now that I should've at least listened to your side.'

Her blue eyes were still hostile, the set of her shoulders stiff with tension. 'Is that all?'

'No, it's not all,' Sam said. 'I took on board what you said about the sacrifices you've made to protect Bella.'

She didn't move or speak, just stood there watching him silently, accusingly.

Sam took another breath and slowly released it. 'I should've realised the adjustments you've had to make,' he said. 'I know more than most how the squeaky wheel gets the oil in families and how other siblings can feel left out or isolated as a result.'

'Fine,' Lexi said. 'Can I go now?'

Sam frowned. 'You're not making this easy on me.'

Her eyes hit his like blue diamonds. 'Why should I?'

'You're right,' Sam said, letting his shoulders down on a sigh. 'Why should you?'

He was still trying to get his head around this new Lexi. Not the party girl but the young woman who loved her sister so much that she put her own interests to one side. It went against everything she had told him about herself back then. During their short fling she had laughed off his comments about her lack of ambition. She had said how much she loved the social circuit, how all she had time for was fun, not boring old stuffy studying. Those had been her exact words. He had thought at the time it was such a waste given that he'd had to work so hard to get to medical school.

Unlike Lexi, he hadn't gone to a fee-paying school with the best resources on hand. He had toughed it out in the bush in between helping his father run their drought-ravaged sheep property. He had missed days, sometimes weeks of school to help nurse his mother through the last stages of her kidney disease. Catching up with his studies had been an added burden eclipsed by worry about his mother's declining health and the quiet desperation he'd seen in his father's sun-weathered face whenever he'd looked at his wife lying listlessly in the bedroom of the rundown homestead.

Hearing Lexi say she had deliberately sabotaged her educational achievements to protect her sister was something that had touched Sam deeply. It had made him take pause. He had not realised what a compassionate person she was. Her shallow party-girl persona was a clever artifice for a sensitive young woman who clearly suffered a lot of survival guilt. She had thrown herself into fundraising for SHH, but what else would she have secretly loved to have done? What dreams and aspirations had she put to one side in order to protect her sister from feeling inadequate?

It was part of his job to deal with the families of transplant patients. He understood the dynamics, the sometimes tricky family situations that fed into the patients' outcomes, whether they liked it or not. He wanted to do a good job on Bella, not just because she was Lexi's older sister but because she was a deserving recipient of a lung donation. But even more than that he wanted to make sure Lexi got her chance to shine. Operating on her sister could well be the most important transplant he had ever performed.

Sam looked at her standing there with a mutinous expression on her beautiful face. Anyone seeing her now would assume she was a sulky spoilt brat but he felt like the scales had been removed from his eyes. He could see the hint of vulnerability in her ocean-blue gaze and the almost imperceptible quiver of her bottom lip, as if she was holding back a storm of emotions. 'Why did you get involved with me?' he asked. 'Why me and not someone else?'

'It wasn't an act of rebellion,' she said. 'It was nothing like that.'

'Then what was it?'

She unfolded her arms and used one of her hands to brush back her hair. 'I can't explain why,' she said. 'It just…it just happened.'

Sam watched as she moved restlessly to the other side of the room, her arms folded protectively across her body. Her cheeks were a delicate shade of pink as if the memory of their time together unsettled her more than she wanted to admit. Her saw her beautiful white teeth sink into the soft fullness of her bottom lip. It was one of her most engaging habits, one he suspected she was largely unaware of. It gave her a look of innocence and guilelessness; the potent mix of sexy woman and innocent girl was totally captivating.

'At the pub the other night you said something that's been niggling at me ever since,' he said. 'What was it you thought I'd always known about you?'

Lexi kept her gaze out of the range of his. 'It doesn't matter now…'

But of course he wouldn't leave it at that. 'It was when I mentioned that we'd been worlds apart in years and experience,' he said. 'Tell me, Lexi. What was it you thought I'd always known about you?'

She pressed her sandpaper-dry lips together. Her throat felt tight, too tight even to swallow. Her stomach was churning so much she could hear it rumble in the prolonged silence. Why had she even mentioned it? What was the point of going over this now?

It was over.

They were over.

She was moving on with her life.

Or trying to…

'Lexi?'

His commanding tone summoned her gaze. 'I didn't just lie about my age,' she said on an expelled breath.

His gaze never wavered; it remained rock-steady on hers, but the darkness of his eyes seemed to deepen another shade. 'What else did you lie about?'

She moistened her lips in order to get them to move again in speech. 'Actually, it wasn't really a lie, not an outright one. It was just that I didn't quite tell you the truth.'

Sam's forehead became a map of frowning lines. 'The truth about what?'

Lexi took a breath and then released it in a rush. 'I was…I was… You were my first lover.'

His face looked as if it had just received an invisible slap. She saw him flinch, every muscle contracting, his eyes widening and his mouth opening and closing as if he couldn't quite locate his voice. *'What?'*

'I was a virgin.' Lexi bit her lip. 'At least technically I was…'

'Technically?' he asked. 'What the hell is that supposed to mean?'

She pulled in another uneven breath. 'I'd had boyfriends in the past,' she said, 'lots of them actually. I just hadn't…you know…done it…gone all the way…'

Sam raked his fingers through his hair as he paced back and forth. 'I can't believe I'm hearing this.' He stopped to glare at her furiously. 'Why on earth didn't you say something?'

'Because I knew if I'd said something you wouldn't have slept with me.'

'You're damn right I wouldn't,' he said. 'What were you thinking, Lexi? You were just a young girl. We had so much sex over those two weeks.' His throat moved up and down over a tight swallow. 'Did I…did I hurt you?'

She shook her head vigorously, perhaps too much so.

'Lexi?' He barked her name at her.

'All right, all right,' she said, her eyes rolling in defeat. 'Just a little bit but it was fine after the first—'

'Oh, dear God,' he said, rubbing a hand over his face.

Lexi stalked to the other side of the room. 'You're making such a big deal out of this,' she said. 'I had to lose my virginity some time. At least it was with a considerate lover. It could've been a lot worse.'

He glared at her again. 'How much worse could it have been? I thought I was sleeping with an experienced party girl who knew all the rules,' he said. 'Now I find out she was an innocent virgin.'

'Not so innocent,' Lexi put in.

He held his head in both of his hands and groaned. 'No wonder your father was ready to nail me to the floor.'

'My father didn't know I was still a virgin,' she said. 'It's not exactly something you discuss over the dinner table.'

'No, but it *is* something you discuss with a potential sexual partner,' he pointed out.

'Not when you're having a meaningless, short-term fling,' she threw back.

He stilled. Not a muscle moved. He was like a statue, frozen. 'So,' he said finally in a voice undergirded with steel. 'Let me get this straight. You just wanted a meaningless short-term fling and I was the handiest candidate. Is that right?'

'No…'

'For heaven's sake, Lexi,' he said bitterly, his voice a harsh rasp of anger. 'You nearly cost me my career. I almost lost everything because of you. Do you realise that? Did you even think about what the consequences would be?'

Lexi turned away from his thunderous expression, her arms going back across her body, tightening like a band to hold herself together. He was a fine one to talk about consequences. He hadn't had to face the biggest consequence of all. 'It wasn't like that,' she said.

'What was it like, damn it?' he asked.

She let out a shaky breath. 'When we met…I felt something.'

'Lust.' There was no mistaking the disdain in his voice.

She threw him a look. 'Not just lust. Before you came along I didn't feel ready for a relationship, not a sexual one at least. But it was different with you. From the first moment we met…'

His eyes hardened to chips of ice. 'Don't,' he said, a warning thread of steel in his tone.

'Don't what?'

'Don't try and dress up what we felt for each other as anything other than what it was,' he said. 'I know it's not the most romantic fact in the world but sometimes sex just happens because of instinct. Chemistry. Animal lust.'

'It wasn't like that for me,' Lexi said quietly.

'Well, it was like that for me,' he snapped back.

Lexi turned away again, not willing to let him see how much he had hurt her. She had hoped…foolishly hoped that he had felt something for her back then, but their brief relationship had meant nothing to him.

She had meant nothing to him.

She had just been another name in his little black book. It was deluded of her to have expected anything else. His career was his priority. It had been back then and it still was now. She had been a temporary distraction that he deeply regretted. The breathtaking magic of their relationship that she had revisited so many times in her mind was an illusion, a flight of fancy on her part, romantic nonsense that had no place in the cold, hard world of reason. Emotion clogged her throat, a cruel strangulation of regret and recriminations. Tears were so close she had to blink to stop them from falling. The tattered remnants of her pride would not allow her to cry in front of him.

She made a move for the door. 'I have to go…'

'Hang on a minute,' Sam said. 'We haven't finished this discussion.'

Lexi slung the strap of her bag over her shoulder from where it had slipped. 'I think we have, Sam. There's nothing more to be said.'

'Wait.'

He caught her arm on the way past, his fingers like a metal band around her wrist as he swung her back to face him, the sudden movement sending a shockwave through her body.

The skin on her wrist sizzled as if he had branded her with his touch. His long, strong fingers were like fire. They burned through the layers of her skin, setting nerves into a crazy, maniacal dance. She felt the strength of his grasp as she tried to pull away and her heart started to pound like a faulty timepiece.

She breathed in the scent of him, the hint of aftershave overridden by the sexy musk of late-in-the-day male. She could see the pinpoints of stubble on his jaw and her fingertips tingled as she remembered how it felt to stroke that sexy regrowth with her own soft skin.

Her lips, too, remembered how it felt to move over

that bristly surface. She wanted to do it now, to remind herself of how he tasted. She wanted to feel her tongue lapping at his skin the way she had in the past.

Lexi looked into his dark, mesmerising eyes and it was like looking into them for the very first time. She felt the same electric shock rush through her, making every single pore of her body acutely aware of him. The raw physicality of it terrified her. It shocked her that her body could want one thing while her mind insisted on another.

Her leg wasn't supposed to be moving forward half a step to bring her body up against the rock wall of his.

Her breasts weren't supposed to be pressed against his chest, the nipples already tightly budded with desire.

Her pelvis wasn't supposed to be anywhere near his, certainly not flush against him and shamelessly responding to the hard ridge of his growing arousal.

Her inner core was pulsing with a longing that felt so intense, so rampantly out of control it was like a fever in her blood.

It was wrong.

Forbidden.

Dangerous...

She dropped her gaze to his sexily sculpted mouth. It was suddenly just a breath away from hers as if her lips had drawn his down through a force of their own. She could see each of the fine vertical creases in his lips, the masculine dryness an intoxicating reminder of how it felt to have his mouth possess her soft, moister one. She could feel the mint-fresh breeze of his breath as it skated across her lips. It was like a feather teasing her, stirring every sensitive nerve until she thought she would go mad if he didn't cover her mouth with the heated pressure of his to assuage the spiralling need.

His mouth moved infinitesimally closer.

Lexi felt his erection, so thick, so powerful and so wickedly tempting against her. She pulled a breath into her lungs but it felt as if she was hauling a road-train along with it. All she had to do was step up on tiptoe and press her mouth to his…

'If you don't step back right now I'm going to do something I swore I wouldn't do,' Sam said in a deep, rough burr that sent a shiver down her spine.

'Why don't *you* step back?'Lexi asked, not because she wanted to win this particular battle but more because she couldn't get her legs to work right at that moment.

'Don't do this, Lexi,' he said, still staring at her mouth, his breath a warm caress on her lips, his body still hot and heavy and aroused against hers.

Lexi felt the hammering of his heart beneath her palm where it was resting on his chest. Its pace was just as hectic and uneven as hers. His hands were gripping her by the upper arms, his warm fingers scorching her flesh. She felt the battle raging in the pulse of his blood, pounding through his fingertips, the war between holding her tighter and letting her go. 'You touched me first,' she said. 'You grabbed my arm.'

'I know,' he said in a gravelly voice. 'It was wrong. I shouldn't have touched you. I don't want this complication right now.'

'So step back.'

His glittering eyes seared hers for a pulsing moment. 'You're enjoying this, aren't you?' he said. 'You're enjoying the fact that you still have this effect on me.'

'You want me to step back?' she asked with a pert look. 'Then let go of my arms.'

His fingers loosened but he didn't release her. 'When I'm good and ready,' he said. And then he brought his mouth down slowly, inexorably towards hers.

Lexi knew she should have moved. She knew she should have pushed against his chest and put some distance between their bodies. She knew she should not have just stood there waiting for his mouth to come down to hers. She knew it, but in that moment she was trapped by her own traitorous need to feel his lips against hers just one more time.

As soon as his lips met hers she felt the electric shock of it through her entire body. It travelled from the sensitive surface of her lips to the innermost core of her where that deep ache of longing was flexing and coiling. Hot pulses of need fired through her as her lips felt the subtle pressure of his. He kept the kiss light at first, experimental almost, as if he was rediscovering the landscape of her lips. It started with a brief touchdown of hard, cool lips on her softer ones. A barely touching brushstroke and then another. He raised his mouth off hers a mere fraction but her lips clung to the rougher surface of his. He pressed down again, slightly harder this time, his lips moving against hers in a gentle exploration.

But then it all changed.

That one searching stroke of his tongue against the seam of her mouth made the kiss became something else entirely. Lexi opened to his command, hungrily feeding at his mouth, brazenly playing with the stab and thrust of his tongue. It was a kiss of passion, of unmet desires, frustration and, yes, maybe even a little bit of anger thrown in for good measure. She tasted the wonderful familiarity of him, a hint of mint, good-quality coffee and that unmistakable maleness she had missed so very much. His tongue was roughly masculine against the softness of hers, stirring in her deep yearnings for the physical completion she had only felt with him.

Being back in his arms felt so right, so perfect, the chemistry so hot and electric it was making her blood hum in her veins. He drew her even closer by placing his hand in the small of her back, a touch full of intimacy and deliciously primal in its intent. She felt the rigid heat of him against her, the unmistakable swelling of his hard male body in response to hers. It was a breathtaking feeling to be back in his embrace, to experience the way her body fitted against the contours of his as if made specifically for him.

His kiss deepened even further as he gave a low growl deep in his throat, and the hand at her back pulled her even closer while his other hand cupped the back of her head, his broad fingers splaying in her hair. Every nerve ending on her scalp fizzed at the contact, sharp arrows of pleasure darting through her from the top of her head to her toes. She had to step up on tiptoe to kiss him back and the movement brought her breasts up against his chest, the friction so wonderful she pressed herself even closer. Below her waist she could feel the hard male ridges of his body, the stark difference that made him so male and her so female.

His mouth continued its sensual assault on hers—hot, moist, urgent, masterful and unbelievably thorough. She kissed him back with all the longing she'd had locked away inside her for five long, heartbreaking years. It was like unleashing a wild beast, and once let loose the unrestrained desire could not be subdued or tamed. Her tongue tangled with his, teasing, flirting and then darting away as he came in search of her. It was a cat-and-mouse game, a battle of wills, a war between two strong opposing forces.

The hand he had placed at the small of her back shifted to cup her bottom. The pressure of his hand drew her pelvis so close to his she felt the complete outline of his potent erection. She felt her stomach drop like an out-of-control elevator as he moved against her. This was what she remembered so well about him. The way he took charge physically, the way he left her breathless with longing, the way his body told her all she needed to know about what he felt about her.

He still wanted her.

Lexi could feel her mouth swelling from the prolonged kissing. She didn't care. She didn't even care that she tasted a hint of blood. She didn't know if it was hers or his. She didn't want the kiss to end. She linked her arms around his neck, her fingers exploring the thick pelt of closely cropped light brown hair on his head.

No one kissed her like Sam did. It was a sensual assault that made her whole body sing and hum with delight. His kiss was erotic and daring, demanding with that edge of hungry desperation in it that suggested he was only just managing to keep control.

Meanwhile, her own control had slipped way out of her grasp. She knew kissing Sam was wrong while she was wearing another man's ring, she knew it and yet she couldn't stop herself responding to the intoxicating magic of his mouth on hers. It was like a drug she knew was forbidden and dangerous but craved anyway. She didn't care about the moral consequences right now. Now was about feeling the red-hot passion Sam incited in her body. Her flesh was tingling and crawling with the need for more of his touch. Her breasts were aching for the caress of his lips and tongue. Her feminine core was pulsing a primal beat that was reverberating throughout her body. It was an unstoppable desire, a longing for the sensual high of passion that she knew he alone could give her. She pushed against him shamelessly, her mouth locked to the bruising pressure of his, wanting more, needing more, aching for more.

Sam suddenly wrenched his mouth off hers, his hands dropping away from her as if she had burned him. 'That should never have happened,' he said, breathing heavily, the fingers of one hand scoring through his hair in agitation.

Lexi took a moment or two to reorient herself. Her senses were spinning so much she felt as if she had just stepped off a merry-go-round that had been going way too fast. Guilt made her go on the attack. 'You started it.'

'You should have stepped back,' he scolded.

She gave him a challenging look, still not ready to accept the total blame. 'Why didn't *you* step back?'

He let out a stiff curse. 'I told myself I wasn't going to do this,' he said, dragging his hand down over his face until it distorted his features. He dropped his hand and glowered at her. 'We should never have got involved,' he said. 'Not then and certainly not now.'

'Who said anything about getting involved?' she said, waving her hand in front of his face. 'I'm engaged, remember?'

The ringing silence was accusing.

Lexi glared at him, directing the anger she felt at herself onto him instead. 'Do you really think I would become involved with you again?' she asked. 'I'm not that much of a fool. You might be happy spending your life passing from one bed to another like a game of musical chairs, but that's not for me. I want stability and certainty.'

'So you picked the richest man in your circle and got yourself engaged to him,' Sam said with a cynical look.

'You don't have any idea of what I want or who I am,' Lexi flashed back. 'You didn't know me five years ago, and you don't know me know. Not the real me. I was just a girl you wanted to sleep with. You didn't want anything else from me. Sex is easy for men like you. It's just a physical thing. Emotions don't come into it at all. I want more than that now. I want the physical and the emotional connection.'

He continued to look at her with his dark, smouldering eyes. 'Are you going to tell your fiancé about that little physical connection we had just now?'

'Let's just forget about it, OK?' Lexi said, hot in the face, even hotter on the inside where the pulse of longing still hummed like a tuning fork struck too hard. 'As far as I'm concerned, it didn't happen.'

Sam thrust his hands deep in his trouser pockets in case he reached for her again. He was sorely tempted. It would be so easy to haul her back against him and force her to admit the need he could see playing out on her features. He could see the battle she was having with herself. He was having it too. Was it because she was now off-limits that this need was so overpowering? He hadn't felt like this with other partners. Each time he had moved on without a backward glance when the relationship had folded. After a couple of months he hadn't even been able to recall their names. But something about Lexi drew him like a bee to a pollen-laden blossom. He ached for her. A bone-deep ache that was as strong as it had ever been. How long was she going to deny what was still between them? Or was this just a game to her, a way of paying him back for leaving without giving her notice

'Are you happy, Lexi?' he asked.

Her blue eyes met his, wariness, uncertainty shining there. 'What do you mean?'

'With this Matthew guy,' he said. 'Are you sure he's the right one for you?'

A defensive glitter came into her eyes. 'Of course he's the right one for me,' she said. 'I wouldn't be marrying him if he wasn't.'

'The way you responded to me just then made me think—'

'I don't want to hear this,' she said, swinging away in irritation.

'You can't just ignore what happened,' he said. 'You can't just push it under the carpet.'

'It meant nothing!' she said. 'I just got a little carried away. We both did.'

'Lexi—'

'Stop it, Sam,' she said with a warning glare. 'Just stop it, will you? I want to forget about it. It was a stupid mistake. You're right. It should never have happened.'

Sam strode over to her, right in front of her, so close he could smell her perfume again. So close he could have touched her. So close he could feel her sweet vanilla-scented breath wafting on his face. 'How can you even *think* of marrying that guy when just minutes ago I could have had you up against that wall?' he asked.

Her hand came up in a flash, connecting with his cheek in a hard slap that cracked through the air like a stockwhip.

Sam held himself very still, his eyes locked on hers. The air pulsated with the combined force of their anger. It was a thundercloud of frustration, a hurricane of hatred and longing, a lethal mix that could explode at any moment. He felt the tension in his body. The wires of his restraint were stretched to the limit.

He had never wanted anyone more in his life.

'Feel better now, do we?' he asked.

Her throat rose and fell over a tight swallow but her eyes still flashed at him with glittering heat. 'You insulted me,' she said. 'You as good as called me a slut.'

'I want you, Lexi,' he said in a low, husky tone. 'And you want me. Deny it if you must but it's not going to go away.'

'It has already gone away,' she said, swallowing again.

'You want me,' he said again. 'Go on, admit it.'

'I will do no such thing!' she said, struggling to put some distance between their bodies. 'You just want me because you can't have me.'

'Oh, I can have you,' he drawled. 'Make no mistake about that, sweetheart. Engaged or not, I can have you and we both know it.'

She pushed away from him, glowering at him with venomous hatred as she wrenched open the door. 'You're wrong, Sam,' she said. 'You're so wrong.'

'Let's see about that, shall we?' he asked.

Lexi closed the door on his mocking smile, running, stumbling down the corridor as if the very devil himself was at her heels.

CHAPTER SIX

EVIE was coming back into the hospital as Lexi was leaving it. 'Hey, what's the rush?' Evie asked. 'You look like you're running from a fire.'

Lexi worked hard to get her flustered features under some semblance of control. 'I have a lot to get done,' she said. 'Things to do, people to see, you know.'

'Have you been to see Bella?' Evie asked.

'Um…no,' Lexi said, averting her gaze. 'I got distracted with…with, er, something else.'

Evie cocked her head. 'What's that on your face?'

'What's what?' Lexi asked, putting a hand up to her hot cheek.

Evie peered closer. 'It looks like some kind of rash…' She straightened and gave Lexi a narrow-eyed look. 'Beard rash. Where the heck would you get beard rash from when your fiancé is several thousand kilometres away, working in a remote Nigerian village?'

'Evie, don't,' Lexi said, releasing an impatient breath. 'I'm really not in the mood for this.'

'It's Sam Bailey, isn't it?' Evie said, frowning.

'Don't be ridiculous.'

'I saw you talking to him the other night at the pub. You were by yourselves for ages, looking all cosy in the corner. What's going on?'

Lexi threw her older sister a look. 'You're a fine one to talk,' she said. 'Everyone was talking about you and Finn that night. Finn was looking at you as if he wanted to strip you naked right then and there. Have you got something going on with him?'

Evie pulled her chin back in disgust. 'Are you crazy? I hate Finn's guts. You know that. He's the most arrogant, bull-headed man I've ever met. He probably left the pub with one of the barmaids. It wouldn't be the first time. That's the sort of jerk he is. Anyway, stop changing the subject. What's going on with you and Sam Bailey?'

'Nothing,' Lexi snapped irritably. 'Why does everyone assume there's something going on just because we were once involved? There's absolutely *nothing* going on. How many times do I have to say it?'

Evie looked at her for a lengthy moment. 'You *are* in love with Matthew, aren't you?' she asked.

'Of course I love him,' Lexi said. And she meant it. She really did. Matthew Brentwood was one of the nicest men she'd ever met. He treated her with respect; he made her feel important and special. It wasn't his fault she didn't enjoy being intimate with him. He hadn't done anything wrong. In fact, he had been incredibly patient with her. She hated herself for disappointing him. So many other men would have ended the relationship but, no, he had insisted it would get better once they were married. She felt safe and secure knowing he would always be there for her in spite of her shortcomings. She felt a treasured part of his loving family. His parents and two sisters had welcomed her with open arms. Her relationship with Matthew would never be a hair-raising, white-knuckle roller-coaster ride; it was more like a safe, gentle cruise on a peaceful lake.

It was what she wanted.

'Loving someone isn't the same as being in love,' Evie said. 'Sometimes a relationship can feel right but be totally wrong.'

'There's nothing wrong with my relationship with Matthew,' Lexi said. 'I just wish people would mind their own business.'

'Sor-ry,' Evie said. 'No need to be so prickly.'

'I'm sorry,' Lexi said, her shoulders going down. 'I'm just dealing with some stuff right now.'

Evie frowned. 'What stuff?'

Lexi gave her sister a direct look. 'Did you know Dad had threatened to end Sam's career five years ago?'

Evie blew out a whooshing breath. 'I thought you might stumble across that sooner or later. I was hoping you wouldn't find out.'

'You knew about it and didn't *tell* me?' Lexi asked.

'I didn't find out about it until the other night at the pub,' Evie said. 'Finn thought it highly amusing to think of Dad trying to suck up to Sam. I asked him what the hell he meant and he told me he'd always suspected Dad had had something to do with Sam leaving. I had no idea he had pulled that sort of stunt. When we heard Sam had left, we all assumed he'd got some sort of scholarship to study overseas. Looking back now, I think Dad encouraged everyone to think that. He wouldn't have wanted anyone accusing him of blackmail.'

'No,' Lexi said bitterly. 'Instead, he made me think Sam had left because he couldn't care less about me. How could he do that? How could he act so despicably and think it wouldn't have consequences?'

'You can't change anything now, Lexi,' Evie said. 'You were so young back then. You wouldn't have stayed with Sam in the long term. Surely you realise that?'

'How do you *know* that?' Lexi asked with a furious glare. 'How can you be so sure of what I would or wouldn't have done?'

Evie frowned again. 'No need to bite my head off, Lexi.'

'I'm tired of everyone interfering,' Lexi said, clenching her hands into tight balls of tension. 'I'm so angry with Dad. I'm angry at Sam. But most of all I'm furiously angry at myself.'

'I don't see why,' Evie said reasonably. 'You thought you were in love and got caught up in the fantasy of it. It's what kids do.'

'I was nineteen, not nine,' Lexi said. 'I was old enough to know my own mind. I should have fought for what I wanted. Why was I so weak? Why didn't I stand up for myself?'

'Lexi…' Evie's tone softened. 'Just let it go, OK? You're going to make yourself miserable in the long run. You can't live your life looking back over your shoulder all the time. You're happy and settled now. Don't go stirring up a hornet's nest just for the heck of it.'

'You don't understand,' Lexi said, fighting tears. 'Dad ruined my life. He's ruined everything.'

'I know it's hard for you to finally realise Dad isn't perfect,' Evie said. 'You've had him on a pedestal for such a long time. And while I don't agree with his methods, I think his motives probably came from the right place. He was worried about you wrecking your life. Sam was so much older and he was battle-scarred. Dad could probably see that and just did what he could to protect you.'

'I wish he'd left me to sort my own life out,' Lexi said bitterly. 'Why did he have to play God?'

'Tread carefully, Lexi,' Evie cautioned. 'You've got enough on your plate with organising the ball as well as your wedding without looking for more drama from home. You know what Dad's like. He can be an absolute bastard if you get on the wrong side of him. I should know. I've done it enough times.'

'I don't care,' Lexi said with a steely look of determination. 'I'm going to have it out with him. I don't care if he gets upset and rants and raves. I want him to face what he's done. He's coming back tonight from his weekend away. I can't just ignore this. I can't let him get away with it. It's my life, my happiness we're talking about here.'

Evie let out a sigh. 'You won't get him to apologise, Lexi. You do know that, don't you?'

Lexi set her mouth into an intractable line. 'I want him to realise you can't use people like chess pieces on a board. You just can't do that.'

'Good luck with it, hon,' Evie said. She paused before she added, 'Oh, and maybe you should try a little concealer on that rash before you go home.'

Sam walked back to his office with the taste of Lexi still fresh on his tongue and the skin of his cheek still stinging from her slap. He knew he had probably deserved it. He had goaded her. He couldn't seem to stop himself from needling her. He had wanted a rise out of her. He had wanted her all stirred up and fiery. It made his blood thrum when she looked at him with those flashing sparks in her big blue eyes and her beautiful breasts heaving in anger.

He *had* wanted to kiss her. No point denying it. He

had wanted to from the first day he'd run into her in the car park. She kept waving that flashy engagement ring under his nose but the way she'd kissed him back just now made him wonder if she was as in tune physically with her fiancé as she was with him.

And that was another thing there was no point denying, even though she seemed stubbornly determined to do so. Their physical chemistry was as strong and overpowering as ever.

He was going to have to watch his step. Having an illicit affair with Lexi now wouldn't be a great career move, not with her engaged to one of the hospital's biggest supporters. But, oh, how he wanted her! It was a constant ache in his flesh. He had only to think of her and he was swelling with need.

He was still having trouble processing the news of her virginity. How had he not noticed that? It made him feel uneasy that he had rushed her into bed without considering the implications. They had mostly practised safe sex. Mostly. He had only once…OK, maybe it had been twice…failed to use a condom in his haste to have her in the shower. His stomach clenched when he thought of how much he had demanded of her back then. She had met those demands with unbridled enthusiasm but it still made him feel he had exploited her. There was so much about Lexi he hadn't known back then. But now he suspected her sassy, smart-mouthed comebacks were a shield she hid behind when she was feeling threatened. She played the nose-in-the-air socialite role so well. The way she looked down her cute little nose at him, calling him country boy as if he still had hay between his teeth. Hell, it only made him want her more!

Maybe he was being overly cautious about the career risk. Maybe a short get-it-out-of-his-system affair would clear the air between them. After it was over—and he knew it would be over within a month at the most because he never played for keeps—he could move on with his life and she could go and marry her millionaire. Of course he knew it was wrong; of course if he were the fiancé and she was having an affair with someone else he wouldn't stand for it; of course it was madness. Sheer madness. But right now he wanted her too much to get tied up in moral knots over it.

Susanne was behind the reception desk when Sam came back in. 'There's an organ retrieval scheduled at Sydney Met at six this evening,' she said. 'The patient's family have decided to withdraw life support. He's a twenty-seven-year-old motorcycle victim who sustained severe head injuries three weeks ago. His kidneys are going to Perth, his heart to Melbourne and his lungs here.'

'Whose blood or tissues match have we got?' Sam asked.

'Mr Baker with the chronic obstructive airways disease,' Susanne said. 'He's been on the priority list the longest.'

'Right,' Sam said. 'You'd better call him and let him know. And organise theatre space. Things are going to get busy around here.'

Lexi was in the main lounge room at the family mansion in Mosman when her father finally walked in. She had been pacing the floor for the last hour, anger roiling inside her like a turbulent tide.

'Hello, beautiful,' Richard Lockheart said as he sauntered in. 'How was your weekend?'

Lexi folded her arms and shot him a glare. 'I've had better.'

Richard moved to the drinks cabinet and poured himself a Scotch. He lifted the lid on the ice bucket to find it was empty. 'Be a darling and get your poor old father some ice, will you?'

'I think you're perfectly capable of getting your own ice,' she said through stiff lips.

Richard smiled indulgently as he looked at her, his dark brown eyes crinkling up at the corners. 'What's up, baby girl? That time of the month?'

Lexi suddenly realised how little she liked her father. Sure, she loved him, but she didn't much like him. Why had it taken her this long to see through his easy charm to the ruthlessly ambitious man beneath? If people got in the way of his plans he removed them. If people displeased him he made sure they lived to regret it.

She had always blamed her mother for deserting the family, but now she wondered if what Bella had said was right. Perhaps her father had had more to do with her mother leaving than anything else. She had heard rumours of his womanising behind her mother's back, but as a little girl she hadn't wanted to think of her father as anything other than blameless. It was a cruel shock to realise how she had been duped. How silly she had been to invest so much emotion and dedication in a parent who had callously used her for his own gain. Her whole life, both childhood and young adulthood, had been nothing but a house of cards that was now tumbling down around her feet.

'I found out about how you blackmailed Sam Bailey five years ago,' she said. 'How could you do that? How could you play with people's lives in such a heartless way?'

Richard's brown eyes hardened. 'You don't know what you're talking about, Lexi.'

'I *do* know what I'm talking about,' she said. 'You issued an ultimatum to Sam. He had no choice but to leave. He could have lost his career, but did you care? No. All you wanted was to get him out of the way so you could keep me under your thumb. You didn't even have the guts to tell me he was being appointed here. I had to find out by myself. How do you think I felt?'

'You're in charge of fundraising,' he said. 'You have nothing to do with the hiring and firing of staff. Anyway, I'd assumed you'd forgotten all about him by now.'

Lexi clenched her hands so tightly her nails dug into her palms. 'Like you do with all of your lovers?' she asked. 'Just how many were there while you were married to Mum? Four? Five? Ten? Or have you *forgotten*?'

Her father's mouth tightened and he put his glass down with a loud thwack on the bar. 'What is all this nonsense, Lexi?' he asked. 'I don't expect to come home after a hard day at the office to this sort of behaviour.'

'You don't know what a hard day's work is,' she tossed back. 'You spend most of your time at boozy business lunches and resort weekends paid for by other people. Grandad did all the hard work. You just sit back and enjoy the benefits. You pay other people to do the dirty work for you, like bring up your children, for instance. You don't even take time out of your busy social schedule to visit Bella in hospital.'

Richard's face was almost puce in colour. 'I will not have you speak to me like this in my own house.'

'You told lies about me to Sam,' Lexi said, her anger rolling in her like a cannonball on a steep slope, and she couldn't have held it back if she tried. 'You told him I was only sleeping with him as part of some sort of teen-age rebellion. How could you have done that?'

Richard thumped his hand down on the nearest surface so hard it made the pictures on the wall behind shake. 'You were too young to know your own mind. I did what I had to do to protect you.'

Lexi felt like screaming. The hurt inside her was like a bottle of soda that had been shaken and was fit to explode. 'You had no right to interfere with my life,' she said. 'Not then and certainly not now.'

Richard gave her a disgusted look. 'I suppose he wants you back in his bed,' he said. 'Is that what this is about? You'd be a fool to jeopardise your engagement to Matthew. Sam Bailey will only use you to get where he wants to go. Don't ever forget that, Lexi. He's a boy from the bush who made good. A society bride like you would be the icing on the cake.'

'You have no idea how much damage you've done,' she said, too angry for tears.

'The only damage you should be worrying about right now is raising sufficient funds for the hospital,' Richard said with a sneer. 'Carrying on like a lovesick teenager while you're supposed to be concentrating on the ball is going to feed into people's doubts that you're not the right person for the job. I had to work hard to convince the board to agree to have you as Head of Events. If you stuff this up now, you'll not only be made a laughing stock but you'll make me look a fool as well.'

'I hardly think you need any help from me in making yourself look a fool,' she said. 'You do a pretty fine job of it all by yourself.'

Realising confrontation wasn't working, Richard put on the charm again. 'Now, now, baby girl,' he said. 'Aren't you being a little bit melodramatic? Forget about

Sam Bailey. He's nothing to you now. You're happy with Matthew. He's perfect for you. You don't want to upset him and his family when they've been so supportive of the hospital, do you?'

Lexi glared at him. 'Why is everything always about money with you?'

'Money is a universal language, Lexi,' Richard said. 'It opens lots of doors and it shuts some others.'

Lexi turned and walked out of the room with her heart feeling as if someone had reached inside her chest and ripped it out. There were doors she could never open again. They were shut tight against her. She had been locked out of her own life by walking through the doors her father had opened for her.

But the most important door of them all she had slammed shut all by herself.

CHAPTER SEVEN

'WHAT do you mean, the venue's been cancelled?' Lexi looked at her assistant Jane in horror a few days later. 'The ball is in two weeks' time!'

Jane grimaced. 'I know,' she said. 'The manager wants to speak to you personally to apologise. He said there was a fire in the kitchen that got out of control last night. There's extensive water damage from the fire hoses. They're doing what they can to redecorate but they've had to cancel all bookings for the next month. Shall I get him on the line for you?'

Lexi nodded and took the call in her small office. It was as bad if not worse than Jane had described. After talking to the manager it was clear that the ball could not go ahead as planned. The kitchen was out of action, for one thing, and the ballroom was the worst hit in terms of water damage.

What a disaster!

Lexi felt as if everything she had worked so hard for had been ripped out from under her. She had put so much of herself into this job. She had invested a great deal emotionally in order to get her life back on track. Her father's cruel taunt came back to haunt her. It wasn't just her own lurking doubts about her ability to make a worthwhile contribution to society; it seemed everyone else felt the same. Everyone saw her as a shallow party girl with no substance. They didn't know half of what she had sacrificed to protect Bella. They didn't know how desperately she wanted to succeed. Bella's future—her life, everything—depended on Lexi getting the funds for the new equipment.

She *had* to prove them wrong. She had to show everyone, including herself, that she was up to the task no matter what last-minute hurdles were thrown at her.

She had to *think*.

She had to think past the thick fog of panic in her head and find a solution. What solution? All the tickets had been sold. The silent auction items were organised and confirmed. Everyone was looking forward to the big night of wining, dining and dancing and now it was not going to go ahead, not unless she could find another venue that could house that number of people at short notice. She spent an hour on the phone in the vain hope of finding a suitable venue but nothing was available. It was wedding season after all.

She pushed back her chair and went back to where Jane was sorting the silent auction placards.

'Any luck?' Jane asked hopefully.

Lexi shook her head in despair. 'Unless someone cancels their wedding at the last minute, I'm totally stuffed. Everyone's going to think it's my fault.'

'I'm sure no one will think that,' Jane consoled her.

Lexi gave her a grim look. 'Won't they?' She paced the floor in agitation. 'I can hear them now: "Lexi Lockheart only got the job because of her father and look at what a rubbish job she did of it."' She stopped pacing to grasp her head between her hands. 'Grr! I can't believe this is happening to me on top of everything else.'

'It's certainly a difficult time for you with Bella in hospital and your wedding so close,' Jane said in empathy.

Lexi stopped pacing and looked at Jane. 'That's it!' she said.

'What's it?' Jane asked, looking shocked. 'You're not thinking of cancelling *your* wedding, are you?'

'The hospital,' Lexi said excitedly. 'We'll have the ball here.'

Jane gaped at her. *'Here?'*

'Yes,' Lexi said, tapping her lips as she thought it through. 'The forecourt is big enough for a marquee. The patients can even be a part of it that way, those that aren't too ill, of course. We can get the caterers to do extra nibbles and desserts for all the patients on the wards. It'll be brilliant!'

'It sounds great but what will the CEO think?' Jane asked.

Lexi snatched up her purse and phone. 'I'll go and speak to him now. Wish me luck.'

'Good luck!' Jane called as Lexi dashed out of the door.

Sam looked up at the clock on the wall. 'Time of death: four-forty-six p.m.,' he said in a flat tone.

'You did your best, Sam,' the anaesthetist said over the body of Ken Baker. 'He'd been on the waiting list too long. He would've died anyway. He went into this knowing there was only the slimmest chance of success.'

Sam stripped off his gloves and threw them in the bin, his expression grim. 'I'll go and speak to the family,' he said, his stomach already in tight knots at the thought.

Losing patients was part of the job. Every surgeon knew it. Sam knew it but he still hated it. He hated the feeling of failure. Even when the odds were stacked against him he went into every operation intent on proving everyone wrong. And he had done it—numerous times. He had won some of the most unwinnable of battles. His professional reputation had been built on his successes. He had lengthened people's lives, given them back to their families, given them back their potential.

But this time he had failed.

And now he had to face the family and still act as if he was in control when he felt anything but. The clinically composed veneer he wore was so thin at times he wondered why relatives didn't see through it.

The family was gathered in one of the relatives' rooms outside the theatre suites. Gloria Baker stood as soon as Sam came in. There was a son and a daughter with her, both teenagers about fourteen and sixteen. The son reminded Sam of himself at the same age: tall and awkward, both physically and socially. 'I have some very bad news for you,' Sam said gently. 'We did everything we could but he wasn't strong enough to survive the surgery. I'm very sorry.'

Gloria Baker's face crumpled. 'Oh, no...'

Megan, the daughter, wept in her mother's arms but the son, Damien, just sat there, expressionless and mute. Sam knew what that felt like. The inability to publicly express the devastation you felt inside. He could imagine what Damien was going through. How he would have to step up to the plate and support his mother and sister. Be the man of the house now his father had died. He would appear to cope outwardly and everyone would marvel at how brave he was being. Sam had done the very same thing but inside he had felt as if a part of him had been lost for ever.

'I'm very sorry for your loss,' Sam said again.

'Can we see him?' Megan asked.

'Of course,' Sam said. 'I'll organise it for you. Take all the time you need.'

Gloria wiped at her eyes. 'Thank you for being so kind,' she said. 'Ken knew he might not make it. He's been sick for so long. I just wish you had been here earlier to help him.'

'I wish that too,' Sam said.

'You can come through now,' one of the scrub nurses said to the family.

Sam stood to one side as the Baker family walked into Theatre to say their final goodbyes. There were some days when he really hated his job. He hated the pain he witnessed, he hated the ravage of disease he couldn't fix, he hated the blood loss he couldn't control, he hated the long hours of tricky, delicate and intricate surgery that ended with a flat line on the heart monitor.

He let out a sigh and turned for the theatre change room.

He couldn't wait for this day to be over.

After a prolonged and difficult meeting with the hospital CEO Lexi had finally been given the go-ahead to restage the ball in the forecourt of the hospital. Her head was full of ideas for how the marquee would look. She still had a heap of things to do but she had already organised the layout and decorations. The caterers were booked and she had selected the menu. A wine supplier had donated several cases of wine and champagne and the hospital florist had offered her services for the table arrangements. Lexi had even sent out emails to all ticket holders on the change of venue and was now in the process of pinning flyers to all the staff notice-boards throughout the hospital. After that horrible panic when she'd first received the news it felt good to be back in control of things.

The lift opened on the doctors' room floor and Lexi stepped out with her bundle of flyers. She ran smack bang into Sam's broad chest and the sheaf of notices went flying. The air was knocked out of her lungs and all she could manage was a breathless 'Oops!'

Sam narrowed his eyes at her. 'Don't you ever look where you're going?' he snapped.

Lexi gave him an arch look. 'I thought you always used the stairs?'

His jaw clenched like a steel trap as he bent to re-trieve the flyers. Lexi watched as his gaze ran over the announcement printed there. 'What's this?' he asked, swinging his nail-hard gaze to hers.

'It's a flyer about the ball,' she said, angling her body haughtily. 'There's been a change of plan.'

His dark brows met above his eyes in a frown. 'You're having the ball here? At the hospital?'

Lexi bent down to pick up the rest of the scattered bundle. 'Yes,' she said, tugging at one of the flyers be-neath his large foot. She looked up at him. 'Do you mind?'

He stepped off it and she straightened, making a point of smoothing the flyer out as if it was a precious parchment he had deliberately soiled with his footprint.

'What happened to the other venue?' Sam asked.

'A fire in the kitchen,' Lexi said. 'The firemen went a bit overboard with the water. The place is a mess.'

Sam was still frowning. 'But surely this isn't the

right place to have a function like that. Where are you going to house all the guests? The boardroom only fits twenty. That's going to put a whole new spin on dancing cheek to cheek. It'll be more like cheek to jowl.'

'I've organised a marquee,' she said with a toss of her head. 'It's all on the flyer if you'd take the time to read it.'

'Have you thought this through properly?' he asked. 'You're going to have people all over the place, some of them heavily inebriated. What about security? What about the disruption to the patients? This isn't a hotel. People are here because they're sick, some of them desperately so.'

Lexi rolled her eyes impatiently. 'I've already been through all this with the CEO. He's given me the all-clear.'

'A busy public hospital is not a party venue,' Sam said. 'It's a ridiculous idea. What were you thinking?'

Lexi was furious. She had only just managed to get the CEO on side. If Sam went up to him and expressed his concerns, the decision might very well be revoked. Her heart started to hammer in panic. She had to make this work. There was no other option. Her reputation was riding on this. She *had* to pull it off. 'Why are you being so obstructive about this?' she asked. 'Is it because I'm the one planning it? Is that it?'

'That has nothing to do with it,' he said with a brooding frown. 'I just don't think you've thought it through properly.'

Lexi glowered at him. 'Have *you* got a better idea, country boy? What about we throw a few hay bales around the local park and have a sausage sizzle and a few kegs of beer? Would you be more comfortable with that? Maybe we could even bring in some sheep and some cows for authenticity, or what about a pig or two? I bet that would make you feel right at home.'

Sam took her by the elbow and marched her out of the way of the interested glances coming their way. 'Will you keep your voice down, for heaven's sake?' he snarled.

She tugged at his hold but his fingers tightened. 'Get your hand off me,' she said. 'I'll call Security. I'll scream. I'll tell everyone you're harassing me. I'll… Hey, where are you taking me?'

Sam opened a storeroom door and dragged her in behind him, closing the door firmly once they were both inside. 'You want to pick a fight with me, young lady, then you do it in private, not out there where patients and their relatives can hear.'

'I suppose you think since you've got me all alone you can kiss me again.' She threw him a blistering glare. 'You just try it and see what happens.'

Sam gave her a taunting smile as he stepped closer. 'I can hardly wait.'

Her eyes rounded and she backed up against the storage cabinet, making it rattle slightly. 'Don't you dare!'

'What are you afraid of, Lexi?' he asked, picking up a strand of her hair and looping it around his fingers. 'That you might kiss me back and enjoy every wicked moment of it?'

He saw her slim throat rise and fall over a swallow and the way she sent the tip of her tongue out over her lips, a quick nervous dart that deposited a fine layer of glistening moisture on their soft pillowy surface. 'I'd rather die,' she said with a hoist of her chin and a flash of her bluer-than-blue eyes.

Sam knew he was not in the right mood to be rational. He knew he should have walked away from her and gone home and wrestled his demons to the ground the way he normally did. Take it out on the ocean where no one could see or hear. But being with Lexi even for a few stolen moments was what he wanted more than anything right now. He threaded his fingers through her hair, which felt like silk, fragrant silk that fell in a skein way past her shoulders. The blood was surging through his body, making him thick and heavy with want. She would feel it if he brought her any closer. Her feet had already bumped against his, her slim thighs just a hair's breadth away. 'Have you told your fiancé about us yet?' he asked.

Her eyes darkened like a thundercloud. 'No, why should I?' she said. 'There is no us. It's all in your head. You're imagining it. I don't even like you. I hate you, in fact. I can't think of a person I hate more. You're despicable, that's what you are. You think you can play games with people. You think you can make them do things they don't want to do. You want to make trouble. You want to mess up my life just when I've finally got it all...'

Sam brought his lips to the shell of her ear, trailing his tongue over the fragrant scent of her skin. 'Am I imagining this?' he asked.

He felt the expansion of her chest against his at her sharp intake of breath, her breasts brushing against him enticingly. 'Stop it,' she said in a whisper-soft voice but she didn't move away.

'And this?' he asked, stroking his tongue over the fullness of her bottom lip.

He felt her lips quiver as she snatched in another uneven breath. 'You shouldn't be doing this,' she said, her voice almost inaudible now. 'I shouldn't be doing this...'

'But you want to, don't you, Lexi?' he said, touching her mouth with his in a teasing brush of lips against lips. 'You want to so badly it's like a drug you know you shouldn't be craving but you can't control your need for it. It consumes you. It keeps you awake at night. Sometimes it's all you can think about during the day.' He teased her lips again, a little more pressure, lingering there a little bit longer until her breath mingled intimately with his. 'That's what it's like, isn't it, Lexi?'

Her eyelids came down, the long mascara-coated lashes screening the ocean-blue of her eyes. 'It's wrong...'

Sam cupped the nape of her neck. He felt her melt against him, like soft caramel under the heat of a flame. Her body meshed against his: her breasts to his chest; her slim hips to his achingly tight pelvis; her feminine mound brushing against the head of his erection, making him crazy with desire.

The sound of a mobile ringing from within the depths of Lexi's bag hanging off her shoulder fractured the moment.

'Are you going to get that?' Sam asked after several jarring peels of the ringtone.

She stepped away from him and fumbled in her bag to answer the phone. She looked at the screen before she answered, her cheeks going a deep shade of pink. 'Matthew...I...I was just going to call you.' She turned her back to Sam and continued, 'I miss you too... Yes... not long now...'

Sam let out a rough curse under his breath and, wrenching open the door stalked out, clipping it shut behind him.

Lexi checked both ways in the corridor before she left the storeroom. She patted her hair into place and walked briskly towards the medical ward to deliver the rest of the flyers as well as call in on Bella. She hoped Sam had already completed his rounds because she didn't want to run into him again, certainly not while she was still feeling so flustered. She had been so close to throwing herself into his arms. It had been a force so strong she had no idea what would have happened if Matthew hadn't called at that point.

Matthew.

Every time she thought of him the guilt was like a gnawing toothache. It just wouldn't go away. She would have to tell him about Sam, but how? How did you say to your loving and faithful fiancé that you were confused about your feelings for an ex? Their wedding was only a matter of weeks away. The dress was made. She had another fitting tomorrow. The invitations had long gone out and most of the RSVPs had been returned. Some people had even dropped in gifts, horrendously expensive ones too. How was she supposed to tell anyone, Matthew especially, that she was getting cold feet?

Lexi pulled herself back into line with a good mental shake. All brides got nervous before their big day. It was normal to have doubts. It was a big decision to get married. It was a huge commitment to promise to share your life with someone, to be faithful to them…

Her stomach flip-flopped as she thought of Sam's aroused body against her, and his mouth with its hot, sexy breath blending erotically with hers. She suppressed a forbidden shiver of delight when she thought about his tongue blazing a trail of fire over her sensitive skin. Her body was still aching from the hunger he had stirred in her. Would it always be this way? How was she going to navigate her way through her career and marriage to Matthew with Sam in the way?

She would be strong, that's how, she decided.

She would garner her self-control.

She would be *determined*.

Bella was thankfully alone when Lexi entered the room. She was receiving oxygen through a nasal prongs tube and resting with her eyes closed, but she opened them as soon as she heard Lexi's footsteps.

'Hi, Lexi,' she said. 'I was wondering if you'd forgotten about me.'

'Sorry, Bells,' Lexi said. 'I've been run off my feet with the charity-ball arrangements. I suppose you heard what happened?'

'Yes, one of the nurses told me,' Bella said.

'It's all under control now…sort of,' Lexi said. She tidied up some fallen rose petals on the bedside chest of drawers. 'Is there anything I can get you? Do you want a proper coffee from the café? More magazines?'

Bella shook her head. 'No, I'm waiting for Mr Bailey to come in. I was in the shower when he came past this morning. He's been busy in Theatre most of the day. His first transplant case, or so one of the nurses said. Have you run into him lately?'

Lexi felt the heat rush to her cheeks and turned back to the flowers, willing some more petals to fall so she could keep her gaze averted. 'Not recently,' she lied.

The skin prickled along her arms as she heard the sound of voices out in the corridor. Sam was speaking to one of the nurses, ordering some bloods and scans for another patient. Lexi would recognise that deep, mellifluous voice anywhere.

'Are you OK, Lexi?' Bella asked.

Lexi painted a bright smile on her face as she turned around with the vase of flowers in her hands. 'I'm going to change the water on these flowers,' she said.

Bella frowned. 'But one of the volunteer ladies already did it this morning.'

'It won't hurt to do it again,' Lexi said. 'I might even get you some new ones from the hospital florist. These are just about past it.' She dashed out of the room and without even giving the nurses' station a glance slipped into the utilities room further down the corridor.

'Your oxygen levels have improved a bit, Bella,' Sam said as he read through her chart. 'The infection seems to have more or less cleared. I'd like you to stay in over the weekend just to make sure things have settled. If everything's fine you can go home on Monday, but you must take things easy. We'll have you on permanent standby in case a donor comes up. Has the transplant co-ordinator talked to you about the routine?'

Bella nodded. 'I have to have a mobile phone with me at all times in case there's a match, and a bag packed for the hospital.'

'Good.' Sam clipped the chart back on the end of the bed. 'Who will be looking after you at home?'

'Um…Lexi mostly,' she said.

Sam felt a frown tug at his forehead. 'You don't have a nurse to come in or a regular physiotherapist?'

'Yes, but Lexi's the one who takes me to all my appointments and helps me get dressed if I'm too breathless.'

Sam thought of Lexi juggling the demands of her job as well as the substantial care of her frail sister. It was another reminder to him of how she hid behind the shallow socialite facade when it suited her. But did she ever get noticed for the personal sacrifices she made? How could she if it drew attention to how much Bella relied on her? It would make Bella feel like an encumbrance, and he suspected that was something Lexi would want to avoid, given no one knew how long Bella would be with them. 'I'll have a word with the nurse about a follow-up appointment in my rooms,' he said. 'I'd like to keep a close eye on things just to be sure that infection doesn't come back.'

'Thank you, Mr Bailey,' Bella said shyly.

Sam gave her a brief smile and left to write up the last of his notes in the nurses' station. On his way out of the ward he ran into Evie, who was presumably on her way to visit Bella.

'Sam, can I have a quick word?' she asked.

'Sure,' he said. 'How about in here?' He gestured to a small waiting area that was currently empty.

'It's about my sister,' Evie began as soon as they were alone.

'I'm discharging her on Monday,' Sam said.

'Not that sister,' Evie said with a direct look. 'I meant Lexi.'

Sam drew in a measured breath. 'I see.'

'Actually, I don't think you do see,' Evie said, shooting him a look. 'Lexi's in a good place right now. She's getting married in a matter of weeks. She doesn't need the complication of an ex turning up and distracting her.'

Sam raised an eyebrow. 'Distracting her?'

Evie narrowed her gaze at him. 'I think you know what I mean.'

'Lexi's an adult,' he said. 'She's entitled to do what she wants.'

Evie's hazel eyes were brittle as they stared into his. 'She doesn't know what she wants,' she said. 'That's half the problem.'

'Then she should be left to decide without the influence of others,' Sam said coolly.

'You don't understand,' she said. 'Lexi had a really rough time after you left. I was very worried about her. I'm sure she didn't tell me even half of what was going on. She didn't tell anyone.'

Sam felt something in his stomach turn over suddenly. 'What do you mean?'

Evie pulled at her bottom lip with her teeth before she answered. 'She was so…different after you left. She was flat, depressed even. She closed off from everybody. It was like a wall was around her. No one could get to her and she wouldn't allow anyone in. It's only been since she's been involved with Matthew that she's started to blossom again.'

'I'm not sure what this has to do with me,' Sam said.

Evie glared at him. 'It has *everything* to do with you. People are starting to talk about you both. They think something's going on between you two. Something serious.'

'Perhaps you've misheard the gossip,' he said. 'The rumours that are circulating are about you and Finn, not me and Lexi.'

A rosy flush stained Evie's cheeks. 'That's complete and utter rubbish!'

Sam cocked his eyebrow again. 'Is it?'

Evie folded her arms across her body, just like her baby sister did when she felt threatened, Sam noted. 'I saw Lexi's face the other day,' she said accusingly. 'She had beard rash.'

Sam kept his face blank. 'So?'

'So?' Evie fumed. 'You have no right to kiss her! She's engaged to another man.'

'I wouldn't kiss any woman who wasn't an active participant,' he said with deadly calm.

Evie's eyes flared with anger. 'So you're saying she actively encouraged you? That's an outright lie! She's not a slut, far from it. In fact, I suspect you were her first lover. Did you know that at the time? I bet that's why you targeted her. Quite a notch on your belt, wasn't it? The youngest Lockheart sister. What a trophy to flash around.'

Sam tightened his mouth. 'I think you should concentrate on your own life and let your sister get on with hers.'

'You're not good for her, Sam,' Evie said. 'You unsettle her. She deserves to be happy. She deserves someone who'll love her, not use her as a stepping stone to get where he wants to go.'

'Is that what you think this is about?' Sam asked, frowning.

'What else could it be?' she asked. 'You don't love her, do you? If you loved her you wouldn't have let anyone stop you from seeing her. You would've fought for her no matter what it cost you personally or professionally.'

Sam gritted his teeth until his jaw ached. 'I don't love anyone like that,' he said.

Evie gave him a pitying look. 'Then maybe you should learn.' And with that she was gone.

CHAPTER EIGHT

For the last couple of weeks Lexi had more or less managed to avoid any lengthy contact with her father. She had worked late and then gone to the gym in the evenings, barely exchanging more than a few desultory words with him before she went to bed at night or left for work in the morning. But on the weekend before the ball she knew it would be harder to keep out of his way unless she had a plan to keep away from the family mansion for most of the time.

She had a dress fitting in the city at ten and rather than drive and struggle with finding somewhere to park she decided to catch a ferry across the harbour. It was one of those perfect Sydney spring days: warm and sunny, with a light breeze with a smell of summer to it. The harbour was dotted with yachts making the most of the wonderful weekend weather. Lexi wondered if Sam was out there somewhere, carving through the sparkling water, but she didn't see any vessel called *Whispering Waves*, even though she looked long and hard.

After the fitting Lexi did a bit of shopping, more than a bit, she thought a little ruefully as she juggled the bags of lingerie, clothes, shoes and make-up in both hands as she made her way back to Circular Quay for the ferry late in the afternoon. Rather than go straight home she wandered for a while along the Neutral Bay marina, looking at the million-dollar yachts moored there. There were a couple of yachties about doing maintenance, the smell of fresh paint in the air. The distinctive clanging sound of the rigging knocking against the masts in the breeze made her think of how wonderful it would be to just hop on a boat and sail away into the sunset, away from all of life's complexities. She wondered if that was what Sam did to relax after complicated surgery. She could picture him standing at the helm, his strong, tanned arms hauling sails and spinnakers up and down, enjoying the challenge of conquering the powerful and sometimes unpredictable conditions.

At the far end of the marina Lexi saw a white yacht with dark blue lines painted on the sides and in simple cursive the name *Whispering Waves*. There was no sign of anyone about so she walked closer. It was a beautiful vessel, not top-end luxury but close to it. It was at least forty feet long and well maintained, the paintwork looked fresh and the decks were varnished a rich jarrah red.

Lexi checked if anyone was watching before she climbed aboard, her shopping making the task a little more difficult for her, but somehow she managed to get on deck in one piece with all her shopping still safe. She had a quick look around; rationalising that it was her duty as Head of Events to ensure the yacht was suitable for a party of eight for lunch.

To her surprise the door to below deck was unlocked. She had a little battle with her conscience as she thought about having a quick peek around. It was trespassing, she knew that. But then she knew Sam. That kind of made a difference, didn't it? Anyway, she'd only take

a minute to two. He would never even know she had
been on board.

She strained her ears for any sound below, and once
she was certain all was clear, she went down the steps
to look inside. It was so much more spacious than she
had imagined. There was a kitchen with all the latest
appliances off the lounge and dining area. There was
plenty of storage along the sides of the living area and
a bar with a drinks fridge set in next to a sound system.
There was a bathroom and toilet complete with shower
and vanity. She opened another door and found the master bedroom with its own en suite. The bed was made
up with white linen with a black trim, and black and
white patterned scatter cushions were placed neatly in
front of the large soft pillows.

Lexi was about to test the bed when she heard a foot-
fall on the deck above. Her heart gave a little flutter as
she considered her options.

Come out or hide.

How was she going to explain being in his bedroom?
Why, oh, why hadn't she thought about the possibility
of him returning? He had probably only stepped off
the yacht for a few minutes. It was going to take quite
some talking to get herself out of this sticky situation.
She could just imagine the conclusions he would jump
to. There was only one thing to do…

She chose to hide.

There was a row of tall cupboards on one side of
the master bedroom. The first one she opened was
filled with drawers that weren't big enough to hide her
things so she quickly opened the next one. She stuffed
her shopping bags below some of Sam's wet-weather
gear, closing the door as softly as she could. Her heart
was still galloping as she opened another closet. It had
more hanging space and was just big enough for her to

squeeze in amongst Sam's casual shirts. But while it was an excellent hiding place, she decided against closing the door completely as the lock was a one-way affair. While she wouldn't go as far as describing herself as claustrophobic, the thought of spending the next hour or two—or longer—locked inside a dark cupboard didn't hold much appeal, so instead she hooked the tip of her index finger around the edge to keep the door ajar.

Lexi heard Sam move about above deck. She pictured him doing maintenance like the other men she'd seen. Scrubbing the decks or fixing the stay ropes or some such thing. He probably wouldn't stay long. It was coming on for six p.m. He'd probably leave in a half an hour, tops. Maybe even fifteen minutes. Ten if there was someone watching over her.

Sam frowned as he released the mooring ropes. Did he really have it so bad that he could smell Lexi's perfume wherever he went? He breathed in again, deeper this time. No, he was imagining it. All he could smell was the briny ocean, which was exactly what he needed right now. This was where he could forget about yesterday's failure. He had the rest of the weekend to be alone out on the harbour, to sail, to fish, to think, to find that inner calm he badly needed right now.

He started the engine and motored out of the marina, giving a wave to one of the young lads who'd helped him rig up a new sail the other day.

He had just enough time before sundown to get to his favourite hideaway. He could already taste that first refreshing sip of beer.

OK. Lexi tried to talk herself out of panic when she felt the yacht moving away from the marina. He was probably just taking it out for a test run. That's what yacht owners did sometimes. They didn't always go out for the whole weekend. He would come back and she could slip away without him noticing. It'd be a piece of cake. He would never know he'd had a stowaway on board.

After a while she lost track of time. How far was he going for pity's sake? New Zealand? The Cook Islands? She was hungry, so hungry her stomach was making noises not unlike the growl of the yacht's engine.

Finally, after what seemed like hours, the movement stopped. There was the mechanical sound of an anchor being released and then silence all but for the gentle slip-slap of water and the mewling cry of a seagull passing overhead.

Lexi's finger was aching from being curled around the cupboard door for so long. Her need for the bathroom had long overtaken her need for food. She would have crossed her legs if there had been room.

Sam's footsteps sounded again, closer this time. Lexi held her breath, her heart beating so hard and fast it was like a roaring in her ears.

She heard the sound of clothes being removed, and then—heaven help her bladder—the sound of the shower running. After the longest three minutes of her life she heard Sam towel himself dry and then open the cupboard with the drawers inside.

Beads of perspiration were trickling between Lexi's breasts. Her breathing was now so ragged she felt like her lungs were going to collapse. She looked down at the sliver of light coming through the gap where her finger was keeping the door ajar. She very carefully and very slowly brought her finger out of sight, holding her breath as she closed the cupboard with a soft click. She fought against the panic of being locked in a confined space.

It was dark.

Very, very dark.

Another cupboard opened further along the wall and she heard the rustle of fabric and then a slide of a zipper. Lexi knew what was next. He had just put on his jeans, now he would come looking for a shirt. There was no point in cowering in the dark in the hope he wouldn't see her. Of course he would see her. She would have to brazen it out and think of a very good excuse, like in about two seconds flat, for why she was in his shirt cupboard.

Sam opened the cupboard door and reared back in shock, a swear word slipping out before he could stop it. 'What the freaking hell are you doing?' he asked.

Lexi stepped out of the cupboard with a yellow shirt in one hand and a blue one in the other. 'I'm thinking the blue,' she said, holding it up against his shoulder, her head tilted on one side musingly. 'It goes better with your eyes. Yellow is so not your colour. It washes you out. Makes you look anaemic.'

Sam was still trying to get his heart rate under control. He really wondered for a moment if he was suffering a hallucination. But, no, it was Lexi in the flesh all right, every gorgeous inch of her, on his boat, alone with him. A hint of devilry made his mouth kick up at the corners. She was alone with him for the rest of the weekend. 'I hope you've packed a toothbrush because I'm not turning back to take you home,' he said.

'You have to take me home,' she said dropping the shirts, her sassy facade slipping. 'You have to turn back right now. Right this instant. I had no idea you were planning to sail to Tahiti or wherever it is you've taken me.'

Sam gave a soft chuckle. 'Tahiti sounds nice,' he said. 'I've never been there—have you?'

Lexi pushed past him to the en suite. She turned and glared at him before she went in. 'Do you mind giving me a little privacy?'

He folded his arms across his naked chest, jeans-clad legs slightly apart. 'Don't mind me,' he said. 'I've heard it all before.'

She narrowed her eyes to paper-thin slits. 'I hate you, do you realise that? I positively loathe you.'

'Probably a good thing considering you're engaged to someone else and we're stuck on this boat together until tomorrow evening at sundown,' he said.

Lexi's eyes went wide in horror. 'You're *kidnapping* me?'

'I'm not asking for a ransom so, no, I'm not kidnapping you,' he said. 'You invited yourself on board so you'll have to obey the captain. That's me, if you haven't already figured it out.'

Lexi flung herself into the en suite and snapped the lock into place. She wanted to drum her fists on the door and scream like a banshee. If anyone found out she was on Sam's yacht for the weekend her life would be over. She would never live it down. The gossip would be unbearable.

No one needs to find out.

The traitorous thought slipped into her mind like a curl of smoke under a door. She had her mobile phone with her. She could text her sisters to say she was away for the weekend with a friend. She didn't have to say which friend. She didn't have to say it was her worst enemy. Hopefully they wouldn't put two and two together. Evie and Bella both knew she was trying to keep her distance from their father. They would assume she was staying out of town or something to avoid him.

Lexi came out of the en suite to find Sam had gone on deck. She made her way up to the bridge where he was standing looking towards the west, where the sun was sinking. The sky was a rich palette of red and ochre and gold. A flock of fruit bats flew past on their way to feed on the native trees and shrubs of the bushland on the shore about fifty metres away. It was a picturesque spot and the tranquillity after the hectic pace of the city earlier was not lost on Lexi. She breathed in deep, salty breaths and the scent of eucalypts that had spent all day being warmed by the sun.

Sam turned to look at her. 'Would you like a drink?' he asked.

Lexi folded her arms crossly. 'I suppose you always keep champagne on ice in case you get lucky.'

His eyes smouldered as they held hers. 'Always.'

Lexi glared at him defensively. 'I was doing an inspection. I happened to be in the area and saw your boat so I decided to have a look around.'

'Did it pass muster?' he asked with a teasing glint, 'or do you think the closet is too small?'

She tightened her mouth. 'You could definitely do with some more hanging space.'

He bent to pick up a loose rope, coiling it expertly in his hands as he continued to look at her. 'I think we both know you weren't really doing an inspection,' he said. 'You must have known I was about. The boat wasn't locked up. You were having a little snoop and then you heard me come back on board so you went into hiding.'

She threw him a petulant look. 'I wasn't *hiding*.'

He elevated one dark eyebrow. 'What were you doing?' he asked. 'Colour co-ordinating my shirts?'

Lexi brushed some hair back off her too-hot face. 'It was a knee-jerk reaction,' she said. 'I didn't know who was coming. It might have been a robber or a vandal or…or something…'

'Or a kidnapper.' A lazy smile played around the corners of his mouth.

Lexi bit her lip. 'Did you mean it when you said you won't take me back home until tomorrow evening?'

He stepped over a guy rope and came to stand closer to her. 'This is the first free weekend I've had in months,' he said. 'I wanted to spend it out on the water. Commune with nature. Relax, chill, unwind.'

'I'm sure you'd much rather be alone so if you just set me off somewhere I'll catch a cab back,' Lexi said.

Sam laughed. 'You see any cabs along this part of the coast?' he asked.

Lexi looked at the coastal reserve that fringed the shore for miles along the headland, and frowned. She swung her gaze back to Sam's amused one. 'You have no right to keep me here against my will. I bet you're doing this on purpose to ruin my reputation. That's what this is about, isn't it?'

'No,' he said, taking her by the upper arms and bringing her flush against his rock-hard chest. 'This is what it's about.' And then he covered her mouth with the blazing fire of his.

It was an earth-moving kiss. Lexi felt her legs weaken like overcooked spaghetti as his mouth crushed hers in a deeply passionate assault on her senses. His tongue was a sensual sword that divided her lips to receive him. There was no denying him access. She had no willpower. No self-control. No determination. All she had was red-hot need. So hot it was burning from the soles of her feet, running up her legs, racing up her spine like a flame following a pathway of spilt gasoline. His tongue tangled with hers, teasing it into a sexy dance, taming it with the commanding thrust of his. She whimpered against his lips, her need for him so consuming she was almost sobbing with it. Her feminine folds were heavy with longing, the walls of her womanhood moist with the heat of hungry, rapacious desire.

Sam's grizzled jaw grazed the soft skin around her mouth as he shifted position. He cupped her face with his hands, his tongue snaking around hers in an erotic tangle that sent a rush of heat over her skin.

'I want you so badly,' he said against her swollen lips. 'I've never wanted anyone more than I want you right now.'

Lexi could feel the potent power of his erection against her belly. She could feel her body responding to his just as it had in the past. There was no need for words even if she could have found her voice. She let her body communicate all the pent-up longing she felt. She pushed herself against him, her breasts tight and sensitive, and her feminine mound contracting with a pulse of longing so strong she felt her legs sway beneath her.

Sam's hands gripped her hips, holding her against him, the friction of his arousal a torment to her senses. She welcomed the heat of him, rubbing against him shamelessly to assuage the ache that consumed her.

He slipped a warm hand beneath her top, pushing her bra aside to tease her nipple with the broad pad of his thumb. It was exquisite torture to feel him reclaim her flesh with the blistering heat of his touch. She gave a soft cry as he replaced his thumb with his mouth, his tongue swirling and stroking before he sucked on her with just the right amount of pressure.

She threw back her head in wanton abandon, arching her spine to give him greater access to her breasts. He moved from one breast to the other and back again, ramping up her desire until it was an all-consuming wave that threatened to sweep her away completely.

Lexi placed her hands on his chest, her mouth teasing his with little kittenish bites. Right now she was not the Lexi who was engaged to Matthew Brentwood. She had turned into a wild tigress of a woman eager to mate with her alpha male. Her body was Sam's and Sam's alone. It responded to his with a fervour that was unmatched by anything else in her experience.

Sam's mouth took control of the kiss, one of his hands in the small of her back while the other worked on removing the rest of her clothes. Lexi stepped away from the soft pile of her garments, her mouth still locked on the fire of his. She felt the warm brush of his fingers against the hot wet heart of her. Her flesh was so responsive she knew it was too late to call an end to this madness. She felt the overwhelming pull of release deep within her body, all the nerves singing along the tight wires of her muscles as every sensation gathered to that one intimate point. One more stroke of his fingers and she plunged into the abyss, her body shaking with the tremors that rolled through her like the waves against the shore.

Sam held her as she came back from paradise but she could see his body was in urgent need of its own release.

'Condom,' he groaned against her mouth. 'I need to get a condom.'

Lexi was momentarily jolted out of the sensory spell.

She suddenly felt the enormity of what she was doing. Sex was not just about physical needs being satisfied, or at least it wasn't for her. Her hands stalled in their exploration of his chest, her gaze lowered, her teeth sinking into her lip.

Sam lifted her chin to lock her gaze with his. 'You're not comfortable with taking this any further?' he asked. 'We don't have to. I understand. I really do.'

Lexi looked into the darkness of his desire-lit eyes and felt herself drowning. 'It's been such a long time,' she said. 'I'm not sure I can satisfy you the way I did before…'

He brushed her mouth with his, softly. 'Tell me to stop and I'll stop,' he said.

She cupped his face with her hands, her eyes dropping to his mouth. 'I don't want you to stop,' she said, surprised at how much she meant it.

He carried her below deck to his bedroom, placing her gently on the mattress. He looked down at her as she covered herself with her hands, as if she was embarrassed at being naked in front of him. 'You still OK with this?' he asked.

'Don't mind me,' she said. 'I'm just having a fat day.'

Sam smiled. That was what he loved about Lexi, the way she said the opposite of what he was expecting. He reached for a condom and applied it before joining her on the bed. He anchored his weight on his forearms, careful not to crush her. He couldn't help thinking of the first time he had made love to her. It had been rough and fast, over within seconds for both of them. He had hurt her. She had reluctantly admitted that. It tormented him to think he had done that to her. He should have prepared her young body with gentle handling, making sure her tender flesh could accommodate him. He would make up for it this time. He would worship her body the way he should have done the first time.

He started by kissing her mouth in a soft caress that gradually deepened. Her tongue met his and danced with it in a rhythm that was as old as time, a sacred rhythm that spoke of human connection at its most elemental.

Something shifted in his chest as he felt her arms come up around his neck, her fingers delving into his hair as her soft mouth responded to the gentle pressure of his. It was like a slip of a gear, a stumble of the heart that he hadn't been expecting.

She grew impatient beneath him, lifting her slim hips, searching for him. Sam worked hard to control his urge to fill her. He had never had a problem with anyone else. Control came easily to him, but not with Lexi. He felt the magnetic pull of her core. He smelt the feminine fragrance of her, the sexy salt and musk that stirred his senses into overload.

He went back to her breasts with his mouth, teasing her with his lips and tongue until she whimpered and clawed at him. He continued down her body, dipping his tongue in the shallow cave of her belly button before going to her feminine folds. She was wet and swollen, like a precious hothouse flower, fragrant and heady, luscious and exotic.

He teased her apart with his tongue, taking his time, delighting in the cries she tried to suppress, relishing the way her back lifted off the bed as she convulsed.

Sam watched as her breasts rose and fell as she came back down to earth, her blue eyes looking almost shocked at how she had responded. He kissed her inner thigh and worked his way back up her body, taking his time, making sure she was ready for him to possess her.

'Please…' Her voice was a thready sound, an edge of desperation in it. 'Oh, Sam, *please*…'

Sam positioned himself, intending to string out the pleasure a little longer, but Lexi clearly had other ideas. She lifted her hips and he suddenly had nowhere to go but inside her. He surged in with a deep groan of pleasure as her tight body gripped him. He felt the ripples of her flesh, the intimate grasp of her massaging him until he was hovering on the precipitous edge of his control. He increased his pace, delighting in her slippery warmth as she wrapped her legs around his hips. Her supple body thrilled him, the way she had no inhibitions, the way she was so generous with her touch and caresses. Her mouth was soft but demanding, her tongue teasing and playful as it tangoed with his. He was getting closer and closer to the point of no return. It was a force building within him that was so powerful he could feel it roaring through his veins like a bullet train.

He pulled back from the brink to caress her with his fingers, to make sure she was with him when he finally fell. She gasped out loud as he played with her. He knew her body like he knew his own. He knew exactly what pressure and pace she liked, what she needed in order to be fulfilled. He felt the moment when she lost control; he felt the tight spasm of her body around him, milking him of his essence. He lost himself in her, falling, falling, falling into that blessed whirlpool of absolute, ultimate pleasure.

Sam held her close in the aftermath. He listened to the sound of her breathing slowly coming back to normal. For a moment it was easy to forget why he shouldn't have been lying with her breasts crushed against his chest and her legs still hooked around his hips.

'Oh, God,' she said.

Sam propped himself up on his elbows to look at her. 'Was that an "Oh God, I just had amazing sex" or an "Oh God, what have I done?"'

Her teeth pulled at her lip in that engaging way of hers. 'Both…'

He brushed the damp hair off her face with one of his hands. 'It was always going to happen, Lexi,' he said. 'I think we both knew that in the car park that day.'

She rolled out from under him and got off the bed. Her hair was all mussed up and her lips swollen from kissing. She took one of his shirts out of the closet and slipped it over her nakedness. His shirt was too big for her but Sam thought it looked far sexier on her than any lacy negligee.

He dealt with the condom before he went to where she was standing, grasping the edges of his shirt together to cover her body. He touched her on the cheek with one of his fingers. 'Hey,' he said. 'You don't have to hide yourself from me, Lexi. I know everything there is to know about your body.'

She gave him an agonised look. 'You don't…not really…'

He frowned as he looked at her. 'What do you mean?'

'Sam, I feel…I feel so guilty…'

He tipped up her chin with the same finger. 'It was just as much my fault as yours,' he said. 'I should've turned around once I found you on board and then none of this would've happened.'

She pulled his hand down from her face, stepping away from him, her arms wrapping tightly across her body again. 'I'm not talking about just now,' she said.

Sam frowned as he brought her back to face him with his hands on the tops of her shoulders. 'What *are* you talking about?' he asked.

He saw her throat go up and down and her eyes watered up, glistening with tears that threatened to fall any second. She bit her lip again, but still it trembled. Her whole body began to shake as if gripped by a fever.

'Sweetheart, what's wrong?' he asked, holding her steady with his hands on her upper arms.

She looked into his eyes for a long moment. 'Sam…I had a termination,' she said in a broken whisper. 'I had an abortion.'

He looked at her in a dumb silence. It took at least thirty seconds for him to process her words.

An abortion.

Which meant she had been pregnant at some point.

He said the first thing that came into his head. 'Was it mine?'

She turned away as if he had struck her. 'So that's the most important thing for you to establish, is it?' she asked.

Sam was having trouble keeping a lid on his emotions. Lexi had been pregnant. She had been carrying *his* child. He had never envisaged himself as a father. It had always been in the too-hard, too-emotionally-challenging basket. And yet for a brief time, a few weeks, he had been a father, or at least a potential one. 'I'm sorry,' he said. 'That was unforgiveable of me. I wasn't thinking. Of course it was mine.'

'I didn't know what to do,' she said, still not looking at him. 'I was so frightened and alone. I went to your flat but you'd gone. I didn't know who to turn to.'

Sam thought of how it must have been for her, so young, so inexperienced and yet pretending to be so street smart. Her father wouldn't have been much use, or her mother. What else could she have done?

And yet…

He had almost been a father.

He thought of how it would be to have a son or daughter, a combination of their genes. What would their child have been like? His mind raced with images of a platinum-blonde little girl or a light brown haired little boy. Little arms and legs, fingers and toes, soft wispy hair…

'I'm sorry,' he said bringing himself back to the moment with an effort. 'I know it's not enough but I'm truly sorry you had to go through that.'

She looked at him then, her gaze accusatory, incisive. 'You're angry,' she said. 'You think I did the wrong thing. Go on, say it. I can handle it. You think I did the wrong thing.'

Sam felt ambushed by emotion. He wasn't used to dealing with this bombardment of feeling. 'What do you expect me to say?' he asked. 'Congratulations on your abortion? For God's sake, Lexi, I might act all cool and controlled most of the time but you've just laid a whammy on me so you're going have to allow me a minute or two to process it.'

Her eyes were glistening with tears as she glared at him. 'Do you think it was easy to make that decision? I *agonised* over it. I cried and cried for what might have been, for what I wanted. But in the end I felt I had no choice but to do what I did. Do I think I did the right thing? Yes. Do I think I did the wrong thing? Yes. It was both the right and the wrong thing. Sometimes the hardest decisions in life are.'

'The decision to terminate a pregnancy is never an easy one,' Sam said. 'I don't believe any woman goes into it lightly. Even when it's clearly the right decision even on medical grounds it can take years if not a lifetime to resolve the guilt surrounding it. But if it's any comfort, I think you did the right thing, Lexi. You were far too young for that sort of responsibility. And, quite frankly, I'm not sure I would've been much help even if you had been able to tell me. I would've supported you, of course, but it would have been hard for both of us at that point in our lives.'

She let out a wobbly sigh. 'I'm so sorry...'

Sam stepped up to her and cupped her face. 'Don't be,' he said firmly. 'It's in the past. Let it stay there. You can't change it.'

'I'm glad I told you,' she said on another sigh. 'It's been so hard keeping it to myself for all this time.'

Sam frowned. 'You haven't told your fiancé?'

Her cheeks grew pink and her eyes moved away from his. 'I've wanted to...so often, but the time has never seemed right.'

'Lexi,' he said. 'You're marrying this guy in a matter of weeks. You need to tell him everything.'

She flashed him a glare over her shoulder. 'Like what happened here just now?' she said. 'You think I should tell him I had ex sex because I was feeling a bit lonely?'

Sam clenched his jaw. 'Is that what you think?' he asked. 'You were feeling a bit lonely so you jumped into bed with me? Lexi, you know that's not what happened. We had sex because we can't keep our hands off each other. It has nothing to do with loneliness, yours or mine.'

She turned away, her body hunched as if she wanted to curl up and hide. 'I can't imagine you'd ever be lonely,' she said. 'You probably have heaps of women flocking after you wherever you go.'

'I've had relationships,' Sam said. 'Nothing serious and nothing lasting. I guess I'm not built that way.'

She turned and looked at him. 'So you're not thinking of marrying and having a family someday?'

Sam shook his head. 'Not my scene, I'm afraid. With a fifty per cent divorce rate I don't like my chances of getting it right. I don't want to screw up someone else's life as well as my own.'

'But your parents were happy, weren't they?' she asked.

Sam thought of his father and mother and how his mother's chronic illness had had such an impact on their relationship. How his father had limped along for the last twenty years, half alive, isolated with grief and guilt. 'Yes, but their relationship was one of those once-in-a-lifetime ones,' he said. 'Not everyone can achieve that. It's not realistic to expect there's someone out there who will meet all of your physical and emotional needs. And speaking of physical needs, is that your stomach I can hear growling with hunger?'

She put her hand over her stomach. 'You can hear that?'

'No, but I'm starving and I figured you might be too after all that exercise.'

Her face coloured up again. 'Why does being here with you feel so right but wrong as well?' she asked in soft voice.

Sam brushed her cheek with his finger. 'I think what you said a minute ago is very true. Sometimes some of life's hardest decisions are both right and wrong at the same time. Let's just say this is right for now and leave it at that.'

CHAPTER NINE

Lexi had a shower while Sam made dinner. She tried not to think about the moral implications of spending the rest of the weekend with him on his boat. It was as if she had stepped into a parallel universe, one where she and Sam were able to be together, enjoying each other's company, taking things as they came rather than planning too far ahead.

She looked at her engagement ring and felt like she was looking at someone else's hand. She grappled with her conscience before she tugged the diamond off. She had to use some soap to remove it. Was that a sign of some sort? she wondered. She looked at the pale circle of skin where the ring had hidden her flesh from the sun. She knew she would have to talk to Matthew. But she wasn't prepared to do it via email or over the phone. She needed to see him face to face to explain…

To explain what exactly? That she was in love with another man?

Lexi let out a sigh as she reached for a towel. There was only one man she could ever love and that was Sam. She loved him with her heart. She loved him with her mind. She loved him with her body. She felt like her life was incomplete without him in it. Being without him was like only wearing one shoe. Her life felt out of balance. The love she felt for him was the love his parents had felt for each other. A love Sam didn't feel for her. He had made that pretty clear. His relationships were 'nothing serious and nothing lasting'. That included her. What he was offering her was casual and temporary, a weekend of sensual delight, but then what? He would go back to his life and she would go back to hers.

Maybe she wouldn't have to tell Matthew. Maybe she could just let this weekend be her attempt at closure and leave it at that. She would move on with her life, get married and have babies and build a future with a man who loved her, instead of pining after a man who didn't and never would.

Lexi dressed in one of the new outfits she'd bought that day: a white halter-neck top and slim-fitting taupe pants. She bundled her damp hair up in a knot on top of her head, sprayed her wrists with the perfume she carried in her bag, and applied a light layer of lip gloss before joining Sam in the kitchen dining area.

'That smells delicious,' she said, sniffing the air appreciatively.

Sam turned from the pot he was stirring and handed her a glass of wine he had poured. 'Here you go,' he said. 'Dinner won't be long.'

Lexi took the wine and angled her head to see what he was cooking. 'What are you making?' she asked.

'Mediterranean fish casserole,' he said. 'One of my colleagues in the States is married to a chef. She took me on as a project and taught me to cook a little more than the meat-and-three-veg routine I'd grown up with.'

'You obviously enjoy it,' she said.

'Yes, I find it relaxing,' he said, putting the wooden spoon on the counter. 'What about you? Do you cook or leave it to the servants?'

Lexi slipped back into socialite mode. 'Of course,' she said airily. 'Why do something so menial when you can pay someone else to do it and clean up afterwards too?'

'What if you run out of money one day?' he asked.

'As if that's going to happen,' she said. 'I'm marrying a rich man, remember?'

Lexi watched as he turned back to stirring the pot, the line of his back and shoulders now tense. She wished now she hadn't goaded him. The atmosphere had changed to one of enmity and stiffness when before he had been so tender with her over the termination. 'Can I help with anything?' she asked.

'It's cool,' he said. 'I've got it all under control.' He turned and leaned back against the counter to look at her, his eyes running over her in appraisal. 'You look particularly beautiful,' he said. 'That wasn't what you were wearing before.'

'Lucky I did some shopping today,' Lexi said. 'Otherwise I would've had to go naked.'

His eyes smouldered darkly. 'Suits me.'

'I bought just about everything else but I didn't buy a toothbrush,' she said. 'I don't suppose you happen to have a spare?'

'I always keep a supply of basic necessities on board.'

Lexi gave him a cynical look. 'In case you get lucky.'

His mouth tilted in a sexy smile. 'I guess you could say today's been my lucky day.'

Lexi frowned and averted her gaze. 'Sam...'

One of his hands came down on her bare shoulder, the other touching her beneath her chin and forcing her gaze back to his. His eyes were dark and serious. 'If you really want to go back, I'll take you back,' he said.

Lexi didn't want to go back. She didn't ever want to

go back. She wanted to stay on his boat with him for ever without the intrusion of other people telling her what she should and shouldn't do. 'No,' she said in a whisper-soft voice. 'I don't want to go back just yet.'

He brushed her forehead with a kiss before he stepped away to go back to his cooking. 'Good, because I've had a hell of a week and I really need to clear my head.'

Lexi watched as he went back to the simmering pot. He was frowning as he stirred the casserole, the set to his mouth almost grim. 'You want to talk about it?' she asked.

One of his shoulders went up and down. 'It's OK. I deal with this stuff all the time—patients dying on the table because they're too sick to survive the surgery. It's part of the job. You win some. You lose some. But I hate losing. I never get used to it.'

Lexi put her glass down and moved to stand behind him. She wrapped her arms around his waist and pressed her cheek to the hard wall of his back. 'I'm sorry,' she said softly. 'It must be so hard for you. No one thinks of how the surgeon feels. Everyone feels sorry for the patient and the relatives, but what about the surgeon who has to try to sleep at night haunted by all those people he wasn't able to save in time? It must be absolute agony for you.'

He turned in the loop of her arms and brushed a wisp of hair off her forehead with a gentle finger. 'We're supposed to get hardened by it during our training,' he said. 'I'm usually good at keeping my emotions separate. I have to, otherwise it can cloud my judgement. But I lost a patient yesterday. I guess that's why I bawled you out about the change of venue for the ball. I was in a foul mood. I'd just left a family to say goodbye to their husband and father in Theatre. He died during the procedure.'

Lexi looked up at him in distress. 'Oh, Sam, and I was such a cow to you.'

He gave her a rueful smile. 'I probably deserved it. I seem to always be baiting you. I guess I like getting a rise out of you. You're so adorable when you're spitting chips at me.'

Lexi gave him a sheepish look. 'I didn't mean it about the hay bales and farm animals…especially the pigs. That was a bit low.'

He grinned at her and walked her back against the table with his thighs against hers. 'Yes, you did, you little minx,' he growled playfully.

Lexi shivered as his lips found her neck, nipping at the skin in little bites that sent electric shocks throughout her body. He finally came to her mouth, sealing it with a kiss that made every nerve tingle with delight.

'I thought we were going to have dinner,' she said somewhat breathlessly.

'Later,' he said.

Lexi closed her eyes as she gave herself up to his kiss. It was tender and searching, as if he was looking for the young innocent girl she had been, as if he was trying to redress the past by retracing his steps, doing things differently this time. She kissed him back with equal tenderness, enjoying the new-found intimacy that was so much more than two grappling bodies intent on sensual pleasure but more of a meeting of two spirits who found something special and priceless only with each other.

Sam finally eased his mouth off hers and brushed her hair back from her forehead, giving her a bemused smile. 'You constantly surprise me, Lexi Lockheart, do you know that?'

Lexi gave him a shy smile in return. 'Oh, I'm full of surprises, that's for sure.'

He reached for her ring hand, looking down at it before he met her eyes. 'Where's your engagement ring?' he asked.

Lexi couldn't read his masked expression. 'I…I took it off.'

'I don't suppose you tossed it overboard.'

She pulled her hand out of his and stepped away from him. 'Is that what you'd like me to do?' she asked.

He looked at her for a long moment. 'What *are* you going to do?'

Lexi bit her lip. 'I'm not sure…'

'Seems pretty simple and straightforward to me,' Sam said.

'Oh, really?' she said.

'Yeah,' he said. 'You shouldn't be marrying a man who doesn't satisfy you.'

Lexi put her hands on her hips. 'How do you know he doesn't satisfy me?'

He gave a shrug of one shoulder as if he didn't care either way. 'I figure if you were getting what you need from him, you wouldn't be here with me.'

'Maybe I need more than he can give me,' she said. 'You said it yourself. It's hard to find someone who meets all of your physical and emotional needs.'

'Do you love him?' Sam asked.

Lexi let out a snort of derision. 'Who are you to ask me about love?' she said. 'You don't love anything but your career.'

'Do you love him?' He repeated the question, more forcefully this time, which put her back up.

'Of course I love him!' She almost shouted the words.

'And yet you've told him nothing about what happened between us five years ago.'

Lexi glared at him. 'It's in the past. It should stay there.'

'I beg to differ, sweetheart,' he said. 'What's happened over the last couple of hours suggests it's not staying in the past. It's spilling into the here and now and at some point you're going to have to deal with it. You have to tell him.'

She gave him a cutting look. 'What do you want me to say to him? Do you want me to tell him you seduced me when I was barely out of school?'

His brows clamped together in a brooding frown. 'Don't go pulling that card on me, young lady,' he growled. 'You lied to me about your age. I wouldn't have touched you if you hadn't thrown yourself at me like a ten-dollar whore.'

Lexi raised her hand but he intercepted it midair, his fingers so tight, so cruelly tight she felt tears smart in her eyes. 'Let go of me, you bastard!'

'Stop it,' he said in a gritty, deadly calm voice. 'Get control of yourself.'

Lexi flew at him in a rage so intense she even frightened herself. She wanted to hurt him. She wanted him to have physical scars similar to the deep, painful emotional ones she had carried for so long. She fought him, tooth and nail, kicking at him, screaming words of abuse she had never used on anyone before.

But it was all in vain because he was too strong, too determined, too in control.

He held her until the fight went out of her. She went limp in his arms, her energy gone as if someone had pulled out the power source from her body.

She started to cry. Not soft little sobs but great big hulking ones that ripped at her chest like a pair of metallic claws. Tears rolled down her face but she could do nothing to stop them as Sam was still holding her in an iron grip.

But finally he relaxed his hold and the fingers that had bitten into her flesh began to stroke and soothe her instead. 'Hey,' he said softly.

'Don't you "hey" me,' she said, but not with any venom. She was way past that.

Sam drew her close against his body, his arms wrapping around her, his body moving from side to side in a soothing rocking motion, similar to one a loving mother did to a distressed child, not that Lexi had much memory of that experience, but she missed it all the same. 'Shh,' he said gently. 'No more tears, OK? I'm sorry. I didn't mean it. You didn't throw yourself at me.'

Lexi nestled against his strength and solid warmth. 'I did,' she mumbled against his chest. 'I acted like a tart. I'm so ashamed of myself. I don't know what came over me.'

She felt his hand stroke the back of her head, holding it close to his body. 'I could've walked away,' he said. 'I should've walked away.'

Lexi lifted her head off his chest to look at him. 'Why didn't you?'

His eyes were dark and warm, like melted chocolate. 'The same reason I didn't turn this boat around when I found you in my cupboard,' he said. 'I wanted you.'

Lexi felt her heart slip sideways in her chest. He wanted her, but for how long? Should she ask him? Would he put a time line on it? Or should she just take what was on offer and leave everything else to fate? 'I need to freshen up,' she said, lowering her gaze in case he saw the longing in hers.

He gave her a pat on the bottom. 'Take your time,' he said. 'I can hold dinner.'

The night sky was amazing as they sat out on the deck after they had eaten. Sam glanced at Lexi, looking as beautiful as ever though she was wearing one of his warm fleece jackets that swamped her slim frame. The wind had picked up, bringing with it a chill that was a reminder that the long lazy days of summer were still a few weeks away.

So too was Lexi's wedding, he thought with a clench of his gut. She may have taken her ring off but she seemed just as determined as ever to go ahead with the marriage.

He wasn't sure how he was going to deal with that day in November. It wasn't as if he would be invited. He wouldn't accept if he was. What he couldn't understand was why she would still want to marry someone who clearly wasn't meeting her needs.

He hated to think of her marrying for money. It didn't fit well with the Lexi he knew now. The Lexi who put her sister's health and happiness above any of her own needs or desires, the Lexi who worked so tirelessly for the benefit of the hospital charity.

But, then, people married for a host of different reasons: companionship; security; common goals...*children*.

Sam thought back to when he had seen himself following in the footsteps of his father and grandfather and great-grandfather before him. Being a husband, then becoming a father, raising a family, providing for them. In the days before his mother had become so desperately ill he had thought about building a life with someone, having a brood of kids. It had seemed the normal thing to do. But then his mother had got sick and he had watched as his father had struggled to juggle everything: the farm and finances; Sam's needs; and those of his mother. It had broken his father, made him half the man he had been. His strong, tall, capable father had seemed to diminish and age right in front of Sam's eyes. It had terrified Sam to think that might one day happen to him.

Lexi was looking up at the sky. 'I think I can see a satellite,' she said.

'Where?' Sam said, joining her on the cushioned seat at the stern.

She pointed to a moving light in the black velvet of the night sky. 'Can you see it? It's moving from left to right. It's just passing the Saucepan.'

'Got it,' he said, breathing in her fragrance. 'I really missed seeing the southern sky when I was in the States.'

She turned her face towards him. 'What did you miss the most?' she asked.

He put an arm around her shoulders and pulled her closer. 'Lots of things,' he said. 'The smell of the dust when the rain first falls in the bush, the sound of kookaburras at dawn and sunset, the sound of rain falling on a tin roof back at home.'

She traced each of his eyebrows with a fingertip. 'Have you ever thought of working in the bush?' she asked.

He captured her finger and pressed a soft kiss to the end of it. 'Yes, of course, but I'm so highly trained now I'm of more use in the city. It's ironic really as the only reason I became a transplant surgeon was to help people like my mother who couldn't access services in time.'

'Why did you become a heart-lung transplant surgeon?' she asked. 'I thought you were planning on specialising in renal surgery?'

'I had a great mentor in the States,' he said. 'He encouraged me to choose the heart-lung route. He thought my skills were more appropriate for heart-lung transplants. It's more challenging surgery. You need nerves of steel. You need to be able to maintain control under impossible circumstances. You have to be able to switch off your feelings and concentrate on the mechanics of the operation. Not everyone can do it.'

'What if there was a fund to help country people?' she asked.

'There isn't one,' Sam said. 'Bush people mortgage their homes and sell off all their assets to access what city folk take for granted. The expenses are crippling. It's not the medical bills so much but the travel and accommodation. Patients can spend months going back and forth over long distances. It's not within most people's budgets to do that.'

'What if I raised some money for a fund for exactly that purpose?' Lexi asked.

Sam brushed her soft mouth with his thumb. 'Haven't you got enough on your plate already with raising funds for the unit?'

'I can do both,' she said. 'I've already been thinking about raising the funds to buy a house for relatives to stay in, similar to what the children's hospital has. Instead of a fast-food chain funding it, we can do it with charitable donations.'

Sam stroked a finger down the curve of her cheek. 'If

you weren't working for the hospital as Head of Events, what else would you be doing?' he asked.

She lowered her gaze, her fingers toying with the collar of his open-necked shirt. 'I'm not sure…'

'You must have some idea,' he said. 'What did you want to be when you were a little girl?

A faraway look came into her eyes as she looked past his left shoulder. 'I wanted to be a ballerina,' she said. 'I wanted to dance on the world's stage. I used to practise in front of my mother's cheval mirror. I dreamed of wearing a sparkling tutu. I dreamed of dancing at a Royal performance. I pretended I was Cinderella…' Her voice trailed away and her shoulders dropped.

'So what happened?'

She let out a sigh and went back to playing with the buttons on his shirt. 'My feet got sore.'

Sam lifted her chin. 'If that was the case there would be no ballerinas in the world.'

She looked at him with sad blue eyes. 'I couldn't do that to Bella,' she said. 'She used to look at me so wistfully when I got taken to my ballet class by our nanny. She would sit on the sidelines and watch with those sad grey eyes of hers. She didn't do it intentionally. She's not like that. But I felt so guilty. I had to stop. I had to stop a lot of things I loved… It's kind of been the story of my life.'

Sam had heard similar stories throughout his professional life but none had touched him more than Lexi's. She had given up so much to protect her sister. Did anyone realise how much she had sacrificed?

Her father?

Her mother?

Her older sister Evie?

Even Sam hadn't properly understood until now.

There was probably a litany of things she had sacrificed in her effort to protect Bella from feeling inadequate. 'You're a very sweet person, Lexi,' he said. 'But why do you always hide behind that I-don't-give-a-damn-what-you-think facade?'

'Because sometimes it's easier to pretend I don't care,' she said. 'I've got used to putting my feelings to one side.' She gave him a little twisted smile. 'Maybe I'm like you in that regard. I can switch off my feelings when it suits me.'

Sam felt like he had just been hoisted with his own petard. 'It's not always as easy as I make it look,' he said, frowning at her.

'What are you saying, Sam?' she asked with an arch of a slim brow. 'That you sometimes feel more than you let on?'

He held her ocean-blue gaze, determined to outstare her. 'I can't give you what you want,' he said. 'I'm not the right person for you. I've never been the right person.'

She got up and moved a few feet away, finally turning to stand and look at him from the mast, her expression cool and distant. 'Are you the right person for anyone?' she asked.

Sam looked out over the crinkled sea gilded by the silvery moon that had come up. 'When my mother died my father never really got over the loss. I know for a fact he blames himself. They didn't have the money to send her to the city for help. For the last twenty years he's lived like a hermit. I don't think he's ever looked at another woman. Can you imagine that? Twenty years he's lived like a monk because he can't bear the thought of replacing my mother.'

'He must have loved her very much,' Lexi said softly.

Sam let out a hissing breath. 'That's exactly my point,' he said. 'He loved her too much. She wouldn't have wanted him to waste his life like that. She would've wanted him to move on, to find someone else to build a future with, maybe even have another child or two, someone who could take on the farm since I had other plans.'

'Maybe there is no one else who can take your mother's place,' Lexi said. 'Maybe your father has always known that in his heart. Maybe he's perfectly happy living with his memories of their time together.'

Sam frowned at her darkly. 'He should've moved on by now.'

'Why should he?' she asked. 'Is it so hard for you to realise that his love for your mother was enough to satisfy him for a lifetime?'

'I can't imagine loving someone like that,' he said almost savagely. 'It's not what I want for myself.'

'I feel sorry for you, Sam,' Lexi said. 'You've closed yourself off in case you get hurt. But life is all about being hurt. It's not something we can control. There's no switch we can turn off to stop us feeling the pain of losing someone, of loving someone so much we don't feel we can go on without them. We grieve because we love. We might as well be dead if we didn't feel something. It's what makes us all human.'

Sam looked at her standing there, the angles and contours of her beautiful face cast in an ethereal glow by the moonlight. She looked like a mermaid that had come up from the depths of the sea. Her long hair had worked itself loose from the knot she had restrained it in earlier. It was lying about her shoulders and down her back in a silky tangle that his fingers itched to run through. 'Do you love your fiancé like that?' he asked, hating himself for asking it, hating himself even more for wanting to know.

Her eyes moved away from his. She stood stiffly, her gaze on the dark endless sea that moved like a ripple of silk under the caress of the light late-night breeze. 'What I feel for Matthew is nothing to do with you,' she said.

'So you're still going to marry him.'

'Is that a question or a statement?' she asked as she turned and met his gaze, hers diamond-sharp.

'Which would you answer with the truth?' he asked.

She turned away from him to look back to the wrinkled black blanket of the ocean. 'I don't have to tell you anything,' she said. 'I'm just here for now. That's what you want, isn't it? Something casual and temporary. No strings. No feelings. Just a physical connection you could get with anybody.'

'Not just anybody,' he said, coming up behind her to cup her upper arms with his hands. 'It doesn't feel quite like this with anyone else.'

Lexi closed her eyes as she felt his body brush against hers from behind. His mouth was already at her ear lobe, his teeth tugging at her in playful little bites that sent arrows of delight down her spine. He lifted her hair off the nape of her neck and kissed her there in soft movements of his lips against her super-sensitive skin. She shivered in delight, her whole body alert to the proud jut of his erection pressing against her bottom. She leaned back into him, her head lolling to one side as he worked his magical mouth on her neck.

Did he mean it?

Was *she* the only one who made him feel like this?

Lexi didn't know for sure but when she turned in his embrace and offered her mouth to his, she knew with absolute certainty that she would treasure every moment of this weekend with him, for she suspected these memories would be all she would have of him once it was over.

The rest of the time out on the water with Sam was like a fantasy come to life. Sleeping in Sam's arms at night to the gentle rocking of the yacht was like a dream come true. Waking to his caresses, to the hot urgency of his mouth and hands and surging male body had made her soar to the heights of human pleasure.

Watching the sun come up together made her feel close to Sam in a way she had not felt before. She had never seen him in such a relaxed and playful mood. It was as if he was determined to make this short time together as pleasurable for her as possible. There was no further mention of the past or her engagement. It was a no-go area they had seemed to reach by tacit agreement. Lexi was relieved for she knew she had some hard thinking to do in the days ahead, but for now she was content to treasure every precious second with him.

When the wind came up Sam taught her how to sail, showing her how to go about by ducking under the boom and reeling in the ropes. It was an exhilarating experience and one she knew she would never forget. They had a picnic on an isolated beach that Lexi hadn't even known existed. They swam, but not for long as the water hadn't yet warmed up enough to be comfortable, but Lexi soon grew warm again when Sam enveloped her in his arms and made love to her on the sand.

But eventually the weekend drew to a close. It had to.

Sam's relaxed mood seemed to dissipate the closer they got to the marina on Sunday afternoon. His features took on a cast of stone and when he smiled at something she said it didn't reach his eyes.

Lexi watched as he steered the yacht back into its mooring position. Once it was secured and locked up he helped her step onto the marina walkway and carried her bags of shopping for her. They got to the end of the walkway and an awkward silence fell.

'I'll give you a lift home,' Sam said, not looking at her.

'No… Thanks anyway but I'd better make my own way back,' Lexi said.

Another painful silence passed.

'I guess I'll see you at the hospital,' Sam said, his expression still inscrutable.

'Guess so,' Lexi said, forcing brightness into her tone. 'And the ball. I can't believe it's next weekend. Have you got a mask to wear?'

'I'm working on it.'

Lexi shifted her weight from foot to foot. 'I had a great time,' she said, looking up at him. 'Thanks for… for everything…'

'Pleasure.'

Well, there had certainly been plenty of that, Lexi thought. Her body was still tingling inside and out.

She started to walk away but Sam suddenly snagged one of her wrists and turned her back to face him. She looked into his unfathomable dark brown eyes and felt her heart trip. 'I want to see you again,' he said, the words low and deep as if they had been sourced from somewhere deep inside him.

Lexi moistened her suddenly dry lips. 'Sam… This is not exactly easy for me…'

A flinty look came into his eyes. 'What's not easy?'

he asked. 'Hasn't the last day and a half proved anything to you?'

Lexi drew in an uneven breath, hope flickering inside her chest like a tiny candle flame in a stiff breeze. 'I'm not quite sure what it is you're offering…'

'You know damn well what I'm offering,' he said. 'I'm offering you the most passionate, pleasurable experience of your life.'

'An affair.' It wasn't a question or a statement but an expression of heart-wrenching disappointment. Pain hurtled through her like a cannonball, knocking over all her hopes and dreams like ninepins. He didn't want her for ever. He never had. But in spite of the roaring passion that existed between them it still worried her to think he only wanted her now because someone else had already staked a claim.

'I've always been clear on what I can and can't give you, Lexi,' he said. 'I haven't made any false promises to you and I'm not going to make them to you now.'

'I know,' she said on a sigh that prickled her chest. 'I know…'

He brushed her cheek with the back of his bent knuckles, his eyes gentle and warm as they meshed with hers. 'If ever you need a hideaway I'll keep that cupboard empty just for you,' he said.

Lexi gave him a bittersweet smile. 'You do that, country boy.' And then she picked up her bags and left to make her way home.

CHAPTER TEN

FINN Kennedy was just about to go home before his throbbing headache turned into a migraine when he got a call from Evie in A and E. He had been having trouble with his arm all day. He had dropped a coffee cup in the doctors' room but thankfully no one had seen it. The pain behind his eyeballs was like dressmaking pins stabbing at him as he tried to concentrate on what Evie was saying.

'We've got a post-op patient of yours in,' she said. 'A Mr Ian Reid with a swelling in his groin. You did a heart-valve op on him eight days ago. He's in pain and the swelling's getting bigger. I think you need to see him.'

Finn rubbed at his aching temple for a moment. The last thing he wanted to do was head into Theatre feeling the way he did just now. What if his arm let him down at a crucial moment? Dropping a coffee cup was one thing, severing an artery was another. 'I'll be down to see him in a few minutes,' he said. 'I have a patient in ICU I have to check on first.'

'We're pretty busy down here,' Evie said. 'The ambos have rung ahead about a stabbing coming in any minute.'

Finn ground his teeth. 'I said I'd be down there, Evie. Just give me five minutes, OK?'

The phone slammed down in his ear.

Finn walked into the cubicle where Ian Reid was propped up in bed, having just finished a sandwich and a cup of tea. A young nurse, Kate Henderson, was just about to clear the tray away.

'Would you like another drink, Mr Reid?' Kate asked.

Finn glared at the nurse as he indicated for her to leave the cubicle to speak to him away from the patient. 'How could you be so stupid as to have fed this patient?' he roared. 'What the hell are you thinking? He's come in with an obvious hematoma over his femoral puncture site, he's obviously still bleeding, he obviously needs emergency surgery, and you're serving him high tea, for God's sake!'

Kate blushed to the roots of her hair and her chin started to wobble uncontrollably. 'But he was hungry, Dr Kennedy. I didn't know he was going to Theatre.'

'Didn't Dr Lockheart inform you of his condition?' Finn asked, frowning furiously.

'Um…she mentioned to make him comfortable until you arrived,' Kate said.

'Comfortable?' Finn said with a sneer. 'Well, he's not going to be very comfortable if he vomits when he's anesthetised, aspirates and ends up on a ventilator in Intensive Care, is he?'

'But I didn't know he needed Theatre…'

'Well, you damn well should have checked,' Finn said. 'Anyone with any sense and experience could tell he was in dire straits and would've taken the initiative to fast him. What are they teaching you lot at university?'

Kate started to cry, her shoulders shaking as she stood with her head bowed before him.

'Oh, for pity's sake,' Finn said. 'Stop acting like a child and get an orderly down here and have them get this patient up to Theatre before any more harm is done. He'll have to have a crash induction and we'll just have to hope to hell nothing goes wrong before we get this bleeding under control.'

Kate scurried off, still brushing at her eyes as she went.

Evie frowned and followed Finn into the office, closing the door for privacy. 'What was that all about?' she asked.

Finn began writing up his patient notes and didn't even acknowledge her with a look. 'What was what all about?' he asked.

Evie ground her teeth as she took in his devil-may-care demeanour. 'You had no right to speak to that young nurse like that,' she said. 'This is only her second day in the department. She's still finding her feet.'

Finn scrawled his signature on the foot of the page before he cut his hard, ice-blue gaze to hers. 'She can find her feet somewhere else,' he said. 'I haven't got time to babysit silly little schoolgirls.'

'That's hardly fair, Finn, you know how hard it is for the new graduates these days,' Evie said. 'They don't have a lot of on-the-ground experience when they come to us.'

Finn gave her a hard look. 'Then you should be watching for slip-ups like this. It's my name that will be dragged through the courts on a malpractice suit if something goes wrong. What the hell are you doing down here? Running a bloody crèche?'

Evie flattened her mouth in annoyance. 'You really get off on intimidating everyone, don't you?' she asked.

He eyeballed her for so long the air almost started to pulse with tension. 'You want to pick a fight, princess?' he asked. 'Just keep going the way you are.'

She stood her ground, even though her stomach gave a funny little wobble as his ice-pick gaze pinned hers. 'Why do you do it, Finn? Why are you so determined to alienate everyone?'

His eyes were like stone as they held hers, his jaw just as unmalleable. 'I'm not here to win a popularity contest.'

'Maybe not,' she said. 'But it doesn't mean you can't demonstrate a bit of emotional intelligence from time to time, especially with younger members of staff. You're meant to be a role model. Monkey see, monkey do, re-member?'

'Leave it, Evie,' he said, tossing the file on the desk with an impatient flick of his hand, his forehead criss-crossed with a brooding frown.

'No, I will not leave it, Finn,' she said. 'You can't come into my department and throw your weight around, or at least not on my watch.'

His lip curled upwards in a smirk as he stepped to-wards her. 'Your watch?' he asked. 'Since when have you been appointed Department Head?'

Evie was the only thing between him and the door and she was determined not to move until she had said her piece. But it was hard work staring him down when he was so big and so threatening and so very close. She could feel the heat coming off his body. She could smell his scent: one part aftershave and three parts potent, hard-working male. She could feel herself responding to his nearness. She could feel her skin prickling as he sent his gaze on an indolent perusal of her body. Those Antarctic, unreachable, unreadable eyes seemed to be slowly but surely stripping her of every stitch of clothing, leaving spot fires burning in their wake. 'I might not be a head of department but I'm responsible for the staff who work with me,' she said, trying to keep her voice steady. 'It's about being a team. We're meant to be working together, not against one another.'

Finn's hooded gaze burned into hers. 'You want to get out of my way, princess?'

Evie felt a warning shiver scurry down her spine like a small furry animal but she still didn't budge. A perverse desire to get under his skin kept egging her on. 'What are you going to do, Finn?' she asked. 'Throw me over your shoulder, caveman style?'

His eyes gleamed menacingly and she felt his warm breath skate over her uptilted face. 'Now, that sounds like a plan,' he said, planting a hand either side of her head, trapping her within the cage of his strong arms.

Evie sucked in a quick little breath that felt like it had tiny rose thorns attached as he moved just that little bit closer. His hard, muscular chest brushed against the swell of her breasts and his belt buckle poked her in the belly, an erotic hint of what would happen if she allowed him any nearer. Her body flared with heat at his disturbing proximity, her skin tingling with awareness, her scalp prickling all over. His eyes were a deep and dangerous blue sea of male desire as they held hers. Her heart started to flap at the wall of her chest like a shredded truck tyre against bitumen. And her mouth went totally dry as his loomed inexorably closer...

A rumble of voices in the background suddenly lifted Finn's head. 'Might want to open that door, Evie,' he drawled mockingly as he stepped back from her. 'Your *team* might be wondering what's keeping you from doing your job.'

Evie moved aside to let him pass, her heart still flip-flopping against her ribcage as she sent him a contentious glare. 'Go to hell, Finn.'

He flicked her cheek with a lazy finger on the way past. 'Been there, done that and thrown away the T-shirt long, long ago,' he said, and then he left.

'What's been eating at Finn Kennedy lately?' Julie, one of the nurses on duty, asked Evie a little while later as they were clearing up a cubicle after a patient had been transferred to ICU. 'He's been wandering around like a bear with a sore head.'

Evie peeled off her gloves and tossed them in the bin. 'I have no idea,' she said. 'He's always been a law unto himself.'

A head popped through the curtains from the next cubicle. It was one of the other nurses who had worked with Finn earlier. 'That's because he *has* got a sore head,' she said. 'I saw him pop a couple of paracetamol before he left. Mind you, who wouldn't get a headache working here? Patients are lined up three deep in the waiting room and there are no beds.'

Evie frowned. 'Finn had a headache?'

The nurse nodded. 'He saw me looking at him while he was getting the painkillers and said he was fighting a migraine.'

Evie let out a breath and sank her teeth into her bottom lip. 'He should have said something…'

Julie gave a snort as she bundled up the linen in her arms. 'Yeah, right, that sounds like something Finn Kennedy would do.'

Evie took off her stethoscope and ran the rubber tubing through her fingers. Finn had seemed particularly snarly this evening. And she had gone at him all guns blazing. If he was struggling with a migraine it was no wonder he had lost his temper with the junior nurse. And he'd had to take Mr Reid to Theatre. It would have been a nightmare for him if he hadn't been feeling well.

She glanced at her watch. Her shift was nearly over. It was late but not too late to deliver an apology in person.

Finn's penthouse apartment light was on. Evie had checked before she had knocked on the door but it seemed a decade or two before he answered.

The door swung open and he scowled down at her. 'What do you want?'

'How's your headache?' she asked.

His frown deepened. 'What headache?'

'The headache that made you act like an absolute boor in A and E earlier this evening,' she said.

His hand fell away from the door and tunnelled through his hair. 'It's fine,' he said in a gruff tone. 'I've taken something for it. It's almost gone.'

Evie sidled past him in the doorway.

'What are you doing?' he asked, shooting her a glare.

'I've come to apologise.'

'For what?'

'For laying into you the way I did,' she said. 'I didn't realise you were ill.'

His brows snapped together. 'I'm not ill.'

'You have a headache.'

'So?'

'Doesn't that qualify as being ill?'

'Not if it doesn't interfere with my work,' he said.

'But it does interfere with your work,' she argued. 'The way you spoke to that poor girl was—'

He opened the door and jerked his head for her to leave. 'Don't let me keep you.'

Evie ignored the open door. 'Have you had migraines before?' she asked.

'Go home, Evie,' he said grimly. 'I don't need a diagnosis. I had a tension headache. I get them occasionally. Everyone does. Now leave.'

'There have been a number of times at work when I've seen you struggling with your co-ordination,' she said. 'I've seen you drop things. And that facial stitching you abandoned that time? It was like you couldn't get your fingers to work. Now you're having migraines. Have you thought of having some scans done to rule out anything sinister?'

Finn let out an impatient curse. 'I haven't got a brain tumour,' he said. 'I haven't got anything. Now get out of here before I lose my temper.'

Evie moved even further into his apartment, trailing her fingers over the leather sofa as she walked by to look out of the bank of windows overlooking the harbour. She affected an air of calm she was nowhere near feeling. Finn was intimidating at the best of times, but in this mood he was lethal. He reminded her of an alpha wolf who had taken himself away to lick his wounds without the cynosure of critical eyes. The thing she had to establish was if the wound he was hiding was self-inflicted. That was the one question she dreaded asking but ask it she must.

'What the hell do you think you're doing?' Finn asked.

Evie turned and looked at him, taking a deep breath

before she asked, 'Is it alcohol? Have you got a hang-over?'

His expression became thunderous. 'What are you implying?' he asked.

Evie rolled her lips together for a moment. 'You know what people are like, Finn,' she said. 'They talk, gossip, spread rumours.'

'Then they can bloody well talk,' he said. 'I don't drink on the job. Never have, never will.'

'I want to believe you but—'

'I don't give a rat's backside if you believe me or not,' he shot back. 'Now, I'm going to say this one more time. Leave.'

Evie folded her arms and eyeballed him. 'Aren't you going to offer me a cup of coffee or something?'

His face was a blank canvas. 'No.'

'You don't give a damn about anyone, do you?' she asked.

'Not particularly.'

'I'm trying to understand you,' she said, her voice rising in frustration. 'But you're so damned obstruc-tive. Why can't you at least meet me halfway?'

Finn shut the door with a definitive click; the gun-shot sound of it making Evie flinch. She drew in an uneven breath as he sauntered over to where she was standing, his long legs eating up the distance in a mat-ter of strides.

His features were harsh as he looked down at her, his cold, unfathomable eyes nailing hers. 'What is it you really want, Evie?' he asked. 'A cosy chat over coffee or a quick tumble in the sack to let off some steam?'

Evie felt her face flash with heat. 'You think I came here to sleep with you?' she asked.

'Yeah, that's what I think.' His eyes flicked to her

mouth before coming back to mesh with hers, challenging her, provoking her, *arousing* her.

She straightened her spine and sent him a withering look. 'Strange as it may seem, Finn, I don't want to dive headfirst into your bed,' she said. 'Call me picky but I don't care for where you've been just lately.'

He gave her a devilish smile as he stepped into her body space. She tried to move away but the sofa was in the way. He captured some strands of her hair and looped them around his fingertip, a disturbingly intimate tether that sent her heart into an erratic rhythm. 'Liar,' he said. 'We both know why you're here, princess. You want me to finish what I started back in the office.'

Evie ran her tongue out over the chalk-dry surface of her lips. 'Y-you're totally wrong,' she said in a husky whisper that didn't really help her denial one little bit. 'I just wanted to check that you were all right. I was concerned about you.'

He fisted some of her hair in his hands; the tugging should have been painful but instead it was intensely erotic against her scalp. His eyes dipped to her mouth, lingering there for a heart-stopping moment before he came back to her gaze. 'Keep your concern for someone who wants it,' he said. 'I have no need or desire to be taken care of and certainly not by you.'

'Why must you block anyone getting close to you?' Evie asked.

His fist tightened on her hair, making her toes curl inside her shoes. His eyes blazed with heat as they bored into hers. 'I'm not blocking you now, princess,' he drawled. 'You can get as close to me as you want. I won't stop you.'

Evie snatched in a prickly breath. 'I'm not talking about physical closeness.'

He bent his head to her neck, his lips nibbling on her skin in a teasing caress that sent a shiver down the length of her spine. 'It's the only type of closeness I want,' he said. 'And you want it too, don't you, Evie, hmm?'

Evie wished she could deny it but her legs were already folding beneath her as his tongue moved across her lower jaw, making every nerve spring to attention. She tilted her head to one side to give him better access, her eyes closing as ripples of pleasure flowed through her body. He got closer and closer to her mouth without actually touching her lips. It was a torturous assault on her senses. She felt her lips buzzing with need as he advanced and retreated, again and again and again, until with a little whimper of desperation she finally took matters into her own hands and pressed her mouth to his.

Fireworks went off in her body as he took control of the kiss. His lips moved against hers with bruising pressure, his tongue not asking for entry but taking it in one savage thrust that lifted every hair on her head, including the ones he still had fisted in his hand.

He turned her in one deft movement and began walking her backwards to the nearest wall, his muscled thighs moving against hers in a commanding and totally provocative manner. She felt the surge of his erection against her belly as her back hit the wall, the rock-hard length of him pulsing with the drumbeats of raw, primal, male need. Her body was aflame, her feminine core already seeping with the dew of her longing. It was a raging fever in her blood, a full-throttle rush of sexual need on a scale she had never felt before. She felt wanton and wild with his mouth crushing hers. She gave another whimper as his mouth ground against hers with savage intent, his tongue demanding hers submit to his. She fought him every step of the way for supremacy. She used her teeth, small nippy bites and harder ones, but he refused to allow her control.

'Damn you,' he growled against her mouth as he tugged at her top to uncover her breasts. 'Damn you to hell.'

'Damn you right back,' she said as she held her arms up over her head so he could remove her top with a reckless abandon she suspected she might regret later when common sense returned.

He kicked the top away with his foot as his mouth ground against hers, his hands roughly caressing her breasts through the lace of her bra. It was exhilarating to feel his warm hands on her but she wanted more. She wanted to feel him skin on skin. She wanted no barriers between them.

Evie put her hands behind her back to unhook her bra, letting it drop to the floor at her feet. Finn murmured with approval and left her mouth to suck savagely on her right breast. She gasped out loud at the impact of his hot mouth on her puckered flesh. He swirled his tongue round her nipple, his teeth nipping at her, tugging, pulling and teasing in a cycle of pleasure and pain that had her totally at his mercy. His mouth was ruthless, hot and insistent, determined and dangerous as it toyed with her sensitive flesh.

She didn't waste time on his shirt; instead her hands went straight to the waistband of his trousers, fumbling over the fastening in her desperate haste to feel him under her fingertips. He was so hard it made her insides quiver in a combination of anticipation and trepidation.

She could feel the pulsing heart of him pressing against the restraint of the fabric of his underwear as she undid his zipper.

A hot burst enflamed her insides as she finally uncovered him. The arrantly male jut of his body was smooth as satin but as hard as steel. Her hand moved up and down his length, slowly at first, exploring him, delighting in how aroused he was.

He gave a guttural groan and wrenched her hand away, pushing her almost roughly back against the wall as he lifted her skirt, his fingers pushing aside her knickers to slip with devastating thoroughness into the hot, wet heart of her.

Evie arched up in aching need to feel more, to have more of him, to have all of him. She could feel the tension building inside her, the dizzying rush of her blood, the emptying of her brain but for the fiery sensations coursing through her.

His mouth came back to hers in a hard kiss that had an undertow of desperation in it. His tongue duelled with hers in an erotic mimic of how he wanted to possess her. Her body thrilled at the sensual promise, the inner walls of her core pulsing with the need to feel him moving inside her. Every nerve in her body was screaming for more. For more of his touch, for more of his branding kisses, for the release she wanted more than her next breath.

He made another rough male sound deep in his throat as she moved urgently against him. He hoisted one of her legs around his waist, positioning himself before driving so deeply into her silky warmth her head banged against the wall.

Her gasp was swallowed by his mouth as it plundered hers. The friction of his body within hers sent shockwaves of delight through her. She felt pleasure in every part of her from her curling toes to her prickling scalp where one of his hands had locked onto her hair to anchor himself.

It was a rough coupling, a desperate, urgent mating that bordered on animalistic. He thrust deeper and deeper, and harder and harder, his breath a hot gust near her ear as he laboured over her.

Evie felt the first faint flutters of orgasm, the tiny ripples that rolled through her, gathering speed with each pounding movement of his body within hers. She felt her body chase the delicious feeling, all her intimate muscles tensing for the freefall into ecstasy.

Suddenly it consumed her.

It picked her up like a giant wave and thrashed her about before spitting her out the other side, spent and limbless.

She was so sensitised she felt every pulsing moment of Finn's release. She felt the way his body tensed all over before that final explosive plunge into his own paradise. Her inner core felt each and every aftershock and her mouth accepted each and every earthy gasp from his.

Evie felt him slump against her, his head buried against her neck, his breathing ragged and uneven. Her hands slipped under the loose tails of his shirt, her fingertips memorising every knob of his vertebrae. He flinched as she touched him between his shoulder blades so she backed off. But then she felt the puckered flesh of the scar he had sustained during combat and her fingers stalled…

As if he sensed her hesitation he pulled back from her, his expression shuttered as he refastened his trousers. 'You should have gone home when I told you to,' he said.

'I don't like being told what to do,' she said. 'You should know that by now.'

'Here,' he said, tossing her bra and top at her. 'Get dressed.'

Her heart sank. But what had she expected? Evie considered defying him but decided against it. Somehow having a discussion with her topless and him fully clothed didn't really appeal. Once she was decent she turned and searched his features. Was he really so cold he could push her out the door as if nothing had happened between them just now? It might have been rough sex. It might have been rushed and raw and performed with most of their clothes still on, but it had been the best sex she'd ever had. For a brief moment she had felt a connection with him that had superseded the mere physical. She had felt his vulnerability in their passionate embrace, the way he had lost himself in her body as if she was the only one who could reach inside him and soothe and comfort the dark bleakness of his soul.

'Let me see it,' she said softly. 'Let me see your scar.'

He scowled at her menacingly. 'I'm not a freak show, Evie. You got what you came for, now get the hell out of here.'

Evie dug her heels in. Any reaction from him was better than no reaction. Red-hot anger was better than chilly indifference. 'You got that when your brother was killed, didn't you?' she asked. 'You were almost killed as well.'

His jaw clicked as he ground his teeth. 'Get out.'

'You feel guilty that he died instead of you,' she went on. 'That's why you punish yourself by working such crazy hours. You close yourself off from everyone because you don't believe you deserve to be happy because you lived and he didn't.'

She saw his hands clench into fists and a vein bulge in his neck. His eyes were blue chips of ice, hard and unyielding, distant, closed off, angry. 'Get out before I throw you out,' he ground out.

Evie raised her chin. 'I think you care about people way more than you let on,' she said. 'Take me, for instance.'

His lip curled mockingly. 'I just did.'

A dagger pierced her heart but she went on regardless. 'You hate yourself for needing anyone. You keep everything and everyone on a clinical basis. We just had amazing sex and yet you just trivialised it as if it meant nothing. You cheapened it as if I was just another girl you picked up at a bar. But I'm not just another one-night stand. I'm someone who cares about you. Don't ask me why but I do.'

He gave her a flinty look. 'Are you done?'

Evie let out a breath. 'You don't believe me, do you? You don't believe anyone can care about you. Why do you believe that? Why do you think you're so unworthy of love?'

'Love?' He spat the word out as if it was acid. 'Is that how you have to justify what we just did? You're using the wrong four-letter word, princess. What we just did was have a good old fashioned—'

Evie closed her eyes as if that would stop her hearing the coarse word, but of course it didn't. She opened them again to see him looking at her with that same mocking expression. She felt hurt beyond description. She was nothing to him other than a sexual outlet, one of many he had used. Their intimacy hadn't touched him at all. She had imagined it. Her overwhelming attraction to him had distorted her judgement. She felt used, cheap, like a piece of trash he no longer had any use for. 'You really are a piece of work, aren't you, Finn?' she said with an embittered look.

He leaned indolently against the sofa, his eyes running over her lasciviously, smoulderingly. 'You ever feel that itch again, princess, just knock on my door and I'll gladly be of service,' he said.

She turned for the door, wrenching it open before she threw him a glittering look over her shoulder. 'Don't hold your breath,' she said, slamming the door behind her.

Finn pushed himself away from the sofa, cursing. He had just broken his own code with Evie. Evie, of all people! He should have known she wasn't the type of woman to play by his rules. It would never be just sex with Evie Lockheart. She pushed against his boundaries in a hundred different ways with her concerned looks and soft voice and those velvet hands touching him as if he was the most fascinating specimen of manhood. For a moment there he had lost himself in her.

Totally lost himself.

Felt things that he had no right to be feeling.

He didn't do feelings.

He didn't do emotional connection.

He didn't want to feel anything for her. And he certainly didn't want her feeling anything for him. But the sex had been mind-blowing, even if it had lacked finesse. All he had wanted to do was bury himself in her and forget about everything except the way his body felt gripped tightly by hers.

And it had felt incredible.

She had met him physically in a way he had not expected. Her body had been so responsive to his. He had felt every silky ripple of her skin, every tight spasm of her orgasm, every breathless gasp of her breath into his mouth as he'd driven them both into oblivion.

It had been much more than a meeting of bodies in the primal act of mating. He had felt the stirrings of a much deeper bonding that had terrified him. Evie had revealed her vulnerable side, citing feelings for him he had never asked for, never sought, and secretly dreaded.

He had a feeling she could see inside him, the *real* inside—the inside where the ragged edges of his soul barely held him together any more. His emotional centre had been bludgeoned in childhood and then obliterated completely the day Isaac had died.

He was dead inside, dead emotionally. But Evie with her soft hazel eyes kept stroking at the cold heart of him with her looks of concern and her questions about his health. It was as if she was determined to perform cardiac massage on his lifeless soul.

Allowing someone, *anyone*, into the locked and bolted heart of him was unthinkable. He never wanted to feel anything for anyone again. He didn't want anyone to feel anything for him either because he was sure he would only let them down just as he had his brother.

He was used to being alone.

It was the only place where he truly felt safe.

CHAPTER ELEVEN

'You won't believe the juicy piece of gossip I heard on the weekend,' Lexi's assistant Jane said as soon as Lexi came in on Monday morning.

Lexi kept her expression blank but her heart gave a little stumble of panic. 'Oh?' she said offhandedly as she leafed through some donation slips.

'Your sister and Finn Kennedy had a blazing row in A and E,' Jane said. 'They tore strips off each other.'

'So?' Lexi said, privately releasing a sigh of relief the gossip hadn't been about her and Sam. 'It's not the first time they've locked heads and it probably won't be the last.'

'Yes, but that's not all,' Jane said. 'Finn had her backed up against the door in the office and it looked like he was about to kiss her. It was only because one of the staff came past that he didn't.'

'I still don't think that means they're an item,' Lexi said.

Jane leaned forward conspiratorially. 'Not only that. Evie went to his apartment later that night. One of the nurses who lives in the same block saw her.'

Lexi put the donation slips down and gave Jane a look of reproach. 'That doesn't mean anything. She might've gone there to talk about a patient or something, or maybe she went there to try and smooth things over.'

'Can't have worked 'cause they're still at logger-heads,' Jane said. 'Everyone's talking about it. Mind you, I can see what she sees in him. He's seriously gorgeous with that sexy stubble and that haven't-slept-properly-in-weeks look. What woman wouldn't want to jump into bed with him?'

Lexi had her own complicated love life to deal with without getting embroiled in her sister's, but when she happened to run into Evie in one of the staffroom bathrooms a couple of days later it was obvious Evie had something on her mind.

'Lexi, I want a word with you,' Evie said, blocking the main door with her body so no one could disturb them.

'Sure,' Lexi said. 'What's up?'

Evie narrowed her eyes at her. 'What the hell are you up to with Sam Bailey?'

Lexi felt her chest freeze in mid-inhalation. 'I'm not sure what you mean.'

'You don't?' Evie said with a raised brow. 'Well, how about I spell it out for you? I was on late shift last night with an intern who happened to be working on his father's boat at the weekend. He said he saw you getting on Sam's boat on Saturday afternoon. He also said he saw you leaving it the following evening.'

Lexi chewed at the inside of her bottom lip. 'I know it looks bad…'

'Bad?' Evie's tone was incredulous. 'Do you realise what'll happen if this does the rounds of the hospital? You're putting everything in jeopardy. Your engagement, your work for the transplant unit, not to mention Sam's reputation. Do you realise that?'

'What about you?' Lexi said, going on the defensive. 'Everyone is talking about you going to Finn's apartment late at night. Do you want to tell me what time you left or is that no one's business but your own?'

Evie's mouth flattened. 'At least I'm not supposed to be marrying another man next month. You can't have it both ways, Lexi. You have to make up your mind. Matthew doesn't deserve this.'

'I know, I know, but I'm so confused,' Lexi said, fighting tears. 'I can't get a call through to him to even talk to him. What am I supposed to do? Send him an email or a text and tell him I'm in love with someone else?'

Evie's shoulders dropped as she let out a sigh. 'God, I didn't realise things were that bad,' she said. 'You really love him…Sam, I mean?'

Lexi nodded miserably.

'And what does Sam feel?' Evie asked. 'Does he love you?'

'No…' Lexi's chin wobbled. 'He's never loved me.'

Evie let out another sigh and reached for Lexi, hugging her tightly. 'Then you've got yourself one hell of a problem, hon,' she said.

'Tell me about it,' Lexi said, and burst into tears.

The night of the ball finally arrived. The marquee at the front of the hospital looked spectacular. Starched white linen tablecloths adorned each table set with gleaming silverware and crystal glasses. Black and gold satin ribbons festooned the chairs and crystal candelabra centrepieces gave each table an old-world charm.

The press had arrived to document the event, cameras flashing everywhere just like at a Hollywood premier as the guests walked up the red carpet accompanied by the beautiful music of a string quartet.

The men were dressed in black tie suits, the women

in gorgeous evening gowns, and almost everyone had entered into the spirit of the occasion by donning a mask.

Lexi was wearing a backless silver satin gown, nipped in at the waist and floating to the floor in a small but elegant train. She had chosen a Venetian mask, which covered most of her face, and her hair she'd had professionally styled in a glamorous pile on top of her head.

Evie had arrived and had spoken briefly to Lexi but she seemed to be doing her best to avoid Finn, who looked particularly dashing in a mask that only revealed his piercing ice-blue eyes.

Lexi knew the exact moment when Sam arrived. The fine hairs on the back of her neck lifted and she swung her eyes to the entrance of the marquee where she found him looking straight at her. The slow burn of his gaze made her feel as if he was seeing right through her evening gown to the tiny strip of lace that was her only item of underwear.

He looked magnificent in a black tuxedo, and the black highwayman's mask he was wearing gave him a devilishly sexy look that made a hot flood of desire rush over the floor of her stomach and flow tantalisingly between her thighs.

He looked away to respond to another guest who had spoken to him, and Lexi took a much-needed sip of her champagne to settle her nerves.

Other guests came in and drinks and canapés were served. Some masks had to be removed for guests to eat and drink, but they were still a great ice-breaker and everyone seemed to be having fun as they perused the silent-auction items set up along one wall of the marquee.

The evening progressed with a fork-food buffet dinner, which Lexi had specifically organised so people could mingle rather than be stuck at one table. The dancing had already started and the music was up-beat and got even the most determined wallflowers up on their feet. Lexi could see Sam dancing with Suzy Carpenter, one of the nurses with a reputation for sleeping around. Lexi wondered if Sam would be one of Suzy's conquests by the time the night was over. It certainly looked like that was Suzy's goal if the way she was draping herself all over him was any indication, Lexi thought, turning away in disgust.

Lexi had so far been too busy seeing that everything ran smoothly to get on the dance floor herself, but then she heard the band strike up the opening bars of the song that had been her first dance with Sam on the night they had met five years ago. A rush of emotion filled her, and she quickly walked out of the marquee, not sure she could bear seeing Sam dance their song with someone else.

She was standing looking at the view of the harbour when she felt someone come up behind her. 'They're playing our song,' Sam said, his broad shoulder brushing hers.

Lexi turned and looked up at him. 'You remembered?'

He held out his arms for her to step into them with a crooked smile on his face. 'How could I forget?'

She stepped into his arms and sighed as her body came up against his. She laid her head on his chest and moved with him as the slow romantic ballad took her back in time. 'I've missed you,' Lexi said. 'I can't stop thinking about the weekend, how wonderful it was.'

Sam rested his chin on the top of her head as the song changed to a poignant minor key. 'I've missed you too,' he said, his legs moving in time with hers.

They danced through another number, a slow waltz

that made Lexi feel like she was floating on air instead of dancing with her feet firmly on the ground. It always felt like that in Sam's arms. Her worries and cares slipped to the back of her mind when his arms held her close against him. She felt protected and safe, his arms like a shield to keep the world and all its disappointments away from her. He might not love her the way she wanted to be loved but she was sure he felt something for her, something more than just transient lust. But would it be enough to sustain a relationship between them? And for how long? A week or two? A month? Three months?

And what was she going to do about Matthew? He had promised to match the funds she raised this evening. How could she tell him she no longer wanted to marry him? How could she reach him before she went any further with Sam?

Lexi felt Sam's lips moving against her hair. 'What are you doing after this is over?' he asked. 'Do you want to come and spend the night with me on my yacht? Tomorrow we could go out on the water. Just the two of us. No interruptions.'

Lexi looked up into his handsome face. 'Sam...'

A frown settled between his brows. 'You haven't told your fiancé yet, have you?'

She lowered her gaze, staring at the bow tie at his neck rather than meet his gaze. 'I have responsibilities, Sam. I've made a commitment to the hospital and I can't just walk away. It's not that simple. People are relying on me.'

Sam's features darkened with cynicism. 'It's about the money, isn't it?' he said. 'You'd do anything for Brentwood's money, wouldn't you? You'd even sell your soul.'

Lexi stepped back and hugged her upper arms against the light chill in the air. 'Sam, you're asking too much and giving too little,' she said. 'You want me to give up my life for you but what are you promising in return?'

His eyes glittered darkly. 'Isn't what we have together enough for now?' he asked.

Lexi opened her mouth to answer when she heard the sound of footsteps and two male voices approaching.

One was her father's.

'I think she went out there,' Richard said. 'She's probably gone off to the kitchen to sort something out with the caterers. She won't be far away. Do you want me to call her on her mobile? I'm pretty sure she has it switched on.'

The other voice was her fiancé's.

'No,' Matthew Brentwood said, anticipation and excitement evident in his voice. 'Don't do that. She has no idea I'm here. She walked past me three times already and didn't recognise me. I want it to be a surprise when I finally take off my mask.'

Lexi looked at Sam in wide-eyed panic. *Matthew was here?* Her heart threatened to beat its way out of her chest. She couldn't breathe. She felt trapped. Claustrophobic. Her stomach was churning. She wasn't prepared. She needed more time. She needed to get her emotions in check.

Sam gave her a look that cut her to ribbons. 'Thank you for the dance,' he said. 'I hope you enjoy the rest of your evening.' And without another word he strode away, not back into the marquee where all the laughter and music and frivolity was happening but into the anonymous darkness of the night.

CHAPTER TWELVE

It took Lexi over a week to find the courage to tell Matthew their engagement was over. It was the worst feeling in the world to have broken someone's heart, and not just Matthew's heart but his parents' and sisters' too.

After she had said spoken to Matthew she stood outside the Brentwoods' lovely family home, the house she had come to think of as her second home, and knew she would never be back.

It would have been easier if Matthew had been angry at her, furious with her for betraying him. But instead he had just been sad, utterly and indescribably sad. His grey-blue eyes had looked stricken as she had told him she couldn't marry him. He hadn't shouted. He hadn't hurled abuse at her. He hadn't even withdrawn his offer of matching the amount of money she had raised for the transplant unit. He had honoured his promise, which made the breaking of hers that much harder for her to do without feeling appallingly guilty, even though she knew deep in her heart she was doing the right thing.

As soon as Lexi's father found out he told her to pack her bags and leave. He ranted and raved, shouting and swearing, thumping his fists on the table, reminding Lexi of a child having a tantrum because he couldn't have his own way. Unable to bear it any longer, she packed a few things before she made her way to Sam's apartment.

She rang the doorbell but there was no answer. A sickening feeling of déjà vu assailed her. Surely he hadn't left without telling her? But of course not, she reassured herself. He was working at the hospital. He had a two-year contract with an option for five. He was probably on call or something.

Sam wasn't at the hospital either, Susanne, his practice manager, informed her. 'He had a heart-lung transplant this morning,' she said. 'He did his rounds straight after he saw a few patients in the rooms. You might find him down at the marina. He's probably gone out for a quick sail. He should be just about back by now.'

'Thanks, Susanne.' Lexi turned to leave.

'Oh, and, Lexi?' Susanne said.

Lexi turned at the door. 'Yes?'

'I'm sorry to hear about your engagement,' Susanne said. 'I heard about it from one of the staff.'

'Thank you,' Lexi said. 'But I think it's for the best.'

It was almost sundown by the time Lexi got to the marina. Her heart sank when she couldn't see Sam's boat anywhere in sight. Then in the distance she could see his yacht motoring back to the marina. She drank in the sight of him. She hadn't seen him since the night of the ball. He looked so gorgeous standing at the helm of his boat, steering it into its mooring place.

She stood with her bags at her feet, waiting for him, her heart beating hard and fast in excitement and longing.

He looked up and saw her, a frown carving into his forehead when his gaze went to the bags at her feet. Once the boat was tied up securely he jumped down on the marina to face her. 'What are you doing here, Lexi?' he asked, still frowning formidably.

Lexi's stomach did a queasy little turnover. 'I've come to tell you I've called off my engagement,' she said.

'I already heard about that in the doctors' room this morning,' he said, as if it was the most insignificant news, like the current price of milk or bread.

Lexi licked her dry lips. 'I would've liked you to have been the first to know but my father took it upon himself to tell everyone what a disappointment for a daughter I've become because I cancelled my wedding within a couple of weeks of the ceremony.'

'It's your life, not his,' he said, his face set like marble.

Lexi let out a rattling breath. 'Sam? Is everything all right?'

His eyes were blank. 'Sure? Why wouldn't it be?'

She bit her lip. 'I just thought you'd be more…more excited about me ending things with Matthew. I thought you'd be thrilled we can be together now. I'm free, Sam. It can be just you and me. We can be together all the time.'

Sam glanced at her bags before returning his gaze to hers. 'I offered you an affair, not a place to stay,' he said. 'Nothing serious and nothing long term, remember?'

Lexi looked at his mouth speaking those cruel, heartbreaking words and wondered if she had misheard him. She moistened her lips again. 'Sam, I love you. Surely you know that by now? I love you and I want to be with you.'

His jaw was tight, his eyes hard and impenetrable. 'I don't love you, Lexi. I've never loved you. I'm happy to enjoy an affair with you but that's it. Take or leave it.'

Inside Lexi's chest she felt her heart had broken off in a thousand sharp-edged pieces, each one scoring at her lungs every time she took a breath. 'You can't mean that, Sam,' she said, tears building up in her eyes. 'I've given up everything for you. I can't imagine life without you. How can you do this to me?'

Sam's expression was still locked down. 'I haven't done anything to you, Lexi. You've done it to yourself.'

'You asked me to end my engagement!' She didn't care that her voice was shrill.

'I didn't ask you to do any such thing,' he said in a steely voice. 'I just asked you how you could possibly think of marrying a man who didn't satisfy you. You were marrying him for all the wrong reasons. I did not at any point offer to take his place at the altar.'

Lexi swallowed her anguish with an effort. Pride was the only thing she had left and she clung to it with the desperation a drowning person did a life raft. She would have to walk away. She would have to rebuild her life. She would have to learn to be happy without Sam, the only man she had ever loved, the only man she *could* ever love. There would be no happy ending. No marriage and making babies together. It had all been a fantasy that she had mistaken for the real thing. *Again.* Yet again she had been duped by her own foolish, romantic dreams. 'I hope you find what you're looking for, Sam,' she said in a cold, hard voice. 'And then when you find it, I hope it gets snatched away from you and you never get it back.' And then she picked up her bags and walked back up the marina, out of his life for good.

Sam watched her walk away, the words to call her back lodged in the middle of his throat where a choking knot had formed. Seeing Lexi on the wharf with her bags packed, ready to move into his life, had made him panic. But, then, ever since he had heard she had called off her engagement he had felt conflicted. He had felt the same gut-wrenching agitation the night of the ball when he'd heard the sound of her fiancé's voice.

Up until that point Sam had assumed Matthew Brentwood was one of those rich, shallow guys who had plucked the prettiest girl from his social set and got engaged to her because it was the thing to do. But hearing Matthew's excitement at seeing Lexi again had hit Sam in the gut like a wildly flung bowling ball.

The man loved her, *really* loved her.

Sam needed time to think, to process what it meant now Lexi was free. He felt uncomfortable with the prospect of being forever labelled as the man who had come between her and her fiancé, especially when he wasn't sure he could offer her more than a resumption of their affair. He *wanted* to offer more but he didn't know if he was capable of opening up that part of him that had closed down so long ago.

Lexi deserved better than another casual fling with him. She deserved to be loved totally and completely, but he wasn't sure he was ready to make that sort of emotional commitment, or at least not yet.

Sam threw himself into work over the next couple of weeks but even after the most gruelling days he still hadn't been able to sleep at night. He thought about Lexi all the time. He hadn't seen her at the hospital. He had heard via one of the nurses that she had taken some leave. The days seemed so long and pointless without the anticipation of running into her in one of the corridors or on the ward. He hadn't realised how much he had looked forward to those offchance meetings, those little verbal stoushes that had made his blood bubble with sexual excitement in his veins.

Even being out on his boat wasn't the same any more. He could still smell the fragrance of her perfume. It had seemed to permeate the very woodwork of its every surface, torturing him with a thousand little reminders of her: the way she had squealed as she had jumped into the cold water of the ocean; the way her naked body had been wrapped around his on the hot sand as he'd possessed her; the way her soft mouth had pleasured him; the way she had stroked and caressed every inch of his body until he had thought of nothing but the incredible release he felt with her. Even his shirts smelled like her. Wearing them was like wrapping himself in her.

He wanted to rewind the clock, to go back to the marina and do it all differently. But every time he called her phone it went straight to the answering service. And each time he hadn't said anything. Not a word. Hell, it was so pathetic. He had been as tongue-tied as any shy young teenager asking a girl on a first date.

Sam drove up to visit his father on the weekend to distract himself from the habit he'd developed lately of incessantly checking his phone for texts or missed calls. He was acting like some of the teenagers he saw around town, their phones never out of their hands, their fingers constantly texting or scrolling.

Jack Bailey enveloped him in a bear hug as soon as he arrived. 'I hope you don't mind, Sam, but I've invited a young lady to join us for dinner,' he said.

'Come on, Dad,' Sam said with an edge of irritation. 'You know I hate it when you try and hook me up with women. I can find my own dates.' *And lose them, not once but twice.* Would Lexi ever forgive him for that?

he wondered. Probably not. No wonder she wasn't taking his calls.

'This one's not for you, son,' Jack said grinning. 'Jean's my date.'

Sam stared at his father with his mouth open. 'You've got a *date*?'

Jack beamed. 'It's only taken me twenty years to put myself out there but she's great, Sam. She reminds me of your mother. I guess that's why I fell in love with her.'

Sam was still gobsmacked. 'You're in love?'

'Yep, and I'm getting married,' Jack said.

'Married?'

Jack nodded happily but then his expression turned sombre. 'I grieved too long for your mum,' he said. 'I guess I felt so guilty about her dying because I couldn't afford the health cover. But life is short, Sam. You of all people know that. No one knows how long we have on this earth. We each of us have to grab at what happiness we can before it's too late. Your mother would've wanted me to be happy. She would want you to be happy too.'

Sam rubbed one of his hands over his face. 'Yeah, well, I'd like to be happy but you won't believe the mess I've made of things…'

His father listened as Sam told him what had happened. 'Sounds bad, son, especially when she won't even take your calls. What are going to do?'

'What are you doing for the next couple of days?' Sam asked. 'Do you fancy some time out on the boat?'

'Sure,' Jack said with a twinkle in his eyes. 'Are we going fishing?'

'Yeah,' Sam said with a slowly spreading smile. 'You could say that.'

* * *

Lexi was walking along the beach at Noosa on the Sunshine Coast of Queensland when she saw him. At first she thought she had imagined it, conjuring him up out of a bad case of wishful thinking. But the closer he came the faster her heart began to beat until it was even louder than the sound of the waves crashing against the shore.

She wanted to turn and walk back the other way. That's what her head was telling her to do but for some reason her feet weren't co-operating. They were stuck in the soft sand as if it had suddenly turned into concrete.

'Lexi,' Sam said, coming to stand in front of her.

She gave him a brittle look. 'I don't have anything to say to you.'

'Maybe not, but I have something to say to you.'

She rolled her eyes and started walking away. 'I can just imagine what it is,' she said, her bare feet making squeaking noises on the pristine sand. 'You want me to have a sordid little affair with you until you find someone else who interests you more.'

'No,' Sam said. 'That's not what I want to say. Anyway, no one interests me more than you do.'

'Sure, and I believe you,' Lexi said, throwing him a fulminating look over her shoulder.

Sam looked at her flushed features. Her long blond hair was blowing across her face and she kept flicking it back with angry movements of her hands. She looked like a mermaid. His very own gorgeous sea nymph. How could he have ever imagined his life without her in it? 'Don't you want to hear what I've come all this way to say?' he asked.

She frowned at him furiously. 'You think I would

agree to have a relationship with you after the way you treated me?'

'You took me by surprise, turning up at the marina like that,' he said. 'I wasn't prepared. I needed more time to think things over.'

'*I* took you by surprise?' she flashed back. 'I thought you were going to welcome me with open arms and instead you sent me away as if I was nothing to you but an annoying little tramp.'

'I know,' Sam said. 'It was unforgiveable.'

'You've got *that* right, country boy,' she said, stomping away again.

Sam had to trot to keep up. He caught one of her arms and turned her round to face him. 'Lexi—'

'If you don't let me go this instant I'll scream for the lifeguard,' she said. 'I'll say you're attacking me. I'll tell him you're a stalker. I'll tell him you've been calling me about a hundred times and never saying anything, not a single word. I'll tell him…I'll tell him you broke my heart and I'll probably never ever be happy again…' She choked back a little sob.

Sam looked at her with melting eyes. 'Lexi, darling,' he said, holding her close so she couldn't run away again. 'You know how hopeless I am with words. I can only manage one or two when I'm feeling under pressure. I just clam up. But there are three words I wanted to say to your face. I love you.'

'No, you don't.' Her eyes flashed at him. 'I bet you're just saying that to get me back into your bed.'

Sam lifted her chin, a soft smile playing about his mouth. 'I knew you probably wouldn't believe me so that's why I have a back-up plan.'

Lexi wrinkled her forehead. 'A…a what?'

Sam turned her so she was facing the ocean. There

was a yacht out behind the small breakers. Lexi could just make out the name on the side—*Whispering Waves*. 'You sailed all the way up here?' she asked, looking back at him.

'Yeah,' he said. 'What do you say to a few days out there all by ourselves? You, me and the wind.'

Lexi pulled out of his hold. 'I think I'll pass,' she said stiffly, and continued walking.

'Darling, will you just give me a couple of minutes of your time?' he said. 'I have to get back to my yacht before my dad sails it into a reef or something.'

Lexi stopped and looked at him. 'Your dad's out there?'

'Yeah,' he said. 'One of us had to man the boat. I could hardly send him along the beach to ask you to marry me.'

She looked at him with her head at a wary angle. 'What did you say?'

Sam smiled at her. 'Will you marry me, Lexi?'

Lexi's eyes started to tear up. 'You want to marry me?' she asked in a choked-up voice

'Sure do,' he said. 'And I want everyone to know.' He turned her to face the sea. 'See?'

Lexi looked at the mainsail of Sam's yacht as the wind filled it, revealing the words in large blue letters: *Will you marry me, Lexi?*

'So what do you say, darling?' Sam asked. 'Will you be my wife and the mother of my babies? I don't care how many we have. I just know I want to have them with you.'

Lexi blinked back tears, her throat so tight with emotion she could barely speak. 'Yes,' she said, throwing herself into his arms. 'Yes!'

Sam swung her around, holding her tightly against

his body. 'Thank heaven,' he said. 'You had me worried there for a moment.'

Lexi slipped down his body to look up at him. 'What changed your mind? I thought you never wanted to get married? I thought you didn't believe you could love someone enough to spend your whole life with them.'

He cupped her face in his hands. 'I watched my father grieve for my mother for twenty years. I swore I would never love someone that much. But what I've realised is you can never love someone too much.' He pressed a gentle kiss to her mouth. 'You've taught me that, Lexi. Life is about loving with your whole being, not just part of yourself. And I want to spend the rest of my life loving you like that—totally, completely, absolutely.'

Lexi smiled as she looked into his soft dark brown eyes. 'How long do you think your father can handle that boat without you?' she asked.

'Not very long,' Sam said. 'Why?'

She looped her arms around his neck. 'Because I have something to see to first, that's why.'

'Oh?' he said. 'What's that?'

'This,' she said and pressed her mouth to his.

* * * * *

SYDNEY HARBOUR HOSPITAL: HOSPITAL: BELLA'S WISHLIST

BY
EMILY FORBES

To Marion, Alison, Amy, Fiona, Melanie, Fi and Carol.
Thank you for making this such a wonderful experience.
It was an absolute pleasure working with you all!
And to Lucy and Flo, thank you both for all your hard
work in making this series something we can
all be proud of.

PROLOGUE

'LEXI, please, can't you do this for me?' Bella Lockheart begged her younger sister.

Bella was feeling dreadful. Her chest was hurting and every breath she took was a struggle. Her temperature was escalating with every passing minute and it felt as though her forehead was on fire. She wanted to be upstairs, in bed, not sitting at one end of her father's massive dining room table that comfortably seated eighteen people. She wanted to close her eyes and sleep. The only reason she'd agreed to meet with her sisters was because she wanted the chance to try to persuade Lexi to do this one thing for her.

Lexi was sitting at the head of the table with Bella on her left and their older sister Evie on her right. Evie had joined them at Lexi's invitation to begin planning what Lexi described as 'Sydney's society wedding of the decade' and, knowing Lexi and her talent for planning events, her wedding to cardiothoracic surgeon Sam Bailey would be one of the most spectacular events Sydney had witnessed for some time. That was unsurprising really—Lexi had plenty of experience as she was employed by her father's multi-million-dollar empire to run the events side of his company, and Lexi generally got what she wanted. Bella had some doubts about whether Sam was as keen on the idea of a huge wedding as Lexi was but if she'd learnt anything about Sam since he'd proposed to her sister it was that he wouldn't sweat the small stuff, and if an enormous wedding made Lexi happy, that's what she would get. Their father would never quibble either; nothing was ever too much trouble, expense or fuss for Lexi. Richard loved an extravaganza as much as Lexi did.

Bella knew the only way to get Lexi to move quickly on the wedding was to play the only card she had. 'I want to see you get married and the longer you wait the less chance I'll have of being there. Please.'

They all knew the odds of Bella seeing her next birthday weren't good but Bella had *never* played this card before. Not with her father, who had pretty much ignored her for her entire life, or with her mother, who couldn't cope and had replaced her family with bottles of gin, or with her sisters, who had always been there to support and protect her. But she figured if there ever was a time to play this card, it was now.

As Bella watched Lexi, waiting for her response, she was aware that Evie had stopped flicking through the pile of bridal magazines and was watching them both. The highly polished wood surface of the antique table reflected their images. The golden highlights in Evie's brown hair shone in the surface of the table and Lexi's platinum-blonde hair glowed in the reflection, while the dark auburn of Bella's curly locks was absorbed into the wood, making her seem dimmer in comparison. A sigh escaped Bella's lips. Seeing herself as a duller reflection of her sisters was nothing new. She'd had twenty-six years to get used to the idea that she wasn't as beautiful, intelligent or amusing as her two sisters, although she hoped that her kind heart went some way towards redeeming her character.

Not that it seemed to count for anything as far as her parents were concerned. She'd given up trying to mend those relationships, although she was blowed if she would give up on her sisters. They were the most important people in her world and she did not intend to miss out on seeing her younger sister get married. She *had* to convince Lexi to set a date for her wedding and make it soon. She'd missed out on an awful lot of things in her relatively short life and there was no way she was going to sit back and miss out on this. Lexi had to listen to her.

'You only need a month and a day to register. You could be married before Christmas,' she insisted.

'I need time,' Lexi replied.

Time. The one thing Bella didn't have. She knew that. Lexi knew it too, so why wouldn't she agree?

'Time for what?' Bella countered. 'I can't see why you'd want to wait. If I had the chance to get married, I'd grab it.'

All three of them knew what a romantic Bella was. Her favourite pastime was watching romantic movies, comedies, dramas, anything, as long as it had a happy ending. It was looking increasingly unlikely that she would get her own happy ending so she had to enjoy other people's. She adored weddings, she'd been glued to the television for the most recent British Royal wedding and avidly followed the lives of modern-day princesses in the magazines. But her own sister's happy ending was bound to be so much better than anything she could watch on television. Surely Lexi couldn't deny her this?

'I want time to find the perfect dress,' Lexi said.

'I'll design you the perfect dress.' Normally Bella would offer to make it too, but she knew she'd never have time to design and make a wedding dress, not if she wanted the wedding to take place this year. In a parallel universe her dream was to be a fashion designer and to see her sister walk down the aisle in something she'd created would be the icing on the cake for a romantic like her. But she'd have to settle for designing the dress and have someone else make it. Their father would probably fly Lexi to Hong Kong or even Paris to get it made. Money was no object. Richard Lockheart was phenomenally wealthy and Lexi was the apple of his eye. Everybody knew that.

'Look,' Bella said as she opened the sketch book that was lying on the table in front of her. Her sketch book was never far from her side. She turned some pages and then spun the book to face Lexi. 'I've already started.' The large page was covered with half a dozen wedding dresses—a halterneck, a strapless version, some with full skirts, some in figure-skimming satin. 'You just need to tell me which bits you like and I promise you'll be the most beautiful bride but, please, don't wait too long. You *know* time is running out for me, Sam told you that. If you won't listen to me, would you at least listen to him?' Bella paused to catch her breath. She could feel her chest tightening and could hear herself wheezing. 'What do you think, Evie? You agree with me, don't you?'

'I think you have a valid point but it is Lexi and Sam's decision. It's their wedding.' Bella would have argued if she'd had the breath to spare but the end of Evie's answer was partially drowned out by a coughing fit. Bella's slim frame shook with each spasm.

Lexi stood up. 'I'll get you a glass of water.'

'It's all right,' Bella replied as the coughs subsided and she caught her breath, 'I can get it.' She pushed her chair back from the table and stood. She looked at Evie and dipped her head slightly towards Lexi, silently imploring Evie to intercede on her behalf. She knew Evie would understand the signal. Having spent so much of their life relying on each other, all three sisters could read each other instinctively.

'Perhaps you should talk it over with Sam,' Bella heard

Evie suggest as she went to the kitchen to pour herself a glass of water and mix up her salt replacement solution. She was feeling quite feverish now and she knew she was in danger of dehydrating more rapidly than usual if she was running a temperature.

Evie waited until Bella had time to reach the kitchen and be out of earshot. As so often happened, her younger sisters deferred to her to solve any difference of opinion between them. At five years older than Bella and seven years older than Lexi she had taken over mothering duties at the tender age of nine when the girls' mother had walked out and left them with their father, to return only sporadically over the ensuing years. There had been a succession of nannies, with varying degrees of success, and Evie had adopted the role of mother and still maintained it twenty-two years later. Evie never minded the responsibility but she did wonder why she needed to act as referee in this case. Why was Lexi so resistant to Bella's request?

'What's the problem, Lex? You know Bella's right. She might not be around in six months. Why do you want to wait?'

Lexi's deep blue eyes shimmered with unshed tears. She fidgeted with Bella's sketch book, which lay on the table in front of her, absentmindedly doodling on the clean pages. 'I can't think like that. I can't stand the thought of Bella not being here.'

'That's why I think you should consider getting married sooner rather than later.'

'But what if we set a date that's soon and Bella gets sick again? She could be in hospital on the day of the wedding. Or what if she's in surgery? If I wait until Bella is okay, we'll all get a happy ending.'

'But Bella might not get her happy ending. You know

that, don't you?' Evie said gently. 'If you wait, Bella might not be there anyway. She's only asking you for one thing.'

Lexi was shaking her head. 'But if I give in then that's like admitting I think she's not going to make it. I don't want to think about her dying. I can't.'

Evie knew Lexi hated the idea of death. She'd been through one traumatic loss already in her life, when she'd terminated a pregnancy, and that made this situation more difficult for her. But she couldn't let her sister bury her head in the sand. Evie had to get her to face reality. 'Please, just agree to talk to Sam about it. If you set a date and you need to change it to accommodate Bella, is that such a big deal? It's certainly not impossible.' Sam knew what Bella's chances were better than anyone, Evie thought. As Bella's specialist and Lexi's fiancé, maybe he would have more success in persuading Lexi.

Before Lexi had a chance to agree or disagree, they were interrupted by the sound of breaking glass coming from the kitchen, followed by a loud thud as something heavy hit the floor. Then there was silence.

'Bella?' Evie and Lexi leapt from their chairs and ran to the kitchen. Broken glass was strewn over the marble bench tops but Bella was nowhere to be seen. Evie raced around the island bench and found Bella collapsed on the tiles surrounded by the remnants of the glass cupboard.

'Bella!' Evie knelt beside her sister, oblivious to the shards of glass that littered the floor. To her relief she could see that Bella was conscious and breathing. 'What happened? Are you hurt?'

Bella's grey eyes were enormous in her pale face. 'Dizzy.' Her words were laboured. 'Cramp.' She was obviously having difficulty with her breathing. 'I grabbed the shelf when I fell. Sorry.'

'Don't worry about the glasses,' Evie said as she brushed

Bella's auburn curls from her face. Her skin was flushed and her forehead was hot. Feverish.

Bella's powdered drink mixture that she used for salt replacement sat on the bench. Evie picked up Bella's wrist and took her pulse, counting the seconds. Her pulse was rapid and Bella's skin under her fingers was dry and lacking its normal elasticity.

Evie ran through Bella's symptoms in her head. A high temperature, dizziness, cramping, rapid pulse rate. 'You're dehydrated,' she said. 'Why didn't you tell us you weren't feeling well?'

Why hadn't she noticed something? Evie accused herself. *She was a doctor, for goodness' sake.*

She knew she'd been distracted by the tension between Lexi and Bella but she still should have known something was wrong. Bella's behaviour should have alerted her. She wasn't normally so insistent or stubborn.

But that didn't explain why she hadn't told them she was feeling unwell. Evie could only assume it was because she didn't want to make a fuss. That was typical of Bella. She'd been unwell more frequently than usual over the past few months and Evie knew she would be trying to pretend everything was normal. But they all knew it wasn't. They all knew Bella's health was going downhill and Evie was furious with herself for not noticing the signs tonight. But there was no time to berate herself now. They needed to get Bella treated, she needed to be in hospital.

'Lexi, ring Sam and tell him to meet us at the hospital,' Evie instructed. 'I'll call an ambulance and then see if you can get a drink into Bella. She needs fluids.'

CHAPTER ONE

BELLA lay on the stretcher in the rear of the ambulance. She was vaguely aware of her surroundings but the activity felt like it was going on around her, independent of her, even though she knew it all related to her. The emergency lights were flashing, it was dark outside and the lights were re-flecting back into the interior of the ambulance, bouncing off the walls. The siren was silent, the traffic a constant background noise. Evie was with her in the ambulance, she could hear her talking with the paramedic. Bella could feel the pressure of the oxygen mask on her face, the grip of the oximeter on her finger, the sting of the IV drip in her elbow. She saw Evie take out her phone and heard her leaving a message for their father.

She was hot and sweaty, flushed with a fever and tired, so tired. She wondered what it would be like just to close her eyes and drift off. To never wake again. But she wasn't ready. There were still things she wanted to do and things she wanted to see.

She felt the ambulance come to a halt and the flashing red and blue lights were replaced by harsh fluorescent strip lighting. She knew where they were—in the emer-gency drop-off zone at Sydney Harbour Hospital. This was where she had spent countless days and nights over the past twenty-six years. It was the closest hospital to the Lockheart family home in the north shore suburb of Mosman and the cardiothoracic ward had become as familiar to Bella as her own bedroom.

But her connection to the hospital went beyond that of a patient. Her great-grandfather had been one of the original founders of the hospital and it was also where Evie worked. Bella couldn't fault the medical care she received here, she just wished she hadn't had to spend so much of her life within these walls.

The rear doors swung open and Bella felt the stretcher moving as she was pulled from the ambulance. A familiar face loomed over her. Sam Bailey, the hospital's newest cardiothoracic surgeon and next big thing, was smiling down at her.

'There you are,' he said. 'I've been stalking the ambulances, waiting for you.'

Sam was her new specialist, but again the connection didn't end there. He was engaged to Lexi, which also made him her future brother-in-law.

Bella tried to smile then realised it wasn't worth the effort as the oxygen mask was hiding her face and she was sure her smile would look more like a grimace. Sam squeezed her hand before he began talking to Evie and the paramedics, getting an update on her condition. Bella lay silently and concentrated on breathing in lungfuls of oxygen. She wasn't required to contribute. She wasn't required to do anything except keep breathing. 'I've notified Cardiothoracics, we'll take her straight up there,' Sam was saying, and Bella closed her eyes against the glare of the fluorescent lights as they began to wheel her inside.

'Evie? Is everything okay?'

Bella heard a familiar voice. She recognised it but her brain was sluggish and she was unable to put a face to the voice. If she opened her eyes she'd solve the mystery but that was too much effort.

'Charlie!'

Evie's reply jogged her memory and Bella was glad she'd kept her eyes closed.

Dr Charlie Maxwell was one of Evie's closest friends and definitely one of her cutest! Bella idolised him. But she kept her eyes closed, not wanting him to see her like this. She pretended that if she couldn't see him, he wouldn't be able to see her.

Charlie was too gorgeous for his own good and she knew she wasn't the only one who thought so. He had a reputation as a charmer and he'd cut a swathe through the female nurses and doctors at Sydney Harbour Hospital and most probably further afield too. Bella had long worshipped him from afar, knowing he'd never look twice at her, certain he saw her just as his friend's little sister. This wasn't a fairy-tale where the handsome prince would suddenly fall in love with the plain girl and sweep her off her feet. This was real life and the safest thing for her to do was to keep her eyes closed and wait for him to go away. That way there was less chance of her embarrassing herself.

'Is everything all right?' he repeated.

'No, not really. It's Bella.'

That was the last thing Bella heard before the paramedics pushed her into the hospital and Evie's voice faded.

Stay with me, Bella wanted to say. She didn't want to be alone even though she knew Evie wouldn't be far behind her.

Bella? Charlie took a second look at the figure on the stretcher. Her face was obscured by the oxygen mask but her hair was distinctive. It could only be Bella, but he hadn't recognised her at first. She had the same curly, dark auburn hair, the same pale, almost translucent skin, but she was thin, painfully thin. What had happened to her?

Charlie knew Bella had a rough time with her cystic fibrosis. She'd had a higher than average number of hospital admissions, but he'd never seen her looking as sick as she looked now.

'What's going on?'

'She's got a high temperature and she's badly dehydrated. I suspect she has another chest infection,' Evie replied.

'Is there anything I can do?' He knew it was unlikely but he wanted to at least offer his help.

Evie shook her head and he could see tears in her eyes. He and Evie had been friends for almost ten years and she was normally so strong, so resilient. Things must be grim.

'You'd better catch up with her but call me if there's anything I can do.' He leant down and gave Evie a quick kiss on the cheek. 'I'll drop into the ward in the morning.'

He watched Evie as she hurried after Bella's stretcher and wished he could offer more than just support. He viewed all three of the Lockheart sisters as his surrogate family. He knew they had a lack of family support and he knew how much of the burden of worry Evie carried on her slim shoulders. He would do what he could to help but he wished there was something more proactive that he could do for Bella too. But he was an orthopaedic surgeon. He was not what she needed.

Evie caught up to Sam and Bella as they waited for the lift. The next half-hour was frantic as Sam ordered a battery of tests and examined Bella. Lexi had driven to the hospital and she joined Evie on the cardiothoracic ward to wait. Together they tried to stay out of Sam's way. Evie had to remind herself she was Bella's sister now, not her doctor.

Sam appeared from Bella's room and motioned for them to join him. 'I'm admitting Bella. She has a temp of thirty-nine point five, which I suspect is the result of another chest infection, and she's lost three kilograms since her last admission. She was supposed to be putting on weight but her BMI is down to seventeen.'

Evie knew Bella was thin. Too thin. Her body mass index should be at least nineteen—although this would still only put her at the bottom end of normal. Evie knew it was difficult for Bella to put on weight, all cystic fibrosis sufferers had the same problem, but Bella should weigh five or six kilograms more than she currently did. Being underweight made it more difficult to fight infection and increased her chances of ending up back in hospital. Which was exactly what had happened.

'Is your father coming in?' Sam asked.

Evie shrugged. Sam's guess was as good as anyone's. 'I've just tried to get in touch with him again. I've left two messages but I don't know where he is.'

She kept one eye on Bella, wondering how she would react to the news that her father was uncontactable. Bella watched her, her grey eyes huge and pensive, but she didn't look surprised. Evie supposed the news didn't surprise any of them. 'Lexi, do you have any other way of contacting him?' Lexi worked with their father so it was possible she would know where to find him.

Lexi shook her head. 'No, he was going out to dinner but it was private, not business related, so I don't know any more details.'

Evie sighed. If Richard was out with one of his female 'acquaintances' it was highly unlikely that he'd answer his phone. It was also highly unlikely that he'd even make it home tonight, and if he did Evie wondered whether he'd even notice that Bella, and possibly Lexi, weren't in their beds.

'Do you think we need to try to find him?' she asked. Was Sam telling them it was important for Richard to get into the hospital tonight or did they have some time up their sleeves?

Sam was shaking his head and Evie breathed a sigh of relief. He couldn't think it was that urgent. 'I just want to try to get Bella stabilised tonight,' he said. 'I'll start a course of IV antibiotics and get her rehydrated. We'll have to see how that goes but this is now her third admission this year. To be honest, things are heading downhill, but she'll make it through the night. I'm sure your father will turn up eventually.'

Until then Evie would stay by Bella's side. Even when Richard decided to join them Evie knew that she and Lexi would be Bella's main support team. She wished things were different, for Bella's sake, but their father and Bella had always had a difficult relationship, he'd never coped very well with his second daughter or her illness.

Evie's own relationship with her father had been tainted by the departure of their mother. Something Evie held her father partially responsible for. She knew her mother had made her own choices but she felt that he could have been more supportive, offered more assistance, made more of an effort to convince her to stay. If he had, the bulk of the responsibility of raising her younger siblings wouldn't have fallen to Evie and she would have had a very different childhood.

But the Lockheart family dynamics weren't going to change overnight and once again Evie opted to set up a folding bed in Bella's room. She sent Lexi home with Sam but she wasn't going to leave Bella alone. She hoped Sam was right, she hoped Bella would make it through the night, but what if he was wrong? Doctors had been wrong before. She knew that better than anybody.

Bella had been awake since the crack of dawn, woken by the nurse who'd come in to take her six-o'clock obs, although in reality she felt as though she'd been awake most of the night. She always slept badly in hospital. Struggling for every breath ruined a good sleep, not to mention two-hourly obs and the fact she was always cold.

Evie had been by her side all night and she'd waited until Lexi arrived before disappearing in search of coffee while promising to be back in time for Sam's early-morning consult.

Evie and Lexi were the two constants in Bella's life. The two people she knew she would always be able to rely on. She knew she was lucky to have them and she'd given up waiting for her parents to give her the same support. But it didn't stop her wishing that things were different. She didn't like to be so dependent on her sisters but it was the way it had always been. She knew her illness was a strain on everybody but she also knew she wouldn't cope without the love and support of her siblings. She wondered sometimes how they managed, especially Evie, who traded looking after Bella for looking after all her other patients at the hospital. Bella knew Evie had a shift in Emergency today but she had no idea how her sister would carry out such a demanding job after spending the night in a chair by her bed. She hoped Evie didn't get any complicated cases.

'I brought something to brighten your day,' Evie said when she returned, carrying a tray of coffee and hot chocolate for her sisters. Bella felt her eyes widen in surprise; Evie wasn't talking about the drinks.

'Charlie Maxwell,' Lexi said in greeting. 'I'd recognise that bald head anywhere.'

Charlie Maxwell was in her room! Bella knew she was staring and she could hear the 'beep beep' of the heart-rate monitor attached to her chest escalate as her autonomic nervous system responded to his presence. Thank goodness he didn't seem to notice. He wasn't looking at her, his attention focussed on Lexi. Bella was used to that. People always noticed Lexi and Evie before they noticed her, and even though she wished, on the odd occasion, that someone would notice her first, today she was pleased to be ignored as it gave her time to try to get her nerves under control.

'Morning, Lexi,' Charlie said with a grin. 'And for your information, I'm not bald,' he protested. 'I do this on purpose. It stops the women from being jealous of my golden locks.'

'You'd have to be the only bloke I know who voluntarily shaves his head,' Lexi retorted, before Evie interrupted them.

'Bella, you remember Charlie, don't you?' she asked as she handed Bella a hot chocolate.

Who could forget him? Bella thought. She knew she never would, not in a million years. He looked as fit, healthy and fabulous as always. Charlie had been a professional surfer in a past life and he certainly had the body of an athlete. Muscular, tanned and perfectly proportioned, he was wearing a white shirt and Bella could see the definition of his biceps and pectoral muscles through the thin fabric. She swallowed hard as she tried to get her mouth to work but she was short of breath and her mouth was dry and parched. Unable to form any words, she nodded instead.

'*Ciao*, Bella,' Charlie said.

He always greeted her in the same way and it never failed to make her feel special, even though she didn't flatter herself that she was the only one on the receiving end of his charm. But therein lay even more of his appeal. He was one of the few people who didn't treat her any differently because of her medical condition. He was a serial flirt and he gave her the same attention he gave to every woman who crossed his path, and to Bella, who was used to either being shielded or ignored, Charlie's attention was a rare delight.

He winked at her and her heart rate jumped again. She felt herself blush and cursed her fair skin.

'How are you feeling?' he asked.

'I've had better days,' she said, finally managing to get some words out. But it wasn't the cystic fibrosis making her short of breath, it was Charlie. She was always shy around anyone other than family and even though Charlie behaved like family he was so damn sexy she'd never managed to overcome her self-consciousness around him, especially when other people were within earshot. One on one she was more comfortable but with other ears around she always worried about making a fool of herself.

He was gorgeous and she always felt so plain by comparison. His facial features combined so perfectly together she'd never really noticed that he shaved his head. Of course she'd noticed he was bald but she'd never wondered about the reality behind it, she was too busy being mesmerised by his other physical attributes—his chocolate-brown eyes that she felt she could melt into, his smooth, tanned skin, which provided the perfect foil for straight, white teeth, even his small, neat ears all combined into an appealing package. But his best feature was his mouth. She could visualise him with sun-bleached surfie hair but it was irrelevant really because her attention was constantly drawn to his lips. They were plump and delicious, full but not hard like a collagen-injected pout, they were juicy and soft, almost too soft for such a masculine face. He was smiling at her, a gorgeous smile, full and open and honest. You'd have to be dead not to be affected by his smile and while she wasn't feeling anywhere near one hundred per cent healthy, she wasn't dead yet.

'So Evie tells me,' Charlie replied, 'but if there's anything you need, just ask me. I know how to make things happen around here.'

He winked at her again and Bella didn't doubt for one minute that Charlie could get whatever he wanted both inside the hospital and out. She knew his reputation as a charmer, she'd heard the nurses talk about him during her numerous admissions, and she knew they competed for his affections and attentions. The combination of his wicked sense of humour, his infectious smile, his gentle nature and his hardened muscles had the female staff members regularly flustered, and Bella herself was no exception.

As far as she knew, only Evie seemed immune to Charlie's charm. Their ten-year friendship had only ever been platonic and for that Bella was grateful. It meant she was free to adore him without feeling as if she was invading her sister's territory. She knew that from the day Evie had first met Charlie she'd thought of him as the older brother she wished she'd had. But Bella's thoughts towards Charlie were far from familial—although she'd never be brave enough to flirt with him, she knew she wasn't experienced enough to handle Charlie Maxwell. So she just nodded dumbly in reply. She'd lost the capacity to speak again, completely tongue-tied at the thought of Charlie doing things for her. Fortunately Sam's arrival saved her from needing to answer. He was followed by a nurse and a couple of interns and suddenly her room was overflowing with people.

A ninth person came into the room and Bella saw Evie's double-take. It was their father.

Bella had assumed Evie had gotten in touch with him during the night, or vice versa, but looking at Evie's expression now it was obvious she'd heard nothing back and hadn't been expecting him.

He looked tired and drawn. Bella wished she could pretend he'd lost sleep worrying about her, his middle daughter, but she knew it was far more likely to be a result of a late night of a different kind. She waited for her father to push through the crowd gathered at the foot of her bed but of course he didn't. He remained standing just inside the doorway, separate and apart from his family. She sighed, wishing for the thousandth time that things were different. At least he was here, which was more than Bella could say for her mother. She nodded in greeting and then proceeded to ignore him as her sisters took up positions on the bed on either side of her. She was tired of always being the one who reached out to make a connection with her father.

Evie took her hand and Bella relaxed, knowing her sisters would try to protect her from harm. Bella saw Sam acknowledge Richard's arrival with a nod of his own before he began his consult. He checked Bella's vital signs, checked her obs, listened to her chest and generally prodded and poked while she tried to pretend she wasn't surrounded by people. The procedure was familiar to her but that didn't make it any less embarrassing. Once he'd finished he spoke to Bella as though they were the only two in the room.

'You've lost weight since I last examined you, that's not what we were hoping for, your admissions are getting more frequent and your lung function tests are down.' Sam was ticking things off on his fingers as he recited the list.

'Is there any good news?' Bella asked hopefully.

'One positive note is that you've made some improvement overnight. You've rehydrated and your temperature has come down but it's still higher than I'd like. You're showing some resistance to the antibiotics and I've had to increase the dosage to try to get your chest infection under control. Individually all these things are not so concerning but combined it means I need to reassess your management.' He paused briefly and Bella knew what he would say next. 'It's time for the next stage.'

Bella couldn't speak. This wasn't unexpected but she didn't know what to say. Sam was watching her, waiting for her to acknowledge his words, and she thought she nodded in response but she couldn't be sure.

Sam looked away from her now, turning to the members of her family, stopping briefly at each and every one as he spoke. 'I know we've talked about this before but the time has come. Bella needs a lung transplant now. She is already on the active transplant list but I have revised her status. This will move her up the list and means she will get the next pair of suitable lungs.'

Bella tightened her grip on Evie's hand. This was really happening. During her last hospital admission Sam had told her she would need a transplant eventually. That was the way things went with cystic fibrosis. But eventually had become now. Her lungs were officially failing.

Out of the corner of her eye she saw Richard collapse into a chair as though his legs would no longer support him. His response surprised her. Her father was a man of action, he always had a solution for everything, a way to deal with everything—except when it came to her and her mother—but he never normally showed any sign of weakness. Was he actually concerned for her? Bella knew there was nothing he could do for her now but she couldn't ever recall seeing him flummoxed. Was he concerned or was he confused?

'What do we do while we wait?' Lexi's voice was unexpectedly loud in her ear and Bella jumped.

'In the meantime, we start the pre-op processes. Physical tests, including blood work and organ function tests, as well as psych assessments,' Sam replied.

'What does the surgery involve?' Richard asked, and his question answered Bella's own. His tone said this was a question from a man who wanted information and clarification, not a question from a concerned father.

'Obviously it is major surgery. Bella will be several hours in Theatre. It can take up to twelve hours. She will be placed on a heart bypass machine while both lungs are transplanted via an incision across the bottom of the diaphragm, then she will be transferred to ICU for at least twenty-four hours and then back to the cardiothoracic surgical ward.'

'What are the survival rates?' As was his style her father was keeping any emotion out of the equation. He preferred to deal with the facts and figures.

'The figures are good. Currently eighty-five per cent of people undergoing bilateral, sequential lung transplants in Australia survive one year and sixty per cent are still alive after five years.'

Bella heard a sharp intake of breath. For a moment she thought she'd made the sound but then she realised it had come from Lexi.

Bella knew the odds. She'd lived and breathed them since her last admission. She knew the statistics were good, for the short term at least, but she also knew that to those who hadn't spent countless hours doing the research she'd done, the odds didn't sound that fantastic.

'These stats are not just for CF sufferers,' Sam clarified. 'They're for everybody and Bella has age on her side. Although she will still have cystic fibrosis, it won't be in her lungs.' Sam looked directly at Bella. 'If your lungs are functioning properly, you should notice a far improved quality of life. You'll have more energy, you should gain weight and you'll be able to be more active.'

'What do you mean, she'll still have CF?' Richard was frowning.

'Bella's lungs will be clear but she will still have CF in her pancreas, sweat glands and reproductive tract. She will still need her enzyme-replacement medication and she will start a course of anti-rejection medication. The transplant is not a cure for the disease, it just eliminates the disease from her lungs, and will hopefully extend her life.' Sam turned to face her. 'Bella, do you have any questions?'

She still hadn't uttered a word.

'How long do I have?'

'A month, maybe two.' Sam's voice was deep and soft but his words were clear and distinct in the absolute silence of the room.

It was already November. Would she see another Christmas?

'What choice do I have?'

Her question put an immediate and definite end to the silence. Lexi started to cry and Evie started to reason with Bella. They both knew her choices were limited.

Bella held up one hand, asking Evie to wait. 'It was just a question,' she said. 'I didn't say I won't have a transplant, I just wanted to hear if I have any other options.'

'Of course you have a choice,' Sam said, 'it's your body. You can choose to have a transplant if we find a suitable donor or you can choose not to. But you don't have any other options.' He spoke to her as though they were alone in the room. 'It's a big decision and I know how daunting this can be but ultimately I wouldn't expect you to find it a hard decision to make. The consequences of your decision are self-evident. You're free to talk to the psychologists and the transplant team in more detail, you can ask them anything you want or need to know, but you don't have a lot of time to decide. Your lungs are failing. Without a transplant you're on borrowed time.'

Borrowed time. She knew that but it made it more important than ever that she get things sorted. There were things she needed to do. She had to prioritise. She needed to think. She closed her eyes. As she'd hoped, Sam took that as a sign to usher everyone out of the room.

'Okay,' he said, 'I need to run a couple more tests and Bella needs to rest. You can come back later.'

Bella thought Lexi was going to argue but she saw her look at Sam before she said anything. Sam gave a slight shake of his head and Lexi stayed quiet. The medical team was leaving the room and Lexi and Evie kissed Bella before they followed. Charlie and Sam were the last ones remaining. Bella looked from one to the other. Charlie was wedged in next to the bathroom doorhandle, he would have to wait until everyone else had left before he'd be able to get out. She needed to ask a favour and if she was running out of time she needed to do it soon. It looked as if Charlie or Sam were her only options. Not that they were bad options. This was a topic she couldn't discuss with her sisters; she'd tried already and failed, but by the same token she didn't think it was something to discuss with Sam either.

Bella needed a sounding board. Charlie had offered his help and even though she knew this wasn't exactly what he'd pictured, perhaps he wouldn't mind. After all, this concerned Evie and he knew her better than most.

Bella hadn't seen Charlie for some time. He had been a frequent visitor to the Lockheart home but since Evie had moved out into an apartment there was no reason for Charlie to drop by. But she knew from experience that

Charlie was a good listener and he could be relied upon
for level-headed advice. She and Charlie had a history of
heart-to-hearts, albeit a very short one, and perhaps he
could help her again.

Besides, she was running out of time and options. He
would have to do.

'Charlie, could I talk to you for a second?' she asked.
She knew he saw himself as family, maybe he could do
this for her.

Bella saw Evie glance back over her shoulder as she left
the room. She'd be wondering what on earth Bella needed
to talk to Charlie about, wondering why she wasn't talking to her, but Bella knew this was one thing Evie couldn't
help her with.

CHAPTER TWO

EVIE hesitated when she heard Bella ask Charlie to stay. She wondered what that was all about but she didn't stop. She had to catch her father before he disappeared again. There were things they needed to talk about.

'Richard,' she called out to him. She hadn't called him 'Dad' since she'd started working at the Harbour Hospital. Evie's paternal great-grandfather had been instrumental in establishing the hospital and Richard was one of its biggest benefactors. Evie hadn't wanted to be accused of nepotism when she'd joined the staff. Although the Lockheart surname was a clear indication that there was a relationship there, she hadn't wanted everyone to know just how close the relationship was.

He turned and waited for her to catch up.

'Where have you been?' Evie asked. She was furious that she'd heard nothing from him all morning. 'Why didn't you return my messages?' She must have left him half a dozen in total.

'I tried. Your mobile is switched off.'

Evie knew there would be no apology. She always switched her phone off at work and Richard knew that. He could have guessed she'd be at the hospital, he could have contacted her through other avenues. 'You could have paged me.'

Never one to back down he said, 'I spoke to Lexi and came straight here. Tell me, how do we fix this? What can I do?'

'You can't buy lungs,' she replied, knowing that Richard's preferred way of dealing with things was just to throw large sums of money at a problem until it went away. That wasn't going to work this time. 'We just have to wait.'

'What is Sam doing about this?'

'There's nothing he can do other than push Bella up the list, which he has done. It's all dependent on having a suitable donor and convincing Bella to go ahead with the surgery once compatible lungs are found. All we can do is support her through this.' Her little sister was in dire straits and while Evie had known this day was inevitable it didn't make it any less heartbreaking.

She hoped Richard was listening. She hoped, for once, he could be there to support his daughter. She hoped he realised he might never get another shot at this. But she and Lexi would be there for Bella even if her parents weren't. Which brought her to the next item on her mental checklist.

'Will you tell Miranda?' Evie asked.

Evie had started calling her mother by her first name when she was fifteen, when she had finally admitted that her mother preferred her bottle of gin to her daughters. Miranda's contact with her offspring was sporadic, associated with brief periods of sobriety mostly, although there had been plenty of times when the girls had seen Miranda far from sober. But despite this Evie felt Miranda needed to know what was happening with her second daughter and she thought it was Richard's job to inform her.

Richard's expression told Evie all she needed to know but she was not going to let him out of this task. 'You need to tell her. Whether she can understand what's going on is not your problem, but she has to be told. I need to get back to work. I'll see you back here later.' Evie's final words were not a question. Someone needed to tell Richard what was required and she was happy to do that. But she'd have to wait and see if he listened.

Bella looked exhausted. She was waiflike, a pale shadow of a figure against the white hospital sheets. She was sitting up in bed and the only exception to her pallor was her auburn curls, which were vibrantly bright against the pillows that were plumped around her. Looking at her, Charlie thought she could pass for eighteen years old but he knew she was in her mid-twenties. She'd been seventeen when they'd first met, almost ten years ago, when he'd gone back to med school and found himself in Evie's class, and that would make her twenty-six now.

He waited until Bella's room had emptied itself of all the other occupants before he dragged a chair closer to the bed and sat. 'What can I do for you?' he asked. When he'd offered his help he hadn't expected there would be anything he could do, but his offer had been made in good faith and if Bella needed assistance he would do his best to give it to her.

'I need an unbiased pair of ears.'

Charlie frowned. Bella wasn't maintaining eye contact. Instead, she was fidgeting with the bed covers, repeatedly pleating them in her fingers before smoothing them out. He wondered what was bothering her. 'Is this about the transplant?'

'Sort of,' she replied.

'You *are* planning on going ahead with it?'

'Yes.' Bella nodded and her auburn curls bounced. 'But I don't want to talk to you about the actual operation or anything medical. I'm worried about Evie.' She looked up at him then but her fingers continued to fiddle with the bed sheets.

'Evie?' He'd expected that she wanted to discuss the transplant. He had expected to advise her to talk to Sam. Charlie was an orthopaedic surgeon. Lung transplants were Sam's area of expertise, not his. 'I don't understand.'

'You heard Sam, I'm on borrowed time. I'm not ready to give up yet but there's no guarantee that a suitable donor will be found in time.'

Her breathing was laboured and when she paused to catch her breath he could hear a faint wheeze. She had an oxygen tube resting on her top lip and out of habit he checked the flow and her oxygen sats on the monitor to make sure she was getting an adequate supply. The flow was fine so he returned his attention to Bella.

'If I'm running out of time,' she was saying, 'I want to make sure my sisters are okay.'

His frowned deepened. 'Sam has just told you that your last hope is to find a suitable donor for new lungs and you're worried about your sisters?' Charlie was amazed. If he were in the same situation he doubted he'd be able to think about anything except whether he was going to live or die.

Bella shrugged. 'There's nothing I can do about finding a donor but making sure Evie is okay might be something I can have some influence over.'

'What's wrong with her?' He hadn't noticed anything amiss but, to be honest, he hadn't seen a lot of Evie lately.

'I know this whole donor thing is stressing Evie out. She feels responsible for me. She always has ever since our mother walked out on us. But, really, this situation isn't unexpected, we all knew this day would come. But Evie doesn't seem to be coping as well as I would have thought.'

Bella stopped, interrupted by a coughing fit, and

Charlie could only watch as her slight frame shuddered with each spasm. She had asked him to stay behind. There must be something she needed. 'What did you want me to do?' he asked as he poured some water into a glass for her and waited while she sipped it.

'Thanks,' she said as she moistened her throat before she continued to speak in a voice that was just louder than a whisper. 'She seems on edge, which isn't like her, and she's been like that for a little while. Something is bothering her but she won't tell me what it is. Have you noticed anything?'

'I haven't seen that much of her lately,' he admitted. But if Bella was right and Evie was troubled, he was pretty sure he knew what the problem was. The sisters were extraordinarily close and he could just imagine how much this situation was tearing Evie apart. 'I imagine she's just worried about you and doesn't want to burden you with her concerns.' He wished he felt like he was doing a better job of comforting Bella but he didn't think he'd be improving her spirits with this clumsy attempt at reassurance.

'I think it's something unrelated to me,' Bella admitted.

'Like what?'

'I don't know. Sometimes it's as though she has the weight of the world on her shoulders and you know what she's like, she doesn't like to burden people with her troubles. A couple of the nurses were talking about Evie and they mentioned Finn Kennedy. I wondered if something had happened between them, something that would upset her. Have you heard anything?'

Bella's earlier nervousness had disappeared. She'd stopped fidgeting and Charlie wondered whether he'd only imagined her to be on edge. He shook his head. 'I've heard nothing. There's been the usual gossip about the staff and usual complaints about the doctors' egos, but I've heard nothing about Evie specifically.'

'Will you promise me that if anything happens to me, you'll look out for her?' Bella asked. 'She needs somebody to take care of her and she's so independent, which makes it tough. At least she might let you close.'

Charlie nodded. 'I promise I'll make sure she's okay.' He could do that. He wished he could tell Bella that she'd be able to keep an eye on Evie herself but they both knew that might not be the case. They both knew what the reality was.

He could hear Bella wheezing as she breathed and he knew she needed to rest. He should leave and let her recover but he needed to know that everything was under control first. 'Is anything else bothering you?' he asked.

'Well, I also want to see Lexi happily married to Sam but I don't think you can help me there.' Bella smiled and Charlie caught a glimpse of humour despite her circumstances.

'Why wouldn't they get married?' he asked.

Bella shook her head. 'I'm sure they will but I want to be there when they do. Lexi wants time to organise a huge circus, and I know it's her wedding…' She smiled. 'Their wedding,' she corrected, 'but I wish she'd agree to hurry things up. I don't want to miss out.'

Her smile had gone and the tension had returned to her shoulders. She had the bed sheet bunched up tight in her right hand and her knuckles were white with the effort. Maybe it had been stress he'd been witnessing all along.

Charlie wished again that there was something he could do to reassure her. 'You need to be positive. You have to believe you will get a second chance.' He knew his words were hopelessly inadequate but he was out of his depth.

'All right, I'll go along with your fairy-tale for now,'

Bella replied. 'Let's say a donor is found in time, before Lexi and Sam have a chance to get married. What if something happens to me during the surgery? That's a risk too. Sam is my surgeon. How do you think that will affect their relationship? I know the idea of me dying terrifies Lexi but if they're already married they'll have to get past it, but if they're not...' Bella paused and shrugged her bony shoulders. 'I don't want to be responsible for something happening and coming between them.'

'How can what happens in surgery be your responsibility?'

'It's my decision to have the surgery and the other alternative if something goes wrong is for it to be Sam's responsibility. If I don't have the surgery then that pressure is removed.'

'If you don't have the surgery, you'll die.' Charlie knew he was being blunt but he also knew Bella understood the facts. 'It's Sam's job to make sure nothing happens to you. He's a surgeon, that goes with the territory.'

'Don't get me wrong. If a donor is found, I will have the transplant, but I'd just prefer it if Lexi and Sam were married first. Does that make sense?'

Charlie nodded. In some strange roundabout way it did make perfect sense. He could understand her logic. 'I assume you've spoken to Lexi about this?'

She nodded. 'But Lexi has a tendency to get her own way and she wants it all to be perfect. In Lexi's mind the wedding will happen when I've had a transplant and life is going on for everyone just as it should. She won't consider the possibility that I might not make it. She won't admit that waiting might mean she doesn't get perfection. She thinks if she ignores the facts, it'll all go away. She thinks wishing it will make it so. I don't want to make a fuss but it's a big deal to me.'

'What about having someone else perform the surgery? Someone other than Sam?'

'Like who?' Bella asked. 'Evie told me Sam is one of the best. If I'm going to have a lung transplant, I want the best odds I can get.'

Charlie thought about Bella's options. Finn Kennedy, Head of Surgery at Sydney Harbour Hospital, was one of the best cardiac surgeons in Australia but he wasn't a heart-lung specialist. If Charlie had needed heart surgery, he'd happily choose Finn to operate on him, but if he needed a lung transplant his money would be on Sam.

'I guess Sam is your man,' he agreed. 'But if Lexi isn't listening, why don't you talk to Sam? See if you can get him to persuade Lexi to speed things up. Get him to explain the urgency to her.'

Bella nodded. 'That makes sense. I wanted Lexi to talk to Sam about it but I don't think she will. Maybe I should approach it from the other angle, from Sam's side.'

Charlie watched as Bella's fist relaxed and her fingers uncurled, releasing the bed sheet. Perhaps his advice had been more effective than he'd anticipated. Could he leave her to rest? 'So you'll talk to Sam?'

'I guess.'

'Shall I come back tomorrow, check up on you?'

'You don't need to do that.'

'Why not? I can be your conscience, make sure you've spoken to Sam. And once you've got your sisters' lives sorted out, I'm interested to know what you want for you.'

'Me?' Her tone suggested she hadn't given any thought to herself and Charlie was astonished by her undemanding, unselfish attitude.

'Yes. What do *you* want?'

She frowned as if she'd never given any consideration to her own desires and her grey eyes darkened. 'Nothing.'

* * *

How could she want nothing? Charlie wondered as he left the cardiothoracic ward. Everyone wanted something. But he supposed the only thing she wanted might be unattainable. Bella's life was in someone else's hands. Actually, it was in someone else's body. Bella's chance at life would come at the expense of someone else's. Was it better then *not* to think about it? Was it better not to put that longing into words?

And what was he doing, offering to come back tomorrow? Offering to be her conscience? Why was he getting involved?

Normally he would steer clear of any sort of involvement. He'd learnt that lesson a long time ago. He yearned for freedom and in his experience that didn't come from involvement with others. But the Lockheart sisters were different. He'd learnt *that* a long time ago too. Almost ten years ago.

Besides, it was too late to ask himself whether he should get involved. He already was. Ever since he'd first met Evie and she'd dragged him into her world and rescued him from the depths of darkness, the Lockheart sisters had become part of his life. They'd been good for him at a time when he'd been disheartened about life and his future. Evie had helped him through that period, and her situation with her parents and with Bella's illness had made his troubles seem less significant.

Now it was his turn to repay that debt. It was his turn to support the girls and he would do what he could to make sure all three of them got through this time with their spirits and hearts intact.

Bella was Evie's little sister. He would help in any way he could. He would be involved but in a practical sense only. This was one woman who was safe from his advances. Not because she was unattractive, far from it, her auburn hair, pale skin and grey eyes were a mesmerising combination, but Bella was Evie's little sister, which meant she was practically family and she was definitely off limits. But he could offer support, he knew they would need it, and that would be the extent of his involvement. She was Evie's little sister and he would be wise to remember that.

With his involvement sorted in his mind, he headed for the bank of elevators to take him up to the orthopaedic wards and was surprised to find Evie waiting in the corridor. He thought everyone would have been long gone.

'Were you waiting for me?' he asked.

Evie shook her head. 'No. I just finished talking to Richard.'

Charlie waited. He knew Evie and her father had a volatile relationship. Sometimes things went smoothly, other times not so much. He wondered how things were at the moment. 'How did that go?'

'No different from the usual,' Evie sighed. 'Bella needs his support, she needs support from all of us right now, and I don't know if any of them understand how serious this is. Richard certainly doesn't seem to grasp just how difficult it is to find suitable donors, Lexi doesn't want to think about the consequences if there is no donor, and don't get me started on my mother.'

'So that leaves you to try to hold it all together?'

'I guess so.'

The burden of Bella's illness had always fallen on Evie and it looked as though that was still the case. Sam was obviously some support but Evie's immediate family sounded as though they were all still in denial, assuming her mother even knew what was going on. He wondered if he'd been right. Was the stress upsetting Evie? Even so, Charlie knew Evie would always be there to support Bella. Maybe Bella was right—if something was bothering Evie, perhaps it was another issue.

'Walk with me?' he invited. 'I need another coffee.'

She was silent as they walked back to the doctors' lounge. He kept quiet too, thinking that if he waited she might tell him what else was on her mind, but she didn't break the silence. He shrugged as he spooned coffee into the machine. He'd never pretended to understand women. Perhaps there wasn't anything else bothering her.

Evie watched as Charlie fiddled with the coffee machine. The doctors' lounge in this ward had a proper coffee machine and the hospital's best coffee. Technically neither of them should be using it as it had been purchased by the cardiothoracic unit for their doctors, but Evie knew Charlie would get away with it, just like he got away with most things, and she wasn't about to argue.

She was silent as the machine gurgled to life. She knew Charlie was watching her, waiting for her to say something, but she didn't know what else to say. She didn't know what she could do.

'It'll be okay, Evie.'

Did he know what she was thinking?

'You don't know that,' she retorted.

'You're right, I don't, but it's all we can hope for. We have to stay positive. Bella needs that from all of us,' he said as the coffee dripped into the cups.

'What did she want to speak to you about?'

'She needed to get some things off her chest.'

'Why didn't she talk to me?' she asked, hating the petulant tone she heard in her voice, but she couldn't help it. For as long as she could remember she'd been Bella's confidante and protector. What made Bella think she couldn't come to her now?

'I think she just needed to talk to someone who isn't quite as invested emotionally in her as you are.'

'But she's always confided in me.'

Not always, he thought. But Evie didn't need to hear that now.

'Don't worry, she's okay.' Charlie's deep brown eyes were sombre as he stepped towards her and wrapped his arms around her, hugging her against his chest. 'The best thing you can do for her right now is just be there. Just like you've always been. She needs you.'

Evie closed her eyes and leant against Charlie's solid chest as she let out a long breath. It felt good to have a hug with no hidden agenda, a straightforward, comforting hug from a friend. It felt good to let someone else worry about her for a change.

'I'm consulting today. Call me if there's anything you need,' he said. 'Anything. I'm here for you, okay?'

His words vibrated in his chest and into Evie but she was also aware of the air in the room moving and she knew someone else had entered the lounge. She opened her eyes and her gaze settled on the last person she expected to see. The last person she wanted to see.

Finn Kennedy.

The last time she'd been in somebody's arms they'd been his. He stood in the doorway, rigid and forbidding, with his usual unfathomable expression on his face. His gaze was locked on her as she was held in Charlie's embrace. He didn't speak and he didn't move. Heat flooded through her, unbidden, unwanted, unplanned, as he watched her with his piercing blue eyes.

Evie stepped back, breaking Charlie's hold on her. 'I'd better go. I need to hit the showers and get downstairs.' She picked up her coffee and stirred milk and sugar into it, resolutely keeping her gaze focussed on her drink.

'I'll see you later,' Charlie said.

She looked up at him as he spoke. The doorway was empty. She and Charlie were alone again.

It was probably just as well, she thought with a sigh. She didn't have the time or the energy to deal with Finn Kennedy, esteemed cardiac surgeon, Head of Surgery and her most recent lover. Although that term was probably too generous. They'd shared one fiery sexual interlude but she couldn't call it lovemaking. It had been steamy, fierce and passionate but without tenderness. It had been raw, impulsive and gratifying but it could not be repeated.

She did *not* have time to think about Finn Kennedy. She needed to stay in control and, where Finn was concerned, she'd already demonstrated an extreme lack of self-control.

She thanked Charlie and kissed his cheek before she left to get on with her day, hoping and praying for it to improve. She showered in Bella's bathroom and changed into surgical scrubs. She hadn't thought to ask Lexi to lend her some clean clothes and there was no way she'd fit into any of Bella's things, even if Lexi had packed some choices other than pyjamas. At five feet nine inches, Evie was four inches taller than Bella and about two dress sizes bigger. While no one would call Evie plump, Bella was as thin as a whippet because of the cystic fibrosis.

She kissed Bella goodbye and headed for the lift to go to A and E. She yawned as she waited. She was halfway through the yawn when the lift doors slid open to reveal one occupant.

Finn.

Obviously she hadn't been wishing hard enough for her day to improve.

All it took was one glance, no more than a second long, before her heart was racing in her chest. Her lips were dry and her face burned under the scrutiny of his gaze. She couldn't let him see how he affected her.

She turned her back to push the button for the ground floor only to find it had already been pressed. No other buttons were lit. Which meant Finn was riding all the way down with her.

'Late night?' Finn's deep, husky voice made her jump. She hadn't expected him to speak to her. The way he'd looked at her earlier with his disapproving, ice-cold blue eyes she would have bet he'd ignore her. What was it about him? When she wanted him to talk he refused to open up to her yet when she wanted to be left in peace and quiet he had to engage her in conversation. He was so infuriating.

'Yes.' She turned to face him as she answered and saw him look her up and down. She knew he would notice what she was wearing.

'I take it you couldn't make it home?'

Yep, he'd noticed, and she knew what he was implying. She was tempted to let him think he was right but she was too tired to play games.

She glared at him. She was tired and worried. She'd let him take the brunt of her bad mood.

'I spent the night in the cardiothoracic ward. Bella is in hospital again. She was admitted last night.' She was happy if her comment made him feel bad. Why should she be the only one who worried about other people's feelings?

He reached out a hand and took half a step towards her before he thought better of it. She could literally see him change his mind. His hand dropped to his side and his tone softened. 'Evie, I'm sorry, I didn't know. Is there anything I can do?'

Don't be nice to me. I don't know how to handle it if you're nice. She was terrified she'd burst into tears in the lift. In front of Finn. 'There's nothing you can do unless you're a miracle worker. She needs a pair of new lungs.' She was snappy and defensive. It was the only way to ensure she didn't crumble.

'I doubt even the Lockheart name can get lungs to order.' His tone was cool now, his blue eyes appraising. 'I meant, is there anything I can do for you?'

'What could you possibly do?'

'I could organise for someone to cover your shift so you could be with Bella.'

Great, Finn hands you an olive branch and you set it on fire before you give it back. That's just great. Well done, Evie.

She would love to take him up on his offer but she couldn't back down now. It wasn't in her nature and she certainly wasn't about to give Finn the satisfaction of having the last word. 'There's nothing I can do for her,' she said. Evie expected Bella to sleep for most of the day and Lexi was going to stay with her. 'I'd rather be busy down here,' she added as the lift doors opened and she stepped out into the emergency department. Work would ensure her mind was occupied. Staying busy was the best way to keep her mind off Bella's situation. And off Finn.

CHAPTER THREE

It was amazing what a difference twenty-four hours and a hefty dose of no-nonsense antibiotics made. After a full day and two nights in hospital Bella was feeling a lot more positive and Sam was pleased with her progress too. She'd broached the topic of hurrying the wedding along with him and he'd seemed amenable to the idea. Now Bella just had her fingers crossed that he could convince Lexi it was a good idea.

Thinking of weddings, Bella's fingers itched to continue sketching. If her plan was to succeed she needed to build Lexi's excitement and feed her imagination about how beautiful this wedding could be. She needed Lexi to be so excited she couldn't wait to get married and would agree to do it soon. She needed to get some more ideas down on paper but her sketch book wasn't there. Lexi hadn't considered it a priority when she'd thrown belongings together the other night and Bella had been too concerned about other things yesterday to miss it. Lexi was bringing it into the hospital this morning but until she arrived Bella would have to make do with scraps of paper.

She was halfway through sketching a sleeveless figure-hugging satin gown with a plunging back when Lexi appeared, carrying a large tote bag.

'Morning,' she said as she dumped the bag onto Bella's

bed before kissing her cheek. 'Sam says things are looking up?'

Bella nodded. 'I'm definitely feeling better today.'

Lexi unzipped the tote bag and began to haul things out of it. 'I've brought the things you asked for. There's plenty to keep you occupied if you get bored,' she said as she deposited Bella's laptop and a stack of DVDs on the bedside cupboard.

'Did you bring my big sketch book and coloured pencils?'

'Yes,' Lexi said as she retrieved the items and put them on the table over the bed. 'Is Charlie coming in to see you today?'

Bella frowned. 'I think so,' she said cautiously. 'Why?' He'd told her he would call in but why was Lexi asking?

'I thought you might need this,' Lexi said as she pulled a wisp of red fabric from the bag. She shook it out and Bella recognised the skimpy red negligee Lexi had bought for her the last time she'd been in hospital. 'It took me ages to find it. Why was it in the back of your wardrobe? You're supposed to wear it.'

Bella looked at the minuscule slip. It was so not her style and she had no intention of wearing it, which was why she'd shoved it to the back of her cupboard.

'I'm not going to wear it in hospital,' she protested. She had no plans to wear it at all, not in hospital or anywhere else. 'You know how cold I always feel in here.' She floated her old excuse past Lexi. Because she was so thin she did feel the cold and she used that as a reason to wear thick winter pyjamas that hid her figure. She couldn't imagine why Lexi would ever think she'd wear something as tiny as that red negligee.

'I knew you'd say that so I brought you this to wear over the top.' Lexi pulled out a little black, cropped bed jacket.

Or something Bella assumed was a bed jacket. It wasn't much bigger than the negligee but it did have sleeves and a fluffy, furry collar, but even so Bella knew it still wouldn't leave much to the imagination. She'd feel like a model in a lingerie catalogue. Lexi might be comfortable in that situation but she certainly wouldn't be.

'I'm in hospital, Lex, not in an adult movie!'

'Come on, Bella,' Lexi pleaded. 'One of the hottest doctors in the hospital is coming to visit and you're in daggy old flannelette PJs. If ever there's a time for some glamour, it's now. You can't wear what you had on yesterday.'

Bella felt her eyebrows shoot up and almost disappear into her hairline. Lexi expected her to wear this in front of Charlie!

She wished she had the confidence to wear something like that. Just once. She knew Lexi had a dozen items just like this one in her own wardrobe. She'd bought herself one too when she'd purchased this for Bella, and Lexi made sure she wore them. But Bella wasn't Lexi. She didn't have her confidence, or her figure, and she couldn't imagine she'd ever feel comfortable in something that revealing.

Bella was shaking her head in protest but Lexi was used to getting her own way and she hadn't given up yet. 'Won't you at least try it on? Look how cute this jacket is.' She held it up against her. The black was a dramatic contrast to her platinum blonde hair and Bella knew the colour would work well against her own auburn curls. Lexi held the negligee and jacket out to her. 'Why don't you go into the bathroom and try it on?'

Bella could tell from Lexi's expression that she wasn't going to let this rest. The quickest way to get some peace and quiet was to give in. She'd try it on and then change straight back into her pyjamas.

She slipped the oxygen tubing over her head and unhooked the IV drip to carry it with her. She sighed. Getting changed wasn't simply a matter of swapping clothes. All the paraphernalia attached to her made the task that much more complicated. She grabbed the clothes and stepped into the bathroom, wondering why she always gave in and Lexi never did. Once again she was letting Lexi get her way while Lexi refused to budge an inch over the wedding date. Bella knew it wasn't quite the same thing but, still, it wouldn't kill Lexi to give in for once.

She hung her pyjamas on a hook behind the door and wriggled into the negligee. The bodice was firm and she had to tug it down over her head. It had built-in support that pushed her breasts together and created the illusion of a cleavage before the silk skimmed her ribs and flared out slightly over her hips. The silk was cool against her skin and as she turned around to try to see the view from the rear the silk swished around her hips and the sound of it made her feel like an actress in one of the 1950s movies she loved so much. But the negligee left very little to the imagination. She felt extremely exposed. She slid her arms into the jacket and tied it together at her throat. It gave her a little bit of cover but not nearly enough. She stuck her head out of the bathroom to catch Lexi's attention. She had no intention of stepping back into her room dressed like this. She waited until she'd caught Lexi's eye before opening the door a little wider.

Her sister looked her up and down. 'It looks gorgeous. Do you like it?'

'It feels fantastic,' Bella admitted. She loved the feel of the silk against her skin but it was far too revealing an outfit for her. 'But I couldn't possibly wear it in here.'

'Not even the jacket?' Lexi asked.

The jacket was rather fun but Bella knew it would look ridiculous over her pyjamas. Maybe she could wear it over a singlet top but she'd still have old pyjama pants on. She shook her head, she had nothing to wear it with, and then she closed the door and swapped glamour for comfort.

She handed the garments to Lexi as she emerged from the bathroom.

'I'm not taking them home,' Lexi said, 'I'll just leave them on the bed in case you change your mind.' Slightly mollified, Lexi laid them across the foot of Bella's bed before she left, promising to come back later in the afternoon.

Bella's morning tea had been delivered but as she ate she couldn't stop thinking about the red negligee. And about how different she was from her sister. Although perhaps their taste in men wasn't so dissimilar, she thought. She had to agree with Lexi, Charlie was hot. But that was where the similarities ended. Bella would be mortified if anyone saw her in that outfit whereas Lexi would lap up the attention. Lexi would have worn the negligee and flicked her platinum locks and flirted up a storm with an attractive man, while Bella would retreat into the safety of her androgynous pyjamas. She reached for the negligee and picked it up, letting the silky fabric run through her fingers before she stroked the soft collar of the jacket. Perhaps she could redesign this into something she might wear. Something a little less flamboyant, a little less show-girl, a little more restrained.

She had one last mouthful of chocolate ice cream and a final bite of the chocolate muffin before she pushed the morning tea tray to one side to start drawing. She looked at the wedding-dress sketch she'd begun on the scrap of paper and ideas based around the little jacket began popping into her mind. She started sketching another wedding dress, pretending it was something she might one day wear but knowing she was kidding herself. It would never be her. She'd spent so much time in and out of hospital in her short life that she'd never even had a proper boyfriend. When she'd been well enough to go to school she'd always been so far behind in her work that her time had been spent trying to catch up. Making matters more complicated was her mild dyslexia, which had made schoolwork even harder. She could have decided not to bother and concentrated on boys and having a good time instead but it wasn't in her nature to give up so she'd struggled on. Besides, it wasn't like the boys had ever been interested in her anyway, not when her gorgeous younger sister had always been nearby.

The only time Bella had ever come close to having a romantic experience had been on a camp run by the cystic fibrosis foundation. That was where she'd had her first, and only, kiss and she didn't kid herself it had been because the boy hadn't been able to resist her. It had happened because it was a teenage camp and most of them had been in the same boat, looking for normal teenage experiences. With her history, walking down the aisle as a bride wasn't something that was likely to happen in her future. She was resigned to being the spinster sister. Lexi was already engaged and even though Evie wasn't showing any signs of settling down yet, Bella knew it would only be a matter of time. Whereas, for her… She sighed, but, she supposed, being unmarried was probably better than being dead. Probably.

She needed to be positive. That's what Charlie had told her. She looked again at the red negligee as she thought about Charlie. She wondered what he would make of it. He'd probably seen more than his fair share of gorgeous, scantily clad women and she wondered how she would compare. Unfavourably, she imagined.

She thought back to their conversation yesterday. She'd amazed herself that she'd actually been able to get the words out, she'd been terribly nervous and had had difficulty stopping herself from fidgeting obsessively, but in the end she'd managed to have a one-on-one conversation with Charlie. It was no small coincidence that the last time she'd had a personal conversation with someone who wasn't related to her or who wasn't her doctor had also been with Charlie. She doubted he even remembered that night, the night of her high-school graduation ball, or more accurately the night she'd missed her high-school ball, but Charlie had made her night considerably better and even if he might have forgotten all about it, she knew she never would. She didn't find it easy to open up to people but Charlie was a good listener. He was always so relaxed and that seemed to relax her. Still not enough to completely eradicate her nerves, but it was a start.

Charlie had wanted to know what she'd wanted. 'Nothing,' she'd said. But that wasn't quite true. There were a lot of things she wanted. Well, not things exactly, experiences would be a better term for it. Because of the cystic fibrosis she'd missed out on so many things her sisters had done and if she could, she'd love a chance to try some of those things for herself.

She wanted to go on a proper date.

She wanted to be held in the arms of a gorgeous man and twirled around the dance floor.

She wanted to wear a fabulous dress with a full skirt that floated around her and a plunging neckline before she had terrible scars.

She wanted to stand under a starry sky and be kissed senseless.

She wanted to stay up all night and watch the sun rise over the ocean.

She wanted to lie on a picnic rug with her head in her boyfriend's lap and eat strawberries and drink champagne.

She wanted to be able to say, 'They're playing our song.'

She wanted someone to look at her as though she was the most desirable woman he'd ever seen.

She wanted to fall in love.

Bella laughed at herself. She couldn't go back in time and she was so unaccustomed to looking forward that she couldn't imagine getting a chance to do any of those things. There were way too many variables.

First she'd have to have the opportunity to meet someone, then she'd have to be brave enough to engage them in conversation, then she'd have to wait and hope for them to ask her out. She wished she could be a bit more like Lexi. Lexi wouldn't wait to be asked out. Lexi never needed to wait.

Bella wished she was confident enough to flirt and chat but even if she was, who would she flirt with? Who was she going to meet in here? Charlie was coming but there was no way she could flirt with him. Even assuming she knew how to flirt, he would wonder what on earth had gotten into her. It was all she could do to have a normal conversation, she'd have to be crazy to push herself any further. She wished she didn't find Charlie quite so attractive. She might be able to flirt with someone she didn't have a crush on, but what was the point in that? She wouldn't want to date anyone she didn't fancy. But did that mean she would date Charlie? She knew she would in a flash and just thinking about it made her blush. It was a ridiculous idea. She couldn't imagine him asking her out any more than she could imagine flirting with him.

'*Ciao*, Bella, you're looking brighter today.'

The sound of his voice made her jump. She'd been a million miles away and for a moment she wondered if she'd imagined him and his familiar greeting, but when she looked up she found him smiling at her and her heart skipped a beat.

He was wearing short-sleeved blue scrubs and had obviously just come from Theatre. His forearms were tanned and muscular but tapered nicely into narrower wrists and the long, slender fingers she always associated with surgeon's hands.

Bella took a deep breath as she willed herself to stay calm. *You've known him for years, he's just a man.*

But he was so gorgeous, was it any wonder she got all flustered? He was standing in front of her, looking hot and sexy, while she was in bed, looking frumpy and pale. They were at opposite ends of the spectrum as far as sex appeal went. Perhaps she should have left the negligee on. It might have been better than her ancient pyjama pants.

The two of them were such a contrast it almost made her laugh out loud. It was ridiculous to even imagine he'd ever ask her out.

Somehow she found her voice. 'I'm feeling much better,' she answered. 'Whatever cocktail Sam has put me on seems to be working.' She knew she had more colour in her cheeks but it wasn't because she was feeling better, it was because she'd been daydreaming about Charlie, and now that he was standing in front of her she felt her cheeks redden further.

Charlie stepped closer and brought the smell of sunshine with him, which overpowered the antiseptic smell of the hospital. Bella took a deep breath and savoured his scent as she tried to commit it to memory.

'Have you had a chance to speak to Sam about the wedding?' he asked.

She nodded.

His brown eyes watched her intently. 'How did that go?'

She smiled, remembering how nervous Sam had seemed. 'He said he'd do his best but I could tell he didn't like his chances. You'd think someone who's feted as being a top-class surgeon would be afraid of nothing, but I think Lexi is calling the shots.'

Charlie burst out laughing. The sound of happiness filled the room and made Bella smile even wider.

'He did say he'll file their notice of intent to marry. They need to have that lodged a month and one day before they can legally tie the knot.'

'That's a start at least,' Charlie said as he reached out his hand and ran a finger lazily around the edge of her almost empty bowl. He slid his finger into his mouth and Bella's eyes were riveted to the sight of it disappearing between his delicious lips as he licked it clean. He raised one eyebrow. 'Chocolate ice cream for morning tea? That's an interesting diet.'

'Don't you know? A high-fat diet is recommended for cystic fibrosis sufferers.'

'Is that right?' His brown eyes caught the light and the tiny flecks of gold in his irises reflected the light back at her.

She nodded. 'There has to be an upside every now and again, and eating dessert at any time of the day or night is one of them.' Never mind the assortment of tablets lined up on her shelf. Pancreatic enzyme replacement tablets, vitamin capsules and salt replacement tablets marched along the wall in an orderly row, ready and waiting to be taken regularly, but fortunately Charlie hadn't noticed them. His attention had moved on from the ice cream to her sketch book, which was lying open on the table.

'What have you been up to?' he asked.

She glanced down at her sketch book, surprised to see the pages covered with drawings.

A full-skirted wedding dress with a fur-trimmed fitted jacket took up most of one page and beside it she'd drawn a pair of intertwined rings. She remembered starting the dress but she didn't recall filling in the rest of the pages. Luckily she could pass the dress off as Lexi's wedding dress but the other sketches had nothing to do with Lexi. While she'd been daydreaming her hand had been transferring her thoughts to the paper. There was a sunrise warming an ocean and casting light onto a sandy beach. She could see footprints in the sand and in the corner of the page, where the footprints stopped, she could see the tasselled fringing of a picnic rug.

In the centre of the other page she'd drawn a pale green silk dress, its neckline similar to that of the negligee but with a full skirt. She'd drawn the skirt so that it was billowing out as if it was spinning to the music made by the notes she'd surrounded it with. She must have continued doodling absent-mindedly and stars, strawberries and music notes were scattered over the page, surrounding the green dress.

Around the edge of this page, framing it in a border, were lips—plump, juicy, soft lips, coloured in shades of pink and red. She blushed as she saw the frame she'd made, a frame of Charlie's lips. But it was too late to close the book, too late to hide her thoughts. Charlie had spun the book around, looking more closely at the pictures.

'Your drawings are really good.'

Please, please, don't let him recognise the lips.

'Is this for Lexi?' he asked, pointing to the wedding dress.

'Mmm,' Bella replied.

'And is this the bridesmaid's dress?'

She shook her head. 'No.'

Could she tell him? Talking about other people was easy, that came much more naturally to her; talking about herself was harder, much harder. But she'd managed to talk to him yesterday. It was silly to be so nervous.

She looked at her sketches. If she wanted any of those things to happen she would have to force herself to bury the introvert within her. Shy, retiring wallflowers didn't get any of those things she wanted, experience had taught her that already. She was twenty-six years old, she'd known Charlie for ever, it was time to start being a little more extroverted.

She took a deep mental breath. 'That's the dress I want to wear to go dancing.'

'Who are you going dancing with?'

She could hear the note of surprise in his voice.

'No one,' she replied. 'I was daydreaming. These are things I'd like to do when I get out of here.'

'You've drawn a "to do" list?' he asked.

Bella shrugged. 'I think in pictures, not words,' she explained. Even before she'd been diagnosed with dyslexia she'd always thought in pictures and found drawing a much easier way of expressing herself. 'And it's not exactly a "to do" list, more a wishlist.'

'So, dancing?'

Bella nodded and Charlie pointed to the next picture.

'I want to stand on the beach and see the sun rise,' she told him. She held her breath as she waited for him to point to the next picture. *Please don't ask about the stars in the sky.* She didn't have the words to explain that she wanted to be properly and thoroughly kissed by someone who knew what they were doing. She relaxed when he pointed to the footprints in the sand that led from the sunrise to the picnic blanket.

'I want to go on a picnic.'

'A picnic?' He was frowning. 'Surely you've been on a picnic?'

'A proper picnic,' she said.

'What on earth is a "proper picnic"?' he asked with a smile which made Bella's heart rate kick up a notch.

'You know, like the ones in movies where there is such an enormous amount of food you wonder how they've managed to fit it all into the basket let alone carry it across the field. Just two people, in a world of their own, no one else around, just peace and quiet.'

'Let me guess.' Charlie laughed. 'The champagne has stayed cold, the salad isn't soggy and the ants aren't trying to share your meal.'

'Laugh if you must, but someday I am going to enjoy a proper, perfect picnic.'

'So you're going to be at Lexi's wedding, watch the sunrise, go on a perfect picnic and dance under the stars?' he said as he turned the page, obviously looking for more pictures. 'Where're the rest?'

'That's it.'

'That's not much. You could knock that all over in one weekend.'

'You might be able to. I'm not sure if I'd have the stamina.'

'So what's this for?' Charlie treated her to a wicked grin as his hand dipped down towards the end of her bed and disappeared behind the table holding the remnants of morning tea. When he lifted his hand back up the red negligee dangled from his index finger. The table positioned across her bed had hidden the negligee from sight and Bella had forgotten it was lying in full view.

Bella blushed furiously. 'Nothing. Lexi was supposed to take it home for me.'

'Pity. I was hoping it had something to do with your list.' The negligee looked particularly minuscule and flimsy hanging from Charlie's finger and Bella couldn't help but recall that this was the same finger that had sampled her ice cream and been licked clean by those luscious lips.

'Like what?' Bella asked, half terrified and half excited to hear what his answer might be.

'It looks like something you might wear for a long lazy weekend in bed...' he paused ever so slightly '...with company. Drinking champagne by moonlight and getting up only to cook scrambled eggs at midday before getting back between the sheets.'

The picture Charlie painted was enough to make her blush. She'd never had a weekend like that, although it sounded as though Charlie was speaking from experience. He was folding the negligee as he waited for her answer and his hands looked strong and masculine tangled up in the flimsy fabric. The sight took any words right out of Bella's head. All she could do was shake her head in reply.

'So that's really it, that's your entire wishlist? What about something more challenging?' Charlie asked.

'Like what?'

'I don't know. Learning a musical instrument, running a marathon, learning another language, all those things other people always talk about doing one day.'

'I'm not sure I'm going to have time to do those sorts of things.'

Charlie frowned. 'Why not?'

'They're all long-term goals,' Bella said.

'What's wrong with that?'

'Nothing.' There was nothing at all wrong with it for other people. 'It's just I've never really thought long-term.'

'Oh.' She could see him connecting the dots.

'I've never got into the habit of long-term goals,' she explained. While things had improved considerably in the past twenty years, cystic fibrosis sufferers still didn't have a long life expectancy.

'But if you're going to have a transplant, surely now's the time to set some long-term goals. There must be something big you want to do?'

'I've learnt not to set unrealistic goals,' she told him. 'Every time I started something that was going to require a large investment of time the wheels would fall off and I'd get sick and never finish anything. I barely even finished high school because I missed so much time. I haven't expanded the list for after surgery because I've never thought long term, I wouldn't know where to start. My goals have always had to be achievable in the short term.' She looked up at him. 'Do *you* have a plan for your future?'

'Most definitely,' he replied.

'So how did you work it out?'

'Trial and error mainly. It's a work in progress.'

'If you thought you only had a few years left, would you be doing anything differently?'

That was an interesting question but not one he wanted to examine too closely. His current goals centred around his medical career. Medicine had served him well, it had given him another option when his life had gone pear-shaped, but if he hadn't had to plan for a long life, if he'd been living on limited time, would he have tried harder to recover a lost passion? A lost love?

Who was he kidding? He could have tried to resurrect those dreams but he never would have succeeded. He shook his head. Those dreams hadn't died, they'd been killed off and he hadn't had a chance to resurrect them.

'I guess I wish some things could have been different,' he answered, 'but they were out of my control. Things happen for a reason. One door closes, another one opens.'

'I'm just worried about doors closing at the moment,' Bella said. 'If I get through the surgery I can make a new list but I thought I'd start with the ones I've missed.'

'Fair enough, but I still think you should put a couple down for post-surgery. Something to look forward to, instead of back. There must be something.'

She didn't answer immediately and Charlie wondered if perhaps she had really never dared to dream of a future. Was there really nothing she wanted? He didn't think he'd ever met anyone as selfless as Bella. She had her head down again, drawing more pictures on her sketch pad. He watched as her hand flew across the page covering it with tiny high-heeled shoes that reminded him of Cinderella. Then, as suddenly as she had started sketching, she stopped and looked up at him.

'Fashion design,' she said, her voice whisper quiet.

'Fashion design?'

She nodded. 'That's my dream. To study fashion design.'

'Why aren't you already doing it?'

'I have to submit a written application.' She also had to submit six examples of her work but that part was easy. She had hundreds of sketches and finished designs to choose from.

'And?'

'I haven't been able to get the written part done.' Because of her dyslexia she'd never been a competent reader or writer and she'd gravitated towards the practical courses like art and design where she could rely on her drawing skills. The idea of writing a submission to a college, one that would determine whether or not she secured a place in their course, terrified her.

'What does the written part involve?'

'I have to explain why I want to do the course, what I hope to get out of it and why I should be accepted.'

'That doesn't sound too bad.'

She couldn't begin to imagine where to start. 'I can draw anything but I'm not good with words.' She wasn't about to admit her struggles to Charlie. She wasn't ready to have that conversation with him.

'I'll help you but you'll have to add it to your wishlist. It's already November—applications for next year will close soon if they haven't already.'

'Next year?'

Charlie was nodding. 'This is perfect. It'll give you something to look forward to. You tell me what this course means to you and I'll write the application letter for you,' he said as his pager began beeping. He took it from his pocket and checked it before adding, 'I'll come back tomorrow and we'll get started.'

He gave her a quick wink and was gone before she could protest. Before she could tell him she couldn't possibly go to college. It wasn't just the submission—how would she manage the written aspect of a serious course?

She picked up the negligee from where he'd dropped it on her bed. She stroked it while she imagined wearing it, imagined wearing it while Charlie's finger slid underneath the strap and pulled it from her shoulder. She imagined him bending his head and pressing his lips to the bare skin over her collarbone. She could almost feel the heat of his soft lips searing her skin.

She opened her eyes and shoved the negligee into one of the drawers beside her bed. That could stay buried along with her fantasies about studying fashion design and her fantasies about Charlie. None of those things needed to see the light of day again.

CHAPTER FOUR

BELLA felt as though she spent the best part of the next day with one eye on the door, waiting for Charlie. Lexi visited, Evie visited, Sam came on his rounds and pronounced her almost ready for discharge again, but Charlie didn't appear.

She didn't want to think about how much she'd been looking forward to seeing him. How often she'd checked the time during the day and as the hours advanced thought he must have forgotten about her. How she'd deliberately changed out of her daggy pyjamas into a slightly more respectable T-shirt and leggings. How she'd made sure the red negligee was still safely stowed out of sight in one of the bedside drawers.

It was late in the afternoon and Evie was visiting for a second time when Bella heard a new set of footsteps approaching. For a moment she let herself hope it was Charlie but she could hear that the steps were slightly uneven and whoever was walking towards her room was wearing high-heeled shoes.

An older version of Lexi tottered into her room. This woman had the same platinum blonde hair and the same bright blue eyes but Bella knew the similarities were only skin deep. This was her mother.

As usual she was immaculately dressed all in black. She had tucked her skinny black pants into high-heeled black patent leather boots and she wore a long black cardigan over a black top. A stranger could be forgiven for thinking Miranda was on her way to a funeral but this was her colour of choice broken up only by her blonde hair and masses of silver jewellery. Her make-up had also been perfectly applied. But underneath the make-up Bella could see the tell-tale redness of Miranda's nose. It wasn't red from crying, it was red from alcohol, and her eyes had a familiar glazed appearance. But otherwise her presentation was flawless.

Even when she's been drinking she's better groomed than I am, Bella thought. She and Evie exchanged a glance. *What is she doing here?* But before either of them had a chance to speak, Miranda broke the silence.

'Bella! My baby!' She leant over to kiss Bella and almost lost her balance. She reached out one hand and steadied herself on the bed. Bella's nose wrinkled under the smell of gin.

'Mum. What are you doing here?'

'I came to see you, of course.'

'I've been in hospital for three days and you're only coming in now?' As usual it was plainly obvious to Bella that she was not high on the list of her mother's priorities.

'Three days! I only just found out. Why didn't someone tell me sooner?'

'Richard has been trying to contact you,' Evie told her.

'Well, he didn't try very hard.' Miranda pouted.

'He's left several messages.'

'Why didn't *you* ring me?' Miranda asked Evie. 'Do you know how much it hurts to think that my own daughters wouldn't contact me?'

Typical, Bella thought. It was always about what was happening in Miranda's world. She had no great regard for anything other than her appearance and her alcohol supply.

Her daughters came a poor third behind her wardrobe and her alcohol addiction. Bella wanted to ask her if she knew how much she'd hurt her daughters. How much her abandonment of them as young children had hurt, how much her selfishness and drinking continued to hurt. But Bella didn't want to create a scene, she always did her utmost to avoid scenes, although that was hard to manage whenever her mother was around.

'We agreed that Richard would contact you,' Evie replied. 'Don't tell me you haven't got his messages. If you've been in no state to answer the phone or listen to your messages, that's no one's fault but your own. There's no need for all of us to be running around after you. Bella needs us now. We've been here for her as much as possible.'

Bella didn't know how Evie stayed strong. Bella wanted to stand up for herself but she wanted her mother to love her even more, and because of that she very rarely took a stand.

Miranda did her best to appear affronted. She drew herself up to her full height of five feet six inches but her heels gave her the extra two inches, which brought her almost up to Evie's height. 'I beg your pardon. I had one pre-dinner drink, you know how much I hate hospitals.'

Bella knew that even if her mother did detest hospitals, which she thought was unlikely, one pre-dinner dinner drink would still have preceded several more and dinner would be forgotten in favour of another glass of gin.

Did their mother have any idea how much her daughters wished she loved them enough to fight her demons? Bella knew Evie had long ago given up praying for that day but Bella hadn't. But there was no point in arguing about it. She wasn't going to change the facts. But she was exhausted and her mother's visit was making her emotional. She wondered if she had the strength to ask her mother to leave. Before one of them said something they might regret.

'Perhaps you should go, then, if hospitals disagree with you so much,' Evie said, coming to Bella's rescue once more.

'I have as much right as you to be here.'

'Actually, you don't,' Evie said. 'Bella needs to rest and as a doctor at this hospital I can ask you to leave. This is not about you. Bella needs positive support. If you can't give her that then you should leave. You need to take responsibility for your actions. Bella doesn't need to listen to your complaints. She doesn't need you to try to make her feel guilty about being in hospital. It's not as if she wants to be here. I'll walk downstairs with you and organise a taxi to take you home.' Evie turned to Bella. 'Will you be all right on your own for a bit?'

Bella nodded. 'I am tired. Perhaps you could come back one morning,' she said to her mother, unable not to make a peace offering, as Evie took a slightly bewildered Miranda gently but firmly by the elbow and steered her towards the door.

Evie kept hold of Miranda partly to make sure she came with her but also partly to prevent her from stumbling. While Miranda was so neatly presented Evie could pretend everything was fine. The girls knew that their mother's fastidiousness with regard to her appearance was all part of her deception but they held onto the hope that while she retained her sense of vanity maybe there was a chance she would one day seek the help she desperately needed. While she knew Miranda's disease wasn't something she could control or be responsible for, Evie wasn't sure that everyone else would see it from her point of view and she didn't want the hospital staff to see her mother in this state. Did that make her complicit in Miranda's problem? Did that make her an accessory to Miranda's addiction? She knew it probably did but she wasn't going to stop and think about it. Not now. She didn't want to be mean but she didn't have the energy to deal with her mother's issues today and she knew Bella didn't need the drama either. She would make sure her mother got safely out of there.

As she reached the doorway she saw Charlie approaching and saw him rapidly assess the situation. But she didn't worry. Other than her immediate family Charlie knew Miranda's history better than anyone. Evie and Charlie had shared many confidences during their final university years but Evie knew Charlie would be discreet, just as she always was with his personal history.

'Is everything okay?'

'Yes,' Evie answered, but she kept walking. She didn't want to stop and give Miranda an opportunity to create a scene. She knew very well just how likely that was. 'Are you on your way to see Bella?' She waited for Charlie to nod. 'Can you stay for a bit?' she asked. She didn't want Bella to be alone. Miranda's impromptu visits were always disturbing and she knew Bella would replay the conversation and stress over it. She needed company and Charlie would be a good distraction.

'Sure.' He knew what was needed.

Charlie continued walking and knocked briefly on Bella's door as he entered her room. She was sitting up in bed. She was still pale but the oxygen tubing had been removed from under her nose and for the first time since she'd been admitted Charlie could see her whole face without obstruction.

'*Ciao*, Bella. Is this a bad time?' he asked. 'I brought chocolate,' he said as he showed her the paper carry bag he held.

Bella's smile lit up her face. 'As far as I'm concerned, there's never a bad time for chocolate.'

Suddenly Charlie didn't notice how pale she was, or how thin—all he noticed was how her grey eyes sparkled and how the shape of her face changed. For someone of such a slight build she had a round face, but when she smiled her face became heart shaped and she looked less like a teenager and more like a woman. She was beautiful.

He'd always thought of Bella as the quiet one, the unobtrusive one. He'd never thought of her as being the pretty one. Tall, slim, glamorous Lexi with her platinum blonde hair and extroverted personality was hard to miss and Evie with her positive, confident attitude and easy smile was always in the midst of whatever was going on. Thinking of them like that, he supposed it wasn't surprising that Bella could slip through the cracks between her sisters and go unnoticed, that she would become lost amongst the dominant characters of her siblings.

But when he looked at her now it was as though he was seeing her properly for the first time. Her grey eyes were luminous, an unusual cool contrast to the fiery colour of her hair, and her skin was slightly flushed now, giving her a healthy glow. Her unusual colouring had always made her interesting to look at but he couldn't believe he'd never noticed her classic beauty.

He shook his head, trying to clear his mind as he handed her the bag of sweet things and pulled a chair up to the bed. Her bed was covered with pencils and sketch books but the red negligee was nowhere to be seen.

Her laptop was on the overbed table and she pushed it to one side before she emptied the contents of the bag, depositing them beside the computer. Chocolate muffins, chocolate cheesecake, caramel slice and chocolate bars covered the surface. 'What would you like?' Bella asked.

'You choose first, it's your treat,' he replied as he searched in the bag for spoons for the cheesecake. Bella was still smiling and he realised that for the first time she didn't seem self-conscious around him. Her smile seemed natural today; perhaps that was why she looked so different. He was amazed she didn't seem more rattled by her mother's visit considering the state she was in but he supposed she was used to it. 'So things haven't improved for Miranda?' he asked.

'No. But I've learnt there's nothing I can do that will change things there,' she said.

He saw her straighten her skinny shoulders, preparing herself. He was finding her more and more admirable. For someone who looked so frail and young and delicate she was showing a remarkable amount of spirit. He liked that about her. The fact she wasn't going to give up.

'My mother has never made any secret of the fact that I have been nothing but a problem. I spent years trying to atone for it but nothing I do has ever made any difference so now I try to ignore her barbs. Although at times I admit it's difficult. But I certainly don't want to dwell on her tonight. She doesn't spend any time worrying about me. I'm going to return the favour.'

The Lockheart sisters were lucky to have each other, he thought; they certainly didn't get a lot of love and attention from their parents. No wonder they were so close. He may not have had the same privileged lifestyle that the girls had had, in fact his family had struggled financially, but he'd never suffered from a lack of love and attention. His family was close, and even though more money would have made a difference to their daily lives, it wouldn't have changed their relationships. Money could never replace love.

Bella reached out and took one of the spoons from his hand as he sat mutely contemplating their differences. 'I suggest we eat chocolate and talk about something else,' she said as she reached for the bottles of tablets, shaking some enzyme-replacement pills into her hand before selecting several, which she swallowed with a mouthful of water.

He tried to stop staring but he was finding it difficult. He didn't want to freak her out but he couldn't think of anything to say and it took him a moment to even remember why he was there. 'Let's talk about your course application. I came to help you submit it.'

Bella looked startled, her grey eyes wide. 'I appreciate your offer but you don't have to help me, you know.'

'Are you going to do it without my help?'

Bella shook her head and her auburn curls bounced around her shoulders. 'No.'

'Did you want me to come back tomorrow instead?'

'Sam thinks I'll be able to go home tomorrow. I'll get Lexi to help me then.'

'No, you won't,' he argued.

'How do you know?'

'If you were going to let Lexi help you, you would have done this ages ago. I've done all the research, we have chocolate, let's get to work.' He'd promised Evie he'd keep an eye on Bella. She needed distracting. Otherwise, despite her protests, he knew she'd dwell on her mother's issues. Working on her application would provide a perfect distraction.

'You've done all the research?'

He nodded. He liked to be prepared in everything he did. He didn't like surprises. In his experience surprises were never a good thing. 'I had a look at it in some more detail last night. It shouldn't take too long to get it together.'

'You looked at it last night?' Bella raised an eyebrow. 'Didn't you have a date?'

Last night had been Wednesday, traditionally a big night with half-price drinks at Pete's Bar, the local watering hole for hospital staff. Normally Charlie would have been at Pete's. It was always a good place to hook up with an attractive woman, there were plenty of them at the hospital and plenty of them frequented Pete's for drinks at the end of a shift. But he had promised to help Bella and he'd been keen to see her reaction when he arrived prepared. Besides, pretty nurses would be at Pete's again the next time he called in.

'Not officially.' He changed the subject, bringing them back to the reason he was there. 'Did you know the cut-off for applications is next week? Have you got samples of your work to send in?'

Bella nodded. 'The practical aspect of things I'm prepared for, it's just the written application that terrifies me. Words aren't my thing.'

Charlie grinned. It felt good to be doing something like this. He enjoyed finding solutions to problems and that was something he loved about medicine too. 'That's why I'm here. Can you log onto the college website?'

Bella opened her laptop and ran her finger over the mouse pad, bringing the computer back to life. She'd forgotten she'd been watching a DVD earlier and before she could minimise the screen the movie reappeared and Charlie immediately recognised it. Normally she'd be embarrassed if someone discovered her watching the romantic comedies she adored but she'd decided that after the episode with the red negligee she wouldn't waste time being embarrassed. Besides, he already knew her deepest, darkest secrets and if he could accept her alcoholic mother, surely he'd accept her penchant for light cinema.

'Good movie,' he said as he sat down.

Bella felt absurdly pleased that he hadn't criticised her taste in movies. She smiled. 'You've seen it?'

'*Pretty Woman*? Of course. Hasn't everyone?' he said. 'If I remember correctly, it's a modern version of the classic fairy-tale. The rich, handsome hero arrives in his chauffeured limousine, climbs the fire escape to the heroine's tower with a rose between his teeth and rescues her from her tortured life. That sounds suspiciously like Snow White, or maybe Sleeping Beauty, don't you think?'

'Careful. You're having a go at one of my favourite movies,' Bella retorted as she closed the program and logged onto the internet. 'I like to think there's more to it than that. Vivienne wants someone who can see past her outer shell, someone who can see the woman underneath.' Bella knew she identified with the character of Vivienne, probably more than was good for her. 'Edward needs someone to make him see the joy in the little things, to make him see that there's more to life than making money. They need each other. That's what I love. There's nothing wrong with a happy ending, is there?'

'No, not at all. I'm only teasing. I meant it when I said it was good, I just didn't know people still watched it.'

'Go ahead, make fun of my taste in movies, but I'm not the only one who loves it.'

He laughed at the expression on her face and the sound of his laugh and the way his brown eyes crinkled at the corners made her forget all about being cross. She could sit there all day and watch him laughing. He looked so comfortable, completely at ease, happy and relaxed. She couldn't remember feeling like that for a long time. Perhaps if she could spend more time in his company some of his joie de vivre would rub off on her.

'Has that website loaded yet?' he asked once he'd finished laughing at her expense.

She turned her attention back to her laptop, pleased to have something to focus on, something to distract herself from those fanciful thoughts.

'Why are you doing this for me?' she asked as she waited for the website to load. Once she was in she followed the links to the page she needed. She knew how to navigate her way around the site; she visited it regularly. She'd just never been brave enough to take the next step of applying online.

'You'll thank me when you've recovered from your op and you've got all those years stretching ahead of you.' He was still grinning at her and she forced herself to concentrate on what he was saying. She knew she was too easily mesmerised by his smile, by his perfect pink lips. 'You'll need something to do. Even Vivienne in *Pretty Woman* has a job. Not that I'm recommending you follow in her footsteps, I think fashion design is a better fit for you.'

There he went again, making jokes at her expense. 'I never realised you were such a comedian,' she said.

'I'm doing this because I want to help. You asked me to keep an eye on Evie and she asked me to do the same for you,' he admitted. 'This is a way I can be useful at the same time.'

That made sense. Charlie was here because Evie had asked him to come.

Bella wanted to be upset that he hadn't come for her sake but if this was the only way of getting him to visit, she wasn't going to complain. She was used to people doing things for Evie, just like she was used to Lexi always getting her own way. It was just how things worked around her sisters.

'But I don't mind, I can think of worse things to be than the Lockheart sisters' unofficial guardian,' Charlie added, and he sounded so sincere that, once again, Bella found her irritation disappearing immediately. She couldn't have stayed annoyed with him even if she'd wanted to.

He lifted the laptop off the table and set it on the edge of the bed. 'Now, you need to tell me all the reasons why you're desperate to do this course, what your goals are and why you should be considered as an applicant. Then I'll make you sound so fantastic they won't be able to refuse you entry.'

And, over the course of the next hour, that's exactly what he did. By the end of it Bella didn't recognise herself as the girl who'd barely graduated from high school and struggled to read. Instead she sounded accomplished and talented and Charlie had made it sound as though the college would be lucky to have her. 'Okay, that box is ticked,' he said as he saved the file. 'Once you get home you'll need to choose which examples of your work you want to submit and get everything into the college by the end of next week. What else do we need to organise?'

'I think you've done more than enough,' Bella said gratefully. 'I really appreciate your help but I'm okay. I'll be home tomorrow and then I just have to wait and hope that things don't deteriorate too much more before I get new lungs.'

'What about your wishlist?'

'That was just me being silly. It's not important.' She tried to stifle a yawn, knowing that Charlie would leave if he thought she was tired, but she was unsuccessful.

'Okay,' he said, 'we'll save that discussion for another day.' He stood and gathered up the remnants of their chocolate feast. 'Get some rest. I'll see you again soon.'

Bella didn't know when. She wanted to remind him she'd be going home tomorrow but she didn't want it to sound as though she was begging him to come and see her before she left. Why was it so hard to know what the right thing to say or do was? She'd made good progress over the past couple of days, she could actually talk to Charlie without blushing furiously or stammering, but she still continued to second-guess herself. Why couldn't she be more confident? Why couldn't she be more exuberant? Why couldn't she be more like her sisters?

CHAPTER FIVE

It was late afternoon and Bella had not long woken up from an afternoon nap when she heard the intercom at the front gate buzzing. She wandered into the kitchen, wondering where Rosa was. The succession of nannies the girls had grown up with had long ago been replaced by a succession of housekeepers, but the kitchen was empty, Rosa was nowhere to be seen. The buzzing continued. Bella crossed the room to the intercom. Rosa had left a note on the bench, letting Bella know she'd popped out to the shops, and on the intercom screen Bella could see a courier waiting at the bottom of the driveway. She pressed the button to open the gates and met him at the front door.

'I have a registered letter for Miss Lockheart.'

'Alexis Lockheart?' Bella asked, assuming it was for Lexi, who, as far as she knew, was out of the house. 'Does she have to sign for it?'

The courier checked his records. 'Miss Arabella Lockheart, it says, but anyone can sign.'

Registered mail for *her*? Bella frowned and signed the digital receipt, wondering what it could possibly be. The courier handed her a small envelope. It was thick, glossy cream; it could only be an invitation. The only things Bella ever got invited to were Lockheart Foundation events and she'd never received a formal invitation for those. Her hands were shaking as she closed the front door and slit open the envelope and pulled out the contents.

> *Dr Charles Maxwell*
> *Requests the pleasure of the company of*
> *Miss Arabella Lockheart*
> *On Saturday 17 November*
> *For dinner and dancing*
> *On board the* MV Endeavour 2000
> *Please be ready to depart at 6 p.m.*
> *Dress: After Five*
> *RSVP: None required. Dr Maxwell will not accept*
> *any excuses!*

The invitation *was* for her.

Bella sank onto a chair in the front hallway and read it again just to make sure. Charlie was inviting her out. *Her.*

She couldn't possibly go. Could she? A list of excuses ran through her head. She could think of plenty.

She read the invitation a third time. Then re-read the RSVP. Charlie would not accept any excuses. What was she going to do?

At a few minutes after six on Saturday evening Bella eased herself into the soft, puffy comfort of the leather seats and tried to think of something clever or witty to say. *Quick, think of something, anything, before Charlie gets into the car. Before he realises I'm a dud date.*

But Charlie was already getting into the limousine. His subtle, spicy scent combined with the smell of leather and wood polish and made it impossible for her to think.

She was ridiculously nervous. Her heart was racing in her chest and her palms were clammy. She had thought about trying to get out of the date, not because she didn't want to go but because she didn't want to be disappointed. She knew her expectations of the evening would far surpass anything Charlie could have imagined. But when Lexi had arrived home the other day to find her still sitting by the front door, clutching the invitation in her hand, she had quickly put her 'event coordinator' hat on and organised Bella. Lexi wouldn't hear of her passing up this invitation and Bella had let herself be carried away by Lexi's excitement. To be honest, she'd been glad to let Lexi make the decision for her but now here she was, in a limousine, with Charlie, and no matter how many times she tried to tell herself that this wasn't a real date, that Charlie was just being nice, it didn't work. She still held out the hope that this would be the date she'd always dreamed of.

It was almost a fantasy come to life except for the fact that Charlie hadn't greeted her with a kiss. That should have reminded her this wasn't a real date. At least, not in a romantic sense. That should have settled her nerves but as she looked across to where Charlie sat in his dark navy suit, looking more handsome than she'd ever thought possible, her nervousness kicked up a notch. The cut of his suit was perfect, the back was double-vented, which accommodated Charlie's muscular frame and gave him room to move, and his plain white shirt had French cuffs which he'd fastened with silver cufflinks. She knew most people wouldn't notice little details like that but fashion had been her obsession for as long as she could remember. As she looked at Charlie sitting alongside her, she wondered whether she was becoming just a little bit more obsessed with him than was healthy. He was truly gorgeous.

'Can I pour you a glass of champagne?' His question broke into her thoughts.

She wasn't accustomed to drinking, after seeing its effect on her mother she tended to avoid it, but surely a taste of champagne couldn't hurt? Perhaps it would take the edge off her nervousness. She needed to relax if she was going to fully enjoy the evening.

'Are you still taking antibiotics?' Charlie asked when she didn't reply immediately. 'Would you rather something soft to drink?'

Bella hadn't even considered the medication she was taking. Perhaps it wasn't a good idea? But she felt like celebrating, tonight was a big deal for her. 'Would a small glass be all right, do you think?'

'I think so. I promise to keep a close eye on you and administer first aid if necessary,' he replied with a grin as he rotated the champagne bottle and removed the cork with a satisfying 'pop'.

Bella watched as he poured champagne into flutes. He handed her one before gently clinking their glasses together in a toast.

'Here's to a fun evening. And to you. You look beautiful.'

Had he just told her she was beautiful? She couldn't believe her ears. 'I do?' She swallowed hard, trying to dislodge the lump in her throat so she could speak clearly. If she sipped her champagne now, she knew she'd choke on it.

Charlie nodded. 'It's a big improvement on flannel pyjamas.' He laughed.

Bella's cheeks reddened. Once again he'd managed to make her blush. Being embarrassed seemed to be becoming a permanent state around Charlie. 'It's bad manners to laugh at your own jokes,' she managed to mutter.

'My apologies,' he said, looking anything but apologetic. 'But what happened to the green dress?'

She sipped her champagne and felt the tiny bubbles fizz in the back of her throat. For the life of her Bella couldn't remember what she was wearing. She looked down at her dress and saw silver sequins and white chiffon. Not a trace of green in sight. That's right, she'd borrowed a dress of Lexi's. 'The green dress?'

'The one in your sketch book.'

'That was just a design, I didn't have time to make it!' She'd only just had enough time to take Lexi's dress in at the seams and it was still a little big in the bust, but Lexi had fixed that with a padded bra. It was a beautiful dress, a bodice of silver sequins that would shimmer in the lights and a skirt of white chiffon that was made for dancing, but it definitely wasn't green. 'I need a bit more notice if you expect me to whip something up,' she added as the champagne loosened her tongue.

'I'll remember that next time.' Charlie smiled at her and Bella's heart did a funny flip and collided with her stomach.

She had no idea whether it was the effect of his smile or the champagne or his words that caused her insides to take up gymnastics. *Next time?* She didn't even understand what was happening this time.

'Where are we going tonight?' she asked, barely managing to get another sentence out.

'We will be cruising Sydney Harbour in style,' he replied. 'Dinner and dancing under the stars. I'm sorry it's not a picnic on the beach but I wasn't sure if that was wise given you've just come out of hospital. I thought we could save that for another time.'

There he went again, talking about the next time almost as though he really did have plans to see her again. She couldn't let it go again. 'Why would there be another time?'

'Bella! I'm gravely offended,' he joked, clutching a hand to his chest. 'Most girls wait till the end of the date before deciding they don't want to see me again.'

Bella laughed at his expression and she could feel herself relax. She knew it was his intention to put her at ease. 'Sorry, that's not what I meant. I'm just not sure why you're taking me out tonight, let alone why you might want to do it again.'

'I promised to help you with your wishlist and this cruise had all the things I know you love. Music, dancing, a starry sky and plenty of food.'

It's a pity she suffered from seasickness but she didn't tell Charlie that. She didn't want to hurt his feelings. He was being so sweet. 'You're right, it does sound perfect,' she replied.

She'd had the perfect excuse to get out of the evening, she did get terribly seasick, but he'd said on the invitation he wouldn't accept excuses and she wasn't about to give up what might be her only chance to have a night like this.

'Have you been on this cruise before?' she asked, hoping his answer would be no. She wanted the experience to be a first for both of them. But he was already nodding. It had been a silly question. She knew his reputation. He'd probably done this trip a dozen times, each with a different girl. She felt deflated but his next words cheered her up.

'Once before. The ortho department's Christmas party was on board last year.'

That wasn't so bad, that would have been a totally different experience to tonight. He wouldn't have been dining at a table for two that night, she assumed. Although with Charlie she suspected anything was possible.

The limousine came to a stop and through the glass partition Bella saw the driver get out of his seat. Charlie let himself out and came around the vehicle and waited for her as the driver held her door open. She climbed out as elegantly as she could in her unfamiliar high heels, and when her legs felt a little unsteady she blamed her strappy, silver stilettos and not the champagne.

The driver had delivered them straight to the gangplank of the MV *Endeavour* and Bella looked up at it amazed. It was sleek and white and ultra-modern. She wasn't sure what she'd been expecting but this was very slick. And enormous. It towered above them—she could count three decks rising above the water, and dozens of passengers were making their way on board.

Charlie took her hand as they joined the queue. His hand was warm and strong and secure and she was grateful not only for the emotional support but for the physical support as well. She could just see herself stumbling up the gangplank and making a spectacle of herself.

They made their way to the second deck where a waiter led them to a table beside the window on the starboard side. The dining room stretched the width of the yacht and the windows wrapped right around it. They would get glorious views of the harbour through sunset and into the evening, Bella realised as she sat down while the waiter held her chair for her.

Even seated she still felt a little light-headed and it wasn't until her entrée had been served and she had some food in her stomach that she was able to think clearly. At least, she blamed her hunger for her poor concentration, although it had as much to do with Charlie sitting opposite her. She couldn't quite get used to the sight and she was finding it hard to tear her eyes away from him long enough to look down at her plate or to enjoy the view of the harbour that was passing before them. She had no idea what they spoke about as she ate her prawn dumplings but she knew most of the conversation revolved around her. When their main courses arrived she tried to distract Charlie from the multitude of tablets she needed to take by asking him about himself.

'I think it's time you told me something about you. I've

known you for years through Evie but I don't actually know anything about your life, whereas I feel you know everything about me.'

'Even what you wear to bed,' he teased in reply.

Bella felt herself blushing again. 'See, it's only fair that you tell me something about yourself now.'

'Okay, but if I bore you, you only have yourself to blame.' He paused momentarily as he took some vegetables from a bowl in the centre of the table and added them to the beef fillet on his plate. 'Let's see, I'm the youngest of three siblings, an older brother and an older sister. We grew up in Wollongong, south of Sydney, my dad was a professional fisherman, mum is a nurse. I was a little bit wild as a kid. The Gong has some of the best surf beaches in the country and my mates and I spent just about every afternoon after school in the ocean. That's where I learnt to surf.'

Bella closed her eyes and imagined spending lazy afternoons lying on a warm beach or diving through the waves.

'Am I boring you already?' Charlie laughed.

She opened her eyes and smiled at him. She was happy in his company and happy to listen to him share some of his past with her. It made her feel special. 'No, I'm just imagining what it would have been like to be so lucky. I would have loved to have had that freedom.'

'I was given a long leash partly because of the community we lived in and partly by circumstances,' he told her.

'What do you mean?'

'My father had an accident at work when I was fifteen. He was out at sea, chasing a large school of fish, when a big storm hit. The crane on the fishing boat was damaged and fell onto Dad, fracturing his spine. That was the end of his days as a fisherman. He's in a wheelchair now. You might say I didn't cope very well at the time,' he said with a wry smile. 'Mum was understandably caught up in Dad's needs and I was angry, thinking I'd lost the father I knew. That's when I went a little bit wild. As long as I was home before dark no one minded where I was. I think it was easier if they didn't have to worry about me too. I had always surfed, most of the local kids did, and after Dad's accident I spent more time in the water than out of it. It was an escape. I went looking for freedom. I couldn't stand being cooped up in the house. I think seeing my father confined to a wheelchair, seeing him lose his freedom, made me hungry to make sure I had my own and I found that in surfing.'

'And later did they start to worry about where you were or did you run wild for the rest of your teenage years?' Bella wondered if she and Charlie had something in common after all. Were they both products of emotionally absent parents?

'Eventually things settled down at home, the dad I knew was still there, just physically different. We repaired our relationship. Dad accepted his situation more quickly than I did, he was amazing really. Mum too. Once I learnt to deal with the changes we were okay. Mum got a routine established and I was still allowed a lot of freedom but mum and dad needed to know where I was. By then I was quite a good surfer and I loved it. I think Mum was happy for me to be down at the beach as it meant I burnt off a lot of energy, although I'm not sure they were quite so happy when I won the junior world title and announced I was deferring university to join the professional surfing tour.' He gave her a half-smile and a slight shrug. 'But they didn't try to talk me out of it, just persuaded me to keep my options open. Dad had never had a chance to go to uni, fishing was the only thing he knew, and when that was taken away from him he really pushed the value of getting a good education. He saw it as a form of insurance.'

'So you had your parents' blessing to goof off and travel the world with your surfboard?'

'I did.' He grinned at her then, his smile open and honest. She couldn't see a trace of hurt or disappointment in his dark brown eyes, he looked as though he didn't have a care in the world. But Bella couldn't help but wonder what he'd gone through when his own accident had ended his surfing career, ended the freedom he obviously craved. But their heart-to-heart conversations had always been about her life and she felt it would be too intrusive on her part to ask him how he coped without surfing.

She chose to stay on safer, neutral ground. 'I'm still jealous. I've never travelled anywhere. I feel as though I spent my childhood indoors.'

Charlie was frowning. 'You've never been anywhere? I know Evie went on ski trips and didn't she have a trip to Europe when she finished school? Didn't you do those things too?'

She shook her head, sending her auburn curls dancing around her shoulders. 'Evie and Lexi got to do a lot of things that I never did. Not that I blame them. It wasn't as if it was their fault but it would have been nice to have been at my high-school graduation ball instead of in hospital or to have been sent to Paris when I finished school, but some things are just not meant to be.'

'Didn't I come and see you on the night of your grad ball?

Bella nodded and a warm glow suffused her, spreading from her heart through her body. *He remembered.* That had been the first time she'd ever spoken to Charlie alone. The first time she'd opened up to him, but she couldn't believe he remembered. That was the night she had become infatuated by Charlie.

She had been eighteen at the time and Charlie, at twenty-five, had seemed so mature. He'd travelled the world and was studying medicine. Because she'd taken two years longer than most to finish school, the boys she'd known had all been younger than her and in comparison to Charlie they'd seemed immature and silly. Charlie had entertained her with stories about his fellow students and their university pranks and Bella had thought how wonderful it all sounded compared to the drudgery of school. For the first time she'd found herself comfortable talking to someone who wasn't family. In Charlie's company she was able to relax and he'd managed to make her forget all about the graduation ball. Her adoration of him had started that evening and it had never stopped.

'You brought me flowers and chocolate,' she said. She didn't admit she still had the chocolate wrappers and the pressed flowers in a box in her wardrobe. In a box that contained very few keepsakes from her youth but ones that were precious nonetheless.

He grinned. 'I knew the way to a woman's heart even back then.'

Especially this one, she thought.

'You've earned your reputation as a charmer, that's for sure, but I still don't know how you happened to be there that night.'

'Evie and I were meant to be studying for our end-of-year exams but Evie was stressing because while you and Lexi should have been going to the ball together, Lexi was going and you were in hospital. Evie wanted to be in two places at once. She wanted to be with you both but that was clearly impossible. I figured we weren't going to get any studying done so I might as well come to the rescue. I couldn't help Lexi get ready so I volunteered to keep you company instead.'

'That doesn't seem fair.'

'On whom?'

'On you. Getting stuck with the hospital visit instead of the fun.'

'It was fine,' he said with a smile that took the sting out of his words. She wanted it to be better than fine. 'According to you, it wasn't fair that you were missing out on your high-school grad ball so keeping you company seemed like a small sacrifice.'

Bella winced. 'Did I complain an awful lot?'

'Actually, you didn't, even though, in my opinion, you would have been entitled to. You seemed to accept it as par for the course. You couldn't have behaved too terribly. I'm still here, eight years later.'

Yes, he was, but once again it had nothing to do with her and everything to do with his relationship with Evie. He'd promised Evie he'd look after her and Bella knew that was the real reason he'd agreed to help her with her list. That was the real reason they were here tonight.

'But I didn't realise,' he was saying, 'that along with missing your high-school graduation ball you never went on a ski trip or a school camp either.'

'I did get to go on one camp when I was about fifteen,' she admitted, 'but only because it was run by the cystic fibrosis association and Dad felt it would be okay. A whole bunch of us went away for a weekend and it wasn't too bad. Actually, it was quite good to be with other kids who were all going through the same issues but then the camps were stopped because there seemed to be an increase in the number of hospitalisations after the camps and the medicos were worried about cross-infection between the kids.'

'I can imagine what it was like, a camp full of teenagers with raging hormones. It's no wonder kids got sick!' Charlie laughed.

'I know.' Bella knew exactly why kids caught infections. After experiencing her first, and only, proper kiss on that camp she was one of the ones who had ended up in hospital. 'The trouble was we couldn't afford to be sharing germs around so that was the end of that.'

'Well, that's why I'm here. I'm going to make sure you get to try all those things you missed out on.'

'I think it's a bit late for school ski trips and my high-school graduation,' she said.

'Maybe,' he agreed. 'But will you invite me to your college graduation ceremony when you finish fashion design?'

Bella didn't imagine for a minute that Charlie was serious but she was touched that he asked. She smiled, 'Yes. I will.'

'Great. Now finish your dessert so I can take you dancing.'

Bella realised then that the band was moving from dinner music into dance music. 'Aren't you going to finish yours?'

When Charlie shook his head Bella finished her dark chocolate mousse, minus a spoonful which she gave to Charlie to taste, and then polished off most of his Eton mess before she let him take her from the table.

He took her hand and led her past the dance floor and out onto the large open-air deck on the bow of the yacht. The music followed them.

'Why are we out here?'

'Wasn't dancing under the stars one of the things on your wishlist?' Charlie asked.

Actually, she wanted to be thoroughly and properly kissed under the stars but no way was she going to tell him that! 'Yes, yes, it was,' she said as she stepped into his arms. She closed her eyes and let the music flow over her as she blocked out the thought of other people on the deck watching them. She didn't care, she wasn't going to think about them, she was going to savour the moment, the feel of Charlie's hand on her back, his breath on her skin. This was nearly as good as being kissed and she was determined to enjoy every second and commit the sensation to memory.

Charlie's embrace was warm and solid, making her feel as light as air on her high heels. The skirt of her dress swirled around her calves, just as she'd pictured it, the evening air was warm and the music was the perfect tempo. Bella closed her eyes and relaxed and pretended the night was never-ending as Charlie guided her around the deck. He was a graceful dancer. He danced like he walked, fluid of movement and light of foot. Bella supposed his graceful movement was a legacy of his surfing days—he would have needed good balance and smooth changes of direction—and she gave herself over to his lead as the songs blurred into one another.

'Look, the Opera House.' His voice was soft in her ear.

She opened her eyes as the yacht cruised past the Opera House. The white sails, backlit by the city lights, glowed against the evening sky. Even though she could see the Opera House from her own bedroom window, seeing the famous roof from within Charlie's arms made her feel as though she was seeing its beauty for the first time.

'It's magnificent, isn't it?' he said.

And it was. But it was poignant too because it reminded her they were now on their way back to Darling Harbour, and the night was almost over.

As if the band was in sync with her thoughts the music ended and the guests inside applauded. 'It sounds as though that's the end of our dancing,' Charlie said. 'Come.' He kept hold of her hand as they made their way back to the table. 'We have time for one last drink before our evening ends.'

The champagne was on ice and Charlie poured the last of it into their glasses as the dance floor cleared. 'So,' he asked, 'as far as dates go, did tonight meet with your approval or is now the point in time when you tell me you never want to see me again?'

She looked across the table at him. 'It was one of the best dates I've ever had,' she said honestly. She couldn't possibly tell him this was her first proper date. Not unless she wanted to confirm she was a total failure in the romance stakes. 'But to be honest, I haven't a lot to compare it to.'

Charlie laughed. 'Careful, woman, you're doing serious damage to my ego tonight. I was hoping to take home the prize for best night ever because it was fabulous, not because of a lack of competition.'

'We haven't all got as many notches in the bedpost as you reportedly have.'

'None of them serious, though,' Charlie told her.

'How come? What's been wrong with them?' She was genuinely curious and she knew a small part of her wanted to know in case the pitfalls were easily avoided.

'Some of them have been lovely but I've always measured my relationships against my passion for surfing.'

'What does that mean?'

'When I was surfing, if I wouldn't choose to spend time with a girl instead of hitting the waves, I decided I wasn't serious about her and that relationship never lasted long. I didn't see the point. If she wasn't special enough to make me give up an early-morning surf then she wasn't for me. Even when I couldn't surf, I still had that mindset. If I'm being honest, I probably thought even more about it. Surfing was a passion, the sense of freedom, the danger, the escape. A girl had to be something special to rival surfing. And when I couldn't surf any more I had to find a new passion and I found it in medicine, not relationships.'

'I can see how you could have a passion for medicine but it can't be similar to surfing in terms of freedom, surely?'

'You'd be surprised. Being in the operating theatre is a lot like being in the zone when you're surfing. I have to be in control because, if I lose it, things go wrong. But at least I am in control. I had to make split-second decisions while I was surfing and I have to do that when I'm operating too, but they are my choices. Everything that happens is up to me and that's a kind of freedom.'

'Does the same apply to your relationships—do you like to have total control, a sense you can get out of it whenever you choose?' It didn't take a rocket scientist to deduce that Charlie still craved freedom and making sure he didn't restrict himself by getting tied down in a serious relationship would ensure that. Even so, Bella was surprised to hear herself actually ask the question. The champagne must have loosened her tongue, she thought, she'd never normally be so forthright. Did she imagine a very slight hesitation before Charlie shook his head?

'Don't get me wrong. I haven't always been the one to end relationships. Sometimes the girl has done it first.'

That surprised her too. 'Why?' she asked.

'Usually because of my hours. Some of them have felt as though they haven't been my priority. They've been right, but...' he shrugged '...I never promised them my undivided attention. I still haven't found a girl whom I'd choose before surfing or my work.'

* * *

She raised her glass to her lips and looked over the rim at him. Her eyes were huge and it seemed to take her a second or two to focus on him. He wondered briefly if she'd had too much to drink before he dismissed the notion as ridiculous. She'd only had two glasses of champagne over four hours and even though she was taking antibiotics it wasn't as though she'd been drinking on an empty stomach.

She sipped her champagne and smiled at him and her grey eyes shone silver. Charlie relaxed. Perhaps she was just tired. Even though it was relatively early, she hadn't long been out of hospital. But he'd have her home, in bed, very shortly. Looking at her creamy skin, her warm hair and her flushed cheeks, he thought it was a pity she'd be in bed alone.

Where did that thought spring from? he wondered. That wasn't what the evening had been about.

He'd arranged tonight as a way of repaying a debt of gratitude he felt he owed the Lockheart family and also because he'd wanted to do something nice for Bella. It hadn't been about feathering his own nest. But old habits died hard and he couldn't pretend he didn't find her attractive. Couldn't pretend he hadn't noticed Evie's little sister had grown up. But that was the problem. She was Evie's little sister. She was off limits.

Tonight was about helping make some of Bella's dreams come true but now it was time to get her home.

She was a little unsteady on her feet as they left the yacht and, as he put his arm around her, keeping her upright, he wondered again about the wisdom of mixing antibiotics with even a small amount of alcohol. He was a doctor, he'd promised to keep her safe. He hoped he hadn't failed to keep his word.

Their limousine was waiting and Charlie bundled Bella into the warm interior. There was another bottle of champagne on ice but he ignored that and poured them both a glass of water instead. Bella drained hers in a few seconds and Charlie could feel her staring at him while he refilled her glass.

'Why did you shave your head?' she asked.

Yep. He'd definitely let her down. That didn't sound like something a sober Bella would ask. It was far too personal.

'It was time for a change.' That was partially true but the whole truth was far more complicated than that and tonight was about Bella. It wasn't the time to tell her about Pippa.

'You've had a shaved head for as long as I've known you and how long's that? Nine years? You don't change things very often, do you?'

'I guess not.'

'So what was the calatyst? I mean the cat-a-lyst,' she repeated, enunciating the word very slowly.

This was a story he normally avoided telling but he figured she was going through something much worse than the drama he'd experienced. She would probably understand—if she even remembered this conversation in the morning.

'I was on holiday in Bali, on my way home from a surfing tournament, and I was getting around the island on a scooter. The Balinese are not known for their good road safety record and I was young with a foolish sense of invincibility so I guess I was an accident waiting to happen. I got cleaned up by a truck on a mountain road and ended up in hospital with a collapsed lung and a shattered knee. That and torn cruciate ligaments put an end to my career as a professional surfer.' He spoke as though it hadn't been an extremely dark period in his life. It had taken him over a year to accept the fact his surfing days were over. The only thing that had stopped him from losing hope altogether had been going back to uni and meeting Evie. 'When I eventually got back to Australia and went back to uni I didn't want to be reminded of what I'd lost every time I looked in the mirror.' He'd lost more than his surfing career in the accident. It had also cost him his relationship with the first woman he'd ever loved. 'My hair reminded me of surfing and Bali and the accident. So I shaved it off.'

Bella reached out and ran her hand over his head. 'I think it suits you.'

Her hand was cool and soft against his skull and her touch sent a shiver of desire through him. 'You've got lovely lips too. They look sho shoft.' She was slurring her words ever so slightly and Charlie was mortified. Was she drunk? He couldn't believe he'd got her drunk. She lifted her hand again and Charlie waited, certain she was going to put her fingers on his lips, but her hand fell to her side as though she had no control over it any more.

'Didyouknow…' she was mumbling now and her words were running together and Charlie had to concentrate to work out what she was saying '…I've only been kished oncebefore. I'd like to be kished properly.'

Charlie felt Bella lean her head on his shoulder as she finished speaking. Had she just said she'd like to be kissed? He peered down at her, waiting, listening for more. But there was no more. Her eyes were closed and her breathing was slow and deep. Was she asleep?

He shifted in his seat and turned to face her, moving his arm to wrap it around her so she settled against his chest, telling himself he was doing it because it would be more comfortable for her than bouncing around on his hard shoulder. He hoped she was sleeping because she was exhausted, not because she'd passed out. Out of habit and concern he counted her respirations and took her pulse. Both were normal and Charlie breathed a sigh of relief.

Bella's handbag was lying on the seat between them

and feeling only slightly guilty he opened it, looking for her phone. He scrolled through her contacts list, looking for Lexi's number, hoping and praying she was home as he called.

Lexi was waiting at the front door when the limousine pulled to a stop. She raced over and yanked open the door. 'What happened? Is she all right?'

'She's okay, she's asleep. I'm hoping she's just tired but…' he winced as he finished the sentence '…she might be drunk.'

'Drunk!'

A wave of guilt and embarrassment swept over Charlie. 'I'm so sorry, she only had two glasses of champagne and she had plenty to eat.'

'She's not used to drinking—'

'I know,' Charlie interrupted. He knew this was his fault. 'And I know she's on antibiotics but I really thought she'd be okay.'

'That wasn't a criticism,' Lexi said. 'I was just going to say that the motion-sickness tablets she took tonight probably didn't help.'

Charlie frowned. 'What?'

'She gets seasick,' Lexi explained, 'and she took a couple of pills for that before you picked her up.'

This was going from bad to worse. 'Seasick? Why didn't she tell me? I would have cancelled.'

'That's exactly why she didn't tell you. She was so excited about tonight. It would have killed her if you'd pulled the pin.'

At least the extra medication explained why she'd been so affected by the champagne. The motion-sickness tablets would have dehydrated her more than normal and made her more susceptible to the alcohol. Perhaps he wasn't as negligent as he'd feared. 'We'll need to get plenty of water into her to counteract the dehydration from those tablets. Do you want me to organise a drip?'

'No. I'll keep an eye on her,' Lexi said, and Charlie wasn't sure if she was implying he was incapable or irresponsible or whether she thought she couldn't rely on him. He couldn't blame her, he hadn't given her a reason to think otherwise. 'Can you bring her inside?' she asked.

He scooped Bella up in his arms, surprised at how light she was, and followed Lexi up the stairs to Bella's room. Even carrying her upstairs was no problem.

'I'm really sorry, Lexi, are you sure there's nothing else I can do?'

'We'll be fine.'

'Her heart rate and respiration rate are normal but please ring me if you're worried at all,' he said as he scribbled his number on one of Bella's sketch books, which was lying beside her bed.

There wasn't anything else he could do. He let himself out of the house and climbed back into the limo for the trip home. He couldn't believe he'd let this happen; he couldn't believe he hadn't taken better care of her.

CHAPTER SIX

CHARLIE woke frequently through the night, constantly checking his mobile phone to see if Lexi had called him, but there was nothing. As soon as the sun rose the next morning he was out of bed, too restless and remorseful to sleep. He wanted to check on Bella but, if she was sleeping, which he hoped she was, it was far too early for a house call. He needed to clear his head, he needed to get into the water.

Even though his knee injury had cut short his professional surfing career he was still able to bodysurf for fun, but the surf this morning was flat and not at all appealing so he hit the Kirribilli pool. At this early hour only the keen swimmers were in the water and he joined their ranks, slipping into the fast lane and swimming hard for close to an hour. Swimming normally gave him a chance to clear his mind but it wasn't working today. Thoughts kept swirling around in his head. How could he have been so irresponsible?

There he was telling her an edited version of his life story while she was trying to combat seasickness. The tablets had certainly done their job, she hadn't shown any signs of queasiness. He smiled as he finished another lap, thinking about how much Bella had managed to eat. With everything she'd eaten he couldn't understand how the two glasses of champagne had affected her so badly. Perhaps she'd taken more tablets than she needed to?

But that didn't exonerate him from his responsibilities. He should have taken better care of her. But he'd been both distracted by her and absorbed in her and he hadn't been able to think clearly. She was virtually a stranger to him yet he felt as though he already knew her intimately through Evie. He was comfortable with Bella, he could be himself, just as he was in Evie's company, and that was a novelty for him. He was able to let his defences down. He climbed out of the pool and towelled himself dry as he wondered what it was about the Lockheart sisters that struck a chord with him.

Out of habit he scanned the other swimmers, looking for familiar faces. Finn Kennedy was just getting into the pool and Charlie nodded in greeting as he headed for the change rooms. He saw Finn fairly regularly at the pool but they rarely stopped and chatted, Finn always seemed so intent on his exercise that Charlie didn't like to delay him.

Charlie showered and changed quickly before leaving the pool. Sunday-morning traffic over the Harbour Bridge was just starting to increase as he walked out into the street and he looked up at the bridge as it stretched away overhead, spanning the water, before he turned away and headed back towards Mosman. To Bella.

The sun was high in the sky before Bella felt well enough to open her eyes properly and keep them open. Her tongue felt swollen and her lips were dry. She could remember Lexi forcing her to drink a glass of water every time she'd stirred in the night but still it felt as though her tongue was sticking to the roof of her mouth. She sat up, and she could see the indentation from Lexi's head in the pillow next to her. She knew Lexi had slept there but she was alone now.

She reached for the glass beside her bed as she tried to piece together what had happened last night.

She remembered dancing with Charlie, the feeling of his strong arms encircling her, making her feel as though her feet weren't touching the floor, as though she was floating across the deck. She remembered having a half a glass of champagne as the yacht came into dock. She remembered stroking Charlie's head.

Oh, my God, I didn't really do that, did I? But she knew the answer. She could still recall just how his head had felt, the short regrowth soft and fuzzy under her hand.

She slid down in the bed, burying herself under her quilt. How would she ever face him again?

She supposed she wouldn't have to. After last night he probably wanted nothing more to do with her.

She heard her door open. She couldn't face anyone right now. Maybe she could just stay under the covers and never come out again.

'Bella? Are you awake?' Lexi's voice was quiet. 'Charlie sent you flowers.'

That got her attention. She pushed the quilt away from her face and peered out. Lexi was half-hidden behind a mass of sunny, happy sunflowers. Just seeing their cheery, yellow petals made Bella feel brighter.

'He sent flowers?'

'He brought them around this morning, while you were asleep.'

'I thought he'd never want to speak to me again,' Bella said. 'I must have looked like a complete fool, passing out like I did.'

'I think he thought it was his fault. He felt terrible because he'd been plying you with champagne.'

'Hardly plying. I only had two glasses.'

'I know. I told him about the motion-sickness tablets

but I guess he still feels terrible,' Lexi said as she put the vase of flowers on Bella's chest of drawers. 'There's a card here,' she said as she removed the card and passed it to Bella. 'What does it say?'

Bella opened the little envelope and slid the card out to read the inscription. *'Ciao, Bella, I'm sorry I didn't take better care of you. Can I make it up to you on dry land? Charlie.'*

Suddenly she felt a whole lot better. He hadn't written her off, he was going to give her another chance.

'Charlie! I'm glad I found you.'

Charlie turned around at the sound of Evie's voice. She didn't look pleased to see him, she looked mad. He'd been keeping a low profile until he could organise to make up for his faux pas with Bella but he had been expecting Evie to track him down and haul him over the coals for leading her baby sister astray. He'd spoken to Bella, he'd apologised, she'd blamed herself and they'd agreed to forget about it and try a second 'date'. It would be something else from her wishlist but this time Charlie intended to keep to dry land.

Evie did not look happy. Not that he blamed her for wanting to tear strips off him. As far as he was concerned, he deserved it, but he still thought he'd try to minimise the fallout by apologising quickly. He held his hands up in surrender. 'I know, I'm sorry, it won't happen again.'

He watched as her expression changed from cross to puzzled. 'What are you talking about?' she asked.

'I assume you want to give me a bollocking over what happened with Bella?'

'No. She's fine. She's a bit embarrassed but she hasn't stopped talking about what a great night she had, right up until she fell asleep. There's something else I wanted to talk to you about. How well do you know Finn?'

'Finn Kennedy?'

'Of course,' she replied in a voice that suggested he'd lost his mind.

Charlie shrugged. 'As well as anyone can know him, I suppose. I see him at the pool a bit but we really only exchange greetings. He's never been one to socialise much, not even with the surgeons. Why?'

'I wanted to ask his opinion about Bella but he seems rather moody, more so than usual, as though he's angry with the world and everyone in it. I didn't know whether it would be wise, especially after what's happened today. And I just wanted to get your take on things, see if you knew about anything that might be going on that could have put him in a bad mood. See if you think I'm going to get my head bitten off for even going near him.'

'What happened today?'

'He went missing in action.'

'Finn did?'

She was nodding and she looked cross again but now it was obvious she was mad with Finn, not him. 'I had a patient who came in with a penetrating chest wound and I was trying to find Finn. I thought being an ex-army surgeon he'd be the one to call in for a consult, but no one knew where he was.'

'How's the patient?'

'We managed to keep him alive and he's gone to Theatre but it's very out of character and I'm a bit concerned. I need him to be on top of his game.'

'Why?'

'Because I need to ask him about Bella,' she replied, giving him a look that very clearly said, *Keep up!* 'And if he's got problems of his own, I don't want to risk it.'

'Risk what?' Now Charlie even felt like he was missing the bigger picture.

'Would you let him operate on you?'

'I thought Sam would do Bella's transplant...' He let his sentence tail off. He didn't want to state the obvious, which meant assuming compatible lungs were found in time.

'I was going to ask him if he'd assist,' Evie explained, finally allowing Charlie to catch up with her train of thought. 'Do you think there's anything to worry about, given that he's gone missing today and generally seems to be out of sorts, or would you let him operate on you?'

'I haven't noticed anything off. He might not be the most personable of people but he's a damn good doctor. You don't get to be Head of Surgery without being something a bit special.'

'That's what I thought but that was before he vanished in the middle of the day.'

'If you want my advice, it would be to stay out of Finn Kennedy's personal life. He may have had a perfectly good reason to take off in the middle of the day.'

'Don't you think he should have told someone where he was going? No one knew where he was.'

'And I imagine that's how he wants it to stay. You said yourself he doesn't confide in anyone. He's a loner and I think he likes it that way. I'm sure he's fine and I'm sure that even if there is something going on with him, he wouldn't let it affect his surgical skills.'

Charlie couldn't understand her concerns. In his mind they were unfounded. As far as he knew, Finn had never disappeared from the hospital before and just because Evie hadn't been able to track him down it didn't mean Finn had gone missing. He could have told someone where he was, and perhaps Evie didn't ask the right people in time.

But while he couldn't understand her concerns, he could

understand her logic in asking Finn to assist with the operation. While Charlie thought Sam was perfectly capable of performing Bella's surgery without Finn's help, Sam would need assistance and he guessed having two experts operating together was better than one. Whether or not Sam and Finn saw it the same way was something Evie would have to sort out, but until lungs were found it was all hypothetical and, in the meantime, Charlie had some plans of his own to arrange.

He had three days to organise his apology.

Bella hung her car keys on the hook and mixed herself a salt-replacement drink before wandering through to the conservatory. She'd had a long day at the hospital with several appointments all related to her transplant work-up and she couldn't afford to get dehydrated. She was exhausted and her chest felt tight but she put it all down to a long and tiring day. Rosa had pots simmering on the stove and Bella could see trays in the ovens and the kitchen benches were groaning under the weight of several other dishes covered with foil or teatowels. She lifted one corner of a teatowel. This platter held smoked salmon, pâté and other antipasto assortments. Her stomach growled with hunger but she needed to rest for a bit. She'd kick her shoes off and sit down for a few minutes and then she'd come back and see if she could sample whatever yummy things Rosa was making.

The conservatory overlooked the garden and the harbour. As Bella entered the room her attention was caught by the sight of a white marquee sitting in the centre of the lawn. That hadn't been there when she'd left the house this morning. It was the smallest of several her father had, and this one was sometimes used for garden parties. Bella wondered why it had been put up in the middle of the week. Initially all her attention was focussed on the tent and it wasn't until Lexi spoke that she noticed she was in the room.

'Good, you're back.'

Lexi was sitting on one of the day lounges, feet curled up underneath her, flicking through a bridal magazine.

'What's going on?' Bella inclined her head towards the garden and the marquee.

Lexi stood and tossed the magazine onto the table. 'Where have you been?' she said, ignoring Bella's question.

'At the hospital.'

'I expected you ages ago. You'll have to hurry now if you're going to be ready in time.'

'Ready in time for what?' Bella had no idea what was happening. Was there a function she was supposed to know about that had slipped her mind? That would explain the quantity of food in the kitchen.

'Charlie will be here in half an hour. He's organised another date. That's what the marquee is for.'

'What do you mean, "he's organised another date"?' Bella was frowning as she was looking out of the conservatory windows. The marquee was for Charlie? 'How did he do this?' she asked, waving one hand in the general direction of the garden. 'And how do you know so much about it—did you help him?'

Lexi was nodding. 'Rosa and I agreed to help.'

'You should be spending your time organising your wedding,' Bella argued. Lexi was constantly telling her how much time it was going to take to organise the wedding so she should be spending every spare minute on that, then the wedding might actually happen sooner rather than later.

'Charlie can be very charming and persuasive when

he wants to be,' Lexi replied. 'I thought this was more important.'

Bella knew she should argue but she couldn't think straight. Charlie had organised another date for them? She was getting a second chance? She forgot all about being tired as she ran upstairs to get changed. Lexi had said he'd be there soon. Bella had to get it right this time.

When she emerged from the shower she found that Lexi had selected an outfit for her. She assumed Lexi knew what the date entailed so she dressed in the clothes that were laid out on her bed. She'd chosen white cotton trousers, a white camisole and a lightweight caftan to wear over the top. The caftan was made from sheer cotton that had been printed with a pale green and white pattern with a scattering of beads hand sewn onto it. She teamed the outfit with flat sandals and put her medications into a small silver purse. She left her freshly washed hair loose, the curls cascading around her shoulders, and applied the bare minimum of make-up, mascara, lip gloss and a touch of blush.

'*Ciao*, Bella.' Charlie was waiting for her in the conservatory when she came back downstairs and hearing his familiar greeting made her catch her breath. He stood and came to meet her and she watched as his plump, juicy lips spread into a wide smile. He was casually dressed in denim jeans and a T-shirt that moulded nicely to his chest and his chocolate-brown eyes shone with good humour.

He kissed her on the cheek, pressing his delicious lips against her skin, and a tingle of desire shot through her, warming her from the inside. 'Thank you for giving me another chance. I promise to take better care of you this time,' he said.

Not for one moment had she blamed Charlie for her

condition the other night. It hadn't been his fault at all but she couldn't formulate the words to tell him so.

He cocked one elbow and waited for her to slide her arm through the gap before he covered her hand with his. She trembled under his touch.

'Shall we?' he asked.

She took a deep breath and nodded, eager to find out what lay in store for her tonight. With arms linked, they stepped into the garden and walked across the lawn towards the marquee. The grass sloped gently away from the house towards the harbour and the expanse was large enough for the water to still be visible past the marquee. Ferries criss-crossed the water, leaving a trail of white behind in their wakes, and a very slight breeze carried the sound of ferries tooting as they docked and departed from the Mosman Bay wharf to the west of the Lockheart home. The breeze also carried the perfume from the frangipani trees that hugged the boundary fence and had just started flowering. Across the water Bella could see the city lights and the shining white sails of the Opera House. The tent was enclosed on three sides and had been positioned with the open side facing the harbour. Bella knew they would have views of the city from within but the views paled into insignificance as Charlie led her around to the front of the marquee and took her inside.

'Oh, it looks beautiful,' she sighed.

The interior of the marquee had been set up to resemble a picnic. The space inside the small marquee was intimate but dominated by a massive Persian rug which had been laid out in the centre of the tent. The carpet was scattered with brightly patterned, oversize cushions and cashmere blankets, and fat candles and hurricane lamps were grouped in the corners of the marquee, casting a warm glow around the space. Fairy-lights had been strung up against the ceiling, giving the illusion they would be dining under the stars. Music was playing softly in the background and picnic baskets were lined up along one wall beside a large metal tub filled with ice that held an assortment of drinks.

'I thought we'd stay on dry land this time,' Charlie said as Bella stood, fixed to the spot, mesmerised by the colour and light and amazed by the effort Charlie had gone to. Somehow he'd managed to create a little oasis in the middle of a suburban garden in the centre of the city. 'Make yourself comfortable,' he said as he guided her towards the pile of cushions. 'I'm going to mix us a couple of baby Bellinis.'

Bella was about to protest, she wasn't planning on touching a drop of alcohol tonight, but Charlie interrupted her. 'It's okay, I'm using non-alcoholic cider, not champagne,' he said as he retrieved the peach nectar from the tub of ice. 'These will be perfect for our picnic.'

From the middle of the tent Bella could still see across the harbour but she had the sense they had the world to themselves, everything and everyone else seemed so far away.

'How on earth did you manage to organise all this?' she asked as he handed her a champagne glass.

'I can't take all the credit. I had some inside help. Evie told me you'd be out most of the day, Lexi got the marquee set up and Rosa has spent the day cooking your favourite things. I just told them what I had in mind. My only concern was that you'd be wiped out after your day of appointments.'

Her earlier fatigue had vanished in the excitement of the evening. 'I'm good, just starving,' she said as she slipped her sandals off and sat cross-legged on a cushion. Charlie stretched out beside her and his hand rested inches from her thigh. She wanted to pick his hand up and put it on her leg but before she had a chance he was on the move again.

'I haven't known you to be anything but hungry,' he said as he jumped up and searched through the picnic baskets, returning with two platters of appetisers, one warm and one cold. Pâté, smoked salmon and grapes on one, filo pastries and spring rolls on the other. Rosa must have transferred the food from the kitchen to the marquee while she had been in the shower. But surely all that food couldn't have been for them?

'How was your day?' he asked as he put the platters on the carpet between them.

'Interesting,' she replied.

'Who did you see?'

'I had a few tests, blood work, lung function, the usual, and saw Marco D'Avello and John Allen. At least John didn't tell me I'm crazy,' she said as she spread pâté onto a biscuit.

Charlie smiled. 'That would be a psychiatrist's job, John's a psychologist.'

'I know, but it always makes me nervous when someone starts delving into my psyche. It's only a matter of time before someone decides I'm a bit loopy. But he was more interested in whether I've got a good support network— although that could potentially open a whole other can of worms if he expects my parents to come to the party. Luckily I've got Lexi and Evie.'

'You're not expecting your parents to step up?'

Bella shook her head as she swallowed the pâté and biscuit. 'I've learnt it's better not to expect anything, particularly where my mother is concerned. She has very little to do with any of us. It's been that way for years. And she certainly hasn't wanted anything to do with me. I'm not glamorous enough—'

'You can't be serious,' Charlie interrupted. 'That can't be right?'

Bella shrugged. She appreciated his vote of confidence, even though she thought he was wrong. 'I'm sure it's part of it but I also think she can't handle having a sick child. Anything less than perfection isn't allowed in her world. If she could have removed me from her world, I think she would have. Instead, she removed herself from us.'

Charlie couldn't begin to imagine what Bella's life had been like. He knew she'd never wanted for material things but he could hear in her tone how much she longed just to be loved. He wondered how different her life would have been if she'd been healthy, if she hadn't been born with a defective gene. But he guessed they'd never know the answer to that question.

A fierce protectiveness rose up in him, stemming from anger towards Miranda Lockheart. Did she have any idea how her behaviour and her choices had hurt her daughters? Did she have any remorse? He knew Miranda's alcoholism was an illness but it was treatable. Unlike Bella's cystic fibrosis, Miranda could be controlled if treated if only she sought help. But as far as he knew, she hadn't tried and if she wasn't willing to do that then it was obvious her daughters were not her priority. 'What about your father? Have you been able to depend on him?'

'Financially I have, but while he's been in the picture more than Mum he's never really spent any time with me, not like he has with Lexi.' She shrugged again. 'I don't think he knew what to do with me. You heard him in hospital last week, he's used to throwing money at problems to solve them or make them go away, and if something can't be fixed with money, he doesn't know what else to do. With me, he paid for nurses and made me their responsibility so he could ignore the issue, ignore me.'

Charlie may not have had Bella's privileged background but he had a solid, tight-knit family and that included parents who had helped him find his place in the world. Even in his darkest days, when his surfing career had prematurely ended, no one could have taken his family away from him. Bella had her sisters but she deserved more, all three of the girls did.

'My life is what it is,' she said as she selected a slice of smoked salmon. 'Let's talk about something else.'

He was constantly amazed by her selfless nature. Even now she wasn't going to condemn her parents over her upbringing.

She stood up gracefully, unfolding herself from her cross-legged position on the cushion, and wandered over to the picnic baskets. 'What else did Rosa make me to eat?' she asked as she peered into the baskets.

Charlie followed Bella to the picnic baskets. Rosa had left crusty bread, sliced roast meats, mustards, salads, boiled eggs, mini savoury pastries, cheeses, fruit and a whole basket full of chocolate desserts. Looking at the amount of food, he was pleased he'd managed to organise the picnic in Bella's back garden. He knew she'd envisaged a private picnic but he hoped it was more about the company and less about the location—he certainly didn't fancy carrying these heavily laden baskets across a field to set up next to a meandering creek. This was far more civilised; he just hoped it satisfied Bella's expectations. He opened a third basket and handed her a china plate, silver cutlery and a linen napkin, and once she'd made her selection he followed suit before resuming his position on the Persian carpet.

'I put my college application in yesterday,' Bella told him as she sat beside him.

'Good girl.' He was thrilled she'd actually done something for herself for a change. 'How did it feel?'

'Terrifying,' she admitted. 'It's been years since I studied and even then I wasn't very good at it. I was eighteen when I finished school, two years later than I should have. You know Lexi and I did year twelve together and I wouldn't have got through without her help. That's why I was so reluctant to apply for fashion design, I didn't think I'd be able to do it. I still don't. But I'll give it a go.'

He was inexplicably proud of her. Tackling a tertiary degree was obviously a major hurdle for her to overcome. 'Studying a topic you love will be totally different from what you did at school.' He just hoped, having pushed her to apply, that she wouldn't be disappointed. He hoped she'd love it.

'That's what I'm praying for.'

'You're so passionate about design, I'm sure you'll enjoy every minute of it.'

'I hope so. I'm excited as well as terrified, if that makes sense, but you were right, it will be good to have something to look forward to. If I do have this transplant I can't sit around doing nothing for the rest of my life.'

'I'm sure you haven't been doing nothing,' he said as he realised she could have been doing just that for eight years. But that didn't gel with the woman he thought she was or with the woman he wanted her to be.

'I suppose not, but I can't say I've been doing anything terribly worthwhile either, although I do enjoy doing some interior decorating on behalf of the Lockheart Foundation.'

'Interior decorating?'

'Yes. Dad quite regularly buys flats around the hospital. He donates them to the hospital and they use them as short-term accommodation for country families who need somewhere to stay. I get to decorate the ones that need it and furnish them before they're handed over to the hospital. I enjoy doing that.'

'How can you say that's not worthwhile? Think of all the families who benefit from what you've done.'

'I guess, but it's not like your job. You do so much good.'

'Don't be so hard on yourself. You give people somewhere nice to stay when they're going through a tough time and once you've got your fashion design degree you'll be able to help people's self-esteem.'

'That's a lovely thing to say but it's hardly in your league.'

'Don't underestimate the power of self-confidence,' he told her. 'Your designs could give people that.'

She smiled at him. 'You have a knack of making me feel better about myself. Thank you.'

'You're welcome,' he said, as he fetched a bowl of strawberries and a bowl of dipping chocolate. He didn't know about making Bella feel better but her smile made him feel invincible. She groaned and stretched her arms over her head as he returned to the rug. 'Are you all right?'

'Yes. I think I just need to rest before I tackle dessert,' she said as she lay back on the cushion. 'Thank you for organising tonight. No one has ever done anything like this for me before.'

It broke his heart to think of how much Bella had missed out on, how little attention she'd been given. 'I'm glad I could surprise you,' he said as he vowed to do more to help her realise the dreams she had on her wishlist.

'I feel like I've been let loose on the world. No one asking how I feel, or getting me to breathe in and out, no one taking blood samples or poking and prodding. I can pretend I'm just like everyone else,' she said as she shuffled over to make room for him on the rug.

He placed the two bowls by her knees and lay on his side, facing her. They were inches apart. He could see the faint, individual freckles that were scattered across the bridge of her nose and her grey eyes shone silver in the candlelight. She wanted to be like everyone else but she was so different from anyone he knew. And it wasn't because of her illness, although perhaps that had contributed. She had a vulnerability about her but he knew that was deceptive because he'd seen her strength of character time and again; and she had a generosity that was uncommon. She was a selfless person and she made him want to be more selfless too.

He took a strawberry from the bowl and dipped it into the chocolate. 'Can I tempt you?' he asked as he held the strawberry above her lips. She reached up and brought his hand down towards her. She parted her lips and bit into the berry with tiny white teeth.

She rolled onto her side towards him as she swallowed the strawberry. His hand dropped to her hip and then he was motionless. His other hand was supporting his head and he could feel his biceps tighten with the effort. He watched as Bella slowly, hesitantly, stretched out her hand and traced the bulge of his biceps.

In the distance a ferry tooted but the two of them were silent.

Charlie lifted his hand from her hip and threaded his fingers through her auburn curls. They were soft and springy under his touch. He shouldn't be doing this, he shouldn't be touching her like this, she was supposed to be off limits, but he couldn't resist. The movement of his arm made the hem of his T-shirt ride up, exposing his abdominals. He saw Bella's silvery grey eyes drop to his waist and follow the movement of his shirt. She removed her hand from his arm, slid her fingers under his T-shirt and traced the ridge of his abdominal muscles. Her fingers blazed a trail of fire across his skin and made him catch his breath.

He released her curls and caught her hand in his, stilling her movement as he entwined his fingers with hers. Bella held his hand and ran her thumb along his fingers. He tried to fight the attraction that was building in him. He tried to do the right thing but then Bella lifted his hand to her mouth and kissed the tips of his fingers then placed his hand over her heart, holding it against her chest. He could feel the swell of her breast under his palm. Her eyes were enormous. Her lips were parted and he could feel her warm breath on his face.

He knew he should resist but he also knew he was powerless to do so.

They were frozen in time and space. Their gazes locked as they held onto each other, as he tried to fight temptation and tried to resist desire.

He wasn't sure who moved first but suddenly the space between them, which was infinitesimal to begin with, had disappeared. Nothing separated them. Bella's eyes were closed, her lashes dark against her pale cheeks, and then his lips were on hers. Her lips were on his.

Desire and temptation had won.

It was a gentle kiss, a soft exploration, a beginning. He shouldn't be doing this but her lips were so warm, pliable and tender and now that he'd started he didn't want to stop. But he had to stop, he needed to stop. She was Evie's little sister, she wasn't his to conquer. He pulled back, releasing her, and watched as she opened her eyes. They were dark grey now, her pupils had grown so large the silvery grey was barely visible around the edges, and he knew she'd come back for more.

Would that make it all right? If she came to him, would that make it okay?

This time he watched and waited. It had to be Bella's choice.

She closed the gap. He waited until her lips covered his and then he took over. She tasted so sweet. His tongue teased her lips open and she didn't resist. She opened her mouth to him and their tongues met. She tasted like chocolate and strawberries. Warm chocolate.

Her breasts nudged against him and he could feel her nipples, hard against his chest. Her hips pushed into his groin as she slid both her hands under his T-shirt. He felt his own nipples harden as her fingers brushed over them.

Had she really told him she'd only been kissed once before? Maybe he'd misheard her the other night. He was finding it hard to believe right now as she certainly wasn't behaving like a novice. Her fingers were trailing over his abdominals again and then all thoughts of prior conversation fled his mind as he felt her fingers at the waistband of his jeans. She broke the kiss. He could hear her panting and at first he thought she was having difficulty with her breathing but when he looked into her eyes he knew it was simply arousal.

Bella sat up and pulled her shirt over her head. She was wearing a white cotton camisole underneath but no bra. Charlie could see the peaks of her nipples pushing against the fabric and he felt his own arousal stirring in response. She licked her lips. Her pink tongue traced the outline of her mouth and Charlie forced himself not to claim her mouth with his.

She cast her shirt aside and picked up the hem of his T-shirt, pulling it up to expose his stomach. She bent her head and kissed the warm skin on his hip bone, just above the waistband of his jeans. Charlie bit back a groan of desire. He felt her fingers slide behind the button of his jeans as her nails lightly scratched his skin.

'What are you doing?' he asked, and his voice was thick and heavy.

She poised, her fingers on his waistband, and fixed her gaze on him. 'Would you make love to me?'

He could feel her cool fingernails where they rested inside his waistband, against his stomach. He knew she was ready to flick his button undone, ready to make the decision for him, and he nearly didn't need to be asked twice. But then he remembered this was Bella, the girl he'd always thought of as shy, quiet, younger than her years. Had he got her wrong? Did she know what she was doing?

'You want me to make love to you?' he asked. His voice was thick in his throat, his words accompanied only by the sound of Bella's breathing. 'Now?'

She nodded.

'Are you sure?' He had to make certain she knew what she was asking.

'Yes.' Her voice was a whisper. 'I want you to be the first.'

CHAPTER SEVEN

HER first.

He hadn't misunderstood. She wasn't naïve but she was inexperienced.

Did he want to be responsible for this momentous event in Bella's life?

He couldn't do it. There was no way he could make love to her.

Not here, not tonight.

He knew he'd already broken the first rule. She should have been off limits entirely. But he could stop before he made things worse.

He should stop.

He held her hands in his, stilling her, and lifted them from the waistband of his jeans.

He would stop.

He shook his head. 'No.'

'No?' Bella's voice wobbled. 'Why not? Am I not your type? Am I not pretty enough?'

'Oh, Bella.' He shook his head again. 'You're beautiful. So beautiful.' He reached out and slid his fingers into her auburn curls. His suntanned hand was dark against the paleness of her cheek as his fingers rested lightly against her scalp. Her grey eyes watched him, unblinking. 'But I can't.'

'Can't, or won't?'

'Won't.'

'Why not?'

Because I'm not ready for this. He'd never thought that before but he knew this time it was true. Sex was usually about fulfilling a need, a desire. It wasn't something he thought too deeply about. But he wasn't prepared mentally or practically to make love to Bella. She had such a romantic view of the world and she would have expectations that went beyond simply fulfilling a need. This couldn't be a spur-of-the-moment decision.

She'd given up waiting for his reply. 'I know what I want. I want to experience this and I want it to be with you,' she said.

'Why?' Why on earth had she chosen him?

'Because I trust you.'

He almost groaned aloud. That made it ten times worse. It meant he had a duty of care to do it right. Still he hesitated.

'I won't regret this,' she said as he shook his head again.

'It's not because I think you'll regret this.' He'd make certain she didn't. 'But you're Evie's little sister.'

Perhaps saying it out loud would remind him to think of her only in a platonic sense. That was exactly how he used to think of her, but somewhere along the way his feelings had changed, grown and developed, and now he was having difficulty separating his conscience from his desire. He needed to remember that she was Evie's little sister. She was not his for the taking. No matter how nicely she asked.

'So? I'm twenty-six years old. I make my own decisions. Please,' she begged, 'I can't bear the thought that I won't ever know what it's like and I'm not brave enough to go looking for someone else who doesn't know me or care about my reasons.'

He couldn't imagine that either. He couldn't imagine her in bed with someone who didn't care about her or her reasons for wanting this. She was right. Why shouldn't she experience it? And why shouldn't she experience it with someone of her choosing? Half his brain said he should tread carefully but the other half agreed with Bella. Why shouldn't she have this experience while she still could? He knew he could give her pleasure. He knew he'd be able to give her what she wanted, at least physically, but he wasn't going to rush into it. He had to have time to make it special.

He felt an incredible obligation to make it perfect. To fulfil her dreams. It was immensely important that Bella got the experience she dreamed of. Perhaps because there was always a chance that this would be her only experience, it needed to be perfect.

She was looking at him hopefully.

He nodded. 'All right,' he said as his conscience gave up the fight, 'but you have to let me do it my way.'

'What does that mean?'

'It means yes, but not tonight. I want to make it perfect for you. Will you let me arrange it?'

She smiled at him. A glorious, bright smile that turned her grey eyes silver and made him forget about all the reasons he should be letting her down gently instead of agreeing to her crazy request.

'I'm going to Brisbane tomorrow for a weekend conference,' he said. 'You could meet me there? I'll book us a suite in a five-star hotel and we'll have a weekend to remember. You can pack your red negligee,' he suggested.

It had taken all her courage to ask him to make love to her but she was determined not to die a virgin and she couldn't think of anyone better to gift her innocence to than Charlie. She adored him but, better than that, she trusted him too. She knew she might only get one chance at this and she knew Charlie was capable of giving her something to remember. Something to cherish.

But she hadn't expected him not to take advantage of the present opportunity and her emotions felt as though they were on a roller-coaster ride. She'd gone from the high of their kiss to plummeting down the slippery slope when she'd heard 'No' but then he'd lifted her up again to a peak of expectation. She wondered where it would stop.

Brisbane sounded perfect but she couldn't do it. Her heart took another dive, colliding with her stomach, as she realised it wasn't going to happen. Not tonight. And not this weekend. Maybe not ever.

'I can't come with you.' Reality intervened and her euphoria vanished. She hoped it didn't mean she was going to miss her opportunity. 'I need to stay in Sydney in case a donor is found for me.'

'When I get back, then. The anticipation will make it even better, I guarantee it.' He smiled and his brown eyes held all sorts of promises.

He was going to grant her wish! Her emotions rocketed towards the heavens again as she felt her stomach do a lazy somersault when she thought about the things that lay in store for her. She was so close she could almost taste it. She could envisage in glorious detail how she would feel in his arms. How his skin would feel against hers, warm and silky with a firm layer of muscle underneath.

'But if a donor is found for me I'll be in hospital when you get back.'

'Then I'll let you out of our deal. If you have the surgery before we do this, you'll have plenty of time to choose someone else.'

Bella didn't want to choose anyone else but it was pretty obvious she couldn't tell Charlie that. He didn't want to hear how she'd fancied him for ever and that this was a way of making her fantasies a reality. So she had to be content with his promise for now.

'Come on, it's getting late. You should get inside before it gets too cold out here.' Charlie stood and held out his hand, pulling her to her feet. He scooped a cashmere rug up from the carpet and wrapped it around her shoulders before he walked her back to the house. He stopped at the conservatory doors and turned her to face him. He reached out one hand and cupped her chin, tilting it up until his lips met hers. Her mouth opened under his pressure and she felt herself float under his caress. A slow-burning fire was glowing in her belly, awakening every nerve ending in her body. The kiss was full of promise and expectation. It was a kiss that could change her world.

'I'll see you soon,' he said as he broke their contact. Her lips were cold without his touch. 'Wait for me.'

It had been the perfect kiss. And he was promising more. In a few days she would be in Charlie's bed.

Wait for me, he'd said.

She could wait. But only just.

Charlie watched Bella as she slept. Her auburn curls were bright against the white sheets, her lashes dark against her cheeks. He could see the rise and fall of her chest as she breathed in and out and he could see her fingers move as one hand twitched involuntarily. He wondered if she was dreaming.

Her lips were pale pink and he recalled how they'd tasted of strawberries and warm chocolate. He watched as her lips moved and he wondered what she was dreaming about. He wondered if she was making any sound at all but he couldn't tell from where he stood, separated, distant and apart from her.

It had only been three days since he'd seen her but it seemed like a lifetime. So much had changed. So much had slipped away. Would things ever be the same? Would they ever recover what had been lost, the chances they'd had? The chances they hadn't taken. The chances *he* hadn't taken.

He'd left for the conference in Brisbane full of hope. He'd told Bella that anticipation would make the experience even better and that was something he firmly believed. It was one of the things he loved about beginnings. One thing he loved about the start of a new relationship. The build-up of anticipation and expectation that culminated in a crescendo of pleasure. Once that died away he knew he struggled to maintain interest. Once the excitement of new experiences and new challenges had been tasted he had a habit of losing interest, but with Bella things felt different.

He'd spent the last nine years deliberately doing his own thing. Avoiding relationships, avoiding commitment, making sure he always had an escape route, making sure he always had freedom, but when he was with Bella he forgot about running away. Instead, he was thinking about what he could do for her. He wanted to show her things, teach her things, he wanted to see her face light up when she tried something new or made a discovery, he wanted to see her smile when someone did something nice for her.

He was entranced by her. He felt like a different person when he was with her. He was calmer. More content. He wanted to have a connection with her. A connection that went beyond sex, and it felt good to be thinking about someone else for a change. It felt good to be looking forward.

He'd expected to come home from Brisbane to find

Bella eagerly awaiting his arrival. But he hadn't expected to find her here.

He'd called her while he'd been away only to be told she was back in hospital with another chest infection. He couldn't get back soon enough.

And now he stood, watching her from the other side of a glass window. It was fair to say things hadn't turned out quite as he'd planned.

At Sam's insistence Bella had been put into an isolation room. Her immune system had taken a hammering and she couldn't afford to get any other infections, something that was always a risk in hospital.

He watched her as she slept, although he could barely see her for all the leads and tubes she was connected to. He tried to ignore the oxygen tube, the nasogastric tube, the drip, the cardiac monitors and the oximeter. He knew she'd gone downhill rapidly over the past forty-eight hours. He knew it was critical that a donor was found for her; her lungs weren't going to last much longer.

He tried to focus on her hands, her eyes, her hair, her lips, on the parts of her that looked familiar. He wanted to go in to see her, he wanted to tell her he was back, but he wasn't sure if he should. She might not be quite as keen to see him as he was to see her.

He couldn't go into her room without scrubbing. He had to gown and glove first. He turned away from the window as he tried to decide what to do and saw Evie coming towards him.

'Hi,' she said. 'Have you just been in to see Bella?'

Charlie shook his head. 'She's asleep and I'm not sure if I should go in.'

'Why not?'

'I think I've caused enough trouble. I'm probably the last person she'd want to see.'

Evie frowned. 'What are you talking about?'

'I think I might have made her sick.' Logically he knew it was unlikely but he hadn't been able to get the idea out of his head.

'She's got another chest infection,' Evie replied. 'How is that your fault?'

'I kissed her.'

'You did what?'

Charlie cringed inwardly at Evie's tone. 'I kissed her,' he repeated.

'Why? What on earth for?' Evie sounded furious and she hadn't finished yet. 'I thought you were keeping her company, keeping her occupied so she didn't have time to dwell on things. I didn't think you had ulterior motives.'

'It wasn't like that.'

'No? She's not someone you can play with. She's vulnerable, innocent. Don't think of making her one of your conquests.'

He'd thought she was innocent too, until the other night. Now he knew she was just inexperienced and that had put a whole different perspective on things. But he couldn't tell Evie that any more than he could tell Evie how he felt about her little sister. He still wasn't sure himself.

'You'd better have a damn good reason for kissing her.'

'Bella has a list of things she wants to do,' he explained. 'A wishlist she calls it. A kiss was one of the things on her list.'

'So you were doing her a favour?'

Evie sounded sceptical and he couldn't blame her. It was a pretty lame excuse and one he didn't believe himself.

'In a way.'

'Well, don't do her any more favours. She's not worldly enough to handle you. You'll break her heart.'

'It was just a kiss. A consensual one. She asked me to

kiss her and I did,' he said with a shrug as he tried to pretend it hadn't turned his world upside down. 'I have no intention of breaking her heart.'

'No one ever intends to do that but it happens anyway,' Evie argued.

'I don't think her heart's in any danger but if it makes you feel better, I'm sorry. I didn't mean to make her sick.'

'When did you kiss her?'

'Why? What difference does that make?'

'Just answer me.'

'It was Thursday night.'

Evie was shaking her head now. 'Bella was back in hospital on Friday. It would be unusual for her to get sick that quickly, she must have already had the infection. You can't blame yourself for that, but promise me you'll keep your lips to yourself from now on.'

Charlie didn't want to make that promise. He didn't trust himself to keep it. He tried a compromise and hoped Evie wouldn't notice he hadn't agreed to her request. 'Believe me, I have no intention of hurting Bella. If there was anything I could do to help I would. I want to keep her safe. I want to make her better but it's not up to me. Do you know how that feels?'

Evie looked through the window at Bella's inert form. 'I know exactly how that feels,' she said quietly, her earlier anger replaced with a hint of regret.

Of course she would. After all, Bella was her sister. Charlie wrapped one arm around Evie's shoulders and hugged her tightly. 'I'm sorry.' He was sorry she was going through this and sorry there was nothing he could do for Evie or Bella. He hated feeling so powerless.

Evie sighed. 'I'm sorry too,' she said.

* * *

Evie was sorry for a lot of things but she wasn't sorry that Bella had Charlie in her life. Not really. But she hadn't counted on a romantic involvement between them. In her opinion that complicated matters.

Physically Bella was a mess and Evie didn't want to have to worry about her emotional state as well. With their mother's medical history there was always a chance that the girls could have issues as well. Who knew what it might take to push one of them over the edge and into the abyss if they weren't coping? Who knew if Bella was susceptible?

Evie didn't want to find out.

In Evie's mind it didn't matter what was on Bella's wishlist, Charlie should have known better. What had he been thinking? Bella didn't have the emotional strength or experience to handle Charlie.

Evie had to protect her little sister. She couldn't do anything about Bella's lungs but she'd make certain no one trampled on her heart. Not that she thought Charlie would intentionally do that but she knew how Bella worshipped Charlie. Anyone who knew Bella as well as she did would see that. And she also knew Charlie's reputation. He didn't set out to hurt women, he just wasn't prepared to invest in a relationship emotionally. He wasn't prepared for anything serious, and Bella wouldn't handle a casual fling well, not as her first experience. Evie needed to do whatever she could to protect Bella. She acknowledged that Bella's physical state was more serious at the moment than her emotional state but Bella certainly didn't need Charlie, or anyone else, throwing spanners in the works at present. She had enough to deal with.

But no matter what she thought about Charlie kissing Bella she knew he couldn't have made her sick. She'd got sick much too soon afterwards for that. Evie didn't blame

Charlie for giving Bella an infection but she would certainly blame him if he broke Bella's heart.

Although he'd seemed sincere when he'd said he wished there was something he could do for Bella, and Evie knew he meant it, it was just that there wasn't anything practical either of them could do. They were both in the same situation, both useless.

Or was she? she wondered, as the lift doors opened, delivering her to the emergency department, and she saw Finn going into the doctors' lounge. Was she useless or was there something she could do?

She'd been avoiding Finn as much as possible. She was still irritated with him over the disappearing trick he'd pulled, but now she needed to speak to him. Here was her chance.

She followed him into the lounge, hoping he was alone.

As she pushed open the door she saw Finn turn away and shove something into his pocket before he turned back to face her. She glanced around and noted there was no one else besides them in the room. 'Do you have a moment?' she asked.

'What is it?' he barked at her, but Evie chose to ignore his tone. She needed to speak to him and if he was going to bite her head off, that was a chance she was prepared to take.

'I have a favour to ask, a professional favour,' she added before he had a second to object. 'Bella is back in hospital, she has another lung infection and she's deteriorated badly. She's in a critical condition and desperately needs a transplant.' As quickly as she could she explained why she was there—she didn't want Finn to have an opportunity to interrupt. She didn't want him to have time to think of a reason to say no. 'The other day you asked if there was anything you could do. I need to know if your offer still stands.'

'What do you need?'

He was rubbing the outside of his right upper arm while he was speaking to her. His movement was distracting but he didn't seem to be aware of it. She'd noticed this habit on a few occasions, usually when he was in a bad mood, and although his tone wasn't quite as angry as before it was still hardly what she'd call pleasant. But she wasn't going to let him dissuade her and she pushed ahead with her request.

'If—when,' she corrected herself, 'a donor becomes available for Bella, would you assist Sam with the surgery?'

'Why? Sam is more than capable.'

'I know, but I'd feel better if you were both in the theatre. I couldn't think of two better people to have operating.'

'Joe Minnillo would normally assist,' Finn argued. 'What do you plan on telling him? That he's not required?'

Evie shook her head. 'No. He could be there as well. I'd just prefer it if you were there too.'

'It's not all about you, princess.'

She hated it when he called her that but she wasn't about to have that discussion with him now. There were far more important things on her agenda. 'I know that,' she retorted. She felt like stamping her foot or shaking him. Why did he have to be so pig-headed? 'It's about my little sister. Organ transplant is a massive undertaking. You and Sam together are the best in the business. Wouldn't you want to give your sibling every chance if you were in my situation?'

Finn's heart had been so badly damaged a long time ago that he was amazed it could still beat, let alone still be wounded by old memories, but Evie's words were like a knife through his heart and he could feel the air being knocked from his chest. Evie knew he'd lost his brother. How dare she use that against him like this?

The memories flooded back into his consciousness, accompanied by the sensations of a time he'd rather forget. He could almost feel the hot desert wind on his face and taste the gritty sand in his mouth, the sand that had managed to make its way into every crevice, making life uncomfortable, making working conditions even more difficult. But the heat, the noise and the sand had been the least of his problems.

Isaac's face erupted from his subconscious. He closed his eyes but that just made the memories more vivid.

He could hear the whistling of the bombs raining down onto the army base. The deafening explosions as they thudded into the buildings and the ground and the people unlucky enough to be in their way. He could feel the sensation of the earth shuddering as bombs detonated. The screams of the injured, the moans of the dying.

He could smell the scent of death, the sweet, distinctive smell of blood, the putrid, foul scent of torn intestines. He could feel the warm stickiness of fresh blood, his own blood mingling with the blood of others. He could see devastation everywhere he looked. Buildings were reduced to rubble and protruding from that rubble were the limbs of the dead and the dying.

He remembered how it felt to hold someone he loved in his arms and watch as they died. He could recall his final words, begging, pleading, for Isaac to hang on just a little bit longer, until help was at hand.

But it had all been in vain. He'd had to watch as Isaac breathed his final breath, watch as his eyes stared vacantly, seeing nothing. He remembered the awful feeling of helplessness and hopelessness, knowing there was nothing he could do.

At the time his anguish had been so all-consuming it had obliterated his physical pain. He hadn't even registered until much later that he too had been injured.

And even though his injuries had been extensive, his physical pain severe, it had been nothing compared to the pain of losing his brother.

'Finn? Are you okay?'

CHAPTER EIGHT

HE OPENED his eyes to find Evie watching him closely. She was staring at him, a worried expression in her hazel eyes, a narrow crease between her eyebrows as she frowned. She was probably wondering what on earth had got into him. Isaac had died a long time ago but Finn still felt his loss just as keenly today.

A sharp, hot pain burned into his right biceps, shooting from his neck down his arm. This pain was a daily reminder of everything he'd lost. He could feel his thumb going numb and he opened and closed his hand rapidly, trying to encourage his circulation, even though he knew it was a wasted exercise. The numbness wasn't caused by poor circulation—it was all related to a damaged cervical disc—but although the physical pain was coming from his neck, the emotional pain was coming from deep inside him. Rubbing his arm and clenching his fist would do nothing for his discomfort.

'I'm fine,' he lied.

He thought he'd done such a good job of burying his grief. He was surprised to feel the pain of events from years ago resurfacing and shocked by its intensity. He knew he would react just as Evie had in the same situation. He knew he'd try his hardest, try anything, to save his sibling.

He'd been there too. He couldn't blame her for wanting the best.

'There's no point discussing this now, not until a suitable donor is found. I'll talk to Sam then,' he said. He would speak to Sam about assisting him for Bella's operation and, if Sam was agreeable, he would help, but he couldn't see the point in making arrangements until there were lungs for Bella. The pain in his arm—and in his heart—was starting to overwhelm him.

He knew his tone was dismissive but he wanted Evie out of the room. His painkilling tablets were burning a hole in the pocket of his white coat and he needed to take them soon, before his pain worsened, before he developed a headache, but he wasn't about to take them in front of anyone. Especially not Evie. She was bound to ask questions. She didn't seem to know when to leave well enough alone.

Charlie's day had been long and exhausting. He'd had a complicated hip replacement op, which had required total concentration, but he'd found his mind had kept drifting to Bella and fighting to keep his attention focussed in Theatre had only added to his exhaustion. He was looking forward to calling into Pete's Bar for a beer before heading home but he wasn't leaving the hospital without seeing Bella first. If he had to sit beside her and wait for her to wake up, he would. Being with her gave him some respite from the madness of his days. She was always so calm and composed and he found that refreshing. He had a habit of being constantly on the go and Bella made him stop.

Usually he got his downtime in the water. Swimming laps gave him a chance to clear his head. He loved that solitary sensation, the fact that no one could talk to him or expect a conversation as he swam lengths of a pool or dived through the waves, but recently he'd found that Bella's company gave him that sense of peace as well.

He made his way to her room. Through the window he could see Evie sitting with her. A surgical mask covered the lower half of Evie's face but her eyes were puffy and her cheeks, what he could see of them, were tear-stained. She was holding Bella's hand but Bella was very still and very pale and for a moment Charlie thought the worst before he realised all the monitors were still attached and he could see her pulse and blood pressure registering on the screen.

Evie looked up and saw him standing on the other side of the glass. She stood and came to meet him, pulling the mask from her face as she came out of Bella's room.

'What's going on? Why are you crying?' he asked as the worry he'd been battling with all day came flooding back.

'She's gone downhill, I don't know what the matter is, it's almost like she's giving up.' Evie's voice caught in her throat and Charlie knew she was holding back tears.

'Why would she do that?'

'I have no idea.'

'Has Sam been to see her?'

Evie nodded. 'But he didn't have any answers. Physically he says her condition is unchanged.'

'What else has happened today? Has anything happened to upset her?'

'Miranda came to see her.'

'Your mother? Why?' Charlie knew Miranda's presence was always enough to upset any of the Lockheart sisters.

'Apparently Bella asked her to come.'

'What on earth for?'

'I don't know, she wouldn't tell me. She hasn't said anything else. The nurses told me Bella asked them to call Miranda. And now Bella's just lying there. Not speaking.'

'She's awake?'

Evie nodded. 'Would you talk to her, see if you can find out what's going on? She can't give up, she has to keep fighting.'

Charlie agreed with Evie. Bella couldn't give up. 'Bella seems to think your mother left because of her. Because she isn't perfect enough. Is she right?' he asked.

'She told you that?' Evie's voice was incredulous.

Charlie nodded.

'We've never had an explanation as to why she left so I couldn't say if Bella's illness contributed to Miranda's problems, none of us can say, but Bella has always felt it was tied to her. I'm not so sure.' Evie was frowning. 'I can remember, even when I was small, being told she was lying down with a headache and I wasn't to disturb her. That probably started when I was five, around the time Bella was born, and I have wondered whether that was when she started drinking, but I couldn't say for certain because I don't remember anything from a younger age. I do know things escalated when I was nine. That's when Miranda left for the first time. Bella was four, Lexi was two and I was nine.

'I'm really not sure who even made the decision that Miranda would move out,' she continued. 'It could have been our father. He bought her an apartment and he still makes sure she's okay but from then on we were never allowed to spend any time alone with her, not while we were little. Any time she spent with us was always supervised by nannies. Sometimes I wonder whether that was the right decision—children need a mother—but I guess Miranda wasn't the sort of mother Richard wanted for us. Whether it was him or her who decided she'd move out, I know it was Richard who organised the supervision and none of us has an easy or normal relationship with our mother.' Evie shrugged. 'Miranda suffers from depression and an addiction to alcohol. If you want my opinion, I think Miranda would have had problems even without Bella's illness. I think she's one of those people who just finds life itself hard to cope with. Her behaviour has affected us all but in time you learn to ignore it or accept it.'

Charlie didn't think any of the sisters had accepted it and he wasn't sure how successfully they ignored it either. Particularly Bella. 'Bella's made a few references to your mother and I think it's something she hasn't learnt to ignore or accept yet. You and Lexi might have been able to do that but I don't think Bella has. I'll talk to her but there's no guarantee she'll tell me anything.'

'I know, but she's told you a lot of things lately that have surprised me and I don't have any other ideas,' Evie said as she stripped off her gown and threw it into the linen basket as Charlie started to scrub.

Scrubbed and gowned, he hesitated in the doorway of Bella's room. The room looked wrong but it took him a second or two to work out why. There was none of Bella's personality on display. There was no sketch book, no laptop, no DVDs.

Bella's eyes were still closed but some sixth sense must have alerted her to his presence because she opened her eyes as he crossed the room. The expression in them made his heart shrink in his chest. He felt it shrivel with fear. She looked crushed, exhausted, and he realised he'd hoped Evie had been wrong. But she knew Bella better than anyone so of course she'd pick up on her sister's emotions.

Bella looked defeated and his immediate thought was that he had to find a way to restore her spirit. He'd come to rely on her strength and courage and to see this expression of resignation in her eyes was frightening. He was *not* going to watch her give up. Not without a fight.

He mustered up his courage, striving to sound positive as he picked up her hand and brought it to his lips. '*Ciao*, Bella.'

She had so many leads coming off her it was impossible to get near her, and her hand was the only part of her he could get to. He kissed her fingers through his mask. As far as kisses went it was rather unsatisfactory but it was better than nothing.

He got a faint smile in response to his greeting. Her usual warmth was lacking and her smile didn't reach her eyes but he refused to give up. He sat beside her in the chair Evie had recently vacated. He didn't let go of her hand. It was silly but he felt by holding onto her he could anchor her to his world.

'I missed you while I was in Brisbane.'

'You did?' Her voice was hoarse. It sounded like her throat was hurting, which wasn't surprising given the nasogastric tube she had running into her stomach.

'You would have loved it. There was more food than even you would have known what to do with; the drug companies are very generous with their sponsorship of those conferences. I'll take you with me next time.'

'Next time?'

'Unless you've changed your mind. Is all this…' he gestured around the room '…an elaborate ruse to get out of our deal?'

She was shaking her head but even that slight movement seemed like an effort. 'I don't think there's going to be a next time.'

'What do you mean?'

There was a cup filled with ice chips on the table over her bed and she reached out and picked up the spoon, slipping an ice cube into her mouth. Sucking on it, moistening her throat before she answered. Charlie waited, still holding her hand.

'I'm tired. I've had enough.'

His heart, which was already sitting in his chest like a lump of stone, sank to his stomach. 'What? Why? What about all the things you wanted to do?'

'It's too late.'

'No, it's not. You were going to fight. What's happened? Why would you give up now?'

Bella turned her head away from Charlie but not before he saw tears in her eyes. First Evie, now Bella. What was going on? Miranda. It had to be.

He wasn't going to let her ignore him. He wasn't going to let her keep her problems bottled up inside her. That wouldn't do her any good. He needed to know what had happened. He needed to understand what was going on if he was going to be able to help. And there was no other option. He knew that keeping things bottled up allowed the hurt to fester, allowed it to feed on itself until it could take over a person's soul until you couldn't see a way out.

'Evie told me Miranda came to see you today. How did that go?'

She turned her head to face him. 'It was good.'

Charlie felt his eyebrows lift. That wasn't the answer he'd expected. 'Good?'

'I asked my mother to come,' Bella explained. 'There were questions I wanted answered, questions I've never been brave enough to ask. I told her I wanted to know some things before I die.'

'You're not—'

'Don't.' She lifted a hand as she interrupted him. 'I'm struggling, Charlie. I don't want to keep fighting for every breath.'

Charlie couldn't find the words he needed. Why couldn't

he think of something to say? He should have some words of inspiration, words of encouragement, but he had nothing. Bella continued speaking as Charlie sat, mute and confused. 'I got the answers I'd been looking for. It's not my mother's fault they weren't the answers I wanted. I've only got myself to blame.'

'What was it you wanted to know?' he asked, even though he was pretty sure he knew the answer.

'I asked her why she left us.'

Bella pulled her hand from his hold to pick up the cup of ice chips. He thought she was using the cup as an excuse to break the contact but there wasn't much he could do about it.

'And?' Surely she was going to tell him the rest of the story? He could understand why she might not have shared this with Evie, particularly if the tale was unpleasant, but she couldn't leave it here. He had to know more.

'Apparently she had postnatal depression after my birth but it was undiagnosed until after Lexi was born. She says she couldn't cope with any of us, she found motherhood totally overwhelming.'

Charlie breathed a sigh of relief. PND made perfect sense and it meant Miranda's issues couldn't be attributed to Bella. 'There you go. It wasn't your fault. Postnatal depression is not the baby's fault. You are not responsible for your mother's mental health issues.'

But Bella continued as though he hadn't spoken.

'She said she felt guilty because I was sick. She started drinking after I was born. At first it was a gin and tonic when Dad got home from work, to keep him company, but then it became one late in the afternoon while she waited for him and then one after she'd picked Evie up from school. She said she tried to stop when she fell pregnant with Lexi but after a while she started again. She drank gin with lemon and soda, though, because of the side effects of tonic water.' Bella laughed, but her laugh was devoid of humour. 'Ironic, isn't it? She gave up the soft drink because of the side effects but she couldn't give up the alcohol. She would have been worried that Lexi was going to be born with CF too. I don't think she would have cared if she'd suffered a miscarriage. I think that's probably why she kept drinking. So, you see, it all started with me,' she said as she slid another ice chip onto her tongue.

Was Bella right? Had she been the catalyst? Maybe she had but he wasn't about to agree with her.

'Your mother needs to take ownership of her problems.'

'I don't blame myself for my mother's addiction but I do blame myself for her abandonment.'

'How can it be your fault? You were four when she left.'

'There's plenty more to the story. Are you sure you want to hear this?' Bella paused and didn't continue until Charlie nodded. He wasn't certain he wanted to hear what she had to say but he knew he had no choice. 'Apparently she fell pregnant again when Lexi was eighteen months old. The pregnancy was unplanned and she freaked out, worried she couldn't cope with another baby, but especially worried about coping with another child with cystic fibrosis. Genetic testing for CF was very new but she was offered the test and she had it done. The test came back positive. She was going to have another child with CF. She terminated the pregnancy. She didn't want to bring another CF baby into the world. Her depression got worse after that, she says it was the guilt. She couldn't cope with life at all without alcohol to prop her up. And then she left. She abandoned us.'

'But you weren't the trigger for her abandonment.' Charlie tried to get Bella to see reason. Tried and failed.

'Don't you see, if genetic testing had been available

when she was pregnant with me, she would have aborted me. I know she would. But it was too late, she couldn't get rid of me, so she left. I always thought I was the reason she left. Now I know I was right.'

'But she wouldn't have even *known* to be tested for CF with you. She wouldn't have been expecting it.'

'Either way, she wouldn't have wanted me. Doesn't want me. Everything started with me. It would have been better for everyone if I was never born.'

Bella was normally so upbeat, so ridiculously positive despite everything she faced, that he found it quite disturbing to hear her being so negative. Was she depressed? He couldn't blame her if she was, she was critically ill, but he couldn't understand why she was so fixated on her mother. Surely she had more important things to worry about, like whether compatible lungs would be found in time to save her life. He wondered if he should speak to Sam about getting John Allen to assess Bella again but he'd hate to find that a potential transplant was cancelled because of Bella's state of mind. He couldn't instigate something that might put her in that situation. 'How do you figure that?' he asked.

'Life would have been very different for Evie and Lexi if Mum hadn't had me. She might never have got postnatal depression. She might never have left.'

'That's a lot of "mights",' he said. 'She might have got it after Lexi anyway and from where I sit your mother clearly has a lot of issues. You can't blame yourself.'

'I've been waiting to die all my life. I never expected to live to an old age. Having my suspicions confirmed, knowing I wasn't wanted, kind of makes it all seem so pointless.'

'Hang on, your mother never actually said she didn't want you, did she?'

'She said motherhood was overwhelming.'

'I don't think she's alone in that sentiment but it doesn't mean she didn't want you. It just means she couldn't cope and unfortunately her depression wasn't diagnosed early. It's not your fault.'

'I don't care. I'm too tired to care. Lexi and Sam can get married in one week, I just want to last that long.' She'd had enough. She wasn't going to get the happy ending she'd always wanted. No one could give that to her. Not Sam, not her sisters, not her parents and not Charlie.

Her mother would be relieved she didn't have to visit hospitals any more, her father wouldn't even notice she was gone. Her sisters would miss her but Lexi would settle down to her new life with Sam and Evie would be able to lead her own life once the burden of worrying about Bella had been lifted from her slim shoulders. And Charlie, well, Charlie would continue to live his life completely oblivious to the fact that Bella had been in love with him.

She was tired of fighting and she was tired of wishing for things that weren't going to happen.

But Charlie was distraught. Bella had to fight. If she stopped fighting, if she gave up now, she'd be lost. He knew it was only willpower that would keep her going, keep her alive. Lexi's wedding might be enough incentive to get through the next week, but then what? He had to find another reason for her to keep fighting.

'What about your wishlist? What about us? You and I have unfinished business.'

She smiled at him and his heart lifted as he caught a glimpse of the old Bella, the one who had a desire to go out and live her life. She shrugged her skinny shoulders. 'It doesn't matter any more. It'll just be something else on my wishlist that isn't done. It was a stupid list and a stupid idea. There's only one thing I want now and that's to see Lexi and Sam married. That's my last wish. My dying wish.'

CHAPTER NINE

'BELLA, no! Please, you can't give up. You have to find something worth fighting for.'

'It's my time, Charlie, I can feel it.'

'But you're not the type to give up. You just need to hold on for a little bit longer. You'll get new lungs, you have to.'

She gave the tiniest shake of her head. 'I'm so tired.' Her voice caught in her throat. 'I'm tired of fighting to stay out of hospital, I'm tired of fighting to put on weight, I'm tired of taking a thousand tablets, I'm tired of fighting to breathe, I'm tired of wanting my parents to love me.'

So that's what this was all about. He should have known. Bella just wanted to be loved. She needed to be loved.

'I know what it's like to want to give up but you can't, you have to keep fighting. Do it for the people who love you. Do it for Evie and Lexi.'

A reflex almost made him say 'Do it for me' but he hesitated and Bella picked up on his hesitation.

'Yes?'

He shook his head.

'What were you about to say?' she asked.

You're a coward, Charlie Maxwell, his conscience told him, but he couldn't talk about things he didn't understand. He couldn't tell her he couldn't imagine his life without her in it because he wasn't exactly sure what that meant and, if his words could be misconstrued, if he upset Bella, Evie would have him hung, drawn and quartered.

He'd promised Evie he wouldn't break Bella's heart so he swallowed his words and delivered some different ones. Safer ones. 'I was about to tell you a story.'

'Go on.'

He wasn't sure if she was really interested but he had one last chance to convince her to keep fighting. 'I understand what you're going through,' he said. 'I know what it feels like to want to give up but you've got to believe that this is not the end. You've got to believe things will get better. After I had my scooter accident in Bali I struggled to deal with it. I couldn't see what the point in living was once I lost everything that was important to me. At the age of twenty-three I thought my world was over. For some time I wished I'd died in that accident. It ended my surfing career but it also took away the woman I loved.'

He could tell from her expression that he'd shocked her. That was good. It meant she was listening. Maybe he'd get through to her after all.

'Was she killed in the accident?'

'No.' He shook his head. 'I'd fallen in love and fallen hard. We dreamt of travelling the world together, following the surfing tour, living in perpetual sunshine and good times. But after the accident it turned out that Pippa preferred the life of sunshine and good times to a life with me. She followed the tour and left me behind. I'd lost everything. I went home to lick my wounds, wallowing in my misery. Eventually Dad got sick of me and what he saw as my unhealthy, obsessive behaviour and convinced me to find a new interest. He talked me into going back to uni, back to medical school. He told me in no uncertain terms that I had to find a new obsession and a new way of making a living, just as he'd done. I didn't dare argue.

If Dad hadn't given up after his accident, I couldn't. I let him talk me into it and I'm glad I did. Initially it gave me something else to focus on but it soon became my passion. My family pulled me back to living and once I got to uni Evie's friendship pulled me through that first year. It was tough but between my family and Evie I got back on track. Now it's your turn to look to the future.'

'But my family doesn't need me.'

'If you truly believe that then you need to find another reason to keep going. What about going to college? What about your dream?'

'There's no guarantee I'll even be accepted. It all seems so pointless.'

'Let me help you through this,' he offered.

But that wasn't enough to convince her and why should it be? He wasn't offering her what she wanted. He couldn't. He couldn't imagine his life without her in it but that wasn't the same as being in love with her. It couldn't be. People didn't fall in love that quickly.

Charlie turned and started another lap. He'd been swimming for close to an hour but his head had only just started to clear. When he'd left Bella last night he'd been upset and frustrated and he'd stopped at Pete's Bar, where he'd had one too many beers in an attempt to escape the fact there was nothing he could do for Bella. He was paying the price this morning.

He'd tried his best but it wasn't enough. He hadn't been able to get through to her, hadn't known how to, so he'd tried to forget. She was looking for unconditional love. He couldn't help her.

When he eventually climbed out of the pool and towelled himself dry, he saw a message waiting for him on his phone. A message from Evie.

His thoughts immediately turned to Bella. Had something happened?

His hand shook. He didn't want to read the message, he was terrified it would be bad news, but then his brain slowly kicked into gear and he realised she wouldn't text with bad news. But his hand was still shaking as he pushed 'open'.

'We have lungs. Sam prepping Bella now.'

Charlie started pulling on his clothes, not bothering to get properly dry, shoved his things into his bag and ran to his car. Evie had left the message a little over half an hour ago. Bella would be in Theatre now but he needed to be at the hospital. He wasn't working today but he'd wait there. He might as well pace those corridors, it was better than being home alone.

Bella was getting new lungs. It wasn't over yet.

Lexi and Richard were already in the family lounge attached to the cardiothoracic unit when Evie arrived.

'Have I missed Sam?' she asked. She hoped not, she had some urgent questions for him.

Lexi shook her head. 'He should be back soon.'

Three heads swivelled expectantly as a fourth person entered the room. But this person was wearing two-inch heels, was dressed all in black and had platinum blonde hair.

Evie froze. Miranda looked sober, but it was only early.

Richard stepped forward, and for a brief moment Evie wondered if he was going to stop Miranda from coming any further, but then she realised he was positioning himself between her mother and her as if he expected Evie to react badly. He lifted a hand and ushered Miranda into the room, settling her in a chair. 'Hello, Miranda.' His voice was tender as he greeted his wife. As far as Evie knew, neither of her parents had ever contemplated a divorce and it was obvious Richard still cared for Miranda, making Evie wonder again why he hadn't tried harder to help her. Perhaps he'd done all he could.

Miranda sat, clutching her handbag on her lap, holding it in front of her like a protective shield, but it wasn't enough to stop her hands from shaking. But Evie wasn't going to criticise her today, her own hands were shaking too.

Richard spoke to them all next. 'Do you think we could all put our differences aside, just for today at least, and focus on getting through this day? Forget the past and look to the future, one, I hope, will include Bella.' He looked at each of the women in turn but Evie felt his message was directed at her.

Three heads nodded in reply as they all contemplated what this day might bring.

Sam walked into the lounge and if he was surprised by how quiet everyone was, he didn't show it. 'All right, I'm just about to go and see Bella before we start. Is everyone okay here?' he asked. 'Any last-minute questions?'

'Are you sure Bella is strong enough for the surgery? She's not too sick, is she?' Miranda asked, astounding Evie, who'd thought Miranda was too self-involved to even realise how sick Bella was. Had she misjudged her mother?

'This is her best chance,' Sam replied. 'What's making her so sick at present is the infection in her lungs. The transplant will get rid of that, along with her diseased lungs, and I expect she'll feel better almost from the moment she comes out of the anaesthetic.'

'Is Finn going to assist?' Evie asked. That was her urgent question. She needed to know if Finn had kept his word.

'No.' Sam gave her a puzzled look.

'Didn't he speak to you?'

Sam shook his head.

'I asked him if he'd speak to you about assisting. I wanted you both to be there.'

'I haven't heard from him,' Sam said, but he didn't dismiss her query lightly. He put his hands on her shoulders and made her focus on him. 'We don't have time to organise it anyway. I don't need Finn. Bella will be fine.'

Evie knew Sam couldn't guarantee that, she knew he was saying that because it was what they all needed to hear. At the moment she wasn't a doctor, she was Bella's sister. She too needed to believe that modern medicine could work miracles. And she knew miracles did happen. But she also knew they didn't always happen when you wanted them to.

But all she could do was wait and pray and hope Sam was right. But if anything went wrong, if anything happened to Bella, she was going to track Finn Kennedy down and flay him alive. She didn't care if he was the Head of Surgery, all that meant was that if anything did go awry the buck stopped with him and she'd make sure he knew all about it.

'What do you mean, you can't take her off the ventilator?'

After close to nine hours, Bella's surgery was over. It had gone like clockwork, according to Sam, except for one thing.

'Her new lungs are viable, they're inflating perfectly, but Bella isn't breathing independently. I'm positive it's only a temporary measure but obviously we have to keep her breathing. She's ventilated but we have her on the lowest oxygen setting so when she's ready to breathe on her own, we'll know. She's sedated now but we'll wake her for short periods each day to assess her condition.'

Charlie was stunned and judging by the expressions he could see around him the Lockheart family was just as bewildered. This wasn't how the day was supposed to turn out. Bella's life was supposed to be improving. She wasn't supposed to be in ICU on a ventilator, and to make matters worse he knew he wouldn't be able to see her today. It would be family only and even they would only be allowed in one at a time for a few minutes. He was just a family friend. He was a long way down the list.

He didn't want to be at the bottom of that list, he realised, but he couldn't do anything about it at present. He would have to be patient.

Evie visited Bella very briefly, staying just long enough to see for herself that everything was as Sam had said. Bella was fine, if you counted being ventilated fine, and at least her new lungs worked. As long as she didn't reject them, everything would probably be okay. But probably wasn't good enough for Evie. She was angry and upset and looking for someone to take her frustrations out on. She went looking for Finn. He was Head of Surgery, she'd asked him to help, and he'd been nowhere to be seen. He'd better have a very good reason for ignoring her. She could accept it if he'd said he wasn't going to help but he'd told her he would talk to Sam if lungs became available. Yet, when the time had come, when it had mattered, he'd been nowhere to be found. In Evie's opinion that wasn't good enough. Not from any surgeon and especially not from the Head of Surgery.

Finding out that Finn wasn't in the hospital, had in fact not been seen all day, didn't deter her. If the mountain wasn't coming to Mohammed, she'd have to go to him.

Her heart was racing in her chest as she knocked on

his penthouse door. Visions of what had happened the last time she'd knocked on his door came flooding back. She felt a rush of heat to her cheeks as she remembered what had transpired between them then—raw, impulsive, take-no-prisoners sex. The best sex she'd ever had. She still wasn't sure how that was possible. Wasn't sex supposed to be better if there was an emotional connection? Wasn't that why it was called making love? But there had certainly been no love between them. It had simply been sex, down and dirty, and incredible.

'Princess, what a pleasant surprise.' Finn opened his door and greeted her with a voice heavily laden with sarcasm.

Once again she didn't wait to be invited in when the door swung open. 'You think,' she said as she stormed past him into his lounge, resolutely keeping her back turned to the wall where she'd let him claim her the last time she was here.

She didn't give Finn an opportunity to say any more, she didn't want to give him a chance to tell her to leave. 'Bella got new lungs today,' she told him.

'I heard.'

That took the wind out of her sails momentarily.

She frowned. 'How did you hear that?'

He raised one eyebrow in a habit she found intensely irritating but it was only one of his many habits that annoyed her.

'I *am* the Head of Surgery,' he said. 'People tend to keep me in the loop.'

Being told he'd known Bella was having surgery today and he still hadn't bothered keeping his word sent Evie over the edge. 'You said you would speak to Sam. I asked you for help.' She tried desperately to rein in her temper but she knew she could either yell at Finn or burst into tears, and she wasn't going to give him the satisfaction of seeing her cry.

'Sleeping with the head of a department doesn't grant you the right to ask favours.'

Evie clenched her fists, willing herself not to hit something. God, he was infuriating. 'You arrogant bastard, is that why you think I slept with you?'

'I don't know,' he replied. 'Is it?'

'No!' She couldn't stop herself from yelling that time. 'That was an impulsive mistake and I'm sorry it ever happened,' she lied. 'I don't have a good reason for what we did but wanting the liberty of asking favours wasn't it.'

Finn didn't react to her rising temper. In contrast to her heated tone his voice was cool, calm and measured. 'How's Bella doing?'

'You tell me,' Evie snapped. 'I thought you were "in the loop".'

'I've been out of contact a bit today. I haven't caught up on everything I should have.'

'Her new lungs are working, she's in ICU, as expected, but she's on a ventilator. This was supposed to be the start of her new life but she can't even breathe by herself.' Evie could hear her voice wobbling with emotion and she fought to keep things under control.

'That will only be temporary.'

'I know that. But somehow I think if you'd been there it might have turned out differently. If things had gone according to plan.'

'Whose plan?' he asked.

'Mine.'

Finn was shaking his head. 'I'm sorry it hasn't gone as

smoothly as you hoped but I'm sure she'll be fine. Trust me when I tell you it was better for Bella that I wasn't there.'

'Trust you!' Evie retorted. 'I don't think I'll ever trust you.'

Finn sighed. 'Before you get carried away as judge, jury and executioner, there's something you need to hear.' He gestured to his sofa. 'I think you should sit down.'

Evie stomped over to Finn's leather couch. On the coffee table was a tumbler filled with an inch of amber fluid. It looked like whisky. Finn remained standing in front of her. His back was ramrod straight and his hands were thrust deep into the pockets of his jeans. Even in her irritated state she was aware of how the denim of his jeans strained across his thighs, emphasising his long, lean physique, and she was aware too of her own reaction to his maleness. It seemed that being annoyed with him wasn't enough to prevent herself from finding him attractive. Not that she planned to go anywhere near him ever again. Especially not after today.

'There's a reason I wasn't at the hospital today,' he said, and Evie had to drag her eyes away from his hips and back up to his face as he spoke to her. 'Look.' He took his hands out of his pockets and held them out to her. His right hand was shaking badly. 'I didn't avoid surgery today because I didn't want to do it. I avoided it because I didn't want to be a liability. There was no way I could have operated today. You wouldn't want me near Bella like this, would you?'

'Oh, my God!' She tore her eyes away from his hands and looked up at him. She realised the shadow in his blue eyes that she'd thought was anger was, in fact, pain. She'd marched into his home and accused him of all sorts of terrible things when he'd been suffering. She felt dreadful and for a moment she forgot the nasty things he'd said to her in reply. 'What's wrong with you?'

'I have a ruptured cervical disc at five/six.'

'When? How?'

'It happened years ago, ten years ago, when I was in the army.'

'Ten years?'

He nodded. 'But the disc has deteriorated further.'

'Tell me you've been to see someone.'

He nodded. 'I saw Rupert today.'

'Rupert Davidson, the neurosurgeon?'

Finn sat on the couch opposite her but he didn't collapse into the couch as she had. His posture remained stiff, upright and he held his head still as if even the slightest movement was painful. 'He thinks a fragment of the nucleus has broken off and is causing more C-six nerve root impingement.'

'He thinks? Have you seen anyone else, had a second opinion?' she asked, but who else would he see? Like Finn and Sam, Rupert was another one of the Harbour's surgeons who was the best in his field. 'Have you had an MRI scan?'

Finn gave her a wry smile. 'I've had about a dozen opinions. I trust Rupert. And, no, I haven't had an MRI. Remember the scar on my left shoulder?'

Did she remember? She didn't think she'd ever forget how that puckered scar had felt under her fingers or the fact that when she'd felt it they'd just made love. No, they'd just had sex, she corrected herself.

She nodded.

'I still have shrapnel in that shoulder. I can't have MRI scans.'

He had shrapnel in his shoulder and a destroyed cervical disc. No wonder he was always so grumpy. 'What are you going to do?'

'Rupert wants to operate.'

'What does he want to do?'

'He has to remove that fragment but the disc has lost its height so he's talking about trying an artificial disc.'

Evie frowned. 'Isn't that a bit experimental?'

Finn nodded.

'What does he think the odds are of it being successful?' Her earlier antagonism was forgotten as she tried to process what she was hearing.

'He has no idea. He reckons fifty-fifty that I'll even pull through the surgery and no guarantees that it will work, but I can't continue like this. If my condition deteriorates any further, I may never operate again. I don't think I have much choice. So, that's why I wasn't there for Bella today. I'm sorry.'

He was sorry? Evie felt like a complete bitch. She'd known something was wrong with Finn. She'd seen it in the way he rubbed his arm, she'd seen it in his eyes when a shadow crossed them, darkening his piercing blue irises, she'd known he suffered from migraines but she'd done nothing except badger him about her own needs.

Finn stood and Evie watched as he unfolded his limbs and rose from the couch. It seemed their little heart to heart was over. 'Don't let me keep you any longer. I'm sure you want to check on Bella.'

Evie stood too but that brought them standing within a few inches of each other. She was tempted to reach out, to try to wipe the look of pain from his face. It was etched deep into the furrows of his forehead but as if he sensed what she was about to do he took a step backwards, putting some distance between them.

'I'll see you out,' he said, effectively dismissing her.

He led her to the door but paused as he reached for the doorhandle. 'Can I ask you not to mention this to anyone? They'll all find out soon enough if I need to have time off.'

Evie nodded.

'Thank you.'

She thought that was the most sincere she'd ever heard him sound. Perhaps they could be friends after all.

'Don't mention it. I'm glad you told me,' she replied, then impulsively raised herself up on tiptoe to kiss his cheek. She didn't care if her attention was unwanted. He needed to know she would keep his confidence. He needed to know she was in his corner. 'If you need someone to talk to, I think I'm a pretty good listener.'

Finn didn't respond to her invitation but he didn't refuse it either. He held the door for her and Evie pressed the button to call the lift, before deciding to take the fire escape stairs back down to her apartment. She didn't want to share the lift with anyone, she needed to think.

Finn had been carrying this injury for ten years. She understood that it had obviously not always been as incapacitating as it was now but how had he managed not only to keep it quiet but to continue to do the job he did? Bending over an operating table would be hell with a ruptured cervical disc, particularly at the C five/six level.

The pain would account for his bad temper and she wondered what he'd be like if he was pain free. But there was no guarantee that the surgery would be successful. And if it didn't work, what would that mean for Finn? He might lose more upper-limb function and then he wouldn't be able to operate. What would that do to a man like him? One who obviously prided himself on his skills and no doubt measured his worth by his performance as a surgeon? And that wasn't even considering the complications associated with the surgery itself.

She could see the stubborn set of his jaw and recognised in him the same traits of independence and stubbornness she saw in her mother. She knew her mother's issues stemmed from low self-confidence and self-worth. Finn couldn't possibly have some of those same issues, could he? Not someone who seemed so sure of himself.

Whatever his issues, he needed someone to be there for him and Evie would have bet her last dollar that he had no one. Could she do it? Would he let her?

CHAPTER TEN

CHARLIE sat and watched Bella as she slept. He'd been beside her every chance he'd had for the past two days but he felt he could sit there for ever. He'd be there for as long as she needed him.

'*Ciao*, Bella.'

He picked up her hand. It was cool to his touch. He rested his thumb over her wrist, over the pulse that flickered under her skin, and let the beat of her heart vibrate through him.

Her dark eyelashes fluttered against her pale cheeks but her eyes remained closed. She was still sedated. Still ventilated.

He threaded his fingers between hers and gently squeezed her hand. 'Can you hear me?' he asked as he willed her to return his pressure. Just the smallest of movements would have done but there was nothing.

He could have kicked himself for not telling her how he felt when he'd had the chance. He couldn't believe he hadn't told her he needed her in his life. Wanted her in his life.

He couldn't bear the thought of not seeing her smile. Not hearing her laugh. Not seeing her grey eyes turn silver when she asked him to kiss her, asked him to make love to her. He couldn't bear to think he might not have the chance to introduce her to the delights of lovemaking, might not get to have her naked in his arms or take her to the heights of pleasure. That he might not get to hear her cry out in ecstasy as he tasted, teased and thrilled her.

But he didn't regret not seizing the opportunity the other night. Even if it meant he'd missed his chance, he knew the timing had been wrong. He'd wanted to give Bella the attention she deserved and he couldn't have done that. It would have been hurried and hasty, not the languorous experience that he wanted her to have. Even one night wouldn't be enough. Not for her and not for him. He wanted more than that.

If only she'd wake up he could tell her how he felt.

But he could still tell her now. He could accept the theory that comatose or heavily sedated patients were still aware of conversations, sounds and smells around them, even if they were unable to respond. He could tell her how he felt now and he could tell her again later.

He was convinced her depression was due to her mental state prior to the surgery. If she'd wanted to give up then this was a way to let go. But he couldn't let that happen. He needed to get her to fight.

He wound his fingers through her auburn curls and bent his head, burying his face in her curls and breathing in her scent. Even among the hospital odours he could smell her, fresh and sweet.

'Bella?' he whispered. 'Please wake up. I miss you.' He wanted to talk to her, wanted to hear her laugh. He could talk, he could tell her about his day, but it wasn't what she needed to hear. It wasn't going to get her breathing on her own.

He kept his back to the ICU, blocking out the rest of the world as he concentrated on Bella. His words were for Bella alone.

'I'm sorry I didn't make love to you when you asked me to. I don't want to think we've missed our chance. Believe me when I say I was tempted, very tempted, but I wanted to make it perfect for you. You deserve that. You deserve more than a quick tumble on the grass. Not that it wouldn't have been fun,' he said with a smile, 'but I want to spend an entire night with you. More. I want you to wake up in my arms and decide to do it over again. And again. Not to end up cold and sore in the back garden, having to sneak inside like a recalcitrant teenager. I'll make it up to you. I promise you an experience to remember, but first you have to wake up.' He held her hand, connecting them. 'I want to do it properly.

'Did you know I promised Evie I wouldn't break your heart?' he continued. 'She scares me, your big sister. You didn't know I was a coward, did you?' He was only half joking. He wasn't looking forward to the lecture he was expecting from Evie but he would let her have her say, as long as she didn't try to stop him from seeing Bella.

'If you get through this, I promise I'll make it up to you.' He lifted her hand to his lips and kissed her fingertips. 'I'll be waiting for you when you wake up.'

Bella was dozing, trying to piece together the past few days. It was still so hard to believe she'd had a lung transplant, everything felt so vague and distant. When she'd woken she'd been disoriented and she'd had to ask the nurses where she was and what day it was. Apparently it was her third day in the ICU and she'd only been taken off the ventilator that morning.

Her memory was hazy and she kept her eyes closed as she tested out her new lungs. It hurt to breathe in but it was external pain, muscular pain, not her usual tight, blocked, breathless feeling. She put her hand over the base of her ribcage where the pain was worst and felt the dressing. She followed it as it ran across the lower part of her chest and felt where the drain emerged from the dressing and dropped away over the edge of the bed.

Above the dressing, between her breasts, she could feel ECG leads stuck to her chest but there were no bandages higher up. The scar from the surgery was a horizontal one, down low, just as Sam had told her it would be. But she hadn't believed him. She'd been convinced the scar would be between her breasts, visible to everyone any time she wore a V-neck top. Sam told her that was the case for heart surgery, not lung surgery, but she'd been terrified of waking up and finding out he'd been wrong.

She took another deep breath, in, out, in, almost scared to think her new lungs actually worked. She breathed out as she heard two nurses talking as they came towards her bed. She opened her eyes, thinking they were coming to her, but they stopped at the bed beside hers, ready to turn that patient. They continued talking as they worked.

'Has Dr Maxwell been in yet?'

'No. I haven't seen him since he was at Pete's the other night.'

'I told you you should have talked to him then when you had the chance.'

They were talking about Charlie! Did he have a patient in ICU or had he been in to see her? She racked her brain, struggling to see if she had any recollection of a visit from him, but the past few days were nothing but a fuzzy jumble of images and she had no idea which ones were real and which ones were her imagination.

'I was going to but then he disappeared,' the nurse replied.

Bella couldn't believe how much the nurses in this hospital gossiped in front of the patients. They talked about their lives as though all the patients were deaf. Maybe they've forgotten I'm awake, she thought. She opened her eyes, just a fraction. She had to see who this nurse was but she didn't want them to know she was listening. She squinted through her lashes. She could just make out the name on the nurse's nametag. Philippa.

Philippa? Why did that sound familiar?

No, it wasn't Philippa that was familiar. It was Pippa. The ex-girlfriend Charlie had been talking about before Bella had gone in for surgery. She remembered Charlie talking about how he'd given his heart away and lost everything. The girl, his career, his surfing dreams. No wonder he avoided relationships.

Charlie had obviously thought he'd been helping her, telling her he knew how she felt. But all she could think about was how he'd given his heart away once and would probably never do it again.

In Bella's mind Pippa morphed into Philippa—brunette, big busted, long legs—the complete opposite from her. A woman who knew what she wanted and went after it. Not someone who'd have to beg a man to make love to her.

Bella couldn't believe she'd been such a fool. What on earth would Charlie see in someone like her? He'd even told her, more than once, that the reason he spent time with her was because Evie asked him to. He obviously thought of her as Evie's little sister, nothing more. She felt tears welling in her eyes. He'd probably had no intention of making love to her, poor, tragic, inexperienced Bella, not at any time. He'd probably just been trying to let her down gently.

She wanted to fall in love but she couldn't give her heart to Charlie. Not now. Not now she knew about Pippa. Not now she knew why he avoided relationships. That would be asking for trouble. Trusting him with her heart yet knowing he would only break it. She wanted to fall in love but she'd have to make sure it wasn't with Charlie. He'd given his heart away once before, she couldn't expect him to do it again.

Well, she decided, she'd find a way to let him out of their deal. She didn't think she could bear to hear him say no to her again.

'*Ciao*, Bella.'

By the time Charlie arrived in the ICU Bella had planned her strategy, but as soon as she heard his usual greeting she felt her resolve start to crumble.

'You're a sight for sore eyes. You're looking a million dollars,' he said.

She knew he was exaggerating hugely but his effortless charm still made her feel better. His voice was bright and cheery, he sounded happy to see her; she needed to stay strong.

He placed his hand over hers and squeezed her fingers. His hand was warm and Bella drew comfort from his strength. 'You had us all so worried.'

'I did?'

'Of course.' Charlie looked at her as if she'd gone a little mad and Bella mentally rolled her eyes. Of course people would have been concerned. 'This was supposed to be the answer for you but knowing how you were feeling before the surgery I was worried you were going to give in. But I shouldn't have doubted you—you're a fighter, a survivor.'

But she'd come close to giving up. She knew it. She normally made such an effort to be strong and to fight but she'd been so tired, she'd been almost ready to call it quits. Almost. Charlie had been right, she'd needed a reason to get through the surgery and she'd found it. She didn't need

Charlie's assistance and attention any more, she was a survivor and she'd get through this too.

'I have you to thank for getting me past this,' she told him.

'Me?'

She nodded and reached for an envelope that was beside her bed. She grimaced slightly with the stretch and Charlie picked the envelope up and handed it to her. She held it up. 'In here is a letter from the college.' She couldn't stop the grin that spread across her face. 'I've been accepted into fashion design.'

She was about to let Charlie go, to let him out of their deal and possibly out of her life, but she couldn't let him go without telling him the good news. After all, she did have him to thank for it.

'That's fantastic! Congratulations.'

He leant over and kissed her cheek and Bella felt her resolve slipping through her fingers and sliding to the floor. She closed her eyes to block out the sight of him, his gorgeous brown eyes, his smooth olive skin, his perfect ears and his divine lips. But his image was just as clear with her eyes closed and his lips were soft and warm on her cheek. She felt her heart flip-flop in her chest and she forced herself to remember what he'd said about Pippa. How he'd given her his heart and she'd thrown it away. Forced herself to remember he'd said that medicine was his new passion and he didn't need relationships.

'I knew they'd love you. When do you start?'

She opened her eyes as Charlie's lips left her cheek.

'Not until March.'

'You'll be fighting fit by then?'

'I plan to be. I've got a more pressing engagement before then.' She paused and took a deep breath, still surprised at the feeling of freedom, and told him another one of her reasons for living. 'Lexi and Sam have set a date for their wedding.'

'They have? When is it?'

'In three weeks, the Saturday before Christmas.'

'That's not a lot of time. Will you be okay for that?'

'I'm going to make sure I am. Sam seems to think I have a good chance if I focus on my exercises and eating properly and being vigilant with my medication. Studying in March should be a piece of cake if I can get through the next three weeks.'

'Have you got time pencilled in for me some time after you get out of here? I seem to recall we have unfinished business.' His brown eyes were shining and Bella's insides melted as she imagined letting him take her to bed. Just once.

Was he still planning on honouring their deal? He was grinning at her and Bella was very tempted to let their arrangement stand but she knew she couldn't do it. She wanted to be special and Charlie didn't do special, at least not for more than one night at a time. She wanted to be different and the only way to be different was to make sure she wasn't just another notch in his bedpost.

She steeled herself to stick to her plan. Now was her chance to let him off the hook before he could seduce her. Before he could reject her.

She took a deep breath, still amazed that she could actually fill her lungs, even though the wound gave her some discomfort. 'That's not a priority any more. I have three weeks to get well enough for Lexi's wedding, that's my goal.'

'And after the wedding? Are you going to keep working your way through your wishlist?'

'I have a new list now.'

Charlie frowned. 'A new list. What about staying up all night to see the sun rise? Being kissed under the stars?'

'My list wasn't set in stone. I can change it if I like, it's my list.'

'But why would you change it?'

'I've got more time now. I can look further ahead. Do you know how amazing that feels?'

Charlie was grinning at her, his eyes shining. She could tell he knew exactly how she felt. She'd bet he'd got the same thrill of excitement when he'd been surfing. 'What's on your new list?' he asked.

'I'm going to college and I'm going to travel. Halfway through next year I'm taking myself to Paris.'

'Paris?'

'I've always wanted to go to Paris but I thought it was an impossible dream.'

'You're going on your own?'

'Evie will come with me. She doesn't know it yet but she will.'

'You have everything planned but no time for me?' He actually sounded disappointed but Bella knew he'd get over it. There'd be plenty of women eager to take her place, plenty of women eager to be charmed and bedded by Charlie Maxwell.

'I don't want a quick roll in the hay,' she explained. 'I don't want to be just another notch in someone's bedpost. Not that I don't appreciate your offer,' she added, 'it's just that I want more now. I have my life back. I have time to find the things I want and I want a proper relationship. I want to be in love. I want it to be special.' Bella knew she couldn't expect Charlie to choose her over all the other women out there but she wasn't going to agree to a fling.

Movement to her left distracted her. Busty, long-legged Philippa was coming towards them.

'Hello, Dr Maxwell. I didn't realise you knew Bella,' she said as she checked Bella's monitor. She looked back over her shoulder at Charlie as she added, 'My shift is just about finished and I'm heading to Pete's. Will you be there tonight?'

Bella held her breath, waiting for Charlie's answer, as she watched Philippa making cow eyes at him. She wished she could get out of that stupid bed, out of the ICU, as far away as possible from Charlie and all the silly nurses who threw themselves at his feet. But she was stuck, literally tied to the bed by the tubes and leads and drains that Philippa had come to check, and she had no option but to lie there and listen to her flirt with Charlie.

She didn't want Charlie to choose someone else but she especially didn't want to see him do it right in front of her.

'No, I won't be at Pete's,' he said, as he stood up, and Bella let out the breath she'd been holding. He leant over and squeezed Bella's hand, 'I'll see you later,' he said before he left the ICU.

Bella and Philippa both watched him go. Charlie left and took their dreams with him. Philippa sighed in admiration but Bella felt like crying. She could only assume her dreams were very different from Philippa's.

Charlie didn't think he could do special. He'd been prepared to offer Bella amazing, incredible and delightful but only on a temporary basis. But he knew that wasn't what she had in mind. She wanted to fall in love and he couldn't do that. Love meant giving up too much of himself.

He needed to walk away. He needed to make sure he didn't hurt her. She didn't deserve that. And Evie would kill him if he hurt Bella. For everyone's sake he needed to walk away.

He'd made himself take those steps, he'd made himself

leave Bella behind, and he'd kept away because he wasn't what she needed. He wasn't even what she wanted.

But it was a lot harder than he'd expected.

He sat on the beach and let the sand trickle through his fingers as he watched the waves. The sun was warm on his back and the breeze coming off the ocean left the taste of salt water on his lips. He closed his eyes as he let his memories wash over him. Images of him on a scooter in Bali collided with images of Bella. It wasn't Pippa he pictured on the scooter with him, it was Bella. Images of Bella in hospital, her auburn curls bright against the white sheets, her skin pale, overlapped with memories of the two of them dancing under the stars, of her asking him to make love to her, her grey eyes dark like a stormy sea, her skin the colour of pearls, her lips the pink of a perfect sunset.

He'd driven down to Wollongong to try to clear his head. There were only so many laps of the Kirribilli pool he could do before he went completely stir-crazy. The surf was good and he felt the usual pang of regret that he couldn't be out there, but this time that feeling of regret was overshadowed by thoughts of Bella. If he really wanted to, he could body-surf, but that wasn't what he needed either. That wouldn't make things right. He glanced to his left, at the empty sand around him. He knew if Bella was sitting beside him everything would be okay with the world. With his world.

He missed her. He missed the touch of her hand, her laugh, her smile when he said her name.

He wished he could teach her to surf. He wished he could share with her the feeling of freedom and exhilaration surfing could produce. He knew she would love it. But knowing he couldn't surf again was different from accepting that he couldn't teach Bella. For once he wasn't sorry for his sake, he could remember how it felt to be flying down the face of a wave, to feel nothing but the rush of wind and salt spray in his face, to feel the ocean moving under his feet, alternately lifting him up before it did its best to discard him to its watery depths, the feeling of euphoria when he bested a wave, and he was sorry he wouldn't get the chance to share that with Bella.

But there were other things he could share with her. Other things he could show her. He could take her to the ski fields. They could make love in front of a fire and drink hot chocolate while the snow fell outside. He could go with her to Paris and watch the sunset from the Eiffel Tower. They could take an early morning trip to Bondi and watch the sunrise over the ocean. They had a whole world to explore and he knew then he'd rather have that adventure with Bella than surf one more wave.

When he was with her he stopped searching for the next adrenalin rush, the next hit, the rush he used to get from taking on a monster wave and coming out of it unscathed, victorious. The rush he got from performing a difficult operation and doing it successfully. Bella gave him that same rush of excitement but she also made him feel grounded, content, happy. When he was with her he felt comfortable. He felt free.

And that was when he knew. He missed surfing but not as much as he missed Bella.

He'd offered her an experience to remember but he'd been thinking along the lines of a weekend, maybe two. But that wasn't what she wanted and he realised it wasn't what he wanted either. Could he be the man she wanted?

He wasn't sure but he was prepared to try. He wanted Bella more than anything else and he was going to make sure he got her. He stood up from the sand. He had one

week until Lexi and Sam's wedding. One week until he
knew he'd be seeing Bella again. There were things he
needed to do.

CHAPTER ELEVEN

THE wedding was perfect, Bella thought as she watched couples moving to the music on the dance floor. Even though it had been pulled together in a hurry, every tiny element had been attended to. For the past three weeks, in between her exercise and rehab sessions, Bella had been absolutely frantic, helping Lexi with myriad details for the wedding, coordinating dresses, tuxedos, caterers, musicians, florists and the cake, but to see how happy Lexi was made it all worthwhile.

Lexi looked stunning in the dress Bella had designed for her and she watched as Sam guided Lexi expertly around the dance floor. Their eyes hadn't strayed from each other, they were caught up in their own little world, and Bella envied them.

The pale green of Evie's bridesmaid's dress caught her eye as she glided past in the arms of Marco D'Avello. Marco was an obstetrician at the Harbour and one of several doctors Bella had seen in her pre-op work-up, but she was fairly certain he and Evie were nothing but friends.

While Lexi hadn't danced with anyone but Sam, Evie had had a stream of admiring partners. But Bella had seen her constantly stealing glances at Finn—though she could tell Evie was trying desperately to look as if she hadn't noticed him. Bella wondered what was going on between

Evie and Finn. Evie was passionate in her dislike of him yet Bella could sense something else.

Finn was nursing what looked like a glass of whisky and Bella hadn't seen him on the dance floor. He looked like a man who needed a friend and for a moment she thought about going to speak to him before she realised she'd have nothing to say. The song ended and Bella saw Evie cross the dance floor and head towards Finn. She wondered if Evie was planning on rescuing him from his demons. Watching Finn with the whisky in his hand and the 'keep your distance' expression on his face, Bella hoped his weren't the same demons that her mother faced. Evie needed a new project now that Bella was on the mend; she always needed to be helping someone, but none of them had been able to help Miranda, and Bella didn't want Evie to be disappointed all over again by Finn.

She turned back to the dance floor as another song began. The wedding had been perfect and there was nothing she could do now for Evie and Finn so she might as well enjoy the evening. Charlie was in the middle of the floor. She recognised his graceful movements even before she saw his broad shoulders and bald head. His movement was fluid and rhythmical and she could picture him in his surfing days gliding down the face of a wave, at one with the power of the ocean. He looked sensational in a crisp tuxedo and she devoured him with her eyes as he moved past her.

The wedding had been perfect, everything had been perfect, including Charlie.

Especially Charlie.

She'd expected that she'd have been too busy over the past three weeks to even think about him but he'd filled her dreams every night and he'd been the first person she'd seen today as she'd entered the ballroom where the wedding ceremony was going to take place. She hadn't seen him for three weeks but she'd picked him out the moment she'd stood in the doorway waiting to walk down the aisle in front of Lexi. He'd been sitting on the left of the aisle, on the bride's side, and Bella's heart had done its funny little flip-flop thing when she'd seen the back of his bald head. He'd turned as the 'Wedding March' had started and met her gaze. He'd winked at her and grinned as if nothing had changed. As if they'd seen each other only yesterday. How was it that he could behave as if everything was the same? How was it that he could seem so calm and composed and yet her hands had started to shake and her stomach was in knots with just one look?

But if nothing had changed, why had he still not asked her to dance? She'd begun to think he was avoiding her.

Well, she only had herself to blame for that, she thought as she saw him dance past her again. After telling him about her new wishlist, there was no reason for him to seek out her company any more. At least he'd been dancing with lots of different women, at least she hadn't had to watch him pick up one particular woman at Lexi's wedding. She didn't think she could bear to sit through that.

She forced herself to look away from Charlie. No matter how tempting it was to imagine having a quick fling with him, she knew she couldn't do it. Her heart wouldn't survive. She'd made her decision and she needed to stick to it. But now that the wedding was almost over she needed something else to focus her attention on, something else to keep her mind off Charlie. Her fashion design course didn't start for another three months so she had to find something to keep her occupied.

She turned away from the dance floor knowing the only possible way to keep her mind off Charlie was to keep him out of sight.

* * *

Charlie watched Bella as she hovered on the edge of the dance floor, chatting to her father. He felt as though he'd been watching her all evening, waiting for her to be free from her official bridesmaid's duties. Waiting for her to be free for him. Her auburn curls shone under the soft lights and she seemed to float against the background of the other guests. She looked divine in a dress that hugged her chest and then flared out into a full skirt that looked as light as air and floated about her legs as she moved. He recognised the outfit, he'd seen it in her sketch book.

Richard was moving away, leaving Bella alone. He excused himself from his dance partner as politely as possible and went over to her.

'*Ciao*, Bella.' He bent down and kissed her cheek, savouring the softness of her skin under his lips, the slight brush of her curls against her jaw, the lightness of her dress fabric as his hand grazed her hip. 'You're wearing the green dress.'

She smiled at him and his heart soared. 'I told you I just needed time.'

'It's perfect on you.' The pale green was a perfect foil for her colouring and she reminded him of a butterfly— delicate, ethereal and exquisite. 'Would you dance with me?'

She nodded and stepped into his embrace. She felt slight and fragile but he knew she wasn't. She had a strength of character that belied her petite size. He held her in his arms and revelled in the sensation of having her pressed against him. They talked about everything that had happened in her life for the past three weeks—about the wedding preparations, her recovery from the surgery, her rehabilitation. He'd thought there might be awkwardness between them but they slipped easily back into their relationship as though it had only been one day, not twenty, since they'd seen each other.

Everything they discussed was important but it didn't get Charlie any closer to knowing what he needed to know. He felt they talked about everything but nothing because they didn't talk about them. And he needed to know if there could be a 'them'.

'Have you finished your official duties?' he asked as the song ended. 'Do you think anyone would notice if you sneaked outside with me?'

Her eyes sparkled silver and her pink lips broke into a wide smile. 'You're not going to drag me down to the frangipani bushes and take advantage of me, are you?'

'Not unless you want me to,' he teased. 'I have a proposition for you,' he added, 'but I'd like some privacy.'

Bella nodded silently, and then surprised him when she took control, keeping hold of his hand and leading him out into the garden, guiding him along the path. The air was heavy with the scent of frangipani flowers but Bella walked past the bushes and headed for the Moreton Bay fig tree that stood sentinel over the lawn. An old wooden swing hung from its branches, the seat big enough for two, and Bella pulled him down beside her under the canopy of the old tree.

'I'm listening.'

He wondered what was going through her mind. What she was expecting him to say? She seemed so calm. He was a bundle of nerves. It mattered so much to him to get this right. This was the most important conversation he ever expected to have.

He stood up from the swing, too keyed up to sit still, and paced backwards and forwards, working up the courage to start. What if she said no?

He took a deep breath and began. 'This new list of

yours, I was wondering if you'd share it with me, tell me what's on it?'

'What do you mean?'

'The wedding is almost over and you must have close to three months until college starts. What's next on your list?'

She'd been wondering the same thing herself just moments before. She needed to find something to occupy her time until college started otherwise she'd waste it day-dreaming about things that were never going to happen.

'I'm going to go out in the world and experience life,' she told him. Being deliberately vague allowed her to keep her options open but also suited her because she really had no idea what she was going to do. 'I've been given the second chance I've always wanted. Now I can do anything, so I'm going to search out as many new experiences as I can.'

'Do you think I could persuade you to share some of those experiences with me? I want to ask you for another chance.'

She hesitated. She wasn't sure what she'd been expecting but this declaration wasn't it. Or to be more accurate, it wasn't what she'd hoped for. She hadn't hesitated to join him outside but she knew it was because she was eager to have just one more moment with him. It didn't mean she would be okay with a casual relationship. She still wanted Charlie but unless she could have all of him, emotionally and physically, she was better off alone.

She shook her head. 'I don't think you can give me what I'm after. I don't want a casual relationship, I want something deeper. Not that I expect to find that in a hurry but I want my heart intact so that when the time is right I'm ready. I don't think I can risk my heart with you.'

Charlie sat down beside her and his weight made the swing sway on its ropes. 'Don't give up on me.' His brown eyes were unreadable in the darkness but his voice was thick with emotion. 'I promise I won't hurt you. I've already promised Evie I wouldn't break your heart.'

'I'm okay by myself,' she told him. 'I don't want you to ask me out because of my list or because you feel sorry for me or out of some sense of misguided loyalty to me because I'm Evie's little sister. I'll be fine.'

Charlie reached for her hand. 'This has nothing to do with your list and definitely nothing to do with Evie. Just because I see Evie as my little sister it doesn't mean I see you the same way. I'm asking you to let me date you. Give me a chance. Please.'

He hadn't let go of her and her fingers trembled under his touch. She yearned to give in to him but somehow she managed to shake her head again. 'I'm going to use the next few months as a chance to find out where I belong and I don't think I'll be able to do that unless I spend some time by myself. I need to learn to be independent. I need to learn to stand on my own two feet.'

'I get that, but what if I stood beside you? I want to be with you. I want to be the man you're looking for.'

'Why?'

'I've missed you.'

The way he said it, so simply, as though that explained everything, made her want to believe him and almost made her want to give in, but it wasn't enough.

'I've missed your courage and your spirit,' he continued. 'I've missed our conversations. I've missed everything about you. I've missed hearing your name on my lips, I've missed seeing you smile when I walk into a room. I've missed the taste of your mouth, the touch of your hand.' He lifted her hand to his lips and kissed her fingertips. 'I've had plenty of time to think over the past weeks and to work out what's important in my life. And I know now that it's you. I can't imagine my life without you and I want to be a part of your life. I want to be beside you when you see the Eiffel Tower for the first time, I want to be the man you kiss standing on the banks of the Seine under a starry sky, I want to drink champagne with you at midnight and stay up and watch the sun rise.'

'You want to do all that with me?'

He nodded. 'When you were in hospital after your operation I realised if I had to choose between being able to surf for one more day or seeing you, I would choose you. I'm not talking about a casual relationship. I'm ready to make a commitment to you. Not for the next week or the next month but for ever.'

He reached into the pocket of his tuxedo and pulled out a thin envelope. He opened it and removed two sheets of paper, which he handed to Bella.

'What's this?' she asked.

'Two tickets to Paris.'

'Paris? I don't understand.'

'I want to take you to Paris. In July.' He got off the swing and knelt in front of her, holding her hands in his. 'I want to take you to Paris for our honeymoon. I love you, Bella, and I want you to be my wife.'

Bella's heart was racing in her chest and her mouth was dry. He what?

'You don't need to answer me now,' he said. 'I'm prepared to wait, as long as you agree to go on another date with me. Just agree to let me love you.'

'You love me?'

'I do. And I want to be the best man I can be. For you.'

'Are you sure I'm who you want?'

'I've never been more certain of anything in my life. You have made my world a better place and you have given me the freedom to be myself. That's something I've been searching for ever since I had to give up surfing. When you thought I couldn't give you what you wanted you didn't judge me, you left me to be my own person, but I found out I didn't want to be my own man, I wanted to be your man. If I could still surf I would give it up for you, I would give up everything for you, but the only thing I can offer you is my love. I thought I wanted freedom but I don't. I want you.'

The tickets to Paris were resting on Bella's lap. She folded them up and slid them back into their envelope. 'I don't need Paris.'

'But—'

She reached out and put her fingers on Charlie's perfect, plump lips, quietening him.

'I don't *need* Paris but I would love to go and I would love to go with you. I also don't need time to think about us. I don't need anything except you. I used to feel like a fairy-tale princess, locked away watching the world pass by, kept separate and apart from everyone else, restricted by my illness, but you have never treated me as a fragile invalid who needed protection. You are the only person who treats me as if I'm the same as everyone else.'

'I don't want you to feel as though you're just like everyone else. I want you to feel special.'

'I do feel special when I'm with you,' she told him. 'It's funny, I envied you your freedom but you've set me free. You're my very own Prince Charming. I've been waiting for you all my life. I love you and I know where I belong in the world. I belong with you.'

Charlie stood and lifted her off the swing, pulling her to her feet, and kissed her long and hard, and Bella knew that with Charlie by her side, loving her, all her dreams would come true.

'So you'll marry me?' he asked.

Her heart flip-flopped in her chest. 'Yes, I will marry you,' she replied.

'And we can honeymoon in Paris?'

'Definitely.'

'Then I just have one more request,' he said.

'Anything.'

'You have to throw away all your old pyjamas. You're too beautiful to be wearing them. They're not coming to Paris, they're not allowed anywhere near you. From now on it's red negligees only. Agreed?'

'Agreed,' Bella replied, as she sealed her promise with a kiss.

* * * * *

MILLS & BOON®
By Request

RELIVE THE ROMANCE WITH THE BEST OF THE BEST

MILLS & BOON®

**If you enjoyed this story,
you'll love the the full *Revenge Collection!***

**Enjoy the misdemeanours and the sinful world
of revenge with this six-book collection.
Indulge in these riveting 3-in-1 romances
from top Modern Romance authors.**

Order your complete collection today at
www.millsandboon.co.uk/revengecollection

1115_MB517

MILLS & BOON®

Man of the Year

Our winning cover star will be revealed next month!

**Don't miss out on your copy
– order from millsandboon.co.uk**

Read more about Man of the Year 2016 at

www.millsandboon.co.uk/moty2016

**Have you been following our
Man of the Year 2016 campaign?**
🐦 **#MOTY2016**